THIRTEEN RISING

A ZODIAC NOVEL

THIRTEEN RISING

A *ZODIAC* NOVEL

ROMINA RUSSELL

RAZORBILL®

An Imprint of Penguin Random House

RAZORBILL®

An Imprint of Penguin Random House
Penguin.com

RAZORBILL & colophon is a registered trademark of Penguin Random House LLC.

First published in the United States of America by Razorbill,
an imprint of Penguin Random House LLC, 2017

LIBRARY OF CONGRESS CATALOGING-IN-PUBLICATION DATA IS AVAILABLE
ISBN: 9780448493558

Printed in the United States of America

3 5 7 9 10 8 6 4 2

Interior design by Vanessa Han

For you, the unifiers of our universe:

May we work together to heal our worlds.

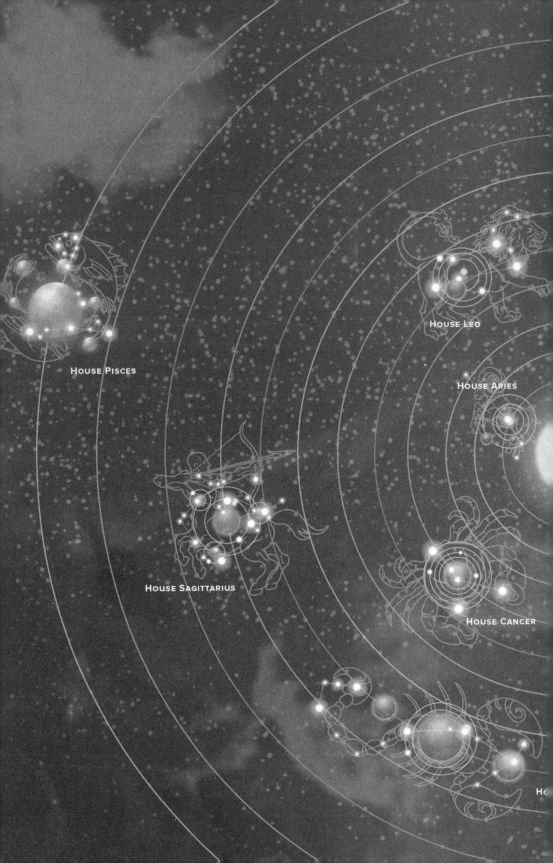

HOUSE PISCES

HOUSE LEO

HOUSE ARIES

HOUSE SAGITTARIUS

HOUSE CANCER

HO

HOUSE VIRGO

HOUSE CAPRICORN

HOUSE TAURUS

HOUSE GEMINI

HOUSE LIBRA

HOUSE AQUARIUS

THE HOUSES OF THE ZODIAC GALAXY

THE FIRST HOUSE:
ARIES, *THE RAM* CONSTELLATION
Strength: Military
Guardian: General Eurek
Flag: Red
Zodai: Majors

THE SECOND HOUSE:
TAURUS, *THE BULL* CONSTELLATION
Strength: Industry
Guardian: Chief Executive Purecell
Flag: Olive green
Zodai: Promisaries

THE THIRD HOUSE:
GEMINI, *THE DOUBLE* CONSTELLATION
Strength: Imagination
Guardians: Twins Caaseum (deceased) and Rubidum
Flag: Orange
Zodai: Dreamcasters

THE FOURTH HOUSE:
CANCER, *THE CRAB* CONSTELLATION
Strength: Nurture
Guardian: Holy Mother Rho
Flag: Blue
Zodai: Lodestars

THE FIFTH HOUSE:
LEO, *THE LION* CONSTELLATION
Strength: Passion
Guardian: Holy Leader Aurelius
Flag: Royal purple
Zodai: Lionhearts

THE SIXTH HOUSE:
VIRGO, *THE TRIPLE VIRGIN* CONSTELLATION
Strength: Sustenance
Guardian: Empress Moira (in critical condition)
Flag: Emerald green
Zodai: Ministers

THE SEVENTH HOUSE:
LIBRA, *THE SCALES OF JUSTICE*
CONSTELLATION

Strength: Justice
Guardian: Lord Hysan
Flag: Yellow
Zodai: Knights

THE EIGHTH HOUSE:
SCORPIO, *THE SCORPION*
CONSTELLATION

Strength: Innovation
Guardian: Chieftain Skiff
Flag: Black
Zodai: Stridents

THE NINTH HOUSE:
SAGITTARIUS, *THE ARCHER*
CONSTELLATION

Strength: Curiosity
Guardian: Guardian Brynda
Flag: Lavender
Zodai: Stargazers

THE TENTH HOUSE:
CAPRICORN, *THE SEAGOAT*
CONSTELLATION

Strength: Wisdom
Guardian: Sage Ferez
Flag: Brown
Zodai: Chroniclers

THE ELEVENTH HOUSE:
AQUARIUS, *THE WATER BEARER*
CONSTELLATION

Strength: Philosophy
Guardian: Supreme Guardian
Gortheaux the Thirty-Third
Flag: Aqua
Zodai: Elders

THE TWELFTH HOUSE:
PISCES,
THE FISH CONSTELLATION

Strength: Spirituality
Guardian: Prophet Marinda
Flag: Silver
Zodai: Disciples

THE THIRTEENTH HOUSE:
OPHIUCHUS, *THE SERPENT*
BEARER CONSTELLATION

Strength: Unity
Guardian: Master Ophiuchus
Flag: White
Zodai: Sires

PROLOGUE

WHEN I THINK OF MY brother, I hear his comforting voice.

Stanton's words have always been my lifeline: They have the power to soothe me, guide me, even save me from my nightmares. I especially love what I call his *Stantonisms*—catchy one-liners he would come up with on the spot whenever I was afraid.

"Don't fear what you can't touch," he told me the night Mom abandoned us. I used to think it was the smartest thing I'd ever heard, but now I know better.

Everything touches us eventually.

The day Mom left us, I stayed up late with Dad and Stan, the three of us huddled on the couch, pretending to watch the wallscreen while we waited for her to come home. At some point I must have dozed off, and Stanton probably carried me to bed. The sky was still dark when I awoke to the sound of my own scream.

The door to my room opened, and my ten-year-old brother's familiar voice said, "Rho, it's okay."

His weight settled beside me on the mattress, and his warm hand closed around my clammy one. "You're safe. Everything's fine."

My entire body was slick with sweat, and my breaths were coming in short spurts. I could still feel the spot on my shoulder where the Maw from my nightmare sank its fangs, the same place where the real Maw had bitten Stan the week before—only in the dream, Mom didn't swim swiftly enough to save me.

And as the monster carried me far from my family, its eyes were no longer glow-in-the-dark red.

They were a bottomless blue.

"Is—is she back yet?" I whispered as I fought to free myself from the nightmare's hold.

Stan squeezed my fingers, but the pressure felt faint, like I hadn't surfaced to full consciousness yet. "No."

"Is she . . . coming back?" I whispered even softer.

He was quiet a long moment, and I grew fully awake as I awaited his answer. Then he slid up and rested his back against the bed's headboard, sighing. "Want to hear a story?"

I exhaled, too, as I nestled under the covers beside him and closed my eyes in anticipation. I'd take a Stan story over pretty much anything on the planet.

"There once was a little girl whose name I can't remember, so let's call her Rho." His comforting voice wrapped around me like a second blanket, and I felt my heartbeat finally slowing down. "Little Rho lived on a tiny planet that was about the size of Kalymnos."

"But how can a world be that small?"

"Are you telling the story, or am I?"

"Sorry," I said quickly.

"Let's try this again: Rho lived alone on a very small planet, in a different galaxy where things like small planets were possible, and if you worry too much about the science, this story will end. Anyway, little Rho knew everything about her world: the name of every nar-clam, the shape of every microbe, the color of every leaf. Her home was her heart, and her heart was her home, just like Helios belongs to the Houses and the Houses belong to Helios."

His words painted pictures in the black space of my mind, burning up the darkness with their light. "But one day," he went on, "a huge storm rolled through her planet, and little Rho was blown into the atmosphere, caught in a whirlwind that tossed her about the cosmos and stranded her on a strange, much larger world."

"But what about her home—"

"It sounds like you don't want to hear the rest of the story," he said, sitting up suddenly, "so I guess I'll just go."

"No, no, I'm sorry, I want to hear it," I pleaded, tipping my head up on the pillow to stare at Stanton's gray profile.

"Then no more interruptions," he warned, settling back against the headboard, and I mimed sealing my lips shut. "Anyway, she landed on a new world, and instead of the sea surrounding her, she stood on a field of feathers."

"*Feathers?*"

"Huge feathers. They grew from the ground like grass, and they were every color and design you can imagine. When Rho walked, the feathers tickled her bare feet so she couldn't keep from smiling with every step."

I squealed with laughter as something soft suddenly brushed the soles of my feet, and I curled into myself and shrieked, "*Stan, stop!*"

"Yeah, she reacted just like that," said my brother, and I could hear the ghost of a smile in his voice.

"Only every time she laughed," he went on, "Rho's mind forced her mouth back down into a frown. She *shouldn't* be happy, not when she was so far from her home. She had to get back. She had to be serious."

"Were there people on that planet who could help her?" I asked—and then I cringed as I suddenly remembered I wasn't supposed to be asking questions.

"Actually," said my brother, "almost as soon as little Rho started walking across the field, she ran into someone. A purple bird that was human-sized and wore a wreath of flowers around its head."

"Whoa."

"Yeah. That's exactly what Rho said. And then the bird spoke to her."

"It *spoke*—?" I asked, awed.

"In a normal—if not slightly squeaky—voice, it said, 'Welcome, friend. Why do you fight yourself?'" I giggled at Stan's high-pitched bird impression. "Little Rho's shock at meeting a talking purple bird turned into confusion as she considered his question, and she asked, 'What do you mean?'"

"The bird pointed with its beak to Rho's feet. 'I can see the ground pleases you, yet you won't allow yourself to feel pleased. Why do you resist the pull of the present in favor of a pain that is clearly past?'"

"That sounds like something Mom would say," I blurted, and then I sucked in my breath at my own boldness.

Stan paused only a second, and in that instant it occurred to me that he probably didn't want to sound like Mom right now.

"Little Rho's shoulders sagged with the weight of her sadness, and she said, 'I'm upset because I've left my home, and now I don't know how to get back.' The bird frowned. 'But why should that be upsetting? Every bird must leave her nest, and once she does, she can never return. The nest dissolves because she doesn't need it anymore.'"

A sense of unease settled in my stomach, and I went from enjoying Stan's tale to not wanting to hear its ending. "I don't like this story. Let's start a new one."

"That's not how life works, Rho," murmured my brother, sounding older now that he wasn't speaking in character. "It's like in a game when you're dealt a hand you don't like, you don't get to ask for a new one. You have to change your hand for yourself."

"How?"

"By playing through it."

I didn't understand what he meant because I didn't want to try. There was only one thing I was waiting to hear from him. "Is Mom coming back?"

He was quiet for a stretch, and in our silence his breaths grew louder, until they rose and fell in rhythm with my own. When at last he spoke, his voice was so low I barely heard it.

"I think our nest is gone."

Tears spilled from my eyes because I knew my brother wouldn't lie to me. Mom wasn't coming back.

Stan crushed me to his side as I cried, and he continued narrating his story in a tone as soft as my sobs. "'That sounds like a terrible life,' little Rho said to the bird, horrified at the thought of never seeing her home again.

"But the bird's beak widened as it smiled and shook its head. 'Judging is a waste of time because most of what happens in our lives is out of our control. The only choice we get is what we do *right now*, with this moment. Every second is a choice we make.'"

I sniffled as I slid my face up on his shirt, which was stained with my tears. "So little Rho can choose to smile or frown as she walks through the feathers," I said.

"Exactly," said my brother. "You can get through anything, Rho. You just have to let go of your fears and keep moving forward."

"How?" I asked.

He was quiet a moment, and then he said, "*Don't fear what you can't touch.*"

I sat up a little, sounding the line out in my mind. There was something empowering about it, and I loved how neatly it declawed the monsters I couldn't fight, like my visions and my nightmares. And I knew then that I would survive the loss of Mom because I had Stan.

My brother was my strength, my guiding star, my anchor. It wasn't just the times he saved me from my nightmares—it was the love and faith and patience he showed me our whole lives.

With Stan by my side, the monsters couldn't touch me.

As long as my brother was safe, my fears weren't real.

1

THIRTEEN MASKED SOLDIERS SURROUND ME in the cadaverous Cathedral on Pisces.

Heart hammering, I search beyond their white uniforms for a sign of my friends, but no one else is here. The lights of the Zodiac constellations hang overhead, and in the center, Helios is already starting to go dark. Half the sun is swallowed in shadow.

"Wandering Star Rhoma Grace," says the Marad soldier directly in front of me. His greasy voice reminds me of Ambassador Charon of Scorpio. "You have been found guilty of Cowardice, Treason, and Murder. For these crimes, we sentence you to instant execution."

My pulse pounds as thirteen cylindrical black weapons are simultaneously trained on my chest.

"Do you have any final words?" asks the Charon-like voice.

I try to speak in my own defense, but my mouth won't open. I try to run, but my legs won't move. I try to pinch myself, but even my fingers are paralyzed. This can't be happening—it isn't real—they can't touch me—

"FIRE!" he cries.

My scream freezes on my lips as blue lights flash from every Murmur and blast into my chest at once, the pain so agonizing it incinerates my insides.

My body collapses to the bone floor, and the force of my fall is so strong that I blow right through the ground and get sucked down to an even deeper dimension of this hell.

I land on a flat field of prickly black feathers that scratch at my bare feet. The charcoal clouds above me darken and swirl, like a storm could blow through any moment.

My Lodestar suit has been replaced with a thin white dress, and the chilly air bites at my skin. A large silhouette materializes in the gray distance, and as it comes closer, the first thing I notice is it's not human.

Its legs are thin as sticks, and tucked into its sides are great feathery wings. Something about the birdlike creature feels familiar, like I should recognize it, but I've never seen anything like it in my life.

Lightning strikes the ground, illuminating the bird-man's features: It's missing an eye, its wings are studded with spikes, and its beak is soaked in blood.

I let out a high-pitched shriek right as thunder shakes the earth. Rain starts pouring down on me as I spin and run in the opposite direction.

My feet slide on the slippery feathers, and the soaked fabric of my dress clings to my skin as a shadow falls over me. I look up to see the bird-man diving down, its talons bearing on my head—

I roll into a ball, and the ground suddenly falls away, sloping down into a sharp descent. The lower I tumble, the faster I go, bumping my elbows, shoulders, and head on the slippery feathers again and again and again, until land runs out, and I roll into a roaring river.

My skin stings when it slaps the water, and I gasp for breath as the current tosses me around. The bird-man's shadow falls over me again, and I dive underwater to escape it.

Almost immediately, the river starts to shrink until it's too shallow to swim. When my head is in the clear, the creature's talons reach down again, too close to evade—

I cry out as sharp nails pierce my shoulders.

Blood leaks out from the gashes, and it gurgles up my throat, my nerve endings searing in maddening agony until I hear my bones snap in the creature's claws—

And then blackness entombs me.

✦ ✦ ✦

I blink a few times at Helios's brightness overhead, and as my vision adjusts, I realize it's a ceiling light.

I'm lying on a bed, my heart racing like I'm still being chased. An incessant beeping in tune with my pulse comes into focus, and when at last my breaths start to slow, so do the mechanical chirps.

I look down to see clear tubes sticking out of my arms, and my vitals flashing across floating holographic screens. I'm in a hospital.

I raise my hands slowly, and my body feels heavy and sore, like I haven't left this bed in weeks. I scan the empty room expecting to see someone. Someone important—only I can't remember whom.

There's one window in the small space, and it shows a dark, starless sky. My muscles are leaden, but I need to know what's happened. Where I am. *Who survived.*

I gradually remove every needle from my veins, and I hug the armrest to pull myself up.

As my feet drop to the icy floor, oblivion beckons in my mind, and the world grows dark for a few beats. I rest my forehead on the bed, and when I feel steadier, I straighten my crinkly white hospital gown and slowly manage to shuffle out of the room.

Even though the shadowy hallway is empty, a prickle of unease climbs up the back of my neck, and I get the sense I'm being watched. Voices murmur somewhere nearby, and I use the metal handrail along the wall to hold myself upright as I walk in the sound's direction.

"Don't know what we'll do if she doesn't wake up soon."

Hysan.

Relief floods through me, heating my skin, and I move as swiftly as my weakened muscles can carry me. My pulse quickens as soon as I spy his golden head through the partly open doorway of an unoccupied hospital room.

But I freeze when I see who's with him.

"You look exhausted," says a statuesque Ariean with flawless bronze brown skin and long cat eyes. *Skarlet Thorne.*

"That's because I am exhausted," he says, and the heavy exhale that follows settles like a physical weight on my heart.

"All we needed was for her to be the face of our movement," he continues, and there's a lack of sunlight in his voice that makes me flash to the half-dark Helios from the Cathedral. "We had everything else covered—the strategizing, the fighting—but still she couldn't help herself. And now the whole Zodiac is at risk just because Rho couldn't handle her emotions."

My jaw drops, and my chest hollows, like I'm being drained of every good emotion I've ever felt.

"I can distract you from all that," purrs Skarlet, moving in until she's too close to him. "I missed you last night."

Air hitches in my throat as her lips trail up his neck to his ear, and she says something that sounds like, "Come tonight."

My heart holds its beat until Hysan answers.

"As you wish."

I cover my mouth so they won't hear my gasp, and I hear her say, "What if your princess wakes up and discovers us?"

"Rho's the most trusting person in the Zodiac," says Hysan, and in the dim lighting his centaur smile looks more like a cruel sneer. "She won't suspect a thing. And if she does, all it takes is a little sweet talking, and she's mine again."

I squeeze my eyes shut and rub my temples, desperately hoping I'm just hallucinating from whatever drugs they've pumped into me. Then I look again, just in time to see Hysan pressing up against Skarlet.

"How about showing me what I missed last night?" he asks huskily, grabbing her by the waist and pushing her onto the countertop.

I turn away as their mouths come together, and then I bury my face in the wall and try to swallow the impulse to cry—but when I hear Skarlet's soft moans, I muster every lingering store of strength within me and force myself to keep moving.

If I'm going to die, I want it to be as far from this room as possible.

I don't slow down until I've made myself nauseous. I *knew* Hysan wasn't trustworthy. I should have heeded my brain's warnings. I should have trusted my fears all along.

The sense that I'm being watched settles over me again, and I push past my pain so I can focus on finding the others. Mathias, Brynda, and Rubi can't be far, and I need to know where I am and how much time has passed.

A flash of blond hair flickers around a corner, and I speed up. "Wait!" I call out, my voice scratchy and unused. "Wait for me!"

The woman turns around, and when I see her face, I try to call for help—but my throat is too dry to make a sound.

"The stars must like me more than I thought," she says in the reptilian voice I remember as she raises a pistol to my chest.

She's me, and she's not. . . . Even on her Cancrian face, Corinthe's smile is still leering.

She takes a step toward me, and I will my legs to move, but my muscles are leaden, my body betraying me. Broken chains dangle from the metal cuffs on her wrists, and I realize she's escaped custody just as the pistol slams into my head.

2

WHEN I COME TO, I'M in a different dim hospital room, and I'm tied to a chair. Just like I was on *Equinox*.

My heart revs with adrenaline, and I struggle against the chains to free myself. I stop when I see Corinthe's face leaning into mine.

She's sitting beside me holding a jagged knife.

"Didn't want to start the *girl talk* until you were awake to enjoy it." Her voice is almost gentle.

She presses the sharp blade to my gown's neckline and cuts down along the crinkly fabric until my chest is bare. "I thought we'd go with a different design today," she whispers, bringing the icy metal up to my throat.

I cry out as pain explodes through me. The knife punctures my skin and slices from my neck to my collarbone, and I start gasping for air.

"Rising into your House has turned me into a romantic," she croons as I suck in ragged inhales and try to fill my lungs.

"When I'm finished, you and your Guide will have matching scars . . . and if that's not a sign of fated love, what is?"

My breathing is labored and high pitched as she carves down the rungs of my ribcage and reaches my stomach. I can't scream or blink or fight. I'm frozen in my torment, my vision blurry, my thoughts swimming, the agony so complete and overwhelming that even if I survive, I know I'm not coming back from this.

"So quiet today, Rho. . . . Aren't you going to tell me how I'm a victim?" She pushes the blade so deep into my gut that my neck swings forward, and I vomit on my lap.

"Aren't you going to tell me how you still plan to plead for the acceptance of Risers?" she hisses in my ear as I hack up my insides. "How I can hurt you all I want, but you'll still forgive me?"

And even if I could speak, I know I couldn't say that.

Because if somehow I live through this, I'm going to kill Corinthe myself.

The door abruptly bursts open, and she leaps back as Mathias storms into the room with a dozen armed Lodestars. "Arrest her!" he booms, pointing to Corinthe, who's backed up against the wall but holding her bloodied knife out threateningly as the Zodai close in around her.

Mathias darts over and immediately starts undoing my bonds, his square shoulders blocking everything else from view. "I'm so sorry, Rho. This wasn't supposed to happen."

As soon as my hands are free, I pull both halves of my gown together to cover the cuts on my chest. But when I look into his soft midnight eyes, I know he's already seen them. We wear the same scars now.

Before Mathias can say anything, Hysan barges into the room. "What's happened?" he demands.

"Corinthe escaped, but she's been captured, and the asset has been recovered," says Mathias, standing ramrod straight and saluting Hysan.

Asset?

When Hysan's eyes land on mine, his face splits into a sun-filled smile that cuts right through the bags under his eyes and the worry lines on his forehead. His green gaze brightens as he takes my limp hand in his warm one, and even though I know better now, my skin still buzzes from his touch.

"I missed you," he whispers, leaning in and pressing a velvety kiss on my lips.

His *concerned boyfriend* act is so convincing that I wonder whether I made up the conversation between him and Skarlet. Then I look closer, and I notice the faded red lipstick on his chin and the crescent nail marks on his neck, and I know I'm not crazy.

"Get away from me," I snap, scrambling toward Mathias. I look up at him and say, "Mathias, please, take me away from here. I don't want to be anywhere near Hysan."

But Mathias doesn't meet my gaze. He's assumed his unshakable Zodai stance.

"He doesn't answer to you anymore," says Hysan, the gentleness gone from his voice. "Mathias is loyal to your heart, and you gave your heart to me. You're both mine now."

I shake my head and grip Mathias's arms to try to force him to look at me. "Mathias—please—snap out of it!"

His blue eyes finally roll down to meet mine, but his irises are now as hard as stone. "You made your choice, Rho."

"Don't do this!"

My plea goes ignored as a couple of Lodestars cuff my wrists and forcefully march me up to Hysan. "Time to deliver on all your promises," he whispers as he leisurely runs a finger along my jawline. "You wanted to die for the Zodiac, didn't you? I'm happy to report that after so many failed suicide missions, the stars have finally judged you worthy of a martyr's death."

Our faces are inches apart, and yet I feel no warmth radiating from his golden skin. His sunny glow never looked so artificial.

"Congratulations, my lady," he huskily breathes into my lips. *"You earned it."*

Mathias comes up beside us, and Hysan turns to him. "After all she put you through, you deserve this more than I do."

"Thank you," says Mathias, bowing his head, "but this is your right as much as mine."

Hysan unsheathes his ceremonial dagger. "Together then?"

Mathias nods and holds up Corinthe's bloodied blade—then they turn and plunge their weapons into me.

"NO!"

I blink, and Hysan and Mathias are gone.

I'm still tied to the chair.

"Welcome back," croaks Corinthe. Her savage and unhinged smile comes into focus, and I look down to see she's slicing lines across my abdomen.

My shredded white gown is patterned with splotches of red blood. "What's happening to me?" I manage to ask, my voice barely more than a breath.

"What do you think?" she asks. "You failed. And now you're dying."

Her blade digs in too far, and my eyes roll back, only this time I don't lose consciousness—I feel my soul floating up from my body and rising to the astral plane, like I'm deeply Centered.

The molecules of air around me transform into the slipstream where I first met Ochus, and I feel a wintry wind of warning before his monstrous form materializes.

I endured torture for an eternity, he booms, hurling his words like hailstones, *and you can't even handle a few nightmares? You are weak—no wonder you failed the Houses.*

I—I don't understand what's happening, I stammer, his frigid Psynergy burning against my open wounds. *Help me, please! I need to get out of here. I need to get back to where my friends are, I have to rescue Nishi—*

You are not listening—you are too late, crab! he thunders at me. *The Zodiac is gone.*

It—it can't be—

What do you think is happening to you? he demands, his Psynergy wrapping around me like a hurricane, sending chills through my body. *You have joined me in the astral plane. Our destinies were always linked, child, and now we are doomed to face forever what we destroyed.*

But I—I didn't do anything—

You played right into the master's hands. The right leader would have stopped him, but you are rash, foolish, fearful—what hope was there ever that you could go up against a star and win?

His icy hands close around my throat, and I'm infected with winter. *Please!* I beg him. *Don't—*

But my veins ice over, freezing my blood, and I can't suck in any oxygen. Spots obscure my vision as I suffocate, and I'm not sure if I'm horrified or relieved that it's all ending.

I'm so tired of dying and reviving, dying and reviving, dying and reviving. . . . I'm ready for it to be over.

"Oh, but I'm not," croaks Corinthe in my ear.

The pressure around my neck vanishes, as does the cold weather, and I blink my eyes open to find I'm back in my body. Only now I'm lying flat on my stomach.

My back is in scorching pain, like there are live flames licking my skin. "I can't let you die before showing you how great these scars are turning out," says Corinthe as she carves across my shoulder blades. Her breath burns my raw skin.

"Please," I whisper, the fire in my body overwhelming. Water wells in my eyes, and pain presses into my mind. "Just . . . finish."

She laughs softly, but there's no mirth in the mousy sound. "I'll never be finished," she rasps in my ear. "You'll never escape this place. You'll always be here with me."

Her blade stabs into my lower spine, and I arch up in a piercing scream.

She pulls the knife out and stabs me with it again and again and again, until I can't make any more sounds.

Then I hear a loud knocking.

My eyes fly open, and I gasp to find I'm no longer lying down. I'm standing upright in my dorm-pod on Elara and wearing my blue Acolyte uniform.

"WHAT THE HELIOS IS HAPPENING TO ME?!" I shout to the room.

The place looks exactly as it did when I saw it last—my bed is unmade, my desk is riddled with clothes I meant to put away, and a uniform identical to the one I'm wearing is draped across my chair from when I changed into my black space suit for our Drowning Diamonds concert.

Someone knocks on my door again.

I yank it open to find a trembling teen girl in a tattered blue uniform. Her knees are slightly bent, shoulders curved in, unkempt dark hair curtaining her features. She looks like she hasn't bathed in months.

First I think she's a new monster I've dreamt up.

Then I glimpse hints of her cinnamon face, and all my other fears fade from mattering.

"Nishi?"

3

FASTER THAN A BREATH, NISHI unsheathes a dagger and shoves me against the wall, pressing the blade under my chin.

"I'm not scared of you, demon," she says in a guttural predator's voice. "So do your worst."

Since speaking means slitting my own throat, I stay completely still, not daring to even swallow. I just stare at the flickers of amber that shine through her matted clumps of black hair.

The terror in her eyes is so primal that she feels realer than the Hysan and Mathias I met in the hospital.

"Say something," she suddenly commands, pulling the knife back slightly.

"I'm going to find you," I say, my voice tight. "Imogen and Blaze took you away from me, but I swear I won't rest until I—"

"Right, you're risking your life to save mine, and now you're going to make me feel like scum for the horrible things I said to you on Aquarius," she says sharply, the dagger in her hand trembling. "And for joining the Tomorrow Party. And for getting Deke killed."

A sob slips through her sharp-edged voice when she says his name. "Aren't you going to tell me again how he—he was free, and his back was only turned because he was freeing me! How I should have been looking out for him—should have warned him—should have taken his place—"

"Nish—stop! I never said any of that because it's not true!" Tears leak from my eyes, and I wish my subconscious had generated a monstrous version of Nishi—like it did with Hysan and Mathias—instead of this broken, beaten girl.

"None of this is your fault," I insist, and I don't care if she stabs me with that blade anymore. I just can't stand seeing her this way. "Please don't think those things, Nish. I love you and will *never* stop searching for you—"

"*Rho?*"

I blink at the abrupt change in her tone. Her voice has dropped about a dozen decibels, and she sounds more fearful than furious.

"It's me, Nish. I don't know what's happening or if any of this is real, but I'm trapped in some kind of nightmare. Everyone's been awful to me, and—"

"Oh, my Helios, it's *you!*"

Nishi throws the dagger aside and crushes me to her chest. We hug so tightly that I can't breathe, but I don't care. I'd rather die right here, clasped in the arms of my best friend, than anywhere else.

I hear her soft sobs in my ear, and soon I'm crying, too. When at last we let go of each other, we wipe our wet faces on our sleeves, and I shove the clutter off my bed so we can sit.

"How is any of this happening?" I ask.

"The Sumber." Now that she's not putting up a violent front, Nishi sounds much weaker than I first realized. "It took me a while to remember, but I finally figured it out," she says, her hands trembling. "The gun Imogen pointed at me was a Sumber. She shot me, and then the nightmares started."

Even though she looks so different, it's comforting to know she's still the same quick study I remember.

"H—how long have we been here, Rho?"

I almost cringe at hearing her sound so brittle and breakable. And as I open my mouth to answer, I realize I have no idea how much time has passed.

"I'm not sure. . . . It feels like—"

"Forever," she finishes for me, and I nod as our eyes meet. "Just try to focus," she orders me, and I'm relieved to hear some of her bossy Nishiness coming back. "What can you remember before the nightmares?"

For a brief moment, the fog lifts a little in my mind, and I see Crompton standing before me, flanked by a Stargazer and a Dreamcaster. As I raised my Scarab to shoot him, the Zodai beside him raised weapons of their own—an Arclight and—

"I was hit by a Sumber, too," I say, piecing it together out loud as I go. "I think it was a few days after you. But how did we find each other here?"

Her gaze loses its intensity as her focus drifts away. "The Sumber's mind control must run off Psynergy . . . and our Psynergy signatures must be naturally drawn to each other. What can you remember from before you fell? Who shot you?"

As usual, while I'm still trying to process the new information, she's pressing us onward. If we were in class, Deke would be groaning and begging our instructor to ban Nishi from the room until the rest of us mastered the lesson.

"Why are you smiling?" she asks in surprise.

"I just really missed you," I say, reeling her in for another, longer hug. Neither of us says anything as we hold each other, and I close my eyes as I breathe in her thick, dark hair. Even now, unwashed and in an alternate dimension, it still holds hints of the expensive, lavender-scented products she imports from Sagittarius. "I'm going to find you," I whisper, tears threatening to overtake me again.

"I know, Rho—"

She cuts out and yanks on my hand, and we leap off the bed just as an explosion blasts above us, and the ceiling comes crashing down on the mattress.

"RUN!" she shouts.

Fingers laced together, we burst out of my room and hurtle down the hallway, ducking our heads and skidding to stops as chunks of the cement compound begin crumbling down around us. "Don't let go!" calls Nishi over the deafening quaking and thundering.

We turn the corner toward the dining hall and freeze as a massive ball of fire rolls our way. She shrieks, and I pull us in a new direction.

The air grows hotter with every breath as the fire burns up more and more of our oxygen until I shove open a searing red door, and we topple into the swimming complex. Sucking in synchronized breaths, we leap into the salt water.

We stay down as long as we can, and when we finally surface for air, there's no trace of fire, not even a wisp of smoke. "What's next?" I ask between breaths.

"Something worse," says Nishi darkly. "It's always something worse."

We climb out of the pool and take each other's hands again as we step through the red door—only we're no longer in the Academy.

The gray hall has turned glossy black, and it extends infinitely in either direction. The feeling that I'm being watched is back, and I pull Nishi along with me through the passage at a quick clip.

"How do we wake up from the Sumber?" I ask as we hurry hand in hand past symmetrical rows of nondescript doors.

"It's not up to us. Whoever has our bodies has to administer the antidote."

I slow down in disgust at the thought of someone else having complete control over me. And suddenly the polished ground rises before us like a black wave.

Nishi's grip on me tightens as we start to slide backwards, and we wheel around to run in the opposite direction—but we skid to a stop as the path ahead starts rising, too.

"What do we do?" I ask.

Nishi yanks open one of the nondescript doors, and we escape into an unknown room. As the door shuts behind us, I look around and see we're standing in the entrance hall to Zodai University.

Every campus includes this identical chamber, a remnant from the days when all our worlds were ruled as one. The mismatched walls are crafted from stone, and they represent the four elements—sapphire for water, tiger-eye for earth, ruby for fire, and gold for air. On the ceiling above us is the ancient crest of the Zodiac Galaxy: a massive Helios with twelve sunbeams, each one pointing to a different House symbol. Within the sun is our old name: *Houses of Helios.*

I used to cut through this place every morning when I visited the solarium.

"Where'd the door go?" asks Nishi.

I turn to see there's no longer the outline of a doorway in the wall made of rubies, and I hear a strange flickering sound. "What is that?"

"Do you smell—"

Nishi's voice cuts out as a blast of red flame blazes out from the wall, like a fiery hand reaching out for us.

We leap across the room, falling back against the wall of cool sapphires. "What's happening?" I shout as water starts to shower down from the blue wall, drowning my words and drenching us both.

Since the fire's flames are still reaching out for us, we tread along the wall of gold to avoid the water and the heat—until a strong gust of wind punches out from behind us, blowing our bodies across the room.

Nishi and I lose hold of each other, and my back hits the tigereye wall, and then I slide down to the floor. Behind me the stones tremble from the impact.

Water is still falling from the sapphire wall, and by now it's about a foot high, so I'm soaked once more. Nishi reaches down to pull me up, and then we back away from the brown wall as its shaking intensifies.

Tigereye stones begin dislodging and rolling down like pebbles, spraying our heads and faces and legs until we're forced to huddle together in the middle of the room, equidistant from all four sides.

"What happens if we die?" I ask Nishi, shouting over all the noise.

"Each time we survive a danger, a new, worse threat is waiting for us," she says, shivering as more of the flames are drowned by the rising water. "And it keeps going until the dream finally kills us, and a new nightmare begins."

I flash to Corinthe's torture; I instantly shove the image away, terrified that the mere thought could re-trigger it.

The water is now up to my waist, and it seems to be pouring in faster and faster. "If we drown, will you and I be separated?"

Nishi doesn't answer, but she tightens her grip on my hand as my feet float off the ground. "When Imogen shot me, how did you escape the Party?"

Whether she's asking from curiosity or just to distract us from our imminent deaths, I'm glad to feel useful one last time. I furrow my brow in concentration, and I find that the more I focus on the past, the better I remember it.

"It was . . . my Mom."

"What?" Nishi's amber irises grow bright with wonder.

"She saved me." As I say the words, the full memory unfurls: "Hysan found her. They were working together in secret for weeks—"

Our heads bob against the Houses of Helios emblem on the ceiling, and we cling to each other as our faces tilt up into the last layer of air. I pull in as deep an inhale as possible before we're sucked under.

It's pitch black all around us, more like Space than underwater, and I feel bubbles streaming from my nostrils as we descend deeper and deeper and deeper. My head starts to pound from the lack of oxygen, and Nishi's hand grows limp in mine, and I know soon this will all be over.

Suddenly my boot brushes against something solid, and I reach down and feel the ground. There's some kind of metal lever sticking up from the floor.

I try to push it down with one hand, but I can't. Nishi must realize what I'm doing because she frees her fingers from mine and wraps both hands around the metal, and together we try shoving it.

The lever gives way, and water begins to whirlpool around us as a drain opens in the floor, and all of it swirls away. As I finally draw breath, I turn to my best friend in relief—and I run out of oxygen again.

Nishi's sprawled on the ground, her long dark hair fanned around her. *Dead*.

4

"NISHI, *NO!*"

I drop down beside her fallen body, her eyes closed and chest unmoving. Remembering my childhood training, I apply chest compressions and administer mouth to mouth, again and again and again. "Don't leave me alone here, Nish, please," I beg as tears well in my eyes, and I press down on her chest yet *again*—

Her eyes fly open, and she starts coughing up water.

Air rushes out of my lungs as quickly as it rushes into hers, and I help her sit up, the tension in my body finally easing. When it's clear she's going to be okay, I finally take note of our surroundings.

We're in a supersized supply closet lined with aisles upon aisles of shelves. Compression suits, helmets, oxygen tanks, and other gear are stacked alongside weapons like Tasers, pistols, and Ripples.

I help Nishi to her feet, and we survey the supplies around us. Then she wordlessly grabs a pistol and starts filling her pockets with extra ammunition, and I raise a Ripple to eye level, resting its butt against my shoulder. It's

House Cancer's signature weapon, but it's considered mostly ceremonial, since Cancrians don't have a violent gene in us.

Unless our loved ones are threatened.

The crossbow device is made of tightly woven strands of Sea Spider silk that propel up to a dozen slender darts whittled from nar-clam shells and dipped in the paralyzing poison of a Maw. The weapon isn't light, but its weight is comfortable, making the device sturdy enough to keep steady.

Even though I've never held one before, it feels familiar. As Nishi hands me extra dart cartridges, she says, "Remember that *Protector of the Planets* holo-game you used to love playing because it always greeted you by announcing to the whole entertainment center that you had one of the highest scores?"

"That's not *why* I loved playing it—"

"The Ripple is just a fancier version of the crossbow you always used in there," she finishes.

It feels like years since the carefree days when I used to hologram myself into that virtual reality world. The game would provide players with a weapons cache that holds twelve devices, and now that I think about it, they all seemed a lot like watered-down versions of the signature weapons of every House.

"I always chose the crossbow," I muse out loud.

Nishi strides up to a different shelf and pulls down a couple of blue space suits with the university's logo. She hands one to me. "In case the walls come down around us," she says with a shrug.

Since she means that literally, we pull the suits on over our uniforms. "So where's your mom been this whole time?" she asks as we change.

"With the Luminaries." It's getting easier to lower my guard with Nishi around, and I continue pushing down on the walls that barricade my memories to keep filling in the blanks. "It's a secret society of people who've Seen the Last Prophecy, which is—"

"Yeah, I've heard of the Last Prophecy," she says dismissively as we clip black helmets to our belts and holster our weapons. "There are tons of conspiracy nuts on Sagittarius who believe in it."

"It's real, Nish. The master himself confirmed it."

She stops working and steps closer to me, staring into my eyes. *"Who's the master?"*

"Crompton." For some reason, I whisper the name. "He's the original Aquarius."

Her face pales, and she begins to shake her head. "No way—"

"It's true, Nish. He betrayed Ophiuchus to the other Guardians and stole his Talisman to keep his immortality for himself—"

An arrow flies over our heads, and we duck.

Without looking back, we hurtle down the aisle, holding hands, running past rows of shelves in search of an exit as more arrows shoot after us. A dart lodges into the wall a hair behind me, and items keep exploding over our heads.

"There!" shouts Nishi, and she pulls me down a row that dead-ends in a metal elevator, its doors opening like it's welcoming us in. An arrow bounces off the helmet clipped to my hip as we slide inside.

Nishi frantically presses the button to close the doors, and while we wait for them to shut, I catch a glimpse of our pursuer. He's in a billowing black cloak, his facial features shrouded in his hood's shadow. And as he marches toward us, I realize he isn't human.

Twin walls of metal swallow the view before I can see more, and I blow out a hard breath as we ascend somewhere—*anywhere.*

"What's the plan?" I ask Nishi. "While we wait for someone to save us, we're just condemned to live out our worst nightmares?"

She shakes her head. "The antidote alone isn't enough." Her voice sounds small again. "Even if you're dosed, you won't escape until you've faced your greatest fear."

"My *greatest fear?* Nish, this *whole place* is one huge fear fest!"

"You don't understand. This is the final thing the nightmare world is keeping from you—it's the blow that breaks you." Her voice grows rough, and she clears her throat.

Deke's death must've been the last memory she recovered. Her greatest fear was probably a future without him.

"That's why some people never awaken from a Sumber dose," she explains. "And I think that's probably why you're still here."

The person I've forgotten clouds my mind again. The one I expected to see at the hospital . . .

The elevator opens.

We raise our weapons quickly but step out slowly. The metal doors shut behind us, and we find ourselves in the place that was literally and figuratively the brightest point of my time on Elara. It's the highest peak in the whole compound, a wide room with windowed walls that curve to form a windowed ceiling.

The solarium.

Silver starlight glints across the collection of moonstone statues that are modeled after our Holy Mothers, and written across the floor beneath them is the Zodai axiom: *Trust Only What You Can Touch.* Any fantasies I ever had about the future were born in this room.

"No way out again," says Nishi, and I realize she's right—the only exit is the elevator. And its doors are opening again.

"*Hide,*" I whisper, and I pull Nishi into the collection of stone statues. I place her behind Mother Crae, and then I hide behind the neighboring sculpture of Mother Origene. I'm in the exact spot where Mathias used to sit when he meditated.

I rest the Ripple against my shoulder, and from the corner of my eye I see Nishi aiming her gun at the elevator as our pursuer steps into the silver light.

I can't tell if the gasp is mine or Nishi's.

The creature's legs are as thin as sticks, and tucked into its sides are great feathery wings. *It's the one-eyed bird-man.*

Its beak is still steeped in blood, and adorning its head is a crown of pointy thorns—they're the arrows it's been shooting at us. Trying to steady my nerves, I lean out the slightest bit and aim my weapon at its chest.

When I see that Nishi's also in position, I shout, *"Now!"* We fire at the same time, and the bird-man immediately goes down.

We approach it carefully, and Nishi hangs back, her pistol pointed at its head, while I make sure it's really dead.

I lean over its cloaked body slowly . . . and it rears up and launches at me.

We crash to the floor, where the creature easily overpowers me. Pinned down, I feel strong hands wrapping around my neck—not wings, but human hands. Blackness drowns my vision as I choke, and my pulse echoes in my ears, my throat afire—

A bullet goes off, and my attacker's hands fall away.

He slumps to the side, and through my blurry vision I see Nishi, her chest rising and falling with adrenaline, her face set in a warrior's scowl.

"Stellar," I say hoarsely, and she reaches down and pulls me up. I rub my throat as we stare at the human man beneath us, facedown on the floor.

"Let's flip him," I say. Nishi takes his feet and I grab his shoulders, and together we turn him over.

Nishi gasps, but I don't understand.

I stare at each individual feature like it's a clue: the blond curls, the sun-kissed skin, the open and glassy green eyes.

Then I blink, and all at once the pieces come together.

And I scream.

5

DESPAIR DROWNS ME, AND I remember the Cathedral, watching my brother and Aryll roll around on the bone floor, struggling to overtake each other. I see Hysan and Mathias running to help Stan, but they're too late.

There's no cry or gunshot or blood—there's only Stan's pale green eyes as they turn toward me, lifeless.

My heart howls in agony, and it feels like every bone in my body is breaking. I'm coming apart bit by bit, painfully, permanently, and even if the heartbreak doesn't kill me, it doesn't matter, because I'll never recover.

I've already lost everything I loved in the Zodiac. My brother, my home, my House. Returning to reality would be the true nightmare now. I'm safer in here, where the horrors aren't real.

"It's okay, Rho, it's okay, calm down. . . ."

Nishi's murmurs of reassurance blow softly into my ear, and as her voice comes into focus, I register that I'm on the floor, sobbing hysterically beside my brother's body, held up only by my best friend's arms.

"It's going to be okay, I promise," she goes on gently. "This isn't real.

Don't let this place destroy you, Rho. I need you. Please, focus—this is just another nightmare."

Nishi's presence is proof I was wrong—I do have a reason to return.

Just one.

"He—Aryll—killed him," I spit out between sobs, my teeth chattering and limbs shivering. "The master told Aryll to take my mom, and my brother attacked him to try to save her. But I don't even know if she—if she made it out—" My muscles feel gelatinous, and I sink down further until my head is pressed into Nishi's chest cavity.

She inhales sharply. "You mean, he's actually . . . oh, Rho. I'm so sorry," she breathes, her voice choking with her own sobs.

"I don't want to go back," I say, shaking my head vehemently against her. "I don't want to go back, I don't want to go back, I don't want to go back—"

"Shhhh," says Nishi, stroking my hair and holding me tighter to her. "Rho, you're the bravest, strongest, most fearless person I know—"

"No, I'm not, Nish! I'm not. I'm foolish and naïve and a *coward*!" The last word comes out as a shout, and it scrapes my throat.

But still I can't lower my volume. "When I was young, my mom trained me to trust my fears, and it's all I've ever done! It doesn't matter if I leave this place or stay here—either way, my fears always rule me. At least this world is more honest about it!"

"You're wrong, Rho. In here, you can only run from your fears. Out there you can *face* them."

Her wisdom reminds me painfully of Stan. He always believed I was strong enough to face my fears, but he never knew *he* was the source of that strength. Because I never told him.

I should have been there for him sooner. I stopped being a kid long ago, but I kept expecting Stan to treat me like one, to watch over me and love me and protect me unconditionally. But who was there to protect *him*?

"Rho, you couldn't save him," says Nishi, like she knows exactly what I'm thinking. The way she reads my thoughts reminds me of the way Stan and I used to understand each other's minds, and my heart hurts so much that I have to gasp to catch my breath.

"Remember that this was all Aryll's doing," she insists.

"But *I'm* the reason Aryll screwed with Stan in the first place!" I break free of her hold, and I'm shouting again. "When the Marad surrounded us, I recognized Aryll, and I called him by his name! I should have realized how Stan would react. If he hadn't known it was Aryll, he wouldn't have attacked—"

"Rho, your brother attacked Aryll because he grabbed your mom!" Nishi's voice rises to match mine. "And if a different soldier had taken her, he would have jumped in just as fast! Stop taking credit for Stan's death. He died the way he lived—on his own terms—and the only choice you have now is to accept that!"

Lines suddenly start spiderwebbing across the solarium's glass walls, like they did in the crystal dome on the day of our concert, and we leap to our feet just as the window shatters.

Neither of us has a helmet on, so my next breath never comes. Shards of glass slice shallow cuts along my skin and suit as I'm sucked out of the compound and onto the moon's soundless surface.

And the instant I leave the solarium, the nightmare changes.

I'm in a familiar gray room, sitting in a chair, and when I try to move, I realize my wrists and ankles are cuffed. There's an empty hospital bed before me, stained with pools of blood.

A woman in white healer's scrubs has her back to me while she sorts through medical tools on a table.

"Where are we?" asks a familiar voice.

I swing my face around in shock to see Nishi sitting next to me. She's also tied to a chair, and a sense of dread blooms in my stomach, keeping me from answering her.

The healer turns around, and I start struggling, desperately fighting against my shackles.

"Rho, what's wrong?" asks Nishi because she doesn't know this Riser wears my face now.

"Welcome back."

Nishi snaps her gaze to the healer, and whether it's the raspy voice or the leering smile, somehow I know she recognizes Corinthe.

This can't be happening.

I can't bring Nishi into this nightmare.

"Our time together being almost over," says Corinthe, holding up an even larger and sharper knife than before, "I wanted one more moment with you to say goodbye."

Our time is almost over?

Suddenly the room begins to shake around us, and Corinthe's image flickers, like I'm streaming a holo-show through a poor connection.

This doesn't seem to be happening within the dream—it's happening without.

"One of us is waking up," says Nishi, our minds arriving at the same realization. "It's you."

"Yes, but you also have a choice," injects Corinthe, bending over us so we're eye-level. Her knife is inches from me, reflecting back my terrified face. "You can choose to stay."

"Ignore her," snarls Nishi.

"Or you can do that," concedes Corinthe, shrugging. "But if you go . . . she replaces you."

Darkness flashes in her familiar pale green eyes. "I'll take out every moment of your absence on her. Every cut, every wound, every nightmare she suffers will be because of you."

My whole body is shivering, and I wish my hands were free so I could punch Corinthe again.

"Rho, don't even think—"

"I'm not going," I say to Nishi, ignoring Corinthe's presence beside us. "I'm sorry, I can't—"

"You're playing right into the Sumber's game!"

Since I know Nishi won't let me stay for her, I reach for another reason. "Crompton could have custody of my body right now! The last thing I remember is shooting him at the same time that I got shot, and if he's still alive, he's not going to be happy with me—"

"And if that's the case, you'll face it," she says, speaking over me. "He's already outed himself, so who knows what his next move will be? You're needed. And whatever you find when you get back, you'll be ready for it. *I know you will.*"

"Don't worry, I won't kill her," says Corinthe, looking at me like I'm being paranoid. "I'll just bring her right up to the point of death. Every time. That way I can keep her with me forever."

The walls around us start to shake again, and this time I feel a forceful pull on my mind, like my thoughts are being vacuumed out of my head.

"*Tick, tock, tick, tock, crab,*" taunts Corinthe as the quaking intensifies.

"*I'm staying,*" I say out loud, hoping it helps me hang on.

"Excellent," says Corinthe as the air settles, and she returns to rooting through the tools on the table, giving us space. Nishi leans closer to me, and I wish our hands were free so I could comfort her.

"Rho, I don't have any siblings—*Helios*, I barely have *parents*. But you're more than a sister . . . you're a part of me. I can't picture my life without you in it."

"I feel the same way—"

"Before we found each other in the nightmare," she goes on, her features drawing together like she's admitting something shameful, "I had given up. I thought I'd be better off in here, where the nightmares aren't real."

She takes a loud breath. "After a while, without the dream of hope, it got harder and harder to hang on to my sanity—on to *me*. I was alone, and tormented, and tired, and afraid—and then you rescued me."

She leans over as far as she can and presses a soft, slow kiss on my forehead. Tears sprout from my eyes. "You reminded me of who I am. Of who *we are*, and why we've committed our lives to this war. For House Cancer. For our classmates. For Deke. *We can't give up.*"

The room shakes for the third time, more violently than before, and Nishi and I press into each other to keep steady. I know my best friend is right—but I also know nothing awaits me in a world without Stanton or Nishi.

"I swear I'm going to get you out of here, Nish," I say as we pull apart, my voice sounding strong to me for the first time. "Just hang on a little longer— and if this place starts to feel like too much again, know that I won't rest until I find you."

Her face softens with relief. "I know you won't, Rho."

Corinthe cuts over to us as she realizes what's happening, and everything begins to flicker like the Sumber is running out of power. "Who's the monster now?" she shouts as I quit resisting reality, and I feel myself being pulled to the surface.

"You'll abandon your best friend to save yourself?" she keeps shouting. "So much for martyrdom, right, Rho? Just remember that for every minute you're up there breathing your free air, she's down here drowning in your nightmares!"

A dizziness engulfs me, and my surroundings begin to fracture. As the room starts to fade, I hear Nishi cry out in agony.

"NO!"

I want to hang on, but I'm too close to consciousness to stall the process, and I try calling out to her, but my voice is gone. The whole scene is slipping through my thoughts, like trying to hold water in my hands.

I don't know who, or what, will be waiting for me when I awaken.

All I know is I have to save Nishi from my nightmares.

And I have to do it *now*.

6

TICK, TOCK, TICK, TOCK, CRAB.

I open my eyes to find four unfamiliar faces peering down at me. All are wearing white healer's scrubs.

"She's awake!" says the youngest-looking healer, who's probably my age—though she's about a foot taller. "Hi, Rho!"

"*Finally*," says a woman who seems only slightly older, her hair so red it looks like it's on fire. "Check out her dumb expression, though. Could be a sign of brain damage."

"Oh, do be quiet, Kenza," says the only man in the group. He's so heavily muscled that he looks like a professional holo-wrestler. I must be on Aries.

I survey the woman closest to me last, and she smiles down gently. "Welcome back, Wandering Star." Her voice is soft and soothing, at odds with the static-style white noise buzzing in my mind.

"Focus on the sound of my voice . . . breathe in deeply, go ahead and inhale, slow and easy, and then exhale, taking your time. Good. Can you feel my hand on yours? Blink for yes."

Most of my body is numb, but I start to feel a small pressure on my hand. I blink.

"Good. Now can you squeeze my fingers?"

It takes me a while to locate my muscle's strings, to remember where to pull and what to push to activate my various joints. But I think I manage to move my fingers a little.

"Good, you're doing great, Rho. Any moment now, the buzzing in your head will fade, and you'll be able to think clearly. Take your time, don't rush, don't panic. Just remember you're safe, and you're awake."

When most of the numbness melts, I feel like I've just surfaced from a deep dive that lasted days. I blink a few times, and then I clench my hands, one of which is still entwined with the fingers of the woman beside me. "Good," she says soothingly. "I'm going to raise your backrest so you can sit up."

The bed gradually begins to curve, and I carefully shift a little, my muscles sore from lack of use. "You're on Aries, and you're among friends," she goes on.

"Hysan is going to be so happy!" squeals the youngest of the women, and then she covers her mouth like she's said something wrong. "Sorry—it's just, he's been sitting here, holding your hand around the clock, and—"

"Th—thank you."

My voice is soft and insubstantial, but it's enough to silence her. I swallow, and the woman holding my hand says, "Would you like some water?" I nod, and the man passes her a glass, which she holds for me as I drink.

The cool liquid relieves the tightness in my throat, and after a few sips, I ask, "How long was I out?"

"Almost three galactic weeks," reports the man.

"Is there any news on Nishi?"

No one answers immediately. Then the fiery-haired Arien asks, "What the Helios is a *Nishi*?"

Scowling, I try to get out of bed, but I feel a slight pressure on my arm. "Slow down," says the woman with the kind voice, as she gently eases me back. "Your friends are in training, but we can summon them here for you if you'd like."

The youngest healer leans forward. "I can go get Hysan—"

"*No*," I say, a little too quickly. "I need a moment . . . please."

"Of course," says the older woman. "We'll give you space to gather yourself. Remember to relax and go slow, okay?"

I nod, and as soon as they're gone I look down at the three lightweight metallic disks clinging to my crinkly white gown like they're magnetized. When I pluck one off, it pulls away easily. It seems to be a noninvasive sensor that reports my vitals to the holographic screens around me, because as I pull each one off, the displays disappear.

It takes a while to trust my feet to hold my weight. Once I'm finally standing barefoot on the cold floor, I have to lean against the bed for a long moment before I can take my first step. I flash back to the hospital from my nightmares, and part of me wonders whether I've actually woken up or if I'm still trapped inside that Sumber.

Maybe I'll never know.

I find my clean Lodestar suit and boots inside the dresser. I strip off the crinkly gown, and when I'm naked, I inspect my reflection in the mirror for any signs of Corinthe's torture from the Sumber. But all I see are the mostly healed scars on my left arm.

The Scarab around my wrist is gone and my nails have grown back, but Sirna's pink pearl necklace still hangs from my neck. I wonder what happened to the other pearl necklace, the one Mom made me a decade ago that Crompton re-created.

I also wonder what happened to Crompton.

And *Mom*.

I crack open the door once I'm dressed, and I step into a rocky passage that's not at all what I expected. It reminds me a bit of the Zodiax, and I get the sense I'm underground. So this can't be Phaetonis; it must be one of the other Ariean planets—Phobos or Phaet—since neither of them has a breathable atmosphere.

The corridor spills into a high-arched, cavernous space that looks like the hollowed-out inside of a mountain. The balconies of higher levels are illuminated by red bonfires that provide most of the light in the place, and all around me Arieans are marching in different directions, most of them lugging weapons and tools and gear.

This has to be Phaet—the smallest Ariean planet. We studied it in school because it houses The Bellow, the highest-security prison in the Zodiac, which is built inside a mountain. Most likely, *this* mountain.

The House's Majors—Ariean Zodai—guard The Bellow. Even when the junta of warlords overturned the government and marginalized the Zodai, they left Phaet alone. It's just a prison planet, and historically, regardless of the power battles happening on Phaetonis, the Zodai have never stopped guarding it.

From the way the Majors are shuffling back and forth, their red suits covered in soot and scratches and burns, this place feels like an underground forge that's in the midst of preparing for war. The mountain is so dark and oppressive that I'm immediately depressed about being stuck inside. After all those nightmares, I need to breathe fresh air.

I need to be outside.

The giant Arieans pay me no attention as I thread through them, and soon I start to feel a light breeze that doesn't belong in the depths of a mountain. I follow it down a small, rocky passage, and as the gust grows stronger, I smell sweet notes that make me think of plantlife.

But when I make it to the end of the hall, there's only a wall and a burly Major blocking it. "What's your business here?" he asks in a harsh tone.

Before I can answer, an assertive voice behind me says, "She's with me."

I turn to see the statuesque Skarlet Thorne, and every muscle in me tightens. Her hair cascades around her flawless face, her skintight red uniform bringing out the enviable curves of her body. She must have been following me.

The man nods. Then he pulls on a lever, and the whole wall slides down.

Orange sunlight spills into the cave, and I hold up a hand to shield my eyes. I follow Skarlet onto a stone outcropping that descends to the earth like a long ramp, providing a panoramic view of Phaet. In addition to the giant, golden Helios, there's a second small sun in the sky that's ruby red, and it's the combination of both colors that's giving everything an orange glare.

The grassy horizon holds three large hills, and massive Rams as large as Pegazi graze along the banks of a dozen blue rivulets that wind around the hills and disappear into the surrounding forest. Each of the three hills is topped with a monumental stone fortress.

"What the hell is going on?" I demand when Skarlet doesn't volunteer an explanation on her own.

She chuckles and starts walking down the ramp. I grudgingly follow, annoyed to find myself suddenly dependent on her.

"Our Zodai terraformed this planet a long time ago." She's so leggy that I have to take two steps for every one of hers. "We never told anyone, not even the rest of our House, and since The Bellow is as much as most people ever see of this planet, we've been able to keep the forest hidden."

"Why?"

She sighs and slows down to keep pace with me. "Because our people are constantly rising up. In the early days of our House, our Zodai decided we would need a failsafe, and since the Majors have always had control of this planet, they terraformed this place so we'd have a haven and a training ground. Over time, we've managed to quietly transfer over the most important pieces of our history here, in case Phaetonis ever falls apart . . . which it very nearly has."

I spot a few groups of Zodai spread out along the landscape, but we're too far to see anyone clearly. Some people seem to be practicing Yarrot, some are speaking in groups, and some are training with weapons. From the range of uniform colors represented, it looks like the whole Zodiac is here.

"Haven't you noticed how a lie grows exponentially more powerful over time?" asks Skarlet, her bronze brown skin shimmering in the suns' light. "When people are repeatedly told the same thing by those in power, they tend to believe it—that is, until a girl raises her voice to prove power wrong."

I think she might be complimenting me, but it's hard to tell since everything that comes out of her mouth sounds like a challenge.

The stone ramp ends, and as we step onto the grassy ground, I turn around to take in the view behind me. Beyond the towering mountain, the woods seem to grow wild, with trees as tall as starscrapers covered in autumnal foliage. Plumes of black smoke rise over the coppery treetops, like a fire getting out of control.

"That's the Everblaze," she says, following my gaze. "It's a fire that's never gone out. Our forebears used to burn our warriors' souls there so their spirits could rise to Helios, and our Zodai still carry on that tradition. Phaet is the most special part of our House," she adds, and I think this is probably as gentle as her voice gets. "It's always been a warrior's world . . . a land where the spirituality of the Zodai and the might of the soldier meet."

I follow her onto a dirt path that unfurls in the direction of the stone fortresses, and I pan my gaze across the closest group of Zodai, their faces growing more distinct as we approach. When their familiar features sharpen, my breath catches as I make out Mathias's dark locks and Hysan's golden head.

They're speaking apart from the others, and I don't see Mom or Pandora or Brynda or Rubi nearby.

Rather than picking up my pace, my legs seem to grow heavier at the sight of the guys, and I stop moving altogether the instant it hits me that Skarlet is taking me right to them.

"Don't you want to see your *boyfriend*?" she asks, her tone almost taunting.

I thought the tension between us was something I brought back from the Sumber, but now I realize it's coming from her, too. I guess Hysan must have told her about us . . . and I don't think she's used to coming in second place.

Rather than answer, I step off the dirt path and cut across the grass in a new direction, away from the crowd. I don't elaborate, and Skarlet doesn't ask.

"Then how about a shower?" she offers instead. I glare at her, and she crinkles her nose. "You smell awful."

Rolling my eyes, I ask, "Do I have a room somewhere?"

"This way." She marches us toward the forest, and I don't look back because I don't want to risk Hysan or Mathias spotting me. So to keep focused on what matters, I ask, "What happened when I shot Crompton?"

"When their master fell, his soldiers prioritized his life over the mission, and they rushed him to safety, leaving you behind. The Guardians knew the master would likely return for you, so you had to be hidden. General Eurek agreed to give you sanctuary here."

When we reach the shade of the tree line, I can't pry my gaze off the oranges and reds and golds of the foliage. I'm so busy looking up that I nearly walk into a pair of giant Rams, and I only steer myself away at the last moment.

Skarlet laughs, and I turn to see that she was watching me—and most likely hoping I'd collide with them. I bite down on my lip to keep from calling her what I think she is, and I take in the two enormous creatures I nearly hit, ogling at their curved ivory horns and muscled backs.

One of them is black furred and white horned, the other white furred and black horned. They look terrifying, but they don't seem the least bit interested in us.

After being asleep for so long, my muscles are sore from all this walking, but I won't give Skarlet the satisfaction of seeing my weakness. Still, I'm relieved when a stone keep comes into view—much smaller than the three fortresses on the hilltops—its doors wide open.

There's no guard by the entrance, nor do I see much in the way of security, not like there was inside the mountain. This whole forest feels like a secret garden where Arieans can let down their armor and just be themselves. It's like the Majors' own version of Zenith and Paloma's hideout.

We step into a cool, dim chamber outfitted with a sitting area of lumpy and mismatched couches, a couple of wallscreens, and dozens of shelves stuffed with ancient-looking paper books. "The dining hall is through there," says Skarlet, pointing to a stone corridor that leads beyond this room, "and the bathrooms are downstairs," she points to a staircase at the other end of the space. "Got it?"

I nod. I guess that's the extent of our tour.

"So where's my stuff?"

"In your lodgings," she says, and she marches across the keep to a door at its other end. When we step through it, we're outside again.

On this side of the structure, the forest's trees are more spaced out, and sitting between them are massive, multihued tents of every fashion—I see a black one studded with silver stars, a rainbow one with color-changing stripes, a hi-tech one that projects a slideshow of holographic captures, and more.

"Every Zodai picks out their tent and chooses where to place it," says Skarlet as we wind through them. I keep waiting for her to slow down, but her pace stays brisk. When I finally think I'm going to pass out, I see flashes of blue, and excitement replaces exhaustion, quickening my steps.

"Hysan set yours up," says Skarlet, and I almost stumble when she says his name. "He thought you would want to be by the water."

As the golden trees thin out, we step into a clearing, and blue overtakes the view. A sparkling cobalt sea hugs the forest, and on its banks, on the outskirts of the woods, stands a silky sapphire tent that's larger and lovelier than all the others I've seen.

I follow Skarlet through the entrance flap into a beautiful domed space with a central, star-shaped ceiling window where the tent's fabric becomes clear and daylight shines through. The ground is blanketed in white feathers, and there's a wide bed with deep blue sheets. There's also a polished wooden desk and a small area that's blocked off by a sapphire curtain; on its other side is a floor-length mirror, a vanity, and a rack of hangers with silky clothes I don't recognize in bright reds, blues, and greens—the primary colors Librans love.

My Wave sits on the vanity's tabletop, my traveling case is on the white-feathered floor, and beside it is Nishi's lavender levlan bag.

Tick, tock, tick, tock, crab.

My gut knots up, and I feel like I'm going to be sick.

"Bathrooms are at the keep, so unless you want to rough it, grab your toiletries and head back up there when you're ready," throws Skarlet over her shoulder as she walks out. "I have to check in with my troop, so I'll see you in the dining hall in an hour for dinner."

I'm starting to see why Arieans are so physically fit if just going to the bathroom is this taxing. When she leaves, I try to gather the energy to trek back up to the keep to bathe, but I can't. My muscles are more drawn to the sea.

So I strip off my Lodestar suit, leave the tent naked, and walk into the cobalt water.

I lose track of the minutes as I float freely on my back, hoping the orange sunlight can penetrate the darkness coating my skin. I want to inhale the salt of the sea and the musk of the trees, but Phaet might as well be another nightmare world. I can touch it, but I can't taste it.

When my fingers look like prunes, I finally swim back to shore. Since I didn't bring a towel with me, I'm naked and dripping wet when I slip inside the sapphire tent—where Hysan is already waiting for me.

7

GLOWING IN HIS GOLDEN KNIGHT suit, Hysan holds a red robe open in his hands. His vivid green eyes fill with light as I approach, and his happiness weighs so heavily on me that I have to drop my gaze.

My head is still bowed as I reach him, and I twist around to slide my arms into the silky red sleeves. "I've missed you so much," he murmurs behind me, his breath brushing my ear as I cinch the robe's belt closed.

Even though he's *right here*, his cedary scent smells faint, like I'm only remembering it. I pull away quickly and pad to the tent's opening. Then I breathe in a lungful of fresh air and stare out at the darkening day.

Helios's dimming light combined with the Ariean sun's red rays now dyes the water bloodred and saturates the sky with combustible clouds. It looks like we're boiling inside a cauldron, only I can't feel the fire's flames.

I can't feel anything.

"How are you, Rho?" asks Hysan, who's still standing where I left him. Since he was careful not to touch me while he helped me into the robe, he must already realize something's off between us.

He probably picked up on it as soon as he learned I was awake and didn't go straight to him.

"Can I get you anything?" His tone grows tighter in my prolonged silence. "Would you like some food? Are you in any pain?"

"What happened at the Cathedral?" I ask, still staring at the infernal world beyond this tent.

"Mathias and I reached the hall in time to watch you and Aquarius fall. His soldiers were stunned to see him go down, and all they cared about was hauling him to safety. They left you and Ophiuchus behind . . . but they took your mom."

I close my eyes, snuffing out what's left of the daylight, and the first real feeling since awakening tugs on my chest as I think of my proud, strong mother being held captive. I have to help her after I've saved Nishi.

After all, she only came to the Cathedral to protect me. She had a life she enjoyed among the Luminaries, and she abandoned it to help me with my cause. Because she's always placed her duty to the stars above her own happiness.

Above her House.

Above her *family*.

"The Marad also took Aryll."

Hysan's voice brings me back to the present, and I repeat the name in my head until I remember.

Aryll.

It tastes like venom, and I'm tempted to spit it back out. Swallowing the impulse, I keep my gaze focused outside, on the scarlet sea. "I shot him."

"Yes," says Hysan, the word so soft I barely hear it. I can't tell if it's pity or disappointment dampening his voice—nor do I want to turn around and find out.

"Since the Scarab's poison has a twenty-four-hour grace period," he goes on, "I'm sure the Marad was eager to get out of there and administer the antidote to both Aquarius and Aryll."

"And Nishi?"

At last I spin around in anticipation of the answer I'm seeking above all others. "Where is the Tomorrow Party keeping her? What's the rescue mission? Is Brynda helping with the plan?"

Something like understanding flashes in Hysan's gaze, and his expression clears. Like he's been rifling through all the possible explanations for my mood and has finally found the one that syncs up. Now he can adjust his act accordingly.

"We know the Party left Primitus," he says, bringing up the warmth in his voice, like a musician tuning an instrument. "But we don't know much more than that yet. We're in the midst of forming a galactic army for the first time in a millennium, and new Zodai volunteers are arriving daily. There's a lot going on—but we haven't forgotten her."

I don't know what's going on inside me, but somehow the fact that Hysan thinks he has me all figured out bothers me. I feel like I've become one of his devices: He just has to say the right sequence of words, and I'll fall back in line and follow his lead.

I'll just accept that he's been too busy to put any thought into rescuing Nishi.

"Rho . . . I know you need time to recover, but this base needs you," he says, and even from a few paces away I can see the vulnerability softening his incredible eyes. "The Houses unanimously voted that when you recovered you would be leader and tiebreaker of our operation, reinstating the power of the Wandering Star position. So I'd like to get you caught up on everything as soon as you feel up to it."

Part of me is listening, but most of me is marveling at how he even knows that I need him to stay completely stationary right now. His feet have been locked in place this whole time, like he's trying to limit his presence in my space.

And yet, I feel the same discomfort as when I awoke in the hospital and the youngest healer said he'd been visiting my room daily. The better Hysan behaves, the less certain I am about him.

Even though I know my nightmares in the Sumber weren't real, I can't shake the sense of distrust that slid into my heart. The feeling that I should have trusted my instincts about him.

"So Ophiuchus is here," I say, desperate for anything that will drown the doubt from my skin and mute the memory of Hysan pressing Skarlet against the countertop. *It wasn't real.*

And yet, the distrust I feel now *is* real. Hysan lied to me so easily the night of the ball—that whole time we were together, he knew my mom's story, and he didn't say a word. Worst of all, I don't even know why it's so surprising to me, since he lies to his own people every day.

"He's been unconscious this whole time, like you."

I blink, and it takes me a moment to remember we're now talking about Ophiuchus. "Where is he?"

"We have him secured in the mountain, and healers are monitoring his vitals. He's physically fine, but he's in a medically induced coma because we can't be sure how powerful he is in this form. We also can't be certain he won't contact Aquarius psychically as soon as he's awake. So until we know more, we're keeping him sedated."

I try to care, but I can't even muster up some curiosity. At this instant, Corinthe is carving up Nishi's skin, tormenting her to the point of death and then pulling back so the dream won't end. Nishi will remain in overwhelming pain, without sleep or friends or hope, until I rescue her.

If her subconscious doesn't break her first.

I've already lost my brother and Dad and Deke. I won't lose what's left of my family. There's no care left in me for anyone else.

"Any word from the master?" I ask. "Any more Marad attacks? Anything on that front?"

"Nothing new, and Piscenes are still in their comas. More are dying every day—we still haven't found a way to reverse the Psyphoning's effects."

I let out a heavy exhale. It's getting harder and harder to tell apart the real nightmares from the imagined ones.

"I'm getting the sense you'd rather be alone," says Hysan tentatively, and on the last word his perfectly pitched tone cracks.

I take a step toward him, and for the first time, I notice his face is blanketed in a light layer of stubble, like he hasn't shaved in days. "How's Neith?"

His shoulders slump forward, and his touseled golden locks fall over his eyes. "I have to inhabit him manually without activating his artificial intelligence in case Aquarius tries taking him over again. I've been keeping him disconnected from holographic communications and shielded from the Psy at all times. Since Guardians have to travel Veiled, I've just been claiming he's in flight as often as I can."

He sounds so tired, and a part of me wants to take him in my arms and comfort him. My feet carry me forward another step, but then the thought of his warmth makes my joints lock up in protest, and I come to a halt. "Does the whole Zodiac know Crompton is the original Aquarius yet?"

Hysan looks disappointed at the distance that's still between us, but he answers my question. "The other Guardians present at the Cathedral plead our case to the Plenum and to their Houses. Any Zodai who wants to join our cause is either here or on their way here. But most remain skeptical, and since Aquarius hasn't said anything yet, nor has the Tomorrow Party issued any statement, our accusations have been met with silence, which prolongs people's indecision. I'm mostly worried about what Aquarius is planning during his silence."

This time Hysan takes his first step toward me, and I realize we're now close enough to touch. He holds out his hand for mine, and sucking in a quick breath at the prospect of feeling something, I place my palm on his.

But when our fingers interlock, the pressure feels just as faint as when the healer touched me. Like the numbness from the Sumber hasn't worn off yet.

Or maybe I just came back different.

Less awake.

Less *alive*.

But there could be a way back. . . . Ochus once said the worst possible fate is being truly alone—no hope, or future, or escape, or loved ones— which was how I felt in the Sumber, until I found Nishi. It's how she's feeling now, nonstop, until I get her out of there.

According to Ophiuchus, the only thing that could cure that condition is opening up to someone. And now that Stan is gone . . .

Well, Hysan is all I have left.

Maybe if I confide in him about what I've been through, he'll understand why it's so important we rescue Nishi. *Why she can't wait.*

"In—in the nightmares," I start, staring into his leaf-green eyes, "I saw Nishi."

Hysan's brow scrunches with curiosity and concern. "You're certain it was really her?" When I nod, his expression clears a little, and he says, "I've heard stories of people who claimed their consciousness were linked together in the Sumber, but it's extremely rare—it usually just happens with twins. Your connection with Nishi must be very strong."

I faintly feel his fingers tightening around mine, and I keep my gaze steady on his as I say, "Hysan, you don't know what it's like in there . . . there's no time, no break, no hope. And Corinthe . . . she found me, and she . . ."

Sadness softens his expression, and he tugs on my hand like he wants to pull me into a hug. "I'm so sorry, Rho—"

"This isn't about me," I say quickly, drawing away and releasing his fingers. "Corinthe has Nishi now. She's going to make her suffer until I save her. I don't know how long Nishi can hold on. Every instant is a lifetime for her. We have to help her *now*."

"We're going to help her, Rho," he says seriously. "I swear it. We'll hold a meeting first thing tomorrow to get you up to speed on what's going on, and then we can consult the other Houses on the best strategy for a rescue operation—"

"No, *now*!" I insist, anger coursing through me and making my voice shake. "When Blaze took Nishi, I told you I was afraid the Party would torture her, and you said they wouldn't, that they needed her allegiance too much to hurt her. *You were wrong*. I need your help to fix this, and we can't just *sleep on it*. We need to act!"

Hysan studies my eyes like he's searching for something, and after failing to find it he says, "As you wish, my lady. I'll go make the arrangements."

He takes my hand again and brings it to his lips. Then he presses a soft kiss on my skin.

I wait for the Abyssthe-like rush that usually follows, but I don't feel a thing.

When he goes out through the tent's sapphire flap, I dart to my traveling bag and dig into its pockets until I find what I'm looking for—the Veil collar Hysan loaned me on Aquarius. I slip it around my neck, and without replacing the red robe with real clothes or even throwing on shoes, I activate the invisibility and chase after him.

He moves so swiftly that I have to run to catch up. The soles of my feet sting from stepping on sharp objects, and my sore muscles scream in agony. I'm going to need a pain tonic to sleep tonight.

The clouds above are growing as dark as charcoal, but the red sun is still burning in the twilight sky, its laser-like light a fiery torch illuminating our way. We cut through the woods, and I fall as far back as I can so the crunching of copper leaves won't give me away.

I speed up once we're out in the grassy field, in the shadow of the mountain. Up ahead a dozen rivulets tangle through the hilly landscape, delivering fresh water from the cobalt sea to the three fortresses.

I follow Hysan along the banks of the closest stream. The water wraps around the smallest hill and disappears behind it, and as we trace the curving shoreline, I spy a man in a navy blue Lodestar suit.

Mathias.

I stop moving so they won't hear my heavy breathing. Mathias has trimmed his hair in a Zodai style again, and he's smooth-faced, like the days before his capture. It's Hysan who looks disheveled now, his locks too long and poking into his eyes, his features masked in facial hair.

"How is she?" asks Mathias while Hysan is still far away.

I edge as close to them as I dare, keeping my breaths as subtle as possible. "Devastated," says Hysan once he's in front of Mathias. Sadness floods his voice, and he doesn't sound anything like the person he was moments ago.

"I should go see her," says Mathias, squaring his shoulders like he's ready to march to my tent right now.

"Give her a moment . . . and maybe a head's up," says Hysan, and I wonder if he's picturing the state in which he found me.

Mathias nods, the furrow of his brow forming a wall between his eyes. "Did you ask what she wants to do about the . . . body?"

Everything in me hardens, and I almost gasp. The thought of my brother's corpse makes the world spin around me, and I force myself to fall a few more steps back.

"I couldn't—not yet," says Hysan, and he clears his throat like he's trying to cut a path through a wave of emotion. "He's frozen, so there's no rush to decide."

"What about—"

"*No.*" Hysan's voice is almost forceful as he anticipates whatever Mathias was about to ask. "In fact, I think we should push that news to tomorrow."

"Okay," says Mathias, who's suddenly comfortable taking orders from Hysan. "I'll let her know."

So Hysan and Mathias are working together to keep information from me? I guess my nightmares weren't so far off the mark after all.

I lower my gaze to the green ground to calm the icy storm rising within me. Somewhere in my subconscious, somewhere so deep I needed the Sumber to unlock it, I must have known they never fully trusted me. *And that means they can't be trusted.*

"All she cares about is Nishi," I hear Hysan say, and I look up to see Mathias blowing out a hard breath.

"You were right, then," he says. "For a Cancrian, the loss of a loved one is . . . well, when we succumb to an emotion as powerful as grief, it can completely overtake us if we're not careful. I'd hoped, since she coped so well with her father's death, that she might rise from this loss as well— "

I fall back a few more steps, enough that they can't hear me when I crumple to the ground.

Coped so well? What is he talking about?

"It's too much," says Hysan mournfully. "She's lost too much, she's been put through too much, and now she's drawn the line at Nishi—she's all that anchors her, and Rho's determined to locate her. Once she does, she'll go to her straight away, everyone else be damned."

"So what you're saying," says Mathias almost too softly, "is you don't think we should give her a full report."

My eyes latch on to Hysan's face with an intensity that should be able to ignite fires. His jaw tightens, like he's tasting something bitter, and he says, "We can't tell her where Nishi is . . . not yet."

The rest of my body suddenly comes into sharp focus, shattering the shell of numbness that had been shielding me from this nightmare.

Despair clangs through my bones, and I try to keep listening past the pain, past the déjà vu of the dream that prophesied Hysan and Mathias's betrayal.

"She's not going to like that plan," says Mathias. "And I can't say I'm a fan either."

"Nor I," says Hysan, his voice growing more forceful, "but unless you have a better one, I don't think Rho is in the right mind to hear this information, not when Nishi and Aquarius are in the same place. We can't just show up on Leo and start shooting—Aquarius will See us coming."

Leo.

That's where Nishi is.

"We need a real plan," Hysan goes on, "one we coordinate as a team with the other Houses, and that will take more time."

"Can Rho be convinced of that?" asks Mathias hopefully. "Can we explain the importance of combining Nishi's rescue with our strike on the master?"

Hysan shakes his head, and after a moment Mathias says, "Okay then. I'll talk to the others about redacting the report we give her at tonight's meeting."

I push down on the outrage surging up from my core, and I turn back the way I came. Invisibly, I stalk through the field, then the forest, then the keep, until I'm back inside my sapphire tent, and only then do I bury my face in my pillow and scream.

When my throat is a raw flame of pain, I fall limp on the bed and wait for the aching to crush my heart, for the tears to flood my eyes, for the loneliness to scorch my soul.

But nothing happens.

I'm not even angry anymore.

I'm just *done.*

I'm sick of being handled by the people around me. Since becoming Guardian, everything I've done has been dictated by someone else—Crius, Mathias, Hysan, the Plenum, Ophiuchus, Aquarius. Most of them men, all of them older, and each one convinced they could decide what's best for me.

On Scorpio, Strident Engle told me I've been playing someone else's game, and he was right. Everyone thinks they're so much smarter than me. They're so sure they know better. Even though *I'm* the one who uncovered Ophiuchus. *I'm* the one who Saw the Dark Matter. *I'm* the Wandering Star.

And I'm sick of their condescension. I'm sick of *them*. I'm done being a pawn in everyone else's game—now it's time to make everyone play *my* game.

I don't need Hysan or Mathias or a Zodai army.

I can save Nishi on my own.

8

I MAKE MY WAY TO the keep after changing into my Lodestar suit.

In the entrance hall, I follow Skarlet's instructions and turn down the corridor she pointed to earlier. Red flames flicker from torches bracketed high up on the stone walls, and the passage ends in a vast dining hall lined with long communal tables. I go straight to the buffet bar and stack my plate with hunks of unidentifiable meats and rainbow-colored vegetable cake.

Most people haven't arrived for dinner yet, so I sit at an empty table and dig into my meal. It's been so long since I've eaten solid food that before I know what I've scarfed down, my plate is empty and my stomach is grumbling in discomfort. I have to lie back in my chair to keep the foreign food from making a spectacular exit.

"Wandering Star."

I sit up at the sight of an auburn-haired girl in an aqua-colored Zodai uniform. "Hi, Pandora."

She bows and sets her tray down across from me, and then she reaches over the table to trade the hand touch. "It's wonderful to see you awake," she says as she sits, and there's a lightness in her expression that feels unfamiliar since I've only ever known her at her unhappiest. "Your leadership has been missed."

I observe her silently, but she doesn't seem bothered by my curious gaze. She just gives me a small smile as she brings a bite of the vegetable cake to her mouth. The shadows that haunted her after her capture seem to have retreated, and there's a glow in her ivory skin—a glow I used to be familiar with.

She's at peace.

"Tell me what's happened since the Cathedral," I say. I need the information as much as I need to distract myself from the feeling that's so loudly radiating from her Center.

Her face grows serious, and she puts her fork down. "We left Pisces right after the Marad took off. Every House left a team of Zodai to continue looking after the Piscene people, but the Guardians had to return to their Houses to prepare for whatever the master's planning. Hysan has been instrumental in organizing our resistance—he seems to know people on every House, and it's thanks to him we've been able to rally so many Zodai so quickly."

The food jostles uncomfortably in my stomach again, and I shift positions in my chair. "What have you been up to for the past few weeks?"

"We've set up three camps, each in a different Fort." She holds up a finger for each one. "The first is metaphysical, where seers are trying to find answers in the stars; the second is physical, where we're training in weaponry to face the Marad; and the third is intelligence, where we're using advanced technology to collect clues about the master and the army and the Last Prophecy."

"Have you guys made any progress?"

"Well . . . we don't know much about what's coming, but there has been progress of a different sort."

I tilt my head questioningly, and she says, "None of the teams on Phaet are divided along House lines—people from any House can contribute in whichever way best suits their skills. It doesn't matter where we come from because it's more important that we're here. It makes me think about the kind of world Black Moon would have been."

Her eyes are large and bright as she waits for my reaction, and I try to summon some vestige of excitement. When I can't I ask, "So what have *you* been doing?"

"I've been helping out in metaphysical," she says, deflating slightly. "Mathias is in weaponry, and Hysan is in intelligence. We could definitely use you in the metaphysical camp."

I stare at the crumbs on my empty plate and don't answer because I know I'm never going back into the Psy again. If I do, Aquarius will be able to read me, and he'll know he's won. He'll know I have nothing left.

"Maybe *you'll* actually See something."

I look up. "What?"

"No one's been able to See anything. Not even Guardians." She drops her voice to a low whisper, like she's afraid the Psynergy might overhear us. "The master is doing something to the astral plane. It's like the jitteriness was a precursor, and now everything is pure static. Reports from Primitus are that the Pegazi have vanished into the woods—they're no longer interacting with people. It's like the stars have stopped whispering to them."

She's turning her Philosopher's Stone round and round in her hand, and I remember that the devices are linked to everyone in an Aquarian's Clan, so she probably receives regular updates. I'm sure the Eleventh House has fallen into chaos now that Supreme Advisor Untara is dead and the Guardians are accusing Crompton of being the master. But at least Pandora can be in constant contact with her family. With her *sister*.

My gut burns, and I need to change the subject fast. "You're a Zodai now," I say, admiring her official aqua uniform. "How'd that happen?"

Her glow seems to brighten. "We've all been promoted. Everyone who's come to fight has been declared a full fledged Zodai by the Plenum—"

"*Rho!*"

Mathias sets his tray next to mine, and then he pulls me up into a tight hug. "It's so good to see you awake," he murmurs musically in my ear, his muscled arms pressing into my numb skin. . . . But just as with Hysan, I barely feel his touch.

Mathias flashes me a rare toothy grin when he pulls away and says, "Anything you need, I'm here for you."

I spy him trading shy smiles with Pandora as we sit down, and their expressions don't seem to hold any of the insecurity from before. "We've organized a meeting of senior officers to bring you up to speed right after dinner," Mathias says to me as he cuts himself a bite of pink steak.

"Good," I say, my gaze distracted by a familiar statuesque Ariean sashaying into the dining hall, escorted by an even more familiar golden-haired Knight.

Hysan grins at whatever Skarlet says, and she yammers on even as he pulls out a tray for her, and they start piling food onto their plates. The smile is still on Hysan's face as they turn around and scan the tables for a place to sit.

My hand curls into a fist on my lap. How can he be so carefree when I told him what Nishi's going through?

Hysan grows alert when he sees me, and he and Skarlet stride over to our table. He takes the seat to my other side.

I'm stuck between Hysan and Mathias. How original.

"My lady."

I nod back my greeting and to avoid trading the hand touch, I reach for my glass of water.

"We'll have a full report for you tonight," Hysan goes on in a tense voice. "I've made it clear rescuing Nishi is a top priority, and it's the first operation we'll plan."

Skarlet sits next to Pandora, measuring me through her catlike eyes. I stare back at her just as blatantly, until she smirks and takes a swig of her drink.

"So Brynda and Rubi aren't here?" I ask in general, without meeting anyone's gaze.

"They're organizing their House's defenses and recruiting Zodai for our army," says Hysan. "We need to be careful about whom we approach, since the only advantage we hold is that Aquarius doesn't know Arieans terraformed this planet. The Majors believe the Everblaze protects this world's secrets from the Psy. So if we approach the wrong person, we risk discovery—that's why we have to transport everyone here ourselves."

"What about Ezra and Gyzer?" I ask without looking at him. "You sent them to Aquarius to spy on the Tomorrow Party—have you checked to make sure they're okay?"

Hysan hears the sharpness in my voice because it takes him a moment to answer. "We asked them to join us here, but they . . . they decided it would be better if they infiltrated the Party and became our spies. Ezra and I built a special device with a heavily encrypted code to communicate that should be near-impossible to break."

I sit up. If Ezra and Gyzer are with Imogen and Blaze, that means they're with Nishi, too. "Have you heard from them? Have they told you where the Tomorrow Party is?"

"Not yet," he says, and on my other side Mathias sets down his fork and doesn't meet my gaze.

From the corner of my eye, I notice a tall girl in a brown suit slowing down as she walks past our table. She has dark skin and darker eyes, and she's scrutinizing me so closely that she doesn't seem to realize I'm staring back. Her gaze drifts to Hysan next, and when I look at him, I find he's glaring at her. Like they know each other.

The girl blinks and strides away. Hysan locks eyes with me next, and I see the next lie starting to form on his lips—when I suddenly realize I don't care what he's hiding. Whatever's going on with Hysan and his harem of women, it's just a distraction.

"She's—"

"I don't think I'm up for a meeting tonight after all," I say, cutting him off.

Mathias, Pandora, Skarlet, and Hysan watch me in bewildered silence, until Hysan finally says, "But I thought you said there was no time to waste—"

"I'm tired," I say loudly. "I've been through a lot, don't you think?"

"Of course," Mathias answers, jumping in. I spy him shooting Hysan a warning look over my head. Then he touches his Ring, like he's accessing the Collective Conscious to send out the necessary alerts.

"General Eurek would still like to meet with the rest of us," says Hysan, his gaze as distant as Mathias's, like he's syncing with either the Psy or his Scan.

Skarlet stands, her plate spotlessly clean. "Let's go then."

"Rho, would you like someone to walk you back to your tent?" asks Mathias as he rises, too.

"I can escort you, my lady," injects Hysan, also getting to his feet. His meal is the only one that's untouched.

"That's okay," I say, remaining seated in the space between the guys as I stare after Skarlet, the only one of the group who's started walking away to bus her tray.

"Skarlet will take me."

✦ ✦ ✦

When we leave the dining hall, the others exit the keep through the front door while Skarlet and I head the back way, toward the tents.

As soon as we're alone, she rounds on me. "You don't feel like going to the meeting, *fine*—but you're not the only leader here. I have a duty to my House and the Zodiac, and I didn't sign up to play babysitter."

"Well I need your help."

"With what? Pulling you a bath?" She crosses her arms, her breath blowing down on me like an angry wind. "I know you're used to lady's maids and all that fluff, but that's *not* how things work on Aries."

"Are you refusing a direct order from your superior, Major Thorne?" My voice is thin as ice.

Her nostrils flare as I pull rank on her, and even though she's a head and a half taller and could squash me like a water-fly, she snarls, "*No.*"

"Then you'll do as I say, and you won't tell a soul."

Her fingers fidget toward the weapons holstered to her belt, but she just jerks a nod and says through gritted teeth, "*As you wish.*"

"Stellar."

Skarlet may not like me, but she's an honorable soldier—she won't go back on her word. "I wish for you to take me to see Corinthe. *Immediately.*"

The Ariean's eyebrows shoot up to her hairline.

As she opens her mouth to argue, I add, "And I further wish that you shut the hell up."

9

"I CAN'T BELIEVE YOU'RE MAKING me do this," growls Skarlet as we walk up the stone plank, back into the mouth of the mountain.

By now the night is fully cloaked in darkness; the red sun seems to have set, and the clouds are so opaque that I can't see any stars. Behind us only the shadowy shapes of the forest trees and the three fortresses shade the horizon.

"This is a really stupid idea," Skarlet goes on. She's been complaining the whole way, and her whining is making it hard to concentrate on what I'm going to say to Corinthe. "Do you even have a plan—"

"What part of *shut up* is giving you trouble?" I snap.

"The part where you get to keep interfering with my life and meddling with what's *mine*," she says as we reach the hidden doorway in the mountain.

I roll my eyes. "*He* chose. Get over it."

"I think *he's* the one who's getting over it," she says, glowering at me. "He was just distracted by something new, but I think it's quickly losing its charm."

"Quit baiting me and open this door. I'm going to make you take me to Corinthe's cell no matter how hard you piss me off, so you're wasting your energy."

Skarlet presses her face to a retinal scan, and the world thunders around us as the slab of stone slides down.

"I don't know what you think you're going to get out of this," she says as we stride inside. The wall shuts quickly and deafeningly behind us.

"She won't tell you anything," Skarlet goes on. "Her mind has no reaction to Aquarian truth-telling tonics, and Stridents report that she seems to actually *enjoy* pain"—the sour turn her tone takes when she speaks of Scorpio's methods makes it clear she disapproves of them—"and even the most persuasive of Librans couldn't charm anything out of her."

I wonder what Libran fits that bill.

I stay silent as she leads us into the cavernous heart of the mountain, the place illuminated with red flames, just as it was when I woke up here a few hours ago. Skarlet parades past two Majors stationed at either side of a passage, and my muscles clench in anticipation of an interrogation, but they don't stop us or even ask us for identification. I thought for sure Skarlet would have to do some scheming to get us into The Bellow, but it seems nobody cares where we go.

I'm about to ask her why we haven't been stopped yet, but the question escapes my mind when I see what the guards are protecting: a massive wall of black flames.

"What is that?" I ask in awe.

She turns to me solemnly, the dark fire's reflection dancing in her catlike eyes. "This wall is what makes The Bellow impenetrable. The flames are from the Everblaze, and the wall is called Black Truth. This is the sole entry point to the prison: Every other surface beyond here—floor, wall, ceiling— is armed with enough firepower to bring down this whole mountain."

"So then . . . how do we get in?"

Her manner grows professional, and I'm reminded of how quickly the Leonine Truther Traxon switched to his journalist persona on Aquarius. "If you have any nefarious plots beyond this point—if you plan to murder or break out a prisoner—this fire will burn you when you walk through it. But if you are pure in your purpose, you will walk through unharmed."

I blink, completely at a loss for words. Finally, I manage, "*How?*"

Skarlet doesn't break her official demeanor. "I can only provide this warning: If you wish to turn back, now is your only chance—"

But I'm already marching toward the fire. I don't stop when I hear Skarlet shouting my name or her footsteps thudding behind me as I eagerly rush into the black flames' embrace.

I'm almost disappointed when I don't feel anything.

There's just a slight tickle in the air when the flames touch me, and I get the weird feeling that if I were wearing my Ring, I'd sense the Psynergy's buzz intensify. This fire feels connected to the stars somehow, like the Pegazi of Aquarius or the Cathedral of Pisces.

Skarlet is out of breath by the time she joins me, and she yanks on my arm so I'll face her. "*Helios*, Grace! I've been through that fire tons of times, and it still freaks me out. *You* looked like you couldn't wait to burn!"

I jerk my arm free of her grip. "Fear is a useless emotion. You should really try rising above it."

Skarlet's nostrils flare again, but I don't wait around for her retort. I keep forging ahead, even though I don't know where I'm going, and soon she marches past me to take the lead again. We pass another pair of guards as we turn down an endless rocky hallway illuminated by torches, both walls lined with windowless metal doors.

"Why hasn't anyone stopped us yet?" I finally ask when we're out of earshot of the Majors.

She waits almost a whole minute to answer me, and then she speaks through gritted teeth. "Because as far as this army is concerned, you're the top-ranking person in the Zodiac." She spares me a glare. "Since you woke up, your position is now official."

I try to process what that means, but I can't. It sounds like too much power and responsibility, and I don't want it.

"Don't worry," she adds in a low voice, "when they realize you left your mind back in that Sumber, they'll totally strip you of the title—but hey, at least it'll be a familiar experience."

"I must be getting you in some major trouble," I say without looking at her or breaking stride.

"If someone reports our little visit here," she whispers heatedly, "*I'm* the one who'll be breaking the law, since I didn't disclose this with my commanding officer—"

"Then let's not get discovered," I cut in.

Skarlet starts taking such large strides that I have to double my speed to keep up. By the time we get to Corinthe's cell, I've memorized the number of doors we've passed. The Ariean places her hand against the dark metal, and a laser scans the length of her body. Then she crosses her arms and juts at the door with her chin, like she's telling me to do the same, so I do.

After a noticeable delay, the door slides open, revealing an immaculate white room. The place is so glossy and pristine that it's almost blinding, and I squint on walking in. It takes my eyes a moment to adjust. There's a white bed against the wall and a toilet in the corner. Other than that, the room is empty.

Corinthe sits on the mattress wearing white scrubs, her back stiff as she stares at the blank wall before her. A curtain of blond curls conceals her face.

"What's wrong with her?" I ask, approaching slowly and noting the metal cuffs around her ankles, wrists, and neck.

"Before the cell door opens, a prisoner's mobility is suspended."

When I'm directly in front of Corinthe, I can't repress my gasp. She looks just how I pictured her in my nightmares.

What Skarlet told me on Aquarius is true—Corinthe could be my twin. Except for her mouth.

Her too-long lips look just as they did mid-transformation. When Risers shift too many times, they develop deformities that carry over through different identities; Corinthe's massive mouth seems to be one of those mutations.

Her pale green eyes widen on seeing me, and even though they're the same color as Stan's, they reflect none of his light. Her gaze grows duller and colder as her overlong lips curve into a sinister smile that I'm sure will haunt me long after I leave this room.

I glance at Skarlet and find her standing in a Zodai stance by the closed metal door. She doesn't offer to leave the cell to give us privacy, and I don't feel like arguing, so I decide to ignore her.

Turning back to Corinthe's leering grin, I say softly, "Tell me what Aquarius wants with Nishi."

She blinks but gives no other sign she's heard me.

"Where is his army headquartered?" I try next.

She blinks again.

"What's his plan? How can I stop him? What leverage do I have?"

It's pretty clear she's not going to answer me, so I tip my head toward Skarlet and command, "Major Thorne, hand me your bayonet."

To her credit, Skarlet exhibits no doubt or hesitation as she marches over to me. Carefully turning her back to Corinthe as she faces me, she shoves the levlan handle into my hand and narrows her catlike eyes at me in warning. I close my fingers around the reddish-brown grip and nod in understanding before she returns to her position by the door.

When I turn to Corinthe again, she's watching me without a trace of fear, like she knows I'm only pretending.

"What does the master want with Nishi?"

Corinthe deliberately drops her gaze to my left arm, slowly trailing her eyes down the blue sleeve, like she can see every mark she carved into my skin through the fabric. I set the bayonet down on the bed beside her, and Corinthe's gaze follows it longingly. Her arm quivers slightly, like she's struggling to reach for it.

In a different dimension, an alternate Corinthe is mutilating my best friend's body, and I can't stop her unless I get answers. "Please," I say softly. "Help me."

It's strange how quiet my heart is, almost like it's not even beating.

"I'm trying to save my best friend," I go on, and I take Corinthe's cold hand in my steady one and lovingly stroke her skin. Revulsion flashes across her face. "Your master went out of his way to recruit her into his new army, the Tomorrow Party. Why would he do that?"

She stares at me stoically. My touch grows even gentler, and I tenderly wrap my fingers around her thumb.

Then I squeeze tight and yank her nail off.

Corinthe's scream would awaken the whole mountain if we weren't inside this insulated cell. The nail falls from my fingers as Skarlet pushes me into the wall.

"What's wrong with you?" she hisses at me as I watch Corinthe panting in pain over her shoulder. "The Zodai have more humane ways of extracting information—"

"Well I wasn't making a political statement. This was personal."

"These Risers have been brainwashed—I thought we were in agreement on that!" Skarlet squeezes my chin between her fingers, forcing me to look at her frowning face, and I smell her spicy fireburst scent. "Corinthe isn't the master—she's a person who's never known anything but hate, so that's all she can reflect back. But you're Cancrian—you're privileged enough to know how *real* love feels. You should know better."

"It's so easy to think that way," I say, envying the simplicity of her outrage. "I never appreciated what a luxury it was to see things as black or white. I guess it's harder to do after a Riser has tortured you and branded you and murdered the people you love."

Skarlet's scowl deepens. "I made a mistake bringing you here. What you've endured has made you prejudiced—"

"No," I say, setting my jaw. "It's made me entitled."

"Entitled to what, exactly?"

"*Justice.*"

I go around her and grab the bayonet off the bed, and I stab the blade into Corinthe's arm. Swivelling my neck to look at Skarlet, whose mouth is hanging open, I warn, "Stand back. That's an order."

Corinthe's bloodcurdling scream rings in my ears, and as her blood gushes out, my hand remains on the levlan handle, the blade still buried in her skin. My muscles recoil, and nausea fights its way up my throat, but I don't move away. Her eyes sear with agony, and I start to lose myself in their greenness. I'll never again see Stan's pale irises grow vivid with excitement or shiny with emotion or dark with determination or soft with compassion or—

My head knocks into the wall as Skarlet shoves me back and yanks her bayonet out of Corinthe. Then she holds up the bloody knife in horror and stares at me like I'm the only monster in this cell.

The same horror works its way up from my Center as I stare at Corinthe.

Her smile is large and delirious, her eyes dancing with dark delight. Blood is still streaming down her white-sleeved arm, but she doesn't seem aware of it.

"I knew you weren't better than the rest of us," she rasps, her voice gravelly from lack of use.

Skarlet gasps and spins around at the sound, but Corinthe doesn't break our stare.

"You're not so incorruptible after all."

I step toward the bed. "You're right," I say, coming as close to Corinthe as I was before. "Don't you want to see how dark I go?"

I take her hand in mine again, and I'm pleased to feel her fingers twitching in response to my touch, like she's fighting the technology immobilizing her. "Lucky for us, you have nine more nails to lose. And that's just for starters."

Fear flickers in her eyes, and her smile starts to look fake. "Tell me what your master wants with my best friend," I demand.

A muscle in her jaw quivers, but she doesn't answer.

"Why did he recruit Nishi to lead the Tomorrow Party?"

She doesn't answer again, and I wrap my hand around her next finger in anticipation.

"I don't know his plans," she suddenly growls, and I hear Skarlet step closer to us. "But I know they don't involve your friends. So if he hasn't killed her yet, he's keeping her for another reason."

For me, I realize, and I drop Corinthe's hand.

He's holding Nishi as leverage—*she's a prisoner because of me*.

"But he doesn't want me," I blurt. "Not yet." He said so at the Cathderal— he needed Mom because he wants to find the Luminaries, but he said I wasn't ready to join him yet. So why hasn't he awoken Nishi?

"Where is his full army?" asks Skarlet, coming up beside me.

Corinthe keeps her gaze on me when she answers. "We move somewhere new every month. I don't know where they'd be by now."

"So why don't you tell us what you *do* know?" I ask, leaning in until our noses are almost touching.

"All I know is the Marad was unleashed to cause as much chaos and death and distrust as we can—to make the Houses pay for their sins. As long as two people never come to harm."

One side of her mouth hitches up. "But I've never cared for rules."

"*Who?*" I ask.

Hatred hardens the skin of her face until it looks like she's wearing a mask. "You, *unfortunately* . . . and Ophiuchus."

"Why? What does he want with me?"

"Isn't that just the question of our time?"

She must sense the violence rising within me, because before I can reach for her hand again, she clarifies, "I doubt anyone actually knows."

Then her too-familiar eyes light up with deadly intrigue as she adds, "But judging by his methods, I'm guessing it's the last thing you're willing to give him."

10

WHEN I OPEN MY EYES in the morning, Hysan is in my tent again.

He's clean-shaven and sitting at the end of my bed, wearing an expression too gentle for war. "I came to see how you're feeling," he says in his husky voice, "but I couldn't bring myself to wake you."

I don't speak or sit up. I don't remember falling asleep.

All I remember is staring up through the tent's star-shaped window at the velvety black sky, imagining what new tortures Nishi must be enduring at nightmare-Corinthe's hand. And when glints of gold began burning holes in the darkness, a plan came together in my mind.

"Better," I say, sliding up in my red silk pajamas and propping my back against the bed's headboard. "Thanks for coming by."

"Of course, Rho," says Hysan, his voice fuller now that he knows he's welcome. "Skar said she missed last night's meeting because you asked her to stay with you until you fell asleep. She told me you were scared to be alone."

My jaw instinctively clenches. Of course she would come up with a lie that makes me sound weak.

"I just wish she would have had the forethought to offer you a dreamless sleeping tonic so you could have gotten more rest," he adds, studying what must be the bags under my eyes.

"Yeah, she's not the brightest log in the fire," I say, using a Sagittarian expression Nishi taught me.

Pain pinches my chest at the thought of my best friend, and I fight it down by clearing my throat. "So I guess we should have that meeting now." I pull off the covers and swing a leg off the bed.

"Not yet."

I stop moving as I register Hysan's frown. "Why?"

"There's something you need to know first."

Adrenaline burns the drowsiness from my body, and I ask, "What is it?"

His eyes grow bright, making the golden star in his right iris sparkle, and my stomach tenses from the tender way he's looking at me. "I need you to know I'm truly sorry for lying to you about your mom."

"You already told me that on Pisces." I try to infuse my voice with warmth, but his words produce only ice inside me. I haven't forgiven him yet.

"I know," he says heavily, "but now there's something else you need to know. I should have brought it up yesterday, but I thought you deserved a day to recover."

The same spark of hope I felt when he and I spoke then—that fleeting instant when I thought I might not have to carry this pain alone—flickers in my chest again, threatening to melt my glacial shell of numbness. He's going to tell me he knows Nishi's location.

"Go on," I say eagerly.

"Do you remember that Capricorn girl who walked past us at dinner last night?" he asks.

I nod as I recall the brown-suited girl, and his brow furrows deeper. "She's a Luminary. I've confirmed her identity—she's come to help us."

I try to hide my disappointment by keeping completely still.

This isn't about Nishi.

"Her name is Gamba," he goes on, somehow oblivious to the light that just went out inside me. "And she's helping us because of your mom. They were close."

"What do you mean? That girl is our age."

"I don't know the full story. It sounds like Gamba joined the Luminaries as a child, and Kassandra instinctively started looking after her."

"My mom doesn't have a nurturing bone in her body."

"Well I just want you to be ready . . . because Gamba calls her *mother*."

I blink. *"What?"*

Hysan slides closer to me on the bed. "I didn't want you to be taken by surprise again—"

"I don't understand," I say, my mind abruptly blank.

"She's been cagey with the details—with any details, in fact. But I'm sure she'd be more willing to share them with you." Hysan's voice is soft and soothing, and even through my shock, I realize what he's doing. "I think you should speak to her, Rho."

And report back what I learn, I silently add.

Because Hysan and the other Guardians need to get whatever information they can from this Luminary, and I'm their best tool for extracting it. So is this Hysan my boyfriend or Hysan the diplomat advising me?

"Okay," I say, not meeting his eyes. "I'll talk to her."

"I thought you'd say that," he says, getting to his feet. "I'll have both Gamba and breakfast brought to your tent." He leaves quickly, like he's just as eager as I am to avoid the awkward moment of deciding how to touch each other.

As soon as I'm alone, I sink back into bed and number my breaths. I can't let myself think through what Hysan just revealed, or I'll fall apart. Nishi's counting on me to save her, and I can't let my family drama distract me.

But if this girl's story is true, then Mom didn't just abandon me—
She *replaced* me.

◆ ◆ ◆

When Hysan announces himself outside my tent, I'm already in my blue Lodestar suit, my curls pulled back in a ponytail. "Come in," I say.

He enters with a couple of Majors carrying trays of food and silverware, and they lay out a thick blanket on the white feather floor before setting everything down for an indoor picnic. I fix my gaze on the tall, dark-skinned Capricorn girl with tourmaline eyes.

"Rho, this is Gamba," says Hysan when it's just the three of us. The girl keeps coming closer, until we're face to face.

"We'd like to be alone," I say, staring only at the Capricorn who calls my mother *Mom*. "I'll let you know when we're finished so we can meet with Eurek and the others."

"As you wish."

When Hysan disappears through the tent flap, Gamba immediately starts speaking.

"Sister—"

"*Wandering Star.*"

"Wandering Star," she repeats, correcting herself without hesitation or emotion. "I've been longing to meet you for almost ten years, ever since the stars delivered me to our mother—"

"My mother."

This time she doesn't correct herself. She just stares at me in defiant silence—like she's not going to cede on this one.

"Let's get some air," I suggest, striding past the picnic and slipping out through the tent flap. Like Fernanda, the Guardian of Taurus, I no longer trust rooms that aren't my own.

Outside, a breeze brushes my face and cools my skin. We march across the grass to the cobalt water, and as we walk along the sea's banks, I survey the golden trees that seem to have no end.

"You grew up on Tierre?" I ask, thinking of Ferez, the one adult in my life who's yet to let me down.

"I was born on Tethys of House Virgo," she says, her voice even and measured. "I became a Riser when I was eight—right around the time I saw a vision of the Last Prophecy, and the Luminaries came for me."

She tells her life story like she's reading it from a book, the words devoid of emotion. And I hate how much it reminds me of Mom.

"Why are you here?" I ask, planting my feet and facing her.

"To help rescue our mother."

"She's not your mother."

Gamba doesn't flinch. "That's your perspective."

"What?"

"There are no absolutes. Every truth is relative."

I grit my teeth. "Thanks, but when I need wisdom, I'll Wave Ferez."

She tilts her head, scrutinizing me. "Hysan and the others want you to gain my trust. So why are you mistreating me?"

"I don't really care what Hysan or anyone else wants. I don't know who the hell you are, yet you feel completely comfortable calling me sister and claiming my mother as your own. So no, I'm not interested in gaining your trust—and if you want me to care, maybe you should start by gaining mine."

She doesn't speak immediately, and in her sharp silence I see traces of Mom's discipline. "Fine," she says, for the first time sounding like she's losing her cool. "What do you want to know?"

"Where are the other Luminaries?"

"I can't say."

"So much for trusting you."

I start marching back to my tent, but I stop when she says, "It's not that I don't want to—I don't *know*. Once you enter the compound, you can never leave it again, and if you do, you can never find your way back. As a safety measure, none of us knows our geospacial location."

"Where are the rest of you?" I ask, crossing my arms. "Aren't more coming to help us fight?"

"The Luminaries aren't warriors—we're seers. I've come on behalf of the others. I was dipatched to help the Zodai, and I was told to confide only in you."

"Confide what exactly? I already know what the Last Prophecy is, and you can't tell me where the Luminaries are, so what information could you possibly provide?"

She sucks in a deep breath and scans our surroundings before speaking. "We think we know what Aquarius needs to trigger the Last Prophecy."

"*What?*" I ask, stepping closer to her.

"Not what," she says, shaking her head. "*Who.*"

Her dark eyes drill into mine, and before she can say the name, I hear myself say it for her.

"*Ophiuchus.*"

11

MY BODY HUMS WITH EXCITEMENT now that Gamba's information confirms what I began to suspect after questioning Corinthe. And it cements my commitment to the plan I started outlining last night.

"Do you know where General Eurek is?" I ask Gamba.

"I do."

"Take me to him now, please." I'd rather talk to the Ariean Guardian alone, without Hysan.

"Will you tell him that Ophiuchus would make a better ally than prisoner?" she asks, her dark eyes studying me.

"Will *you?*" I shoot back.

"Luminaries only collect information; we do not share it. Once a fact is free, it can never again be hidden. My orders are to speak only with you, and to trust your wisdom."

"Good." I enter the woods and cut in the direction of the looming mountain. I don't know if Gamba is following until I hear her voice at my side.

"So will you tell him?"

"That's not your concern," I say, and she doesn't speak again.

The orange daylight makes everything glint—the blades of grass, the stone fortresses, the Rams' antlers. I have no idea in which of the three Forts I'll find Eurek, and I turn to see that Gamba has stopped walking a few feet behind me.

"What are you going to do about our mother?" she demands.

I roll my eyes. "I'll just find someone else to take me to Eurek—"

"Don't you care what happens to her?" Gamba's dark face cracks with desperation, and it's the first time I see a bit of myself in her. She reminds me of how protective I used to feel about my family.

Back when I still had a family to protect.

"Once I know the situation, I'll figure out what to do about Mom," I say to end our standoff. "Now take me to General Eurek and stop asking questions."

Gamba doesn't argue as she leads me up the hill into the first fortress, which isn't at all what I expected. We enter a massive chamber with a holographic carousel of the cosmos, where people from every House are spaced out and Centered. It's a massive communal reading room.

We edge around the silent crowd and descend a stone staircase into a meeting space. Weapons of every variety line the walls, like an art exhibit or a military museum, and there's a massive rectangular table where half a dozen Majors are gathered. As soon as we enter, General Eurek's strong voice greets me.

"Welcome to Phaet, Wandering Star."

The Guardian of Aries is decked in bloodred military garb, and as he marches over, I can't help admiring his towering stature and muscular frame. We trade the hand touch, and I say, "Thank you, General."

The Majors all stand up and salute me.

"Wandering Star," says the soldier with the most stripes on his sleeve. "We wanted to commend you for the bravery and sacrifice you showed on Pisces. When faced with the opportunity to take out the enemy's General, even though guns were pointed at you, *you took the shot*. That takes guts of steel."

"Indeed," says Eurek good-naturedly. "By taking out the heart of their operation, you found their place of vulnerability and helped us hold on to Ophiuchus—a definite combat advantage."

I've no idea what to say to any of this, so I just stick with, "Thank you."

"I thought you would be coming by later with Hysan," the Guardian goes on, "but I can summon the senior officers now if you'd—"

"I'd rather speak with you alone."

He nods and jerks his chin toward the door, and all six Majors file out. I look to Gamba, and she follows them, shutting the door behind her.

"I don't mean to be rude, but I'm eager to know what's been going on."

"I would expect no less from you," says Eurek, his orange-red eyes glowing like embers. "Aquarius and his Tomorrow Party have vanished. We've been unable to locate their base of operations, yet we do have Zodai who've infiltrated their ranks and have been reporting back to us when they can. Unfortunately, none have breached his inner circle yet, so we know nothing of value."

"So we don't know that he's on House Leo?"

Eurek's black skin pales as he's caught off guard, and his voice drops several decibels.

"He—he is our primary target, Wandering Star," he says apologetically. "I'm sorry for the subterfuge, but please understand that we can't go there without a real plan, and at the moment we don't have one. He can foresee anything we try, so we have to be very careful. We can't risk the lives of our troops until we have a trained army that has a chance of defeating him—no matter how much his hostages may mean to us."

I square my shoulders and make my voice as strong as I can. "General, I sacrificed my *life* to kill Aquarius. I'm the only one who's come close to destroying him. Do you really think I would do anything to jeopardize the Zodiac's survival?"

"No," he says quickly, tipping his head down a fraction. "I apologize for making assumptions, but your friend Hysan—"

"The Libran has developed feelings for me, so his concern colors his logic."

It's amazing how easy it is to say the words—to betray Hysan. Now I understand how he's been able to lie to me again and again and again. It's really not that difficult, if you can just set aside your emotions.

"I had no idea," says Eurek, frowning. "Thank you for telling me."

"Furthermore," I go on, my voice gaining gravity, "he is *not* a Guardian and does *not* outrank me." If Hysan won't own the title, then he doesn't get the power that comes with it.

Eurek nods and says, "Affirmative."

Hoping that his guard will have weakened now that he's feeling sorry, I ask, "Could you tell me about the Everblaze?"

He seems relieved for the change of subject. "Of course. It's existed since before Phaet was oxygenated because the flames aren't fire but Psynergy—the purest concentration you'll ever come across. It's said that if you can find your Center within the Everblaze, you'll be rewarded with a rare vision that most mortals couldn't See. Few people through history have experienced it because the Psynergy is so powerful that when you try to channel it by Centering, it scorches like real fire. That's why we burn our fallen warriors' bodies there: to free their souls' Psynergy and release it to Empyrean. It's a festival called the Ascension, and the shell that remains is later burned to ashes."

I nod as more pieces of my plan come together. "And the wall of Black Truth—does it really protect The Bellow?"

"We believe the stars would never allow anyone through who means us harm," he says without hesitation.

Careful to keep my voice neutral so I don't sound judgmental, I ask, "General, have you been on this planet the whole time you've been under house arrest?"

He nods. "Affirmative. Only the Zodai of our House know this planet is habitable. Our people have so thoroughly destroyed themselves on Phaetonis that the vast majority would never have the means to travel off-planet. The Bellow and the Zodai who guard it have a fierce reputation that people fear, so most won't come near here. We always transport prisoners ourselves."

The door suddenly swings open, and Hysan strides into the room with Pandora in tow. She bows to me in her aqua Elder uniform, her hair pulled away from her amethyst eyes.

"Wandering Star, General," says Hysan by way of greeting, his green gaze locking on mine. "I thought you were going to send for me when you were ready to meet."

"I decided a one-on-one meeting would be best."

"Any word from Lord Neith?" the Ariean Guardian asks Hysan, his deep voice sharp. The question sounds almost like a challenge, and Hysan wrinkles his brow as he registers the tension in Eurek's tone.

"He's with a team of trained Knights investigating a potential Marad base off a tip we received. The plan is for him to check in when he's at a safe communication point."

"As soon as you hear from him, let him know I'd like a word," says Eurek without offering additional details.

"I'll pass it along," says Hysan politely, and then he faces me again, and I quickly turn back to Eurek.

"General, I'd like to give my brother the proper passing rites." Something lodges in my throat and I swallow twice, but the obstruction won't budge. "I—I'd like to celebrate the Ascension," I say thickly.

Dead silence meets my declaration.

I doubt anyone has ever been put to rest through the funeral rites of a different House, and Eurek and Hysan are staring at me like I've just declared myself a Riser.

"It's the best honor I can offer him," I add softly. "Under the circumstances."

"Of course," says Eurek, his strong voice dipping to a gentle tone. "The Ascension always takes place when Helios sets, so we can pick an evening when—"

"Tonight."

Hysan's hesitation is written all over his face, so I pull on my most pathetic-looking Cancrian expression and fend off his objections by saying, "I really need the closure."

Pity replaces concern in his eyes, and then Eurek says, "I'll have the arrangements made. And afterwards, the body—"

"Should be launched to Helios in the Cancrian tradition," I say quickly before he can even suggest burning my brother's body to ashes. My knees grow shaky, and I know I can't discuss Stan another moment or the reality of his passing will settle over me and I'll never make it to the Lion constellation.

"Would you like me to assemble the senior officers for a meeting now?" offers Hysan.

"No need," I say without meeting his gaze. "I'm going to the weapons camp to train with Mathias."

"We thought you'd want to stay here in the metaphysical camp," counters Hysan, and I can't tell if it's a suggestion or a command. "Pandora will join you—"

"I've been told the astral plane has become inaccessible," I cut in.

"Yes, but perhaps *you*—"

"I need to regain my strength first. I think I should do some physical training. And Yarrot."

"Good strategy," says Eurek, and he stares at Hysan like he's daring him to disagree. But the Libran does no such thing.

"I'll escort you over," he offers instead.

My gut hardens. I don't want to be alone with Hysan, but I also need to be doing a better job of pretending everything's fine. Otherwise, he'll be the first to suspect I'm up to something.

"Actually, I can walk her," says a soft, dreamy voice, and we all turn to look at Pandora. "I'd like to talk to Rho about what's been going on in the Psy. We can regroup for lunch."

Hysan looks like he disagrees, but before he says so out loud, I jump in. "Pandora's right. General, thank you for your time. Hysan, we'll see you later."

I don't look his way as I stride past him, and the last thing I hear is his quiet murmur, "*As you wish.*"

But that's the biggest lie of them all.

Because nothing will ever be as I wish.

Not anymore.

12

"HOW ARE YOU?" ASKS PANDORA as soon as we're outside, bathed in orange daylight.

"You don't have to come with me. You can just point me in the right direction."

"I need to check in with Mathias," she says, leading us down the hill toward the other two fortresses. "And anyway, I agree there's no point in you trying to do a reading. Even if the astral plane weren't collapsing, you still wouldn't See anything."

"What's that supposed to mean?" I ask, the words coming out sharper than I intended.

"You're hiding," she says simply, as though she were commenting on the state of the weather and not my mind. "You're not even interested in recovering yet, so there's no point."

Pandora may not have Hysan's powers of perception, but she's experienced enough horrors firsthand to recognize a dead woman walking. I'll have to do a better job of summoning my emotions.

A rivulet cuts through the valley between the first hill and the next, and we step onto a low stone bridge to get across it. The climb up the second hill is steeper than the first, and my muscles are cramping in pain, my body aching for more recovery time. . . .

But it's nothing compared to what Nishi's body must be enduring.

I fight down that thought by forcing myself to stay present as we enter the second Fort. In place of a communal reading room, the main hall is crammed with dozens of elevated rings where Zodai from every House are practicing sparring with each other using blue-bladed swords.

"Why is everyone using the same weapon?" I ask.

"The Marad's technology is Aquarian," explains Pandora. "The blue light it sends out is an energy wave. The Zodai tested every House's weapons against the Murmurs in our possession, and they found the Barer is the only one capable of shielding people from its blast. But we're also training in *all* Zodai devices, since they're so different."

We stop in front of a display of weapons with holographic tags hovering over each one. The Ripple, the Arclight, and the Scarab are familiar, but this is my first time seeing the other Houses' devices up close. I avoid the Sumber and instead study a couple of the Earth Houses' horn-shaped weapons by reading their text overhead.

The Capricorn Shrill is made from Seagoat horns, the insides of which are carved with a series of ridges using a centuries-old Capricorn technique. When sounded, the Chronicler's breath passes through thousands of intricate airways to emit a sound at a frequency that shuts down the nervous system of anyone who hears it.

The Taurian Tremble is a stout, horn-shaped device that can be plunged into the earth to trigger a small, targeted earthquake. The Tremble is most effective when used in teams of three to create a devastating and contained quake within a triangulated area.

A crowd erupts in celebration, and I turn to look at the training area again. "What's going on there?" I ask, pointing to the Zodai gathered around one of the center rings. Squinting, I recognize the pair of fighters—Skarlet and Mathias.

"They do this all the time," says Pandora, following me as I move in for a closer look. I can't take my eyes off them.

The match is like a sensuous and deadly dance between two beautiful warriors. As they spar, the audience cries out in excitement, and some even seem to be taking bets.

I've never seen Mathias move like this before. Skarlet lunges, and he parries. She flickers around in her red suit like a living flame, moving so stealthily and attacking so suddenly that it takes near superhuman reflexes to deflect her—which Mathias has. His fighting technique reminds me of Yarrot—his movements are smooth and connected and focused—and he only raises his sword to defend himself. He never strikes.

A bell rings, signaling the end of the match, and there's no clear winner. The Zodai seem upset by this, and they start arguing with each other about who owes whom payment, but Skarlet and Mathias are laughing as they step off the ring.

"You're tough for a crab," she says, shoving him roughly.

"You're pleasant enough for a ram," he teases back, and then he actually *smirks*. "Well, some of the time."

She punches him in what was probably supposed to be a playful touch, but Mathias cries out and cradles his arm. "*Ow!* The match was over!"

"I take it back," says Skarlet, letting out a loud laugh. "You don't seem so tough now."

They walk side by side, their bodies tall and muscled and sweaty, and there's a comfortable ease between them that he and I never shared. Studying him, I realize he's less burdened than he used to be, and he's almost emanating the same peaceful aura as Pandora—until he catches me watching.

"Hey, everything okay?" he asks, cutting over to us quickly, his gaze panning from me to Pandora. "Is there news?"

Skarlet comes up behind him, also looking alert.

We're so primed for tragedy that apparently anything out of the ordinary is cause for alarm—like my presence in a physical training area.

"I was hoping to train with you today," I say, looking from Mathias to Skarlet. "That is, if Major Thorne is finished with you."

Skarlet smiles sweetly. "How nice of you to ask for permission this time."

"I guess it's only fair after what we went through last night," I can't help saying. Her eyes widen in warning since we're within earshot of other Majors, and I add, "You know . . . how you stayed by my side until I fell asleep so the monsters couldn't get me?"

Her frown eases a little, but her expression is still tense. "Can we speak alone for a moment, please?"

She seems to tag on the last word unwillingly, and Pandora takes Mathias's arm and pulls him away. "I just spoke with your parents," I hear her tell him as they walk, "and they asked me to tell you a new troop of Zodai from Virgo will be arriving tomorrow morning with Numen and Qima. They'll need lodging. . . ."

As her voice fades, Skarlet says, "I had to call a healer I trust last night to covertly close Corinthe's wound, and then I had to change her scrubs so no one would know anything happened. This whole thing is too risky—I'm telling my commanding officer what we did before it gets out."

"No, you're *not*."

"Then you need to go to Eurek. And after you've explained to him how you forced me to help you, you can tell him what we learned from Corinthe. It might be important."

I wait a few seconds to pretend I'm thinking it over, and then I say, "Fine. But tomorrow."

"No," she says, crossing her arms over her chest. "*Now*."

I blow out a hard breath, and without meeting her gaze, I say, "We're launching my brother to Empyrean tonight. So I would rather not do this now."

After a moment she says, "Tomorrow then."

When she leaves, I find Mathias waiting for me by the weapons display. "Pandora told me about Stan," he says, his musical voice soft. "She said you wanted to take your mind off the Ascension by doing some physical training."

I nod.

"Then let's get you fitted with a Barer," he says with newfound energy, and we step into what seems to be a stockroom of weapons. Mathias rummages through the Barers until we find one with rings that fit my fingers comfortably. Since it's suited to a person's dominant hand, I have to transfer my Zodai Ring to my left hand to make room.

"The Barer's strength is completely dependent on your connection to it," says Mathias as we climb inside an elevated ring to test it out. "It's similar to the Zodai Ring—the more attuned you are to its energy, the easier it will be to call on it when you need it. This is where your Centering skills come in handy—you'll need to be completely focused on the energy you're wielding for it to work the way you want."

"How do I do that?"

"You dig down into the energy you feel buzzing in your hand until you've bonded with the weapon. Unlike the Ripple, the Barer isn't about having good aim—it's about concentration. Generally speaking, those who are best at Centering themselves do best with this weapon—so you have an advantage."

As he talks, I flash back to us on Oceon 6 when he taught me how to use the Ring. I remember the way my emotions jostled my mind then, adding their own voice to the conversation. But I can't remember how those feelings felt.

"Metals in the rings convert energy from the atmosphere into electricity. When you're ready, make a fist and think of the shape you want the energy to take—it can become a sword, or a bow that fires off electric blasts, or brass knuckles that deliver electric jolts every time they connect with your opponent."

I close my eyes and reach inward, toward the humming in my right hand. It's similar to the Psynergy from my Ring, only the electric current in the Barer is more of a physical sensation than a mental one. I can feel my skin tingling and the hairs on my arm stiffening from the static. I concentrate on honing the energy into the long blade of a sword, and then I squeeze my hand into a fist.

I hear a crackling sound, and I open my eyes to see a blue flame.

"I'd be impressed if I weren't so used to you impressing me," says Mathias, his midnight gaze bright with admiration. "The second part is projecting a shield around yourself—that's how you can repel a Murmur attack."

"How does that work?"

"You have to dig deep and pull the Barer's energy through every part of your body. Only thing is you need to Center yourself first so you're protected by a barrier of Psynergy. Otherwise, if the blue energy touches your skin, it will electrocute you. So the first thing you do is access your Center and feel the Psynergy bonding with the Barer's energy, and then you spread the shield through your whole body. It takes supreme concentration, and you have to feel every single inch of yourself, or you'll risk leaving holes—"

"I can practice that on my own time," I say before I shut down from information overload. "I'm more interested in learning your fighting technique. There isn't much of a point to wielding this weapon if I don't know how to use it."

First he teaches me how to turn the Barer into a bow. It takes me longer to envision the right shape to manifest it, but once I do it's easy enough to shoot electric blasts. The sword is hardest for me to wield, and Mathias and

I spar for hours until the muscles of my arms and legs grow leaden. I'm not very good, but that's not important.

I don't plan on fighting fair with it anyway.

When I'm worn out—which doesn't take long—we sit on a bench far from everyone else and fill up on water. As we drink, we watch the dozens of fights going on throughout the space, our thoughts adrift.

"Rho," he says after a long silence, "I'm sorry about your brother."

My throat goes dry even though I've had two glasses of water, and I stand up to pour myself a third. When I sit back down, Mathias says, "I'm sorry I didn't save him."

I take a long drink and don't look at him. "I should go see Hysan," I say after swallowing. "I told him I'd check in by now."

"I'll walk you—"

"No, I'm fine. I could use the alone time."

He nods, and I know he understands. But before I get up, he says, "I missed you."

I stiffen and look at him, and his ivory face grows pink as he goes on. "When I thought I lost you . . . that you'd never wake up . . . I guess I understand how it must have felt when you thought I was dead."

I stare into his indigo eyes, and it feels like the first time since the Sumber that I'm truly seeing someone—or maybe it's just the first time I'm letting someone see me.

"You're my best friend," he says, his gaze strong and steadfast. "And if you want to talk, I'm here. Anytime."

13

AFTER A QUICK SHOWER IN the women's locker room, I pull on the Veil collar I slipped into my pocket this morning and activate its invisibility.

Mathias's heart-to-heart left me feeling raw, like a wound that was scabbing just got exposed, and I don't want to risk running into anyone who might irritate it further. Especially since there's more I need to do before tonight.

The entrance hall in the third fortress is hushed and riddled with semiprivate terminals where Zodai are sitting at screens and pulling up information. A massive wallscreen wraps around the upper half of the room; it's divided into twelve sections, and news from every House is updating in real time. I flatten myself against the wall so that no one runs into me, and I scan the headlines.

The Piscene death count from the master's Psyphoning is nearing half a million. There's a chart showing a correlation: With every wave of Piscene deaths, the hole in the Dark Matter around Ophiuchus expands.

It seems the governments of every House are as divided as their citizens. Most don't want to believe Crompton is the original Aquarius or that he's going to usher in the end of the Zodiac. Capricorn's Chroniclers have been citing the Axis more than ever, noting that this is exactly how the century-long civil wars started. The master is re-creating our past—and without trust in each other, we're doomed to repeat it.

I trail along the room's perimeter and turn into the first passage I come across. Torches bracketed along the stone walls illuminate my way, and soon I reach a crossroads where the corridor splits in three. I pick a direction at random and keep going, until I come upon a lounge with couches and tables and food, where Zodai in different colored uniforms are meeting or snacking or napping.

I trace my way back to the crossroads, and this time I pick a different path. It ends in a set of open doors, where a pair of Majors stands guard. This must be where they keep the more sensitive information.

I close my eyes and reach down to the humming of the Barer's electricity, and I mentally mold it into a bow. When I open my eyes, an arc of blue energy glows before me. I turn to make sure the passage behind me is empty, and then I fire a blast of electricity down the dark hall.

The blue ball of light blazes down the stone corridor, and the guards instantly raise their silver tasers to eye level and charge after the electric arrow.

I dart through the entryway they were protecting and enter a narrower stone passage. A series of doors line both walls, and I carefully crack open the first one. It's an empty room of semi-private terminals, like the ones in the entrance hall. Since no one else is in here, I sit down at a screen and try to pull up the menu—but a retinal scan is required.

Time to see how much power I actually have on this base.

I deactivate my invisibility collar and line my eye up with the scanner. A light flashes, fleetingly blinding me, then the screen dissolves into a navigational menu with headings like *Tomorrow Party*, *Marad*, and *Ophiuchus*. I click on the last one, and holographic surveillance footage beams out.

The Thirteenth Guardian is asleep in a bright white cell that looks just like the one Corinthe is in, with metallic sensors spaced out along his body. Metal cuffs wrap around not just his ankles, wrists, and neck, but also his waist, chest, and knees. A needle sticks out from his neck, hooked up to an IV, presumably what's keeping him sedated.

My breathing stalls when I magnify his face. He's *young*.

He doesn't look a day over eighteen.

His hair is so black it's like Dark Matter, and his skintone seems to shift from light to dark, like he's not one shade but many. Its texture makes me think of snakeskin.

I click on the small map thumbnail, and a holographic rendering of The Bellow replaces the footage of a sleeping Ophiuchus. A red line outlines the path to his cell, and I take a moment to memorize it before shutting the screen down and returning to the main menu.

There's nothing noteworthy under the Marad heading, but there are a number of updates for the Tomorrow Party. It looks like Hysan's encrypted communications with Ezra have paid off because Zodai managed to track the Party to the Artistry Pride of House Leo. It's the preferred destination for controversial figures in hiding, since artists are known to judge the least.

I close my eyes to review what I know. I have a general location for Nishi. I have access to Ophiuchus. And I have the perfect distraction.

I'm leaving for Leo tonight.

I shut down my terminal, and my Barer hand buzzes with static. I study the intricate designs etched into the metal rings, and I don't feel the same initial distrust and disgust I had for the black pearl Scarab a few months ago. Now, having a weapon isn't weakening but empowering—it's the difference between dependence and independence.

I reactivate my Veil, and when I leave the room, a woman's laugh floats down the stone passage. Recognizing the sound I instinctively and invisibly step up to the partly open doorway and peek inside.

My whole body hollows, and it feels like déjà vu.

Hysan is sitting on a bench in a small training space filled with outdated exercise machines. He's in a pair of shorts and no shirt, and sweat gleams across the Ariean-worthy contours of his torso and arms, his chest rising and falling like he's just finished an intense workout.

"Why won't you train with the rest of us in the other Fort?" asks Skarlet, who's also barely clothed, baring every single line and curve of her figure. She's wearing shorts and an athletic bra made from some kind of Ariean sweat-absorbing workout fabric that's so thin and skintight it might as well not be there.

"I was already here," he says, his husky voice choppy from exertion. He stands up to grab a water bottle off a stone counter that juts from the wall and takes a swig.

"Is that really why?" Skarlet edges closer to him and leans into the counter. "See, I think you're here because you're afraid."

Hysan sets the bottle down and arches an eyebrow. "Of?"

"Running into me."

His lips hitch into his crooked smirk even as he takes a step back. "You don't scare me, Major Thorne."

"I know you're tempted," she says seductively, moving in close enough that Hysan's shoulders touch the wall. "We used to have so much fun together."

"Skar," he says softly, his expression sobering, "I told you after the ball. I'm in love with her."

I exhale and wait for my veins to flood with relief. . . . Instead, I find myself wondering how long his resistance will last.

"But are you sure she's in love with you?"

Skarlet asks the question with the same gentle voice she used when describing to me what Phaet means to Arieans.

"I've made it clear I'm challenging her, and she doesn't seem bothered by it. Or, who knows," she adds with the flicker of a dangerous grin, "she might even be open to sharing you."

Hysan's jaw tightens, and his words come out slightly clipped. "Why are you messing with her? I thought you said you admired her."

"I do," she says, shrugging. "You know I only pick on people my own size."

"You have a strange way of making friends."

"What is it about her?" she asks, bringing her mouth right up to his, so close that the slightest movement would bring them together. She's wearing so little clothing that Hysan can't avoid touching her bare skin. "I *know* she's not the best-looking woman in the Zodiac," she adds with a sultry smile.

"But she is the most beautiful," he says, all traces of good humor gone from his voice.

Skarlet takes a surprised step back, and for a moment she just stares at him, while he calmly holds her gaze.

"You really are in love," she says at last, tacking on a small shrug. *"Pity."*

As she sashays past me out the doorway, her expression crumbles with the pain she's too proud to let Hysan see, and I turn back to watch him.

His skin's golden glow is dull, like a lamp that's been put out, and he hasn't moved at all. He seems more affected by Skarlet's presence now that she's gone.

I wonder if he regrets rejecting her, or if he's just thinking of what she revealed about me.

But is it true?

I know on a rational level that I once loved Hysan, yet I've lost the memory of the way it felt. It's like my emotions have been muted; I know they exist, but I can't tap into them. Maybe this is what it's like to be Libran.

I'm so lost in my head that it takes me a moment to realize he's moved. Hysan digs into his bag and removes something I can't see. After pulling on a shirt he'd draped over one of the machines, he turns toward the door to go and looks at me.

I freeze in place, until I remember I'm invisible and he can't see me.

"Hi, Rho."

"What—" I cut myself off when I see the collar he's just fastened around his neck, peeking out from beneath the shirt's neckline. The Veils are networked.

"Been here long?" he asks.

"I—"

"Actually, I'm glad," he says quickly, like he's not at all interested in discussing what I just witnessed. "There's something I'd like to show you— but I should shower first."

"Shower later," I say impatiently. "We're invisible anyway."

"Follow me then," he says, and we take off down the hall, away from the room with the terminals and into a different, smaller space that smells musty and old. "This is where the Zodai keep this House's earliest records, the ones they didn't turn over to the Zodiax. It's all the data from when our ancestors first landed on Phaetonis."

He clicks keys on a screen embedded into the wall, until a hole opens up in the floor at the center of the room. A platform rises up, and all that's on it is an open manuscript, its pages yellowed and wispy and faded. The book is encased in light, and unintelligible words begin to rise from it into the air, a holographic recreation of the text, which is written in some archaic language.

"Do you remember when Sirna read that story to us, *The Chronicles of Hebitsukai-Za, the Serpent Bearer?*"

I'm instantly intrigued, and I start regurgitating what I remember. "Sirna said Holy Mother Crae sent Lodestar Yosme to House Aries seventy-seven years ago to study the first version of the myth, about the time-worm—but the report was buried because there were details too alarming to be made public. Details having to do with *time*."

"You really weren't lying about your infallible memory," says Hysan with a half-smile.

"What have you found?" I press.

"Apparently this story dates back to the days of the Original Guardians," he says, growing businesslike again and not meeting my gaze. "I've found more texts with allusions to Ophiuchus; sometimes he's represented with one snake and sometimes with two, like the Caduceus symbol."

"On Cancer, the Caduceus is just one snake."

"That's because the Thirteenth House's mythology has been so twisted over time that we can't be sure what's true. In the Tale of Hebitsukai-Za, thirteen travelers traverse the time warp to enter the universe, and the last one gets wrapped in the coils of a giant worm biting its own tail—so it looks like *two* snakes, but it's really just one."

"But what's important about this?"

"The fact that this version of events circulated at the beginning of time means there must be more truth to it than we realize." The holographic text begins to translate itself as Hysan recounts the story, and I see the images Sirna once projected for us at the Libran embassy.

"Za was the last to come through, and when he did his body was entwined in the ropey coils of an enormous worm biting its own tail—*Time*. Passing though the time warp created an unstable leak between the old universe and ours, and they were in imminent danger of sliding together and collapsing, so the travelers sealed off the warp, but only after Za had brought the time-worm through. The travelers recognized the chaos this would cause and tried to kill the worm, and by accident bludgeoned Za to death. The worm needed a host, so it reversed time and resurrected Za." It ends with what looks like the glyph of House Ophiuchus.

"I remember all this," I say impatiently, "but I still don't understand why it's been filed as dangerous—"

"Because it's true," he says, his large green eyes sparkling with excitement. "Ophiuchus's Talisman lets him control Time—namely, his own time line. And the other Guardians felt threatened by this, so they killed him. Only the Talisman—the time-worm—never truly let go of Ophiuchus. It resurrected his essence and kept him tied to our universe."

"So you're saying it's just like the Ochus stories of every House—more evidence hidden in our art that there was a thirteenth world—"

"Yes, but I think there's another secret in that story," he says carefully. "Travelers came from another universe through a time warp to settle the Zodiac . . . sounds a lot like the universal myth about the first humans arriving here through a portal in Helios, doesn't it?"

"*Myths speak to us through metaphor*," I whisper, recalling Hysan's words when Sirna first told us this story.

His ears turn pink, but he doesn't comment on my memory again. "Rho, I think the gateway through Helios might be real."

His eyes are entranced, and his golden glow burns brighter. "I think just as they erased House Ophiuchus from history, the Original Guardians also convinced newer generations to believe the portal their ancestors came through was just a legend—so that no one would ever attempt going through it again."

"And *that's* the master's plan," I finish for him as Hysan nods. "Holy Helios. *He's going to turn off the sun by going through it.*"

14

WHEN I GET BACK TO my tent, there's an outfit and fresh food waiting for me.

As I eat and get ready, I'm still thinking of Hysan's theory. If the Last Prophecy is really about Aquarius going through Helios, then it's not a future written in the stars—it's a future written by *a* star.

Our sun is only going dark because the master is going to travel through it.

Aquarius himself said he was the first person to prophesize this future, so he must also have the power to stop it. He just has to make a different choice. He has to abandon his plan to go through Helios.

For the Ascension ceremony, it's tradition for Zodai to don silky robes, and as I'm in mourning, I'll be the only one in white. Everyone else will be in dark colors. Since I don't plan to come back to the tent, I leave on my Lodestar suit beneath my robe, and I stuff my Wave, Vecily's Ephemeris, and my Psy shield into its various pockets. I leave Sirna's necklace behind so that Hysan can't track me.

I wonder where the necklace Aquarius re-created from my childhood went. I'm betting Hysan thought it was a transmitter or weapon of some kind. He lost his parents too young to understand the necklace's true power.

"My lady?"

"Come in," I say as I take one last look in the vanity's mirror to make sure my suit isn't visible. I've closed my robe all the way up to my throat, and my boots are hidden by my silky white train.

I step out to the middle of the white feather floor to meet Hysan, who's dressed in a dark charcoal robe. His hair is brushed back, and in the dying day's light his eyes are a dazzling shade of green. And as I'm absorbing every detail of his face, it strikes me that I might never see him again.

"Everyone is heading to the Everblaze," he says huskily. "I came by to offer to escort you . . . if you'd like the company."

"I'm glad you're here," I say, surprised that I actually mean it.

Hysan seems surprised, too, because he comes closer and strokes my cheekbone.

This time his touch doesn't feel so far away, and I lean into his hand. He moves in, too, until his mouth hovers over mine, and something in my chest dislodges, like a chunk of glacier melting. I part my lips to catch my breath, and he tips his face down, like he's going to kiss me.

"Let's go," I say, exiting the tent quickly to escape Hysan's heat. I let the cool evening breeze stomp out the last cinders of whatever just sparked between us so I can keep my wall of ice in place.

It takes a few moments for Hysan to follow me out, and when he catches up, I ask, "What happened to the necklace Crompton threw at me at the Cathedral?"

"I got rid of it. I thought it could be a recording device." He clears his throat. "So how did it go with Gamba today? Did she have any message from the Luminaries?"

I shake my head. "She's here because she loves my mother. I don't think she knows anything helpful," I lie.

Soon we're engulfed in a massive crowd of robed Zodai from across the galaxy, all of us marching toward the black smoke that rises over the golden trees. Above us, the sky has become a boiling cauldron again, the red sun setting the clouds on fire.

When we reach the clearing where the Everblaze burns, I stare up in awe: The black flames rise so high that they practically lick the stars. The crowd parts for Hysan and me, and many Zodai solemnly stick out a hand to touch me as we pass.

We wade through them slowly, until we make it right up to the fire, where General Eurek is waiting with Mathias and Pandora. Hovering beside them is a body on a metal bed, covered by a thin white sheet.

Hysan wraps a steadying arm around me, but I still feel like I'm floating away. A part of me yearns to throw myself at the flames and join my brother—and I probably would, if that didn't mean abandoning Nishi, my sister.

Pandora and Eurek bow to me, but Mathias pulls me into his blue-robed chest and holds me there tightly. When we part, Eurek murmurs, "Do you wish to say something, Wandering Star?" I shake my head no. "Then if you're ready, I'll commence the ceremony."

I nod in agreement. It's as articulate as I'm going to get.

Eurek raises his voice, and it's so strong and clear that it could be echoing through the entire forest; I notice a volumizer floating near his mouth, amplifying his reach.

"We are here to bid farewell to our fallen brother, honorary Lodestar Stanton Grace. He's the first Cancrian—the first non-Arien—whose soul will rise to Empyrean through the Everblaze, but may he not be the last."

Eurek's bloodred robe flickers in the dimming light, and his dark skin grows darker as night lengthens its shadow. "In Stanton's honor, henceforth, anyone seeking refuge, including Risers, will find a home on Aries."

Gasps of surprise spread through the crowd, and one girl whoops so loudly that people's heads turn in her direction. But Skarlet—in a low-cut black robe—doesn't look the least bit sorry.

I feel like in an alternate universe there's a Rho Grace rejoicing at this news. A Rho Grace who just accomplished something she set out to do a dozen lifetimes ago. But that Rho Grace doesn't live here anymore.

She left this world with Stanton.

I'm just a holo-ghost with unfinished business.

The elevated bed holding Stan starts floating forward until the black flames swallow him whole. Eurek bows his head in prayer, and all the Majors do the same. Pandora and Hysan follow their example, as do the Zodai in the crowd.

Mathias and I lock eyes. When Cancrians launch their dead to Empyrean, we look up, not down.

Maybe I was wrong to do this—I'm deceiving my brother by putting his soul to rest through traditions that aren't his own, all so I can betray everything he stood for to save Nishi.

You're honoring him beyond anything he could have hoped for, says Mathias's voice in my head, my Ring buzzing with the influx of Psynergy. *You've just made him a pioneer—the first of us to truly break barriers and belong not to one House but all of them. He would be proud, Rho.*

I close my eyes and send back, *Thank you.*

My chest feels like a fracturing glacier again, and I suck in another open-mouthed breath to push the wall back in place.

When Stan's blanketed body floats back out, it looks exactly as it did going in—except my brother's really gone now. His essence has moved on to Empyrean.

"Per the Cancrian tradition," says Eurek, "we will now launch Stanton Grace's body to Helios. May he find his place with his father, his people, and all those we've lost, and may he bring us together in Empyrean as he's brought us together now."

Metal walls roll up from either side of the bed and seal around Stan, enclosing him in a Space capsule. Eurek inputs a sequence, and the whole thing tips up until it's perfectly vertical, like a rocket.

Eurek rests a hand on the metal and says, "Go in peace, brother."

Then he stands back, and the rest of us do the same, right as a blast of fire booms out, and the capsule shoots into the sky. My robes flutter as it goes, and in seconds it disappears among the stars.

I love you so much, Stan.

I'm sorry for failing you.

But we'll be together again soon.

15

LIKE SAGITTARIANS, ARIEANS CELEBRATE DEATH—they don't mourn it. So there's a huge party following the Ascension, and it's exactly what I was counting on.

Red bonfires spring up all around us, illuminating the night. Since everything has been so tense until now, most Zodai are already drunk within the first hour. Raucous music blares through the clearing, and the party has an "end of the worlds" feel to it—like no one's sure they'll ever laugh or dance or kiss again after tonight, so they're getting their fill.

Pandora stands close to me while Hysan and Mathias fetch us drinks. "Whatever you're planning, let me help you," she says the instant the guys disappear.

My gut clenches with alarm. "I don't know what you're talking about."

"You've been secretive all day. Hysan can tell something's up." The deep purple of her robe makes her violet irises pop. "I'm offering you my help because I think you need it."

"I'm fine," I say too quickly. Then I turn away from her and distract myself by watching the tables of food that Majors are carrying over from the closest keep's kitchen.

It seems like any Zodai who aren't drinking or dancing or hooking up are leaping into the cobalt sea or standing in the shallows of the Everblaze. A tall Ariean girl enters the black flames, her eyes closed and head tipped up to the sky; I count off the seconds, and when I get to thirteen, she jumps back out like she's been burned.

There are no visible scars, but she's clutching her chest like the fire is inside. When she looks up, she spots me.

"Rho!" she shouts over the loud music, and as she bounds over, I recognize the youngest healer—the one who was eager to summon Hysan for me. "I'm so sorry about your brother. Can I get you anything?"

"Hysan's on it."

Her brown eyes light up and grow even larger. "I'm so glad you guys found each other! He was so worried about you—I swear, I've never seen anyone so distraught before. Just watching him as he watched over you was enough to break even an Ariean's hard heart—"

"What were you doing in there?" I ask, cutting her off and jutting my chin at the fire. I can't hear another word about how perfect Hysan is; not when I alone am keeper of his secrets.

"Oh, that," she says, shrugging. "I was trying to get a vision, but it's impossible. I can count on both hands the number of Arieans in history who've managed it. They're legendary."

Hysan and Mathias come up behind her, and they each hand a drink to Pandora and me. "Hi, Valea," says Hysan, greeting the Ariean. "Can I get you something?"

When the healer looks at him, she freezes like a prisoner in The Bellow whose mobility has been suspended. "I—I—sorry, I mean no, I mean thank you!"

Her face looks radioactive, but Hysan gallantly pretends not to notice the effect he's having on her. "Let me introduce you to some friends," he says, and as Valea trades the hand touch with Mathias and Pandora, I watch Gamba step into the Everblaze.

Tendrils of fire reach up and engulf her brown robe until she's barely visible through the black flames. I count off the seconds, but when I get to thirty, she's still inside. I haven't seen anyone endure it that long.

When she finally reappears, she looks pallid and out of breath, and I wonder if she Saw anything.

She turns to me suddenly, like she feels my stare, and we hold each other's gaze as she walks over to where I'm standing. "Wandering Star. May I have a word?"

I hand off my untouched drink to Valea, and I don't offer her or my friends any explanation as I follow Gamba to the tree line where the forest grows denser. Once the music from the party sounds faint, she stops walking and asks, "So what's the plan to save our mother?"

"Tell me about her."

Her troubled expression slackens, like she's taken aback by the question. "About Mom?" I nod. "What do you want to know?"

"What was she like with you?"

"Insightful. Tough. Protective." She recites adjectives like she's reading a report, not describing a beloved parent. "Honest—"

"*Honest?*" I almost laugh.

"She told me everything. She was my mother by *choice*, not chance."

Even though the subject we're discussing couldn't be more personal, she still speaks in even, measured phrases, like this is an intellectual exercise. And I feel like in this girl I'm seeing who I might have become if Mom had raised me.

"What's *everything*?" I challenge.

"I know her mom was an imbalanced Riser, and she had to fight her for her freedom. I know the night she ran away from her childhood home was the first time she Saw herself Rising. I know that to this day she doesn't know her mother's fate."

I try to interrupt, but my brain feels frozen, like my thoughts can't move beyond this moment. Gamba goes on, and I have no idea if she's aware of how much her words are affecting me because I'm not sure she's capable of comprehending emotions.

If she did have feelings once, Mom drilled them out of her.

"I also know that she was always going to abandon you and your brother and your dad. To protect you, in case she turned out to be too much like her own mother."

I can hardly breathe, much less respond. *Mom trusted her.*

Gamba chose Mom, and Mom chose her back.

"She's *your* mother," I say at last. "*You* save her."

✦ ✦ ✦

The music grows louder as I walk away from Gamba, and I dig my hand under my robe's neckline and activate the Veil collar.

I have to force myself to wall off thoughts of my dysfunctional family so I can focus on tonight. I can't let my mother derail me anymore—Gamba can worry about rescuing her. After all, she's the daughter Kassandra wanted.

When I return to the party, people's guards are down, but there's still tension in the air. Everyone is too ready to switch into Zodai mode at the first sign of trouble. I spy Skarlet in the crowd chugging drinks with a couple of male Majors, and my lip curls—the perfect fuse to set off.

As I make my way over, I nearly topple into Mathias and Pandora, who are filling their plates with food. "I think that's enough, thanks," says Pandora as Mathias keeps piling her plate with desserts.

"Don't be shy," he says, adding yet another chocolate treat to her teetering stack. "I saw what you put away after last night's meeting."

Pandora's eyes grow so large that they're practically bulging out of her head. "What do you mean by that?"

"Just that you have a weakness for sweet things," he says, popping a star-shaped candy into his mouth.

"And you're enabling my addiction."

"Or," he says, leaning in, "maybe I just want to give you everything you want."

Fire rushes to her pale cheeks, but to her credit, she keeps her composure. "How . . . how do you think Rho is doing?"

Mathias's brow furrows down and his lightheartedness is replaced with something heavier. I could slap Pandora for ruining her own moment by bringing me up.

"I don't think even she realizes how much she's suffering," he says. "She's protecting herself from fully feeling the loss of her brother. And she's only making it worse for herself when she finally confronts her pain."

I bite my inner cheek so I won't scream.

Mathias hasn't mentioned Nishi once.

"Do you remember when Corinthe tried using me to get you to denounce Rho?" whispers Pandora, and my breathing stalls.

Mathias doesn't answer, but the color drains from his features, making his dark blue eyes stand out even more.

"Afterwards," she goes on, "while you were setting my shoulders back in place, you told me a story to distract me from the pain. It was about a boy who was in love with a girl he knew he could never have, and yet every day, he woke up and watched her. Even though he knew the more he watched, the harder he'd fall, and the more he'd hurt . . . he couldn't help himself.

"You said pain is one of the side effects of love—we can't feel one without suffering the other."

He nods, just barely, and murmurs, "I remember."

"Rho loved her brother more than most people will ever love anyone," she says, her voice feathery soft. "I don't think she's pushing away her pain. I think she's drowning in it."

I walk away before I can hear more, and once I'm close to Skarlet I deactivate my Veil. While waiting for her to finish another round of chugging, I scan the crowd and spot Hysan. He's speaking with a group of people, but he keeps lifting his gaze, like he's searching for someone. He's not going to let me go.

"He's a great kisser, isn't he?"

I turn to see Skarlet, her smile sloppy and her face shiny. She seems delighted to have caught me off guard, which works for me—if she thinks she got under my skin, that's all the pretext I need to get under hers.

"Maybe you should quit drooling over Hysan and start spending your time on the people of your own House," I say, raising my voice so the nearest Zodai—two Ariean Majors, a Taurian Promisary, and a Leonine Lionheart—can hear me.

"What in Helios is that supposed to mean?" she asks, slurring her words slightly.

"It means your Zodai have this amazing life on this planet, but I've been to Phaetonis, and I've seen how the rest of your people live. In shacks, surrounded by the smell of death and decay—did you not think they might appreciate a place like this?"

"Who do you think built the train system and the Hippodrome and all that stuff on Phaetonis?" she demands, and a Strident from Scorpio and a Minister from Virgo come closer, intrigued by the conversation. "The Majors have tried to promote diplomacy for resolving conflicts, but our people have always preferred war. We're fiery tempered, and we need to let off steam often. It's just our nature!"

I shake my head sadly. "The other Houses used to feel sorry for you. How you're one of the poorest Houses, how your Zodai were exiled from governance, how your Guardian was under house arrest—and yet all this time, you've been in control behind the scenes, living in this paradise. I guess no world is what it seems."

"It *is* pretty selfish," injects the Taurian. "I mean, your people are dirt poor, and you've just abandoned them—"

"She's right, though! Arieans are all hotheaded," argues the Scorp. "You can't help them if they don't help themselves."

"Who the hell are you calling hotheaded, you ugly arachnid?" asks a burly male Major.

The whole group dissolves into a rowdy argument, and now that I've kindled the flame, I let the people around me fan it—helped along by all the alcohol, of course—until most of the party is embroiled in debate. I activate my Veil, but before making my way up to the mountain I turn toward the Everblaze.

All the noise evaporates as I step into its black flames.

The fire crackles around me as it tickles my skin, and I close my eyes. I access my Center and start numbering the seconds, until I'm buzzing too hard to keep count. My Ring starts to burn, and blood begins to boil in my veins, but the heat feels good. Even as it scorches my organs and destroys my insides, I don't mind, because it's a change from the numbness.

Let it burn and consume all I am. . . .

Except it if does, who will save Nishi?

Without Deke or me, who will care enough to go after her?

The fire has become so painful that I can't move my feet. I would scream if I could summon my voice, but my lungs are gone, too, and my knee joints give out until I drop to the grass.

I'm dying and I'm invisible, and no one will find me.

I think only of Nishi as I feel myself fall, only the drop isn't physical— I'm descending to an even deeper Center. Light blasts through the darkness of my mind, until I See a familiar wizened face, her skin so wrinkled it looks sun-dried.

Moira?

The vision vanishes, and the Psynergy chokes me until I'm gagging. I claw at the ground, digging my nails into the grass as I drag myself forward.

The sound blasts back on when at last I make it out.

People are still partying, none of them aware that I'm dying at their feet. I curl into a fetal position, taking in raking breaths until the cool air finally reaches my lungs. And by the time I stand up, all the effects of the fire have worn off, healing as swiftly as Ochus's Psynergy wounds.

Breathless and invisible, I climb uphill into the woods, away from the party and toward the hulking mountain. When I'm at the edge of the tree line, far from the wasted crowd, I turn back to take one last look at the world I'm leaving behind.

And that's when Hysan unVeils before me.

16

HIS EYES ARE DARK AND EXPLOSIVE.

"Did you really think I wouldn't know?" asks Hysan as he deactivates my invisibility. He must have unlinked our collars so I wouldn't see him tailing me. A medley of emotions swirls in his green-gold irises, and I know he's already read everything on my face. All the secrets I thought I'd been so carefully concealing.

"So because you've lost loved ones, it's over?" he goes on, as a chilly breeze blows between us. "What about everyone else who's lost family and friends to this war? Are their sacrifices less meaningful than yours?"

"And what would you know about losing a *loved one?*" I ask, and it's almost a snarl. "You have no family, and you've never been honest enough to have a real friend. *You've never had anyone to lose.*"

His eyes grow round with disbelief, but they quickly revert to their normal size as he reins in his emotions. It's so easy for him to bypass his heart; he doesn't care that abandoning Nishi is killing me because he can't possibly understand the pain I'm going through.

"So your solution is to turn your back on all of humanity?" he asks tonelessly. "To save Nishi you'll damn us all? That's how you'll honor your brother and your father's sacrifices?"

I don't feel the sting of his words because they're not true—but I'm not surprised to learn that's what he's thinking. It's almost liberating to hear the truth from him for once. "If you really believe I would damn you all, then you've never known me."

I used to think Mathias was the one who had no faith in me, but now I see how naïve I was. Hysan was only ever fine following my lead if I was doing what he wanted. This whole time he's never trusted anyone but himself.

A dozen Ariean Majors and Libran Knights suddenly march out from the trees and encircle us, and I realize Hysan must have been hailing them through the Psy. They're armed and in uniform, and they came so quickly that there's no doubt Pandora was right—Hysan already knew I'd make my move tonight.

"Rho is trying to breach The Bellow to break out Ophiuchus and take him to Aquarius," says Hysan, his voice hard and unforgiving. I flash back to the Hysan I met in the Sumber, the one who plunged a knife in my chest, and I'm not sure which one I'm seeing anymore.

"She's not herself right now and needs to be seen by healers."

I can't believe I ever thought I loved him. Darkness fills every part of me, feeding the barricade of numbness protecting me from my feelings until it grows thick enough to completely separate my words from my body.

Until my mouth is no longer connected to my heart.

Until my voice is a weapon.

"Nice try, Hysan."

I don't sound angry or afraid; I sound somber and sad, like a disappointed parent. "No one—including General Eurek or Lord Neith—is going to believe I would *ever* free my sworn enemy, the destroyer of my world, the monster I gave up everything to pursue."

I take a measured step toward him, and the Zodai around us fidget like they're not sure what to do. "The real question is," I say softly, "why were *you* about to free him?"

Hysan is so shocked by my accusation that it takes him a few seconds to respond—enough time to cast doubt on his innocence.

"If that were true, why would I call for reinforcements?" he asks, his voice hoarse. "Why did I ask this team of Zodai to be on guard tonight?"

"Because you knew I was on to you," I say, still speaking in the calm voice of authority that I've heard him use so many times. "But I'm not going to let you get away with this."

Hysan's whole face goes slack, like his brain has suddenly stopped producing thoughts. "Rho . . . you're *lying*."

"*I'm* lying?" I ask incredulously. "I have no secrets! I'm the Wandering Star—everyone across the Zodiac knows everything about me. But who are *you?*"

Hysan's glassy eyes widen with horror, but I don't stop there.

"Where is Lord Neith?" I press. "Why hasn't anyone seen him?"

Most of the Knights turn toward Hysan, and from their suspicious reactions it's clear they've already been discussing this amongst themselves. But rather than try to protect his secret, Hysan just stares at me, open-mouthed yet speechless—like for the first time in his life he's been outplayed.

"I believe Hysan Dax has done something to the Guardian of Libra," I announce, looking to the Ariean and Libran Zodai, "and now he's trying to escape with Ophiuchus. Please hold him for the night, and tomorrow morning Eurek and I will question him. No need to ruin everyone's one night off."

The nearest Major cuffs Hysan's wrists, and his golden face betrays no emotion as he's flanked on all sides; he just keeps staring at me in disbelief.

"And for the record," I add, forcing myself to meet his gaze, "*Cancrians don't lie.*"

Light footsteps approach, and a girl in a purple robe creeps out from the tree line, looking paler than usual.

"Pandora!" Hysan seems to come alive at the sight of her, and he starts struggling against the Majors who are trying to march him away. "Please—tell Mathias Rho was trying to break out Ophiuchus! She's not well. She needs help!"

Her astonished gaze jumps from Hysan to me, her orb-like eyes glowing like stars.

"Pandora—" I start, but she rushes back into the woods before I can explain myself.

I glower at Hysan as the Zodai march him away, and he watches me the whole time. Once he's completely out of view, Pandora steps out from the trees. "Are you good from here?"

Her voice quivers, and I wonder if she's going to sell me out the moment I turn my back.

"Why are you helping me?" I ask.

She takes my hand in her cold one, and her hold is firm and unwavering. "Same reason you're going after Nishi. . . . It's just what friends do for each other."

Her loyalty kindles too much warmth in my chest, and I squeeze her hand before dropping it. "Can you just make sure they let him out by morning?"

She nods. "I'll tell Mathias everything at sunrise. He'll sort it out."

"Thanks, Pandora. Stay safe."

I activate my Veil as she bows. "Good fortune, Wandering Star."

✦ ✦ ✦

I copy everything I saw Skarlet do to enter the mountain and access The Bellow.

Once I'm standing before the wall of Black Truth, I let my silky white robe fall to the ground, and I stay in my blue Lodestar suit. I put away my

Ring so Mathias and the others can't contact me, and then I pull out one of the trinkets I stuffed in my pocket—my only hope for getting into the prison: the turquoise Psy shield Hysan gave me as a birthday present at the Libran embassy.

Until the armada no one but Hysan knew of the existence of Psy shields. And as there's been so much going on since then—and given that the Ariean shields were sabotaged—I doubt the Majors have had time to anticipate this loophole.

This crab-shaped, cristobalite-bead brooch must be one of the few functional Psy shields in existence, since it was created by Hysan himself. I activate it and clutch the crab to my chest as I cross the black flames, bracing myself for more pain, or for an alarm, or for the stars themselves to strike me down.

But nothing happens. The fire doesn't even tickle.

It worked.

I invisibly walk through the prison's passages, following the map I memorized to find my way to Ophiuchus's cell. There are fewer guards than last time, and they've all been drinking. No one has ever broken out of The Bellow in the history of its existence, so why should they sense any threat?

Yet as I near the cell, for the first time, I start reviewing and reconsidering my plan. Whatever Hysan might think of me, I'm not going to doom the Zodiac with my actions. Once I've freed Nishi, I'll do whatever it takes to find out if Aquarius truly plans to go through a portal in Helios—and if he does, I won't leave his side until I've stopped him or he's killed me, whichever comes first.

After that the stars can have what's left of me.

The metal door to Ophiuchus's cell scans me, and then it slides open. I step into the blindingly white room and find the Thirteenth Guardian asleep on his back just as he was in the surveillance footage I saw earlier.

Even though he's in mortal form, he doesn't look human. He's even larger than an Ariean, and the subtle patterning of his textured skin is indescribably delicate.

The metal cuffs confining his movements are still in place, as is the needle keeping him sedated. Once I pull it out, I won't undo his bonds with my Barer until I'm sure he's onboard with my plan; I'm hoping I won't need the weapon for self-defense since last I checked, Ophiuchus and I were on the same side.

Watching him sleep it's hard to reconcile the shape-shifting ice phantom that's been haunting me with this overgrown, otherworldly teenager. And as the seconds tick by, something starts to feel wrong.

I should have woken him up by now, only my hand won't move to the needle. All I can think of is Hysan.

Is he trapped in a cell just like this one? Did they do him the favor of sedating him, too, or is he stuck with nothing but his memories of my betrayal for company?

I had him arrested. I almost divulged his identity. I made him the scapegoat for my sins. Just like Aquarius did to Ophiuchus, and the Plenum did to me.

I'm acting exactly like the crooked leaders I was supposed to replace. I'm going behind everyone's backs to defy a democratic decision just because I believe *I* know better. That's the act of a tyrant, not a leader. And if I keep making the same mistakes as the politicians who came before me, what hope does the Zodiac have?

But I need to save Nishi.

My hand trembles as I reach for the needle, only I still don't touch it. Maybe I can find Mathias and ask for his help. He told me earlier that I could come to him about anything, and I should have spoken up then. He'll understand when I explain to him why Nishi can't wait—after all, he was tortured by Corinthe, too.

I drop my hand, and with a last look at Ophiuchus I turn to go. But a deep, booming voice stops me in my tracks.

"I knew you wouldn't do it."

I gasp and wheel around. Ophiuchus is still lying in bed, his face angled up at the ceiling, but he's awake.

"Though I also didn't think you would make it this far."

My throat dry, I take a few steps closer and meet a pair of eyes that are wider and longer than any human being's, with vertical slits for pupils. "You know why I'm here?" I ask, my voice insubstantial when compared to his.

"Undo my binds and let's go," he commands.

"I c—can't," I stammer, my skin breaking into a chilly sweat. "I changed my mind."

His silver irises glow like starlight, and flecks of platinum swirl around his pupils, like worlds orbiting elliptical black holes. "Are you certain?" he asks, his words reverberating through me long after he's spoken.

I think of Nishi, and most of me wants to scream NO. But I force myself to jerk a nod instead.

Without warning Ophiuchus sits bolt upright.

A mere flexing of his muscles and he blasts apart the metal cuffs holding him. I leap back until I'm pressed against the wall, too stunned to run out or raise my Barer.

"Y—you had the power to escape this whole time?"

His bare feet fall to the floor, and he tugs off his crinkly hospital gown and tosses it aside. I drop my gaze to the ground to avoid staring at his naked body, and I notice his toenails are curved like claws.

In the fringe of my vision, I watch him dig into a hidden drawer beneath the bed and pull out white healer's scrubs. The textured patterns of his skin gleam in the room's blinding brightness, and once he's stepped into the too-short pants, I look up again.

"Why didn't you leave before now?" I ask as he pulls on the shirt. His body is so powerful that his muscles ripple through the fabric, straining every thread.

"I was weak. While I waited for you, I focused on regaining my strength."

"For *me*? You foresaw I'd come?"

His starry eyes lock onto mine, and the shading of his thick skin shifts from light to dark as he moves toward me.

I try retreating even further into the wall until the back of my skull starts to ache from the effort. "W—why do you need me?"

"If I'm going to bargain for my House," he rumbles, "I'm going to need something Aquarius wants."

I have to tilt my chin up to keep my eyes on his. "Your plan is to use me?"

"Just as yours is to use me."

"No."

And before he comes any closer, I raise my right hand to his face, tapping into the Barer's buzzing until my fist grows a set of electric brass knuckles. "I came to my senses in time. I'm not going with you."

Hands as strong as stone grip my arms, and my head bashes into the wall.

Pain blasts through me, and the Barer fizzes out as my body is pinned in place, my scalp stinging and eyes streaming tears. A boulder presses into my chest, knocking the air from my lungs, and through my bleary vision I see Ophiuchus, his body pushed up against me, his lustrous snakeskin face just inches from mine.

"I'm not one of your little boyfriends," he hisses, his swirling silver irises rampaging with rage. *"You don't turn me down."*

17

MY HEART RACES, AND ITS ferocious pounding feels foreign and new. I can't remember the last time I heard it this clearly.

Fear coats my tongue, releasing gallons of adrenaline through my veins. And though my head is in agony, this is the first time I've felt something real since the Sumber.

The first time I've felt *alive*.

Ophiuchus steps back, and without him to hold me up I crumple to the floor. My pulse fades away, and as the emotions recede I'm left even emptier than I was before.

He reaches down for me again, and I scream as he bundles up my limbs as if I'm weightless. He cradles me to his chest like a newborn, wrapping me completely in his arms, and then he rams his back into the cell's door.

The slab of metal goes flying and slams into the rocky passage.

And then we're racing through the mountain, and I feel like I'm moving as swiftly as when Candor carried me. Ophiuchus pushes my head down with his chin, and I'm like a turtle being shoved into her shell until I can't see anything. An instant later shots explode all around us, and I squeeze my eyes shut, waiting for a bullet to lodge into me.

Soon the air changes from warm and musty to cool and earthy, like we're aboveground and soaring across Phaet's surface. Ophiuchus's grip is as firm as stone, his hold steady and his stride stable, but I can't see what's going on.

When he finally slows down, I peek my head up. We're on a landing pad filled with ships from across the Zodiac. He sets me down roughly, and I'm dizzy on my feet, so I drop to the ground and close my eyes to get my bearings.

"There's no time for weakness," he barks, and I glare up at him. But he's not watching me—he's looking behind us. I follow his gaze, but I don't see anything.

"They're coming. The Bellow's guards have alerted the whole base. We only have minutes. Let's go."

He strides up to a round red ship with twisty wings that look like ram horns, and as I get up to follow him, I notice the Ariean pilot pointing his pistol at Ophiuchus's chest.

Even though the man is nearly a giant by human standards, he's still a full head shorter than the Thirteenth Guardian. "Stand back!" he warns him, his hand trembling.

But Ophiuchus keeps moving forward, and the man begins to discharge his weapon. The bullets burn through the white healer's scrubs but bounce right off of Ophiuchus. When he's just a foot away, the man throws the whole gun at the Guardian's head, but the latter merely tilts his face to avoid it.

Then he curls his fingers around the man's neck, and the Ariean's knees buckle as he runs out of air. I want to tell him to stop, but I can't find my voice. When the man finally faints, Ophiuchus lets go, opening the ship's door with brute force and motioning for me to follow.

I feel like I'm wading through water as I wind around the man's comatose body. Part of me wants to drop to the floor and make sure he's still breathing—but a smaller, newer part of me wonders if it even matters.

Everyone here has committed their lives to this cause. Didn't Fernanda say teamwork meant making sacrifices for the greater good? Besides, if I can't defeat Aquarius, we'll *all* be blown to pieces and none of this will matter.

I board the ship, which is much smaller than *Equinox*, and Ophiuchus shuts the door behind me. But instead of accessing the control helm, he turns toward the nose's glass window and closes his eyes. He looks like he's Centering.

The engine fires up.

He's not touching any buttons or speaking any commands—*he's navigating the ship with his mind.*

"How are you doing that?" I ask, clinging onto a handrail as we shoot into the air.

"I've told you before," he says, his eyes still shut. *"Everything is Psynergy."*

I hold on tightly as the ship shudders through Phaet's atmosphere, and I'm relieved when my feet don't float off the floor. Though the walls are shaking, Ophiuchus stays completely still, even without holding onto anything. Once we jump into hyperspeed and the ride stabilizes, I finally let go of the railing, and while Ophiuchus remains Centered, I check out the rest of the ship.

My tour is brief: All I see is a lavatory, a galley, and a cabin. This is clearly a one-person military vessel.

I take a moment in the cabin to catch my breath. The Zodai were right to sedate and restrain Ophiuchus, but they should have realized that if he's really as powerful as they feared, those measures might not be enough.

Since the master already knows everything about me, I decide to learn everything I can about him, from the only being alive who knows the true Aquarius. So I return to the front of the ship, determined to yank Ophiuchus out of the astral plane and back to reality—but when I see him, I freeze.

A shadow has fallen over Ochus, and he's curved and hunched over, the way he was when time took its toll on him in our battle during the armada. I keep as far back from him as possible as he suffers in soundless torture, his expression contorted with misery, and I desperately hope this doesn't affect his ability to navigate the spacecraft.

I don't know how many hours pass, but gradually, Ophiuchus reverts to his full strength. When the process finishes, he's breathing heavily and his eyes fly open.

"What was that?" I whisper from my spot on the floor against the far wall. We've been silent for so long that the sound of my voice feels intrusive.

"All power has a price," he murmurs, his gaze turned toward the stars.

"So—does that mean—Aquarius has a weakness, too?"

"Whatever he's doing is warping the Psy and undoing the astral plane. I have no idea what he's capable of, or how to stop him."

I think of Hysan's theory about the portal through Helios. I'm sitting next to one of the only two souls still around to confirm or debunk it.

"Where do humans come from?"

A dreamy expression relaxes Ophiuchus's features, and he closes his eyes again. He's silent for so long that he's either asleep or deeply Centered, and I'm about to call out to him when the ship goes completely dark.

"What's happening?" I whisper.

The darkness begins to recede from the center of the room, like curtains being drawn, and a rocky landscape unfolds around us. I feel like I'm viewing a Snow Globe.

The nose fully vanishes as the memory overtakes everything, and I get to my feet and scan the vast, barren terrain. Above us is a high-tension fabric dome that seems to be held aloft by air pressure, like the domes of Phaetonis.

That's where we are. Where history says the humans first landed.

As soon as I have the thought, I begin to notice an antiquated fleet of ships on the far horizon, high above the dome's protection. There must be thousands of vessels. They look like metallic insects getting ready to launch an attack.

Time takes one stride forward, and now the people have disembarked and they're packed inside the dome. There must be a million of them.

I'm not sure how I come up with the number—it's like I'm not simply seeing our history, but *embodying* it. Hysan once told me the Guardian's Talismans contain the essence of a survival skill—the meaning of the thing itself. And that's how this feels.

Which makes sense, since Ophiuchus is a living representation of his Talisman.

The humans are all standing around anxiously, as though they're waiting for something. They were invited here, I realize. Some still have their air masks on, like they distrust this dome. I look around me just as they do, trying to find the reason for this gathering. And then I see them.

Fourteen silhouettes grow clearer in the distance beyond the dome, all equally spaced out and encircling the whole human population. Through some trick of Psynergy, they've made it so that every person has a clear view of every Original Guardian, even if that person is short and standing in the middle of a million-person crowd.

I turn in a slow circle, observing them—the Geminin Twins are so perfectly identical they look like clones—and I see that the humans around me are doing the same thing. Some Guardians look more masculine and others more feminine, but most are so androgynous they don't seem to have a gender. And just like the ice carving of Sagittarius that Nishi showed me in Starry City, these mortal stars have an amalgamation of features that probably represent the ultimate evolution of their people. No human I've seen in modern times looks anything like them, yet somehow I can still find traces of all my friends' faces in theirs.

I stop studying the fallen stars and stare instead at the humans around me. Unlike the Guardians, these beings all look more or less the same. They have a small range of skin tones, and hair shades, and eye colors, and body types. They're not all that distinguishable from each other—they must hail from a single planet.

Earth.

At least our history records seem to have gotten that much right.

The humans also look unhealthy. Thin, tense, tired, terrified, tiny—and as they behold the majestic Guardians and their magic tricks, they don't seem all that inclined to trust them.

"Welcome to the Zodiac Solar System," says the tallest Guardian, who's draped in red fabric. I get the sense that everyone understands him, like he's somehow speaking to them in their own language. "When our Thirteen Constellations foresaw your arrival through Helios, each of our Houses gave up its Guardian Star—*us.*"

Gasps rise from the crowd, but when he speaks again, a million people fall to instant silence.

"We shooting stars crashed onto planets in our own Houses, and we arose in human form, each of us with a Star Stone, or Talisman, that stores our particular power—the strength we bring to the Zodiac."

I thought the Talismans were secrets entrusted only to the Guardian of each House—and yet Aries is freely telling everyone about them. Is this another one of Aquarius's manipulations? Did it occur to him that knowledge of these Talismans would one day inspire another ambitious soul to attempt the same theft he committed?

"In these mortal forms, we have been charged by the stars to work together and harness the powers of our Stones to protect our planets, and, hopefully—if you'll have us—our *people.*"

I can barely process any of this.

Humans came through Helios—Hysan was right. Which means there's really a portal in our sun, and it could lead anywhere. This might not even be the largest solar system—our Zodiac could be another offshoot from something bigger.

And *that* has to be what Aquarius is dying to find out.

18

A DIFFERENT GUARDIAN STEPS FORWARD and enters the dome, walking through the barrier like it's not even there. I know I didn't notice him earlier, because if I had I wouldn't have been able to take my eyes off him.

My amazed reaction is reproduced through the crowd, as everyone's eyes find Ophiuchus. If his appearance is striking now, it's nothing to what he looked like then, in his original form. He's as tall as Aries, maybe taller, and his skin seems to contain every color imaginable and unimaginable. When he moves, he glimmers and shines like he's made of pure light—even the day's shadows don't seem to touch him.

"Friends, I have come to tell you that you have nothing to fear from us," he says in a voice that emanates strength and warmth and trust. "If you choose to form your own society, we will honor your wishes and leave you in peace."

Murmurs of shock and relief break out, but they die down as soon as he speaks again.

"We have no desire to hurt or control you. We are the stars of the Zodiac, and we are here to watch over you. It's our fate to steer you toward your passions and your purpose and your soul mates—but ultimately, your destiny is designed by your decisions."

He bestows on the humans a dazzlingly brilliant smile that could make the sun swoon. "We would never take your free will from you. Nor are we unknown to you. We are manifestations of universal concepts, and if you search yourselves, you'll find you're more drawn to one pursuit or pastime or value than all others, and therein you will find yourself and your Center.

"For my part, I seek only to promote Unity—a skill you do not yet possess. You are divided by man-made barriers that you have been born into; yet we are offering you a chance to choose your own identity. It's a right I hope you will be humble enough to extend to your children when they're old enough, and that they will one day extend to their children, and so on."

I can't believe how far we've strayed from Ophiuchus's vision for our future. It's only now that I can fully appreciate his original purpose in our galaxy.

The earthlings were ultimately swayed by him, and we zoom forward in time to see how the Guardians took turns addressing the population, each one sharing what strengths they most valued and describing what kind of world their House would one day become. It took centuries to colonize some of the more topographically complex planets, like Sconcion of Scorpio and Kythera of Libra, so for many generations, people of different Houses shared their land and resources with each other. They elected representatives for a galactic government, and though they'd just divided themselves into thirteen new nationalities, the humans felt united.

They were a homeless people who'd found a new home to inhabit.

They were *survivors*.

Over time, people evolved to better suit or reflect the environment around them. In the deepest waterworlds of Scorpio, humans developed red eyes that cut through darkness. On the rough streets of Aries, people grew buff enough to hold their own. On the swampy Ophiuchan planet, teens developed scaly skin when they reached puberty that protected them from the bites of most poisonous creatures.

Each House designed its own system of rules, but those laws were superseded by the Zodiac's universal government. The Original Guardians acted in an advisory role for the humans, and they continued to meet in the astral plane to work together to ensure the Zodiac's wellbeing. They read the future together, traded resources, dispensed advice, ensured harmony, and planned for tomorrow.

The scenery shifts, and as I skim through a montage of these Guardian meetings, I realize there's one fallen star with whom Ophiuchus appears to be particularly close.

Aquarius and Ophiuchus are constantly presenting opposing viewpoints, and since they're so well matched, there's rarely a clear winner. Yet instead of getting on each other's nerves, they seem to share a deep mutual admiration and respect; when one of them makes a particularly compelling point against the other, I can see it secretly makes the other one proud.

I notice the two of them sometimes linger longer in the astral plane after the others have returned to their bodies, but Ophiuchus moves us quickly through those memories, so I can't explore those moments. Until time slows down again, in the midst of another meeting during which Ophiuchus and Aquarius are having one of their signature arguments.

Aquarius has Crompton's pink sunset eyes, but that's where their similarities end. In his original form, the somewhat androgynous-looking Guardian has ivory skin that glows like moonlight, silver hair that shines like starlight, and a sculpted face that looks like a carefully crafted work of art.

"Do you realize these mortals have seen more of our universe than we have?" he demands of the other fallen stars. "I propose we go through the portal ourselves to see what else is out there."

Ophiuchus frowns, for the first time not getting pleasure from his friend's words. "You jest, of course. Using the portal will destroy this reality, just as the earthlings' passage destroyed theirs."

"Do we know that for certain?" asks Aquarius, only concern and curiosity in his voice. "That is just what the humans *claim* they saw, but they do not possess our keen senses."

"They told us not all their ships made it because their universe began to collapse as soon as the first vessel went through," says Ophiuchus, his tone conveying complete trust of the humans. "I believe them. Why would they lie about that?"

"They are small and fallible," says Aquarius simply, no judgment in his voice. "They come from an ordinary dimension. *We* are sentient stars. To these humans, we are gods. The portal might work differently from this side."

A couple of Guardians look intrigued by Aquarius's words, but most seem to find them as unpleasant as the Thirteenth.

"I have foreseen that the right cosmic conditions to reactivate the tunnel will not repeat themselves for at least three millennia, and these semi-mortal bodies we're in will decay long before then," continues Aquarius, his voice gaining strength. "We must act now before our window closes. This is our shot to discover a different dimension of existence, a new reality! We are stars—we are not meant for small deaths. When we die, we redesign the sky."

The silence that follows feels charged.

Only Ophiuchus dares break it.

"We will not abandon these humans," he says with an authority that chills the air, even among this group of gods. "Nor will we destroy our home."

The scene suddenly fades to darkness, and we're back on the Ariean ship. Ophiuchus is wide-eyed and staring at the ground, his breaths shallow. He's lost his Center.

"You knew," I whisper, glaring down at him from where I'm standing. "You've always known. Only one being could have had the cruelty and nerve and access to you to pull this off. It's been three millennia, so either you're so stupid you still don't see it, or you've been *protecting* him."

I spit the word out.

He doesn't meet my gaze, so I keep going. "You made me feel bad for being weak before, but the truth is *you're* weak. Love's turned you into a murderer and a monster and the Zodiac's ultimate *fool*."

Ophiuchus lunges at me, and the whole ship tilts to the side as he shoves me into the wall. "You have no idea what you're talking about," he growls, his lethal jaws at my neck.

His starry eyes sear into mine with such fury that I know in my gut he could kill me right now.

My heartbeat grows more present with every breath, and I can't deny it feels good to hear it again. I'm afraid, but I'm also excited . . . because deep down I crave the death he offers.

He lets go of me suddenly, and as the ship straightens I dig my back into the wall so I won't fall to the ground again.

"If Helios goes dark, so does this whole universe," I warn as my pulse fades into the void in my chest once more. "That means your precious people go, too. So if you really care about your House, talk to me about the portal and the Last Prophecy. How do we stop Aquarius?"

He stands with his back to me and stares out at the blackness looming ahead. "We keep him from activating the portal."

"Why? What happens when he activates it?"

"The Zodiac's days will be numbered. *Seven*, to be exact."

"What happens after seven days?" I press.

"That's how long it takes for the portal to fully open. The instant the first ship goes through, the solar system will begin to fall."

"And how exactly does he plan to activate the portal?"

Still turned away, Ophiuchus says, "He's going to sacrifice me."

19

THE THIRTEENTH GUARDIAN SITS ON the floor and tunnels deep into his Center for the rest of the trip. I've asked him a dozen follow-up questions, but he hasn't answered any of them. Not that I think he'd tell me the truth anyway.

I dig through the galley for a squeeze tube of protein, and then I try to sleep a little in the cabin. I wake up just a couple of hours later, drenched in sweat, the skin on my chest burning like it's been freshly carved, and I don't close my eyes again.

Ophiuchus doesn't seem to have any needs, because he doesn't move again until the Lion constellation flies into view.

The House has one planet, Leo; two moons, Lion and Leon; and a small sun. Its people are divided into nine Prides: Power, Courage, Honor, Leadership, Truth, Adventure, Competition, Sensuality, and Artistry. I've read that much of the planet is covered in harsh terrain—mountain ridges, jungles, marsh—and even the moons have strange topographies: Lion has forests and a lake that is the House's largest store of freshwater, and Leon is a vast glacier with mountains made from crystals.

Since I'm not wearing my Ring or checking my Wave—so Hysan can't locate me—all I have for company as we travel are the memories Ophiuchus shared with me. I keep picturing the beautiful god he started out as and comparing it to the lethal beast he's become. And what frightens me most is how much of myself and Hysan and Ferez I saw in him in his early years.

When he addressed our ancestors, Ophiuchus was nurturing and wise and just, and his intentions to lead and protect humanity appeared selfless and pure. He seemed the embodiment of hope.

Just as with Aryll, it was easier to hate Ochus before seeing his beginnings, and something Lord Neith once told me comes to mind. He said the symbol for Justice is a set of scales, because good and bad exist in equal quantities and to eradicate one is to eradicate both.

I wonder if that's because the bad can never truly be separated from the good, since each of us harbors the potential for both.

We are all Grey Gowan. We are all Ophiuchus.

We are all the heroes and the villains of our own stories.

"I can't locate Aquarius's Psynergy signature." The Thirteenth Guardian breaks our silence, his eyes still shut. "Where does your army believe he is?"

"The Artistry Pride."

He finally meets my gaze, and I know why he's frowning. Supposedly, nothing stays in place in Artistry because the scenery is always changing. We could never hope to navigate that world without a guide.

I sigh. There's only one Leonine I know who might be willing to help us. But I really hate having to call on him.

✦ ✦ ✦

I send Traxon Harwing an encrypted message from my Wave, and I hope to Helios that Hysan can't trace the transmission.

The Truther agrees to meet me at the *Friend* gate outside the Artistry spaceport. Before disembarking, Ophiuchus changes into a red Major uniform. He couldn't fit into one suit, so we had to sew two together. I also give him my invisibility collar, and before disembarking I activate it.

I wish we had two so that I could vanish with him.

We walk into a terminal swarming with eclectic Leonines showing off a dizzying array of traveling styles—pajamas, courtsuits, floor-length dresses, animal costumes, beachwear—and we hang back from the crowd so that no one runs into Ophiuchus's boulder-like body. I feel the heat of his giant presence at my side as we follow the flow of passengers toward the main transportation hub, and my gaze finds the brilliant blue sky beyond the windowed wall.

Like Aries, Leo has a small secondary sun, but instead of red this one is golden and looks like a mini Helios. Mountaintops break through the foamy white clouds in the distance, and I watch what looks like planes or large birds diving off the tallest peak and soaring toward the small sun. Then I squint for a closer look as the birds or planes begin to drop off, freefalling like they've been shot down, and disappear from view.

It takes me a moment to realize they're people.

"Sun-sailing!" says an excitable Leonine in a constellation-patterned jumpsuit. She suddenly slings an arm around my shoulder and pulls me up to the window, and I spy a half-moon tattoo on her cheekbone.

"See that point there?" she asks, touching a spot on the glass. "That's Mount Luz. It's our planet's highest peak. We have a sport called sun-sailing where you change into these protective suits with wings and try to catch a solar ray and ride its energy wave. There's a net waiting to catch you when you fall!"

She turns to me, and I notice the crescent tattoo on her cheekbone has shape-shifted. It's now phased into a full moon. "Interested? I can get you a discount—"

An invisible grip yanks on my arm, pulling me away from the girl and the window. "If you buy tickets, tell the salesperson I sent you!" she calls after me. "Name's *Solay!*"

I stay close to Ophiuchus as we're funneled down a winding path that dead-ends in two queues: one is for Leonines, the other is for out-of-House visitors.

I'll meet you on the other side. I hear Ophiuchus's voice in my head as his hand pulls away.

"Thumb out, please," says the Leonine sitting behind the podium of the visitors' queue. The holographic nameplate on her purple uniform reads HERRA, and I'm mesmerized by how the color of her afro changes with every customer. When she helped the Sagittarian couple ahead of me, her hair was bright blond, but now it's turned inky black.

Her device registers my identity, and the words WANDERING STAR RHOMA GRACE flash before us. I guess my location isn't a secret anymore.

Herra shoots to her feet, and panic flares in my chest as she surveys the area around us like she's searching for a Zodai. Then she looks at me again, and her face splits into a broad grin.

She tugs on her right sleeve, revealing a tattoo on her wrist: It's the glyph of me wrangling the snake into submission that I saw on Centaurion.

"It's an honor to meet you, ma'am," she says, her afro now a shocking shade of pink. "Welcome to the Lion."

"Thank you."

I'm still trying to process what happened as I step forward into the main transportation hub, when a bloodcurdling scream pierces the air.

The crowd around me parts in half, and my brain stalls as a troop of Marad soldiers marches toward me. They must have set up an alert for my astrological fingerprint.

I stand frozen, my pulse materializing in my throat, as the porcelain-faced army comes closer and closer. *Where the Helios is Ophiuchus?*

The soldier in the lead lifts his Murmur. I will my legs to move, but I'm paralyzed in place, the way I was when I faced the Marad tribunal in my nightmares. I squeeze my eyes shut as he aims his weapon—

"CUT!"

The Marad soldiers groan and talking abruptly breaks out all around me. I open my eyes to see stylists approaching the soldiers to adjust their masks, while some people in the crowd pull up holographic scripts to review.

"Who is this girl in the middle of my shot?" demands the same man who yelled "cut." "Why is she just standing there? Can somebody get this crab to scuttle off my set? NOW!"

When I realize he's talking about me, my muscles grow even more leaden, like my body skipped over the fight-or-flight debate and went straight for surrender.

An invisible hand wraps around my arm, and when Ophiuchus tugs, my legs miraculously work again. I turn away in time to avoid the handful of harried Leonines who were running over to chase me off.

I'm relieved when Ophiuchus leads us through the exit, and at last I can breathe fresh air again. I have no idea where the *Friend* gate is, but the Thirteenth Guardian seems to know the way because we're charging through the crowd.

WELCOME TO ARTISTRY

I look up at the huge, color-changing holographic sign hovering high in the bright, dual-sun sky. All around me, hundreds upon hundreds of people are posing for holo-captures with the words in the air behind them. Since the plaza is so packed, eventually Ophiuchus has to slow down to keep everyone from noticing the violent ghost in their midst.

He's already knocked at least five people to the ground.

Holograms of the most famous stars in Zodiac cinema float through the tourists, telling them about the Artistry Pride. "Ever wish your life was more like a movie?" asks the hologram of the Cancrian actress who plays

Amara in the galaxy's most popular holo-show. It follows the love triangle of the last human survivors after the Zodiac has been wiped out, and the characters are inspired by the three Guardians behind the Trinary Axis.

"When you're in Artistry, you can be anyone you want to be," she says, and while some people walk through her, most stop and try to snap holo-captures with her image. "You're entering the land where the art you love is created. Want to drop by the set of your favorite holo-show and be an extra for a scene or two? Want to bid on an exclusive invitation to dine with the cast? Want the chance to purchase new merchandise far before it's available to the rest of the Zodiac? If this sounds like Empyrean to you, then you'll want to enter through the *Meet the Stars* gate." Winking, she adds, "I'll see you there."

Her hologram wends past me in the crowd, but I can still hear her because her voice is amplified to carry. "Or perhaps you'd rather be the star of your own adventure. Do you often fantasize about saving the universe? Have you always longed to solve a crime? Would you relish the chance to safely channel your darker impulses by stepping into a villain's shoes? Then enter through the *Be the Star* gate and purchase the Storyline that's right for you!"

I finally see where the towering wall that surrounds this Pride breaks for a series of gates. *Friend* is the smallest of them; it's closed and locked and there's no official nearby.

A large holographic sign says: ARTISTRY LAW STATES THAT VISITORS MUST BE ACCOMPANIED BY A LEONINE AT ALL TIMES, OR YOU RISK ARREST. PLEASE WAIT HERE UNTIL YOUR NAME IS CALLED.

The gate suddenly opens, and a Lionheart peeks her head out. "Thumb, please."

I press my finger to the reader she holds out, and a moment later my name appears.

The opening widens, and the Leonine Zodai holds the door for me. I feel Ophiuchus move ahead, and I think he must brush her as he goes by because she looks around like she felt something.

I hurry through and follow her down a long, dark tunnel that cuts through the extra-thick black wall that encloses Artistry. This Pride certainly takes its privacy seriously.

When we get to the other side, we're on what looks like a fake street. The storefronts are too squat and bright, and the holographic graffiti on the walls is too evenly spaced. This must be an old filming set they don't use anymore.

A troop of Zodai is standing guard nearby, and a guy with a bushy brown mane and pierced eyebrows waits among them. Traxon is wearing the white outfit he wore when I first met him on Taurus, when he spoke on a panel with other members of 13.

"We release you into Traxon Harwing's custody," says the Lionheart who let me in, scrutinizing me curiously through rainbow-colored eyelashes. "Enjoy your stay, and we wish you a happy ending!"

As soon as I trade the hand touch with Traxon, his feet start moving and his mouth starts running. "Rho, always exciting to see you! I'm glad you decided to do the honorable thing and hold up your end of our bargain, but you could have given me more of a head's up." His feet work at the speed of his words, and I hurry to keep up with him. "I had a speaking engagement for 13 today that I had to walk out on—"

"I'm not here for—"

"But it doesn't matter because this interview will be worth it! Obviously, I would have much rather done this in my studio on the Truth Pride, but at least Artistry is crawling with production hands. We've managed to improvise a decent setup—but here, you can see for yourself!"

Beaming, he pulls open the door to one of the abandoned storefronts, and we step into a small, dark space. Only a couple of chairs and camera equipment have been set up, and there's two Leonines dressing the set with flowers and water glasses.

"Okay, so we should be ready to go in a few minutes, but in the meantime, maybe you can run me through the main talking points—"

"Trax, *stop*," I say, stepping up to him so he'll see *me* and not a headline. "I'm here for something else."

He furrows his decorated brow. "We had a deal. I kept up my end, I told you who was funding the Tomorrow Party, and you—"

"Look, I'll give you an exclusive. I will. Just not now, okay? First I really need your help."

"No," he says, crossing his arms over his chest. "We do the interview first, and then I help you."

I clench my jaw and try not to snap. *"Can we talk in private?"*

He wordlessly turns to his two production hands, who've stopped working to watch our argument, and they step outside.

"I need you to take me to the Tomorrow Party," I say once we're alone. "They're hiding somewhere on this Pride."

My request seems to stump Traxon, and he looks more confused than upset. "What makes you think I can find them?"

"Because you're an incredible investigator."

Rather than appease him, the compliment seems to inflate his ego, and his chest swells with pride. "Well I'm not interested unless you do this interview. You and your Aquarian friend were so pleased with yourselves when you offered me an ultimatum last time we met, remember? Now I'm offering you one: If you want my help, do my interview."

"There are more important things going on!" I shout.

"Great!" he roars. "Let's hear about them!"

"You're being a *child*—"

Traxon's eyes suddenly shift away from me, and the dark tan drains from his skin until he looks as pale as an Aquarian. His mouth opens and closes, like he's finally run out of words, and I know better than to believe I could have that effect on him.

I wheel around and see that Ophiuchus has deactivated his collar.

20

IN HIS TOO-SMALL UNIFORM, WITH his too-wide eyes and his too-big clawed feet, the Thirteenth Guardian looks too large for this world.

Tears streak down Traxon's cheeks, and he bends into a low bow that goes on for an uncomfortably long time. When he straightens, he says, "Your holiness, I—"

"Traxon, we need to go *now*," I say, my hands curling with impatience. "There's no time for this!"

But he still isn't looking at me, nor does he appear to be listening. "Your holiness, I want to apologize on behalf of the Zodiac for what's happened to you and your House," he murmurs, hanging his head.

"Thank you," rumbles Ophiuchus, his booming voice shaking the walls of the small space. Then he turns to me and says, "He will get us where we need to go."

"Stellar. Then let's move," I command. "You should reactivate your collar—"

"No need," says Trax, looking away from Ophiuchus long enough to remember my presence. "Everyone's always playing a character here—people will just assume you have killer costumes."

When we're outside, Traxon dismisses the two production hands, and he reaches out to his sources to inquire about the Party. Ophiuchus and I hang around a few moments while Trax consults his Lighter, and then he says, "This way."

"Have you found the Party?" I ask as we hurry down the street.

Traxon clings so close to Ophiuchus that he reminds me of the tiny fish that hitch rides with crab-sharks. "I have a friend who lives nearby. Whatever's going on, he'll know."

Soon we arrive at a busy shopping district filled with restaurants and stores and theaters and street performers. More holograms of Zodiac celebrities float through the crowd offering additional services.

"The present is so fleeting!" I hear one of them say. "Don't let your Storyline end when your vacation does—relive the experience again and again and again by purchasing the film!"

"Isn't there a faster way to get there?" I ask Traxon. "Some kind of public transportation system?"

"It'd take us longer to reach the wall than it would to cut through the crowd," he says, and seeing my confusion he explains. "There's a train that runs inside the wall enclosing this Pride. But like I said, walking will be faster."

I look to Ophiuchus to see if he's as exasperated as I am, but his expression is distant and detached, like Trax and I are kids at an amusement park and he's the parent with bigger things on his mind.

I glimpse a young Taurian girl eagerly unwrapping a purple chew candy at a treat stand and shoving it into her mouth. "Slow down," chides her mom as the girl's jaw works exra hard to eat it quickly. When she swallows, her parents and the salesperson all stare at her expectantly.

Suddenly she releases a shockingly loud burp, blasting her parents' faces with purple smoke.

The little girl and the Leonine salesperson are in hysterics, but her parents don't look amused. I look up at the holographic sign over the stand: PURPLE URPLES—YOU'LL BURP PURPLE SMOKE!

"Please, I want them!" I hear her begging her mom long after we've passed them. *"Pleeeease!"*

I fall back a step as a man in an inconspicuous black getup sidles up to Trax. "I'm hiring people for a major jewel heist. Max told me you're the man for the job."

Trax glares at the Leonine and adopts a deep, husky voice unlike his usual one. "I've got other plans today, old man. Now scram, and don't breathe a word about me to Max. I'm undercover, understand?"

The man nods and hurries away.

"What the Helios was that?" I ask.

Traxon shrugs. "People don't come to Leo for judgment—they come to give in to their passions. Sometimes you need to shed your inhibitions and let your weirdness out, so when you hear a Storyline you like, you *take* it."

I feel like under other circumstances, I might be charmed by the playful nature of this world, but right now I just want to find the Party and awaken Nishi.

"Your holiness," Traxon says, turning to Ophiuchus, "I would be honored if I could ask you a few questions, if you're feeling up to it. I have a show dedicated to exposing politicians' lies, to keep them from doing to others what was once done to you—"

I roll my eyes so hard I think I see the back of my head.

"You see," Trax blathers on, "it's been my life's dream to find proof of your existence and help you reclaim your place in the Zodiac, and now— well, you can't imagine what meeting you means to me."

As Traxon professes his adoration, I'm relieved to see he's steered us away from the tourist district and onto a quieter street that looks like a real residential area. No one seems to be selling anything here, and the Leonines entering and exiting buildings are dressed up for dramatically different occasions, like the travelers at the spaceport.

I dodge a woman wearing a pink tutu and ballerina shoes who's dancing her way down the street, and a block later I edge around a painter who's planted himself in the middle of everything to capture the scene with his brush. Then a man in a top hat emerges from his townhome, sucks in a huge breath, and starts belting out a song:

> *Life is a story*
> *About seeking glory*
> *Whose plot isn't always so clear . . .*

He strides up the street, tipping his hat to people as he sings, and some of the passersby join his song, like they're familiar with the lyrics.

> *So when they told me*
> *To pick who I would be,*
> *I asked for a heart with no fear!*

A group of girls starts dancing around him, and soon there's a mobile musical number making its way down the street. Some people join in by playing their instruments from their balconies, and others contribute by drumming on windows and walls. Even those who are too busy to participate don't look put out by what's happening—performing seems to be as natural as breathing here.

"He must've just gotten some great news," says Trax, like that justifies the man's decision to burst into song in public.

"Is this whole Pride just one big production?"

Right as I pose the question, Traxon stops before a rundown townhouse and knocks on the door. After a moment, a disheveled teen guy opens it and studies us. "Traxon."

"Tomás."

Both guys nod and trade a complicated hand touch greeting, then Tomás stands back to let us in. His home is small but cozy: We step into a narrow sitting area that's adjacent to a kitchen and a study, and in the back of the space a staircase spirals up.

The seating area has a couch and two armchairs around a coffee table, and all the furniture looks beat-up and heavily used. Tangible paper books line the shelves that were built into every wall, and painted canvases of every size and at varying stages of completion clutter the floor. When I look at Tomás again, I notice the paint on the underside of his hands and the back of his neck.

"Tomás is a member of 13," says Trax, swinging an arm around his friend's shoulders. "In exchange for helping us, I've promised him a secret."

"A *secret*?" I ask.

"Truthers trade in secrets," he explains. "It's the most valuable currency we can offer. So, Tomás—my secret is this." He turns to Ophiuchus, who's standing beside me, and says, "*That*, my dear fellow, is the one and only Ophiuchus."

Tomás's eyes widen with awe as mine fill with fury and fear. "Are you *insane*?" I shout at Traxon.

"A Leonine always pays his debts," he says simply, no apology in his voice. I turn to Ophiuchus for backup, but now he's sitting on the floor beside the coffee table, his eyes closing like he's descending to his Center. *Perfect.*

Tomás orbits the Thirteenth Guardian, scrutinizing him closely like a collector evaluating a new piece. "Incredible," he murmurs every few seconds. When he finally looks at us again, his eyes are just as shiny as Traxon's.

"Given that you're all about the *truth*," I say to Traxon, "you must hate this Pride since everything seems to be a performance."

Tomás answers in place of his friend, frowning at me. "This is a land of *performers*. That's not the same as a *performance*, which is something you put on for others. Simply put: Performers perform. Making art is just how we live our lives. We're not doing it for an audience, but if people want to consume our art because it makes their lives meaningful or enjoyable or even bearable, we welcome them."

Tomás's speech sounds rehearsed, like he's defended his profession before, and I wonder if he realizes that even now he's performing.

Then again, I'm probably the last person to know what's real anymore. I'm no longer sure any of us can be completely certain where performances end and truth begins.

"So can you help us find the Tomorrow Party?" Traxon asks his friend.

"I might have a lead. But you and I should go alone—any non-Leonines would be suspicious."

Trax nods and turns to me. "We'll be back soon."

Alone with Ophiuchus, I sit on one of the faded couches and try not to think about how much time has already passed. How much pain Nishi has already endured.

Tick, tock, tick, tock, crab.

I distract myself by contemplating the Thirteenth Guardian. Even though he's nothing like the godlike being he was in his original form, he's no mere mortal either. Being around him feels like I'm in the presence of something holy, yet undeniably dark.

He's a fallen god who succumbed to the worst kind of evil.

A broken star.

The front door opens, and I'm relieved the guys were so quick. I stand up in anticipation—only instead of Trax and Tomás, a dozen masked Marad soldiers in white uniforms march inside, training their Murmurs on us.

I can almost delude myself that it's just a bunch of Leonine actors, but then a thirteenth Lion strides into the room.

The leader of the Tomorrow Party.

21

I RAISE MY HAND AND make a fist, releasing the blue sword of my Barer. "Wake up!" I shout at Ophiuchus, but he remains on the floor, deep in his Center.

Blaze Jansun eases in with the same conqueror's confidence he always exudes—like every room he enters instantly becomes part of his domain. He's wearing a royal purple Lionheart uniform, and his russet eyes and bright brown skin glow against his newly dyed white hair.

"I'll kill you," I warn as he walks closer, holding the sword as steady as I can. "Your master wants me alive, so you can't hurt me," I remind him.

"I have no intention of hurting you, Rho," he says, sounding wounded by the mere suggestion. He settles into the center couch cushion, stretching his limbs and taking up the whole thing. "These weapons are for your friend."

"Did you hurt Trax?"

Traxon comes forward from behind the wall of soldiers, and for the first time I hear how truly gullible I am.

"We knew you spoke with Traxon on Aquarius because we saw you meeting with him in the Pegazi stables," says Blaze. "So once you left, I found him and offered to hand over the one thing he's always wanted from both of us."

The truth.

Traxon doesn't shrink from my glower because by his standards, he didn't do anything wrong. He's stayed true to his own code—*truth above all*—and he probably sees *me* as the one in the wrong for manipulating him. And maybe I am.

Every truth is relative. I hear Gamba's words in my mind, but I shake them off by digging into Blaze. "And what version of *the truth* did you give him?"

"We told him *everything.*" From the way Blaze says the word, it's clear that Traxon's knowledge of the Party now far surpasses mine. "And in exchange, we asked that he tell you Untara was funding Black Moon—which, full disclosure, was all along just a ploy to draw you in and steal your followers."

Fire flames inside me at the thought of how they used Nishi, but for her sake I keep it tamed. I need to save her first—I'll worry about making them pay for what they did after.

"I thought you were honorable," I growl at Traxon.

"I don't go back on my deals," he says, glaring back at me just as angrily, and in his hurt expression, I see the pain of my refusal to trust him. "Besides, you wanted me to take you to the Party, and now I've brought the Party to you."

I lower my hand but don't turn off my Barer. Instead, I transform the energy into electric brass knuckles, and I keep my arm ready to swing if the need arises. "So what exactly are you doing for Aquarius, Blaze?"

"It's what *he's* doing for us, Rho," he says, sitting up with excitement. "He's freeing us from the old ways and the old politicians and the old prejudices—he's giving us a chance to re-create our universe. To make it the way it ought to be. All of us living as one, not twelve or thirteen."

"That's inspiring, but I'm curious: How does murder play into that utopia?"

"That's what you Cancrians don't understand," he says, shaking his head. "*Sacrifice.*"

I hear Fernanda's accusation in his words: *On Cancer you believe the loss of one life is as unacceptable as the loss of ten thousand—but on Taurus, we're team players and we believe in making sacrifices for the greater good.*

"Sometimes a broken building can't be repaired," he goes on. "Sometimes you have to blow up its foundation and build it anew."

This time, it's Deke I hear: *To change the norm, you have to break it.*

Words can be so easily manipulated—all you have to do is assign them new meanings, and the message changes. They're as inconstant as the streets of the Artistry Pride, and that's what Aquarius—a wordsmith by nature—realized. It's what he's used to change the Zodiac.

Words have always been his weapon of choice.

But they've also been mine.

"So what are we waiting for?" I ask, and the electricity snuffs out from my Barer. "Take us to him."

"You friend is a little large to carry," says Blaze. "We'll wait for him to wake up."

Ophiuchus's silver eyes open, and he rises to his impressive height.

"Well then." Even though Blaze is still playing it cool, there's a tense note in his voice now. "As they say in Artistry: *It's time to meet the director.*"

✦ ✦ ✦

Rather than marching us out, Blaze and his soldiers force Ophiuchus and me upstairs, and then they open a hatch in the ceiling and make us climb onto the rooftop. Traxon and Tomás stay behind.

A machine that looks like a massive silver cat lands lightly and soundlessly before us, and I gasp.

A Panthera plane.

Everyone in the Zodiac has heard of Panthera planes, but hardly anyone has ever seen one. Only the highest level of Leonine government officials have access to them because of their stealth—since the ships don't exactly fly, they have no real engine and operate on minimal technology, so they slip past almost every kind of detection.

Panthera planes play a big part in pretty much every Leonine action film, so on Cancer every kid grew up wanting one. Even Dad used to talk about them.

The craft operates on four powerfully springy legs that silently leap from rooftop to rooftop. The only windows are in the plane's catlike head, where the driver sits, guiding the legs' direction.

An entryway opens in the silver cat's round belly, and Ophiuchus and I follow Blaze inside, Murmurs aimed at our backs. The space is dark and velvety, without windows or wallscreens, and each of us straps into a seat. Then the mechanical cat extends its legs, and the craft barely shakes as we leap from roof to roof.

With nothing to watch or listen to, all I have to think about is the meeting that's coming. If Traxon's betrayal did anything, it cemented that I was right not to trust anyone but myself. It's not like any of this changes my plan anyway: I was always going to go before Aquarius and beg for Nishi's life. I was just hoping to show up on my terms, not dragged in at gunpoint.

My stomach tickles as the Panthera makes an especially low jump, and as soon as we land, Blaze and the soldiers get to their feet. When we deplane, I turn around quickly to watch the huge silver cat leap away.

We're on the banks of a vast body of water, and docked on the blue shore is a piece of home I never thought I'd see.

A giant ridged shell reaches up on either side of the iconic Cancrian vessel we called the *Mothership*. It's the floating residence where our Holy Mothers used to live. Aquarius must have moved the Party's headquarters here for *me*.

I've always dreamt of seeing this place up close. I studied it so much as a kid that I memorized everything about it, and Mom promised to take me one day if I trained hard enough.

The top part of the ship is domed and crystalized, and it looks like a pearl caught in a giant nar-clam's jaws. This Leonine replica is smaller than the real vessel, but it still looks sizable enough to hold a few hundred people.

Even though it's a knockoff, I still feel a chill as I step onto the boarding ramp, like I'm entering the holiest home on House Cancer. Since it's an abridged version, the Leonines only included the parts that are best known to us, so we step directly into one of the most famous places in the ship—the Family Room.

It's a hall decorated with the crests of Cancer's twelve founding families, and it's where Mother Origene used to hold her beloved "seaside chats."

She would sail to different parts of the planet and invite families from all levels of society to sit with her and discuss everything and anything. Then she'd listen to questions and complaints from anyone, even kids, and Lodestars would broadcast the chat to the whole planet. I wanted so badly to attend one so I could show her everything Mom taught me and make both of them proud.

Which inspiring initiatives will Cancrians remember from my tenure as Guardian? The way I ran away from the Crab constellation right after my coronation, or how I led an armada of Zodai to their deaths?

I try to keep focused on the present as we climb up a spiral staircase that's polished and pink, like the inside of a seashell. It goes on for so long that my muscles start screaming in agony, reminding me that my body hasn't fully recovered from the Sumber yet.

I breathe a sigh of relief when we finally reach the top, and I lean against the wall to catch my breath. We're in a domed room encased in crystal, a place few people have ever seen—the Holy Mother's reading room.

The Marad soldiers are no longer with us, and now it's just Blaze, Ophiuchus, and . . . Aquarius.

He stands before us in a billowing aqua cloak, but he's not looking at me. He and Ophiuchus are staring at each other like Blaze and I don't exist.

It's strange to see the Original Guardians in these bodies—Aquarius as a forty-something man and Ophiuchus as a teen. Yet both are really fallen stars who've shared an eternity together.

Ophiuchus's silver eyes gleam with emotion, like he's finally yanked his head out of the astral plane and joined us in reality. Aquarius moves toward him until they're standing face to face.

"I meant for you to leave Pisces with me. But when I was hit, my people chose to save me rather than follow my orders to bring you with us. I'm sorry."

"Your eyes."

Ophiuchus's voice is so soft it's almost a whisper. "They're the only part of you that hasn't changed."

Aquarius reaches into his robe and pulls out the diamond-bright Talisman he brought to the Cathedral—Ophiuchus's Star Stone. The Thirteenth Guardian stares at it in muted shock, and I spy his jaw clenching.

But Aquarius doesn't notice his reaction because he closes his eyes and holds the Talisman between his hands, concentrating so hard that a vein bulges on his forehead, and he seems to be in terrible pain. After a moment, his face relaxes and he lowers his hands.

When he opens his eyes, his ivory features glow, a ghost of the moonlight he gave off long ago. His silver hair grows silkier, and even his voice sounds different, more velvety than before. He looks ageless and otherworldly, like he's shed his human skin at last.

"Does this please you more?" he murmurs as he slips the Stone back inside his cloak.

Ophiuchus exhales heavily. "You know I never cared for such things. It was your soul I admired, not your shell."

"Where's Nishi?"

Aquarius jerks his face to me, like he's just noticing I'm here.

"Wandering Star, welcome!" He gives me a bow that only serves to remind me of how little power I actually have in this room. "Thank you for coming."

"I'm not here for tea," I say, my voice a low growl. "I came to bring you Ophiuchus in exchange for my friend. Now free Nishi."

"You're quite wrong," says Aquarius pleasantly. "Ophiuchus came to me of his own accord, same as you . . . but you have other things to barter with."

I cross my arms. "What do you want?"

"When you're *really* ready to listen," he says in a maddeningly condescending tone, "I'll tell you."

I ball my hands into fists at my sides and try to restrain the Barer from activating. "*Please*—I can't wait anymore. Every moment she's in there, Nishi's suffering."

My voice cracks, and though my gut hardens in disgust, I fall to my knees before him.

"Take me instead. Let me take her place in the nightmare world. I'll do anything—just get her out of there. Please. Name your price and I'll pay it, but don't make her stay in there another moment. *I'm begging you—*"

"Rho."

Aquarius frowns, and to my shock he drops to his knees before me, too. His pink eyes look so concerned that a more trusting version of myself might have believed he actually cares. "I told my army to avoid inflicting pain on her at all costs. They should have used the Sumber's dream chamber, not nightmare. Were *you* also—?"

He reads the answer on my face because he grows even more pallid. "I'm so sorry . . . I have forgotten how frail mortal minds can be. We will have her awoken immediately, and you can go to her straightaway."

The whole Zodiac suddenly fades to background noise.

"I can go *now*?"

"Absolutely." He looks to Blaze. "Please see that this is done immediately, and let Rho have some privacy with her friend. I expect Nishi to receive the best care possible, and I will personally see to anyone who disobeys me. Clear?"

Blaze nods. "On my honor."

I take one last glance at Ophiuchus, who's still staring at Aquarius and looking hopeful for the first time, and though part of me would like to stay to hear what's said between them, nothing matters more than Nishi. So I run after Blaze, who's climbing down a different spiral staircase.

I remember from my studies that the Mothership has four wings, just like the Cancrian embassy has four bungalows, but what's new are all the books stuffed into every shelf and nook and cranny—the paper kind that are rarely sold on most Houses anymore, since everything went holographic centuries ago.

"Aquarius is quite the reader," Blaze explains as we step into a sitting area crammed with more manuscripts. "He's read every single book every Zodai on every House has ever published."

As I pass the rows of spines, I wonder how we stand a chance against someone who knows us better than we know ourselves.

At the other end of the sitting area is a set of swinging double doors. Inside is a medical bay with curtains hanging from the ceiling between hospital beds, but only one set is drawn around the sole patient.

I race past Blaze and shove back the black curtains.

Nishi.

I drape myself over her chest and clutch her to me, my breaths loud and labored. I found her. She's alive.

We're together, and it's *real*.

"Rho, move back so they can help her," says Blaze, and I look up to see a pair of Leonine healers coming over. I step aside without letting go of

Nishi's hand, and I watch as they inject something into her system. Nishi suddenly grips my fingers, and I gasp—but the others don't seem surprised.

"It just means the injection's kicked in," explains Blaze. "Now it's up to Nishi's mind to wake up."

"I remember," I say through gritted teeth. "Leave us."

"But Aquarius said to offer her the best care—"

"And I will," I say, glaring at him. "I want you all out of here. Go tell Aquarius if you want, but I'm sure he'll instruct you to follow my wishes."

"Okay, then," says Blaze. "Let's go."

I shut the curtains around us and sit next to Nishi, taking her hand again. Since she's already faced her worst fear, the antidote shouldn't take long to work. But I watch her for hours, and her eyes never open.

At one point, Blaze comes by and drops off food for me, but I don't touch it. He offers to escort me to my quarters, but I ignore him until he goes away.

"Please, Nish," I whisper, late into the night when the lights have been dimmed and the whole place is silent. "Please wake up. I'm so sorry I left you for so long, but you're safe now, I promise. You have to fight for this. *Please fight.* I need you."

I must doze off at some point, because the next thing I know I jerk awake to find Nishi's eyelids blinking open.

"Nish?" I whisper, my voice thick with hope.

Her amber irises find mine, and her hand twitches, so I squeeze her fingers. "I'm here," I say, cupping her face with my free hand. "You're okay. Just follow the sound of my voice," I go on, repeating everything I remember the Ariean healer saying to me. "Inhale deeply, then exhale, but take your time. Blink once if you can feel my hand squeezing yours."

She blinks.

"Good. Can you try squeezing back?" I wait to feel something, but nothing happens. "It's okay," I say soothingly. "You're okay."

Her fingers suddenly clamp down on mine, and my face splits into its first smile since Pisces. My shoulders fall and a pressure eases behind my eyes, and only now do I realize how tightly wound I've been this whole time.

Then Nishi's lips part, and she whispers hoarsely, "I knew you'd find me, Rho."

22

THE SECOND THING NISHI SAYS is, "You're not real." Her expression falls, and what little color she had recovered begins to fade.

"I am, Nish, I promise," I whisper, squeezing her hand firmly, but her fingers are limp and panic is exploding in her eyes.

"Nish," I plead as gently as I can. "You're safe, I swear it."

Her whole body stiffens, her shoulders peaking up, her hand twitching in mine. She doesn't trust me. "I know you're scared," I say, stroking her dark hair. "So how about we just sit here and wait for a bit?"

Nishi nods her head slightly but doesn't say a word. After almost an hour of holding hands in silence, she finally seems to relax, and I try talking to her again. "How do you feel?"

"Confused," she finally answers, sitting up. I grab the glass I left on the counter, and I slowly tip the water into her mouth. When she wraps her own hands around the glass, I let go.

After a few sips she asks, "Where are we?"

"With the Tomorrow Party."

"Why did they let you come to me?"

"What do you remember from what I told you in the Sumber?" I ask tentatively.

She takes another drink of water. Then she hands the glass back to me and says, "Crompton is the master."

I nod. "He gave me permission to see you. I don't know why—but I'm not questioning it. I just want to get you back to the others."

Her eyes grow alarmed. "Rho, we have to get out of here now, before the Party members come for us. The master will never let us go—"

"Shhh, calm down," I say. "First you have to recover your strength. We'll worry about everything else once you're better. We're safe for now."

"How? *How are we safe, Rho?* These are the same people who shot us with the Sumber in the first place—"

"Just trust me, Nish," I say, my voice firmer than before. "I'll protect you—*I swear it on my mother's life.*"

The ceiling lights suddenly brighten, and I hear footsteps. I get to my feet and position myself in front of the bed, my Barer at the ready in case I need to defend Nishi.

One of the healers pokes her head in through the curtains. When she sees that Nishi's awake, she looks pleased. "May I check her vitals?" she asks me.

I nod, and she comes in and reviews the data flashing on the holographic screens. "Everything looks good," she says at last. "But you've been under for so long that your muscles need rehabilitation. We can pop you into a healing pod if you'd like to expedite things—otherwise, you're looking at a couple more days in here."

"She'll take the healing pod," I say before Nishi can speak. There's no time for an extended hospital stay.

"Actually, *she'll heal naturally*," says Nishi testily.

I turn to her. "You need to get better faster than that."

"I'm *not* going inside the healing pod," she says, her voice loud but shaky.

"Why not?"

She drops her gaze, and suddenly I realize I know the answer. She doesn't want to go back to sleep.

How could I not anticipate that fear when it's tormented me, too?

"We have dreamless sleeping tonics," says the healer gently, understanding the problem as well.

Nishi perks up a bit at this news, but then she abruptly turns to me, concern resurfacing in her eyes. "I'll be right here when you wake up," I assure her. "I promise."

She nods in agreement, and the nurse and I carry Nishi between us. Once she's sealed inside, the pod runs a scan, and then the total time it will take to heal Nishi flashes on a screen. While the nurse sets the program to begin, I step through the double doors and leave the medical bay.

In the sitting area, I spot a small stone table with two plushy armchairs on either side, and Aquarius is sitting in one of them, reading the holographic news projecting from his Philosopher's Stone. His skin is still glowing like a star.

"I brought you breakfast," he says, gesturing to the tray of food on the table. "How long do you have?"

I frown at his generosity and guardedly say, "The healing pod opens in fifteen hours."

"Excellent." He waves the holographic screens aside and takes a sip of his tea. "Then we'll make the most of our time together before you have to return. Would you like a nap or a shower?"

"No."

It's actually pretty liberating not to care about myself anymore. I'm free to run my body down completely because I have no future to save it for. Once I get Nishi away from here, all that matters is gaining Aquarius's trust and thwarting his plans, or relaying what I learn to my friends so they can stop him.

"So, any more questions, or are we about done with the *dullatry*?" I ask.

His pink eyes sparkle with delight when he hears me using his vocabulary. "You eat, I'll talk," he says, and he waits for me to take a bite of toast before he keeps going, as though to remind me that all the power lies on his side of the table.

"I'm sorry it's proven so difficult for us to get together. I'd meant to avoid that by giving you the pearl necklace at the Cathedral."

"The necklace?"

"It was a Psynergy device of my own design that enabled us to communicate privately."

Hysan was right. As usual.

"I'm guessing your boyfriend interfered."

I cross my arms. "How did you know about Lord Neith?"

"Now *that* was a clever trick," he says, sitting up and leaning forward. A strand of silver hair falls over his face, and he brushes it back. "I can't believe it got by me for so long. Any other era and I would never have been caught unaware by a human, but, as you know, I've been a bit . . . distracted." He smiles indulgently, like I'm an amusing pet he loves but doesn't respect.

"I figured it out the day Neith malfunctioned at the Hippodrome, when he answered *Insufficient data*. At first I thought Neith had built a robot decoy for his own protection at Plenum meetings—so I watched him closely after that, and soon a golden-haired boy caught my eye. It wasn't hard to figure the rest out."

I think back to that day on Aries, my second attempt to convince the Plenum that Ophiuchus was real. Hysan got Tasered when he tried standing up for me, so he has no idea what happened while he was unconscious. I should have mentioned Neith's malfunction to him.

Why didn't I say something?

"I managed to get my hands on Neith for a day," Aquarius goes on, and I know he's now referring to the day Hysan was supposed to fly me to meet the Marad, when Twain replaced him as 'Nox's pilot. "When I inspected the android, I realized the Psynergy around him was being artificially attracted to cover for the fact that he has no soul. His insides were designed to look human—only instead of blood, his heart pumps Abyssthe through his veins. It's really quite clever."

The day Hysan started helping me, his own life starting falling apart.

I've done nothing to aid him.

I've done nothing to deserve him.

"After all, androids are my specialty," he adds, and I stare at him in wonder. "How else could I be multiple people at once?"

"You mean you had android versions of Morscerta and Crompton?"

"Naturally. Only unlike Neith, I don't imbue them with artificial intelligence—I inhabit them myself through the Psy. It took me centuries of training and studying to perfect my technique, and unfortunately I haven't found a way to permanently install my essence in a more sustainable vessel, but no matter. I won't need to do that anymore now that my secret is out."

What the Helios is happening here? I feel like I've entered some kind of alternate dimension. Why is my enemy being more honest with me than my own friends?

He nudges my plate closer to me, and I look down at my toast; I've taken exactly one bite. "Would you like to see your mom?"

"What do you want from her?" I ask, forcing the bread to my mouth, even though my stomach's sealed itself off.

"Information she doesn't possess," he says dismissively, looking disappointedly at my plate.

I swallow, and the bite of bread slowly descends down my dry throat. "Did you hurt her?" I ask, my tone tight.

"That approach would have been a waste of time," he says matter-of-factly. "You can't break someone who has always been broken."

I don't like thinking of Mom that way, and suddenly I want to see her.

"Well, if you're not going to eat, shall we get started?" he asks, linking his hands together on the cold table. "This has been a charming chat, but I would hope you have more important questions to ask me, and I'd like to get through most of my answers before your fifteen-hour window closes."

I make a point of pushing the plate aside, scraping it across the stone, and I lean forward. "Really?" I ask dryly. "You're actually going to answer my questions and tell me everything I want to know?"

He leans in, too. "*Try me.*"

"Okay," I say, sitting back. "What's your master plan?"

"Like your ancestors, I am going to travel through the portal in Helios to colonize a new galaxy, and I hope to save as many samples of the Zodiac's species as possible when I go. Because Helios is dying."

"Our sun isn't dying!" I snap, straightening my spine. "*You're* killing it."

He sighs and says, "You've already come this far. Will you at least hear my side before condemning me?"

I'm not going to get anything I want by antagonizing him, so I force myself to nod. "Okay."

He seems to think for a moment and then rises. "Let's speak elsewhere."

I follow him up the closest pink spiral staircase, and we cut through a series of passages to the north wing. The Mothership's sand-and-seashell floors and walls remind me so much of Cancer that by the time we step out onto a higher deck of the ship, I could be convinced that I'm actually home—if not for the second sun in the sky.

The deck is secured with a crystal railing, and the space is small enough that there's only room for a handful of benches. We're so high up that we can see the curving tops of the giant shells on either side of the ship, and I realize we've been moving this whole time.

I lean against the crystal railing, and the wind blows strands of my hair in my eyes as we sail into the blue horizon. Aquarius joins me, and he's so tall that he has to fold half his body down to lean on the banister.

"At the turn of the first millennium," he says, his pink eyes gazing at Helios, "I began to notice a change in our solar system that was brought on by the presence of Dark Matter. Helios was losing her strength—the Dark Matter was sucking her energy, and her light was dimming. I alone noticed her weakening. I, who had watched her all this time. I hoped it was only my imagination, but then came the year when Helios's Halo stopped taking place altogether."

Despite my hatred for him and everything he stands for, I'm instantly sucked into his story. I flash back to when I asked Sirna why she thought that phenomenon had vanished from the sky, and she said, *I think it's because we don't look up as often as we used to.*

She was kind of right.

If we had looked up, maybe we would have seen the disappearance of Helios's Halo as an omen—a sign of the deeper darkness that would one day steal all our light.

"I knew the cosmic conditions for the portal's activation wouldn't repeat themselves until this millennium, so I had to wait." Aquarius straightens his spine and turns to face me, resting his hip against the crystal and crossing his arms over his chest. "In that time, I prepared. I remembered how the first humans described a fleet ten times the size of the one they came with, but the portal didn't stay open long enough for all of them to get through. I knew there would be no way to save the entire Zodiac."

"So why did you decide to blow Cancer, Virgo, and Gemini off the map first?" I ask tonelessly.

His shoulders sag, but he doesn't defend himself. "The quantum fusion experiments Origene, Moira, and Caaseum were conducting had a Psynergetic component to them—something only the three of them knew about. The Houses had exhausted every attempt to study Dark Matter, but they were unable to learn much about it, other than the fact that it could suck the energy from a planet. But these three Guardians were convinced they could find more answers using Psynergy. What they didn't realize is that they were disturbing the Dark Matter, and to keep it from reaching Helios and killing us all, I had to divert it. Alone I couldn't move it, but with Ophiuchus I could."

He furrows his brow. "Rho, I don't expect you to see this from my perspective—that would be like asking the ocean tides to consider the moon's point of view. But when it comes to protecting an entire population, sometimes sacrifices must be made."

I tune into the singing surf of the sea because I don't want to process his words. I don't want to think of my beautiful blue planet as expendable. I don't want to think of Dad as an acceptable loss.

And yet as my mind waits for my heart's counterargument, it doesn't offer one.

I can't hear its beat.

"I have spent the better part of my immortality looking for a way around the Last Prophecy, but the Dark Matter we created will destroy us." Aquarius's voice is gentle, and again I don't know how to reconcile his warmth and openness with everything I know about the master. "There is no possible way to save everyone. All I can offer is the chance to save *some*."

"That's why you started the Tomorrow Party." I don't know if I'm asking or telling him. "So the Marad members are expendable to you, but the Zodai of the Tomorrow Party are worth saving?"

He shakes his head. "I have a separate deal with the Marad. Believe me, everyone is getting what they want."

Seeing the confusion on my face, he explains, "I'm doing what any scientist, or *god*, would do: I'm taking my best samples, my optimal representative group of the species, to build a new and better world. But that isn't enough."

My confusion only grows after his explanation. "What do you mean?"

"It's taken me millennia, but I've finally understood how your species lost its way," he says, and he walks over to one of the benches and sits down.

"I understand why Ophiuchus's presence was so important. Your lives are so brief that hope is often short-lived among people. You forget your history when it's unpleasant, yet you obstinately cling to outdated values and belief systems, because the only thing you fear more than facing the darkness of your past is confronting a future that's unknown.

"You need *inspiration*. People don't need to be told what they're capable of—they need to *know* it. They need proof they can touch: an example to emulate, a leader worth following, a person who speaks out even in the face of injustice, who stays honest even when tempted with power, who embodies the best of what an individual is capable of even when it seems everyone is at their worst."

His pink eyes stare into mine, and I suddenly realize: "You're talking about *me?*"

He nods, and this is so outrageous that I have to sit down at the other end of his bench.

"I foresaw you," he goes on. "A seer who could actually detect Dark Matter and who would warn the worlds of their doom."

Mom's vision that someone in her bloodline would be the harbinger of the Zodiac's demise, and Empress Moira's declaration that she'd long been expecting me—if they both predicted my arrival, of course Aquarius did, too.

"I Saw that most would be too blinded by this seer's light to see her for what she was, but the rare few who did would be the best of their species. Only those who believe in you are worthy of surviving—all who did not heed your warnings will be left behind."

It's the first time he truly seems like a parent, in the realest sense—a lion protecting his cub.

"You were my vision's first ambassador, Rho."

I have to let the salty air fill my lungs to keep from drowning in this newest revelation. Aquarius used me as bait—he dangled me out to the Zodiac to lure his chosen ones.

"But first I had to be sure *you* were worthy."

I glare at him. After all my experiences with Guardians, I know exactly what that means. "You tested me."

"Naturally. First thing I did was set Ophiuchus on your tail."

My eyes widen in horror, but since calling Aquarius a sociopath won't help me free Nishi, I clamp my mouth shut.

"And, as I'd hoped, you survived his numerous attempts on your life."

"He stopped trying to kill me as soon as he realized I would make a better ally to escape you," I say, desperately trying to wound him even a little.

But he only sits up straighter. "That was after he saw your strength, which proves my point.

"Next, I had to learn what part of you I needed to enlist. I had to discover whom you needed me to be so I could give you what you were missing. For this test, I had to hack away at your shell, removing the armor you hide behind and stripping you down to your essence. That required another kind of tool; not a blunt object but a fine blade."

"*Aryll*," I growl. "And what exactly did he teach you about me?"

"That your pity betrays you," he says, like he's analyzing a character from a book he's reading. "You find infinite value in every man, every soul. You fail to grasp what my eternal existence allows me to know—that humans are a brief phase of biological evolution who exist but for a minute, in a galaxy that is but a drop of water in an ever-expanding ocean. And *none* of you can be saved."

"That's one hell of a pitch."

"It's not a pitch—I'm not selling you anything. I want to open your eyes so you can decide for yourself."

I swallow, remembering when Hysan said something similar to me on Centaurion.

Aquarius leans in, his pink eyes glinting in the sunlight. "The prime directive of your organism is to die; death is the *only* thing life guarantees you. The truth is, the length of time a random individual lives matters little to the stars, or even to most members of your species. And yet, even an unknown, faceless person can imprint forever on your soul."

In his eyes I see the small Cancrian girl's pink spacesuit that's been branded into my mind since Elara.

He knows *everything*.

All I've felt, all I've known, all I've wanted. I feel exposed. And I also feel trapped, like there are no moves I can make because I'm playing against an opponent who sees how the game will end before it's even begun.

"It's not your fault you're like this," he goes on. "The potential is there; you just haven't had the right upbringing. And that is where I can help you. See, I've studied you closer than even you have. I've seen your mind's corners, its curves, its contradictions . . . and beneath your Wandering Star luster, you are held up by an unshakable Cancrian core."

He takes my hand in his, and though my Barer buzzes, my fingers feel limp, like my body's tired of resisting.

"I can give you the thing you've always felt you were missing," he whispers. "I can be your true parent, Rho. One who knows you, who puts you first, who never abandons you. I've been there for all of your most important moments, even if you didn't know it. When you faced the Plenum. When you were disgraced. When you returned triumphant. I've watched you grow. I was so proud when I got to crown you Wandering Star."

His warm eyes grow shiny, and I realize that even though he caused the tragedies that led to these moments, he still believes he means these words.

"Let me teach you what I know. Men are mortal, but I am a star, an everlasting part of this galaxy. Let me help you feed your flame so that for the blink of an eye you're here, you can blaze brighter than Helios herself."

23

"I STILL DON'T UNDERSTAND WHAT you want from me." My voice sounds so small, it feels like it's coming from light-years away.

Aquarius's sunset eyes stare steadfastly into mine. "When we go through that portal, I want you at the helm of the first ship. I want you to lead humanity into a united tomorrow—and I want to be the star that guides you."

I shake my head in complete confusion. "But—you've been trying to kill me this whole time."

"No, I've been providing you with opportunities to understand your own strength," he says, like that's a perfectly acceptable justification. "You were never in any danger, not if you were the person I believed you to be."

"That's quite a gamble to make."

"Which came first, fate or free will?" he asks, smiling paternally. "That's the universal question."

This whole conversation makes as much sense as the nightmares in the Sumber, and I don't know how to begin digesting anything he's said, so

I blurt, *"But why did you put me through the worst moments of my life if you wanted me on your side?"*

His expression grows pitying, which only irritates me further. "Heart, mind, and soul . . . that's what you Cancrians test for the Guardianship, right? I already knew you had the soul of a star because you could See Dark Matter. I knew you had the mind of a leader because you succeeded in bringing the Houses closer together than they've been in millennia. But how do you test the heart of the most forgiving person in the Zodiac?"

"Do you always answer questions with riddles?"

His pink stare grows grave, and for a moment I worry I've pushed him too far.

"First you take everything from her," he says, and I'm beyond certain my heart has stopped. "Then you dare her to forgive you."

◆ ◆ ◆

I've already been sitting by the healing pod a couple of hours when at last the countdown reaches zero and the lid opens.

I don't know what time it is, but it's late into the night. After my talk with Aquarius, Blaze took me on a tour through the Mothership and introduced me to Party members, and I tried to take as many mental notes as I could—but I was still in too much of a daze from everything the master revealed.

Now that I know what he wants—my trust—I finally have leverage over him. All I have to do is make him think he's earned it, and then he'll confide in me the specific details of his plan. But I can't reach out to Hysan until I know something that can actually help the Zodai defeat Aquarius; otherwise, I'll risk the master discovering my duplicity before I've had a chance to be useful.

I grow instantly alert as Nishi sits upright, and I'm relieved to see that warmth has returned to her cinnamon skin.

When her eyes find mine, I spy a familiar shrewdness in their amber depths. "Something's wrong."

"Should I call a healer?" I ask, leaping to my feet.

"Why are you here, Rho?" She narrows her gaze, and her suspicious expression is further proof that the old Nishi is back.

And the old Nishi will be impossible to fool.

"I can't talk in here," I say softly, barely moving my lips, which is at least true. I have no idea if the Party has installed hidden surveillance—and since I'm playing both sides, that means trusting no one.

Nishi nods in understanding. "So, what's next?" she asks tentatively.

"We get out of here and get you back with the others."

She wrinkles her brow. "We. *We* have to get back to the others. Why didn't they come with you?"

"Nish, I can't talk," I say, again dropping my voice to barely a whisper.

She blows out a hard breath, but at least she doesn't press me. I guess truth is the most convincing lie.

"Wandering Star?"

I turn to see the healer from earlier poking her head through the privacy curtains. "May I see to our patient?"

"She's fine," I say.

"Your presence has been requested at dinner. Blaze said a change of clothes awaits you in your suite."

"I'm not hungry. And it's late."

"But Aquarius specifically requested—"

"I don't care."

"She'll be there," announces Nishi, and when I glower at her, she's already glowering back. "We just need a moment," she tells the healer, who nods in relief and retreats.

"You have to go, Rho," she says in a firm tone. "If you let me distract you from defeating him, I'll never forgive myself."

I swallow and turn away so she won't see the guilt on my face. "I'll come back right after," I toss over my shoulder.

"Maybe you should get some sleep right after."

I whirl around, and she winces at my wounded expression. "I'm sorry, Rho, it's not that I don't want to see you. It's just—you look like you could use some rest. You can tell me all about the dinner first thing in the morning."

I shrug and say, "Here's hoping they don't poison my food."

"Hey, *you're* the chosen one; you have nothing to worry about." Her feral grin makes me think of the warrior Nishi from the Sumber. "If you don't piss anyone off too much, I'll probably be fine, too."

I smile at her innocently.

"Then I guess I'll have to be on my *best* behavior."

✦ ✦ ✦

I search for room number nine, and when I turn the key Blaze gave me, I enter a spacious suite outfitted with sparse furniture. The few pieces in here are all silver with a pearl finish, and they look exquisite and expensive. The minimalist aesthetic reminds me of Aquarius's office at the royal palace, and it seems to suit his philosophies well—if you're chasing tomorrow, you probably want to pack light.

A sparkly dress has been laid out for me on the seashell-patterned bedspread, and by now I'm so used to people telling me what to wear and when to wear it that I don't even care how it looks. Since I have to put it on to curry Aquarius's favor, there's no point in having an opinion.

I force myself to take a quick shower so I can pretend to care about tonight, and I've just pulled on the dress when there's a knock on my door.

I open it to find Blaze in a hot-pink suit, his white hair twisted into a bun atop his head.

"Now *that's* a Wandering Star," he says gallantly, admiring me. "Let me just fix your hair."

Without waiting for permission, he comes around me and corrals my wet curls behind my neck, weaving them into one long, loose braid.

"Did you dye your hair white because you're desperate to be Aquarian?" I ask as he works. "Or do you honestly think that looks good on you?"

He faces me and plucks a few curls free to frame my face. "Are you this charming with all your admirers, or do I warrant special treatment?"

"My *admirer*—"

But my outrage is cut short because he disappears into my bathroom and returns with a tin of tiny diamond pins that he starts inserting into my hair. I ignore what he's doing so I won't give him the satisfaction of a reaction, and I pick up where I left off. "You and Imogen attacked Nishi and me just weeks ago—"

"We didn't kill you, nor would we."

He stops working and looks me in the eye, his handsome face creasing with concern. The expression is so full of Aquarius's magnetic sincerity that I can see why these two fell in with each other. "These are times of war, Rho—but you should know that, as you were the one who sounded the alarm months ago."

"*Sounded the alarm?*" I don't care if I blow my cover anymore, because anger is setting my gut ablaze.

"If we're going to have a real talk," I say fiercely, "then let's start by calling things by their real names. My home planet was *demolished*—and it was Aquarius's doing. He destroyed my entire world and murdered my people, and that's in addition to what he did to Virgo, Gemini, Pisces, Capricorn, the armada—can you *understand* that, or are you just too damned brainwashed?"

Blaze's brown skin pales, and the confident light fades from his russet eyes. "Okay . . . let's talk honestly."

Even his voice sounds different, deeper. "I want an existence where we're all allowed to be whom we want. I think what happened to Cancer—and Virgo and Gemini and Pisces and all the other lives lost—is abhorrent and devastating and I'm *sick* about it. *I'm sick about it*," he repeats, his voice growing guttural.

"But I'm not a god."

He blinks, and his eyes are bright again. "A human who judges Aquarius is like the lion who judges man. We can never know what it's like to be stars."

Blaze raises his arm and offers me his elbow. I hesitate, and on seeing my indecision he adds, "Gods create and destroy—it's the nature of their condition. We can't have life without death, or fortune without misfortune. That's just the way things are."

I have no choice but to play along, so I give in and link my arm through his. As soon as I do, he pulls me in close and murmurs in my ear, "Rho, you should know there's no tomorrow without you."

I tilt my head back to look into his eyes. "What?"

He seems completely serious. "The Tomorrow Party believes in your Sight *and* your vision, and we will follow you to any universe."

"Except this one," I say.

His eyes flash and his arm tightens around mine. "Don't you understand? *We're leaving the Zodiac because we don't want to die.* This solar system is coming to an end: Our sun will burn out. As hateful as his actions seem—and as distasteful as this sounds—what Aquarius is offering us isn't doom."

Blaze brushes back one of my flyaway curls and buries it in my braid.

"It's *hope*."

✦ ✦ ✦

We head to the south wing of the ship and enter a semi-dark room, and immediately I understand why we're clothed the way we are: My sparkly dress and Blaze's neon-pink suit are giving off their own light. There are probably a hundred people here, and they all look like different-colored stars. The effect is dreamy and romantic and otherworldly.

Something bright flits in the corner of my eye, and I look behind me. There's a mirror hanging on the wall, and I catch my own reflection.

The dress hangs above my knees but has a long train in the back, and glimmers of silver trail in the air behind me. The silky fabric isn't visible—all that can be seen of my silhouette are the constellations of sparkles that adorn the bodice and the twinkling of the diamonds Blaze placed in my hair.

A Scorp girl walks up to us, and I stare at her in awe. Her blue dress swirls like it was sewn from actual water, and her translucent skin glows with light, like Aquarius's. She hands Blaze and me glasses with a glow-in-the-dark white drink. Blaze clinks his glass with mine and tips the substance into his mouth. Without waiting to see what happens, I down mine, too.

I feel a warm sensation spread through me, and I look down to see my *skin* is lighting up.

I turn to Blaze. He's also glowing. He flashes me one of his winning smiles and says, "The idea is to look past people's shells to the light they carry within."

But as I gaze out at the hundred or so senior Party members here, all I see is the darkness surrounding the lights. The souls who had to be snuffed out for Aquarius to shine even brighter.

In this solar system of people, it's not hard to spot the sun. Aquarius's light is so authentic that he's obviously the only real star among imitators.

Students flock around him, soaking up his wisdom like he's their favorite Academy instructor, and it looks incredibly inviting to be one of his followers. To be that inspired, that hopeful, that wholly devoted . . . It seems like it makes everything so much easier.

Even through the crowd of shimmering bodies, his eyes find mine and his voice suddenly rises high enough to cut through the conversations, silencing everyone at once.

"What you all blame on the stars," he declares, "is something you impose on yourselves."

There isn't a sound in the room.

"The stars do not decide which House you are born into—your parents do that, as did their parents before them, and their parents before them. It's your dependence on ancestral memory—your delusional insistence on chaining your future to your past—that hinders you."

He steps forward, toward me, bringing the crowd with him.

"But every so often, a star is born from beyond the universal chaos, free from the call of a single constellation, who can see things as they truly are. She needn't be a conqueror or a genius, but in possession of a soul so pure that she shines a light on the human condition for us all. And when her brightness reaches so far that all are illuminated by her splendor, we see each other as we truly are.

"The presence of such a star amongst us is like the light before the storm. We are forced to see our own reflection and decide who we are. We have been shocked into a growth spurt, and so we must evolve. Once touched by such a light, one cannot abide the dark. And in that instant when the brightness blinds us, when it wraps around us so that even those in power look away for a moment, forgetting to jealously guard it—the universal clock takes one tick forward.

"The tick echoes in Space's silence like thunder, and now everyone sees the light for what it truly was: *Lightning*. And by the time this storm moves on, what was present will become past, and what was already past will fall another notch farther from us. That is how today becomes *Tomorrow*."

He's in front of me now, and as he holds out his hand for mine, everyone is watching.

I place my palm on his, and the whole room breaks into applause. Aquarius leans in and says, "Welcome to Tomorrow, Wandering Star."

24

THE NIGHT IS A WHIRLWIND of introductions.

Most members are in their late teens and early-to-midtwenties, and they've already distinguished themselves in some way. Stan was right: This Party is as elitist at it gets. But now that I know Aquarius's plans, I understand why.

He's admitted he's a scientist, and since he has no idea what's on the other side of the portal or how long it will take to find a habitable planet, it makes sense to fly with a young and talented crew. I also understand why he wouldn't want to go alone: He may have the soul of a star, but he's in the body of a man. He has no chance of surviving on his own.

Besides, it's in an Aquarian's nature to be a social architect—he wouldn't derive any pleasure from surviving alone. He'd rather lead the chosen to a new world.

"This is Barg," says Aquarius, introducing me to a Scorp with red eyes.

"It's an honor to meet you, Wandering Star," says Barg, trading the hand touch with me.

"I visited your House," I say, angling my head curiously. "I've found most Scorps want nothing to do with the rest of us."

"I know." He hangs his head a little. "I've never fully fit in there. When I was eight, I used to talk about how I wanted to meet people from other Houses and see more of our solar system, and my classmates started calling me a *Riser*. I was bullied by my family for lacking proper Scorp pride, until I finally gave in and stopped dreaming of other worlds."

"I'm sorry that happened to you," I say.

"But then I watched you speak of a united Zodiac, and I saw how people's hatred and ignorance didn't stomp out your fire—it only fueled it." He raises his chin. "And I felt hopeful for the first time in years."

Blaze wraps an arm around Barg's shoulders. "You're home now, brother," he says, and Barg beams.

"Barg has synthesized a regenerative formula from an underwater plant on Scorpio that can reverse years of aging without any of the painful procedures of the Geminin methods," says Aquarius proudly, and Barg's face seems to radiate even more light as he basks in the Guardian's admiration. "We're honored to welcome him to our family."

"I heard my House mentioned," says a new voice, and I turn to see a curvy, tawny-skinned Geminin with glowing red lips.

"Imogen," says Aquarius, tipping his head to her. He cautiously pans his gaze to me and back to her and says, "I hope the two of you might consider beginning anew tonight. In the spirit of the unity we're trying to foment, I think we should leave the past where it belongs and move forward unburdened by the pain we've suffered to get here."

"I agree," I say, relishing how easy it is to lie now that my heart is mute. I hold out my hand for the greeting, all the while envisioning stabbing her with a bayonet the way I did to Corinthe. Then doing it again and again and again.

She'll pay for what she did to Nishi.

I smile sweetly.

Imogen merely bumps her fist with me, but I don't let her stop there—I make her go through the whole elaborate choreography of knocking knuckles, bumping elbows, and slapping hands. She seems annoyed that I've co-opted her greeting style, and my smile widens.

"So you're coming with us?" she asks in a dry voice.

"I'm here for Nishi," I say, opting to use the truth to lie again. "The leader you admired so much that you shot her. I'm not sold on anything else yet."

"And you're fine with leaving Hysan and the others behind to die?" she presses.

"No—but if there's one thing you taught me, it's that I can't save everyone. I have to let my friends choose their own fates."

Everyone nods approvingly.

"What about you guys?" I ask, turning the question around on them. "You're fine with leaving your families behind?"

"Party members may bring their families if they wish," says Aquarius. "It's painful enough to leave everything we know—but it would be inhumane to leave behind our loved ones. There are still spaces free for your friends, if they should change their minds."

I'm speechless but not for long, because more and more Zodai are coming up to introduce themselves. I keep expecting to see Ezra and Gyzer, but they're not here. Eurek mentioned they haven't been able to breach Aquarius's inner circle yet, so they're probably not high ranking enough to be invited tonight.

"Rho!"

A couple of people come over, and I recognize the girl who called out to me as Geneva of Taurus, Blaze's date to the royal ball. "The youngest Promisary in Taurian history," I say, and she burns bright red.

"Wow, you remembered."

Blaze also looks pleased, and he flashes me a smile.

"Hi, June," I say to the Libran in the medical hover-chair who's come over with Geneva.

"*Helios*, is my face as red as Geneva's right now?" she asks, and everyone laughs. "I can't believe you remembered me!"

I notice a third person behind them, and when I see her, I'm thrown back in time to Helios's Halo, the first time I ever saw the Zodiac come together, the night before we set off in the armada.

"*Mallie?*"

"Okay, you can stop showing off your memory now," says Blaze, and everyone chuckles once more.

"It's an honor to see you again, Wandering Star," says the Aquarian Mallie, and her orb-like eyes make me think of Pandora. "Have you designed your universe yet?"

"My universe?"

"Everyone's submitted a prediction of what they think the universe we land in will be like. Come do yours quickly before they're all screened," she says eagerly, and I'm led away from the group toward the back of the space where there are a dozen enclosed white booths. She hands me a black drink in a shot glass.

"Take as long as you need. You paint a detailed picture in your mind of what you think we'll see as soon as we go through the portal, and when the image is clearest, down this drink. Whatever you envision will imprint on the walls around you for an instant and then disappear. But it will be re-created holographically in a different terminal so that you can actually see what you imagined."

"What is it?" I ask, sniffing the telltale licorice scent of Abyssthe.

"It's an aural tonic."

My hand shakes at the name. Immediately, I see Stan and Aryll, when they tried these at the Taurian festival after I was given the title of Wandering Star.

Stan's soul projection was an image of our home and our family.

"I don't want to," I say, handing it back to her. She looks confused yet curious, and before she can press me, I ask, "Did Pandora tell you about the Tomorrow Party?"

I remember Pandora mentioning it was Mallie who inspired her to sign up for the armada in the first place.

"No, I haven't seen her since Helios's Halo. I came because I Saw myself joining. I'm one of the newest members."

"You *Saw* yourself?"

"Back when we could still See visions in the Psy . . . yes, I foresaw that I would join this Party. And of course it's not surprising to find you here. If I had any doubts about any of this, they're quieted knowing it has the Wandering Star's blessing."

She bows her head slightly, and I feel a line of sweat forming along my hairline. I know I should keep quiet, but my conscience is shouting at me, and I can't help myself.

"Mallie, the truth is I don't—"

The place falls silent so abruptly that I stop speaking. I survey the room, and I gasp along with everyone else as hundreds of silver bubbles are released at once, and they float into the air above us. As they glide gently along the ceiling, I see that each one contains a different imagined galaxy. They're everyone's visions of various universes.

Colors and shapes swirl within each bubble, and as they dance together they create an ethereal and entrancing light show. I see blue worlds and new constellations and unknown stars, and I think of the earthlings when they washed up on Phaetonis, tiny and tired and terrified. I try to picture how it would feel to peel back a layer of existence and glimpse a larger universe.

And I'm ashamed to admit that a small part of me is intrigued.

✦ ✦ ✦

When the party ends, Aquarius offers to escort me back to my room. While we walk, I want to say something about the people I met, something that will make him think I'm coming around so he'll tell me more about the portal. But instead I ask, "Why are you being so open with me? How do you know I'm not a double agent?"

I instantly bite my lip, regretting my bluntness, but to my shock, Aquarius laughs. "Because you're so honest that you can't help yourself," he says, still smiling. "Also because trust is a two-man operation: It won't work unless we both feel it. And, more to the point, because you trusted me with a secret about your mother even when you didn't know who I was or whether I was trustworthy."

"How can you expect me to listen to anything you say when just yesterday you had my world destroyed and my family and friends killed?" I try to keep the hatred out of my voice, but it's an especially impossible feat when I'm walking through sand-and-seashell halls that are constant reminders of what he's taken from me.

He stops and faces me, just a few feet shy of the east wing staircase. The light under my skin is feeble since by now the drink's glowing effect has mostly worn off, but Aquarius still shines as luminously as a full moon in a black sky.

"I am sorry for your pain, Rho."

I'm not sure he's capable of remorse, but even if it's a performance, the apology sounds real.

"I understand this makes me a monster in your eyes, but you are the first human whose life I have felt invested in. I don't think I ever fully understood the weight of mortal emotions until now, when for the first time in millennia, I have something to lose.

"Ophiuchus . . . he was different." His voice grows so soft that it feels steeped in memories. "He had a vulnerability to him, a special ability to access the purest parts of his core, and it enabled him to think as both man and god."

"Do you regret what you did to him?" I chance.

He doesn't answer, but he doesn't look upset so much as pensive. He starts climbing up the polished pink staircase, and I follow a step behind.

"I don't see the past the same way you do, so I don't have regrets," he says as we spiral upward.

"What do you mean?"

"There's a reason there are no lines in nature. There are only circles. O's. Everything works in cycles, even immortality, because everything is happening simultaneously: We are all growing, we are all dying. *Time* is just how we give small moments meaning. It contextualizes our existence. But it's like a railing on a staircase: On its own, it's nothing."

We step off the spiral stairs and pad down another sand-and-seashell passage. "We're so obsessed with the future and the past," he goes on, "but neither of them truly exist. There is only the present. *This moment.*"

His words send me plummeting back in time, to the day Mom left. Stan's story about a little girl who got lost on a new planet and wouldn't let herself enjoy it because she couldn't let go of her home. And a different Stantonism jumps out at me from that story instead of the usual one.

Every second is a choice we make.

Aquarius stops outside suite number nine, and the concerned way his sunset eyes sweep my face makes me think of Dad the morning after Mom left us. He looks like a parent trying to explain something difficult to their child.

"Rho, we can never be free of Time's rule because none of us are truly immortal—not even the stars in the sky. But life *is* forever. Existence is eternal. Your compassion for your fellow humans is admirable, but the Zodiac's thirteen skills were divided among thirteen worlds, not people, because it's the survival of the species, not individuals, that matters."

I don't want to think that way.

I could never think that way.

So I cut directly to what I want to know. "What will you take for Nishi's freedom?"

His brow furrows and his expression grows puzzled. "I don't understand. I want her to survive the Last Prophecy. I want her to come with us. Don't you?"

Blood drains from my face, and I drop my gaze as I spot the flaw in my plan. If I push too hard for her to go, I'm showing him my hand—so I need to soften my approach. "I think she needs to get away from here and decide for herself . . . or she'll always feel like a prisoner."

"What do you propose?"

"I'd like to send her back to our friends. Who knows, maybe she'll even bring some of them over to our side." I didn't mean to say "our side," so I stop speaking abruptly when I hear the words fly from my mouth.

Aquarius nods like he's considering my viewpoint, but then he grows resolute again. "This is war, Rho, and exceptions are weaknesses. If those opposing us regain Nishi—a powerful ally—then we must have something equally powerful in exchange."

From the calculating way he's looking me, I can sense another test coming on, and I steel my gut.

"You asked me what I want from the Luminaries earlier. I'm after a prophecy they're concealing from me—a vision of the universe that awaits us through the portal. I will grant you Nishi's freedom if you can procure me another Luminary."

"But—you said Mom didn't know anything. Why would a different Luminary know more?"

"Your mother is a hard woman to get information from."

That's the understatement of my lifetime.

"How do you know this prophecy even exists?" I press.

"I've come close to Seeing it enough times over the centuries that I know it's there, and it's being blocked by the same power that lets the Luminaries hide from me in the Psy. Any time I've been able to locate a member, I Psyphon their Psynergy to try to glimpse the prophecy, but so far it hasn't worked."

He Psyphoned Mom.

My stomach hardens with disgust at the violation even as my chest relaxes with relief that she wasn't physically tortured.

"Until now," he goes on in his velvety voice, "I'd only ever managed to Psyphon former Luminaries or recruits I've been able to capture before they vanish from existence, but I've never read a current Luminary, one who hasn't severed her connection to the society. Tomorrow morning, I want you to convince your mother to reach out to them and ask them to send someone to help. Once the Luminary arrives, you have my word that one of our ships will fly Nishi anywhere she wants."

I cross my arms. "How can I trust that when you've already gone after everyone I love? Why would you suddenly leave her alone now?"

"Haven't you noticed that my army hasn't attacked the Zodiac in months?" he asks, his expression open, his gaze direct. "We haven't even bothered tracking down your resistance because it's not our concern—those are Zodai affairs, and this solar system won't exist for much longer. I swear to you that we will not go after any of your friends or the Zodai they're working with—and I would not want to risk your friendship or your trust by betraying you. The only two beings in the Zodiac I want by my side are already here . . . Ophiuchus and *you*."

"Sir."

I spin around to see that Blaze has just come up behind us, and I spy something wild in his eyes when he looks at me, but he quickly tames it down when Aquarius turns. I wonder if he heard the last thing the Original Guardian said.

"I'm coming, Blaze." Aquarius gives me a small bow. "Good night, Wandering Star."

He starts walking away.

The longer I take to make this decision, the longer it will take to get Nishi out of here because they'll have to fly to Aries first. And I don't want my best friend here another moment.

If—or *when*—Aquarius discovers I'm a double agent, he'll definitely use her to punish me. I need her as far away from here as possible.

Gamba's face forces its way to the forefront of my mind even though I've been trying to push it back this whole conversation. Am I really considering handing over an innocent girl to the same monsters that tortured and traumatized me and Nishi and Mathias and Pandora?

But I already committed to free Nishi, and that's what I intend to do. Gamba can take care of herself. She chose to be a Luminary, and she took herself out of hiding to get involved—but Nishi never asked for any of this. She was only sticking by my side.

She's endured enough.

"*Wait*," I say, and Blaze and Aquarius stop by the staircase. I swallow, hard. "I know where you can find another Luminary."

25

I TRY TO GET SOME sleep like Nishi suggested, but when blue dawn light streams in through the window, I'm not sure I ever even closed my eyes. Sitting upright, my head is heavy on my neck and my left eyelid feels twitchy.

I open the room's closet and pull on a royal purple pantsuit. I'm not surprised to find it fits me perfectly; I might as well be living in the virtual world of a holo-game. Or the nightmare world of the Sumber.

These theories are further reinforced when I step out of my room and glimpse a familiar face with a headful of braids.

I instinctively take off after Ezra as she rounds the corner, but when I get to the end of the hall, she's gone. I follow in the direction where she disappeared, peeking into a couple of alcoves and common spaces, but they're all empty.

I turn to head back when I notice a door that's slightly ajar, like someone thought they closed it but the lock didn't catch. I swing it open slowly and slip inside a large supply closet with a few rows of shelves that house cleaners and maintenance tools.

"Ezra?" I call out, looking between the aisles. Is she hiding in here?

There's a small door at the back of the space, and since it's also ajar, I pull it open. It's an empty lavatory.

I give up and turn around to leave, but I stumble back at the sight of a grave, golden face glaring at me.

"Hysan—*what are you doing here?*" I whisper when I've recovered my breath.

Since it takes him a moment to react, I know he's a hologram—but his transmission is remarkably clear, like he's only a few rooms over. Ezra must be projecting his call through whatever special comm device they designed.

She set me up.

The anger lining his frozen face transforms into raw concern when his hologram activates. "Rho, are you okay?"

I'm guessing I look like total sharkshit.

"I'm fine."

"Has he hurt you?"

"Hysan, stop," I snap, staring at the shelves behind him to avoid his gaze. "Why do you even care after what I did to you?"

"Believe me, I had every intention of being angry," he says, and even without looking, I can feel his eyes scrutinizing me closely. "But you're not yourself. Ezra's working on a plan to get you and Nishi out of there—"

My stomach flips itself, and I say, "We don't need Ezra's help. I've got it handled."

Every part of me itches to warn him of what I've done, but I can't form the words, and I can't bear to see his face when he learns how badly I've betrayed him and everyone else on Phaet. There's no coming back from what I've done.

But I wasn't coming back anyway.

"How?" he demands. "What's your strategy?"

"Why is it so hard for you to trust my decisions?" I shoot back.

And since I know he's going to try to sweet-talk me into opening up, I strike first.

"I told you I wasn't ready to lead the armada when we were on the Hippodrome stage, but you insisted I was. It didn't matter to you that I didn't want that role. Then you pushed me again on Centaurion by recruiting an entire army of teens using my name without even asking whether or not I wanted the charge! And on Phaet you claimed I would lead us, but you were totally fine with censoring my reports. You've gotten so used to being the puppeteer behind the scenes that you treat me like one of your androids!"

He flinches at my words like they're projectiles, and before he can defend himself, I say, "I know what I'm doing. And if you really believe all the things you've said about me, then you'll respect my choices."

I walk through him to leave, and since he's a hologram, he can't follow. "Rho—wait!"

But I don't.

I have no idea how private that conversation was—if he and Ezra haven't been caught yet, then maybe we weren't either. But what if Aquarius knows all about Ezra and Gyzer, and he's just playing along for now? Either way, I'm pretty sure nothing I said could make Aquarius distrustful.

I hope.

When I get to the medical bay, breakfast is brought in for us. Nishi wants to hear all about dinner and everything that's happened since the Sumber. So I tell her in detail about Pisces, from my reunion with Mom to what went down in the Cathedral, and then I fill her in on the Artistry Pride. I pretend I can't talk about the Zodai army so I won't give away their headquarters, even though I already have.

Whenever Nishi asks about the deal I struck with the master to be here or begins to reference an escape plan for breaking out, I change the subject to remind her we're being watched. We visit my quarters in the afternoon, where there's a matching purple suit in Nishi's size waiting for her. We take turns showering, and right as we're flipping on the wallscreen to check the news, there's a knock on my door.

"Nishi's transport is here," announces Blaze.

"What—what's going on?" Nishi turns to me in alarm.

"We're leaving," I say. *It's half-true.*

We follow Blaze downstairs, and I keep up with him so that Nishi can't try talking to me. We step outdoors onto a hangar deck in the back of the vessel where there are three small black bullet-ships, but only one of them has its engine running.

Aquarius must have spacecraft positioned all over the galaxy if he picked up Gamba this quickly—and they must fly exceedingly fast.

"What's happening?" Nishi asks me again, and she doesn't bother keeping her voice down. She knows something's wrong, and I know I can't hide it from her anymore.

I pull her in for a hug and whisper all I dare say into her ear. "I can't go with you yet. Find Hysan. Tell him it's Dark Matter that will make the sun go dark, not the portal, and that's why Aquarius is leaving. See if Hysan can disprove it."

She stares at me in awe as we pull apart, her long, slanted eyes bright with disbelief. She seems ready to cause a scene, but something in my expression shuts down the impulse, and instead she says, "Be careful, Rho. *You might not like yourself when this is over.*"

They're the same words I said to her on Aquarius. I nod like I agree, but she doesn't realize that for me it's already over.

The only reason I'm still fighting is for *her.*

Tears fall from Nishi's eyes, but mine don't even burn. I'm so numb that it shouldn't be hard to convince Aquarius I'm ready to embrace his plans. I just have to be like one of those razed buildings Blaze described that's ready to be designed anew.

I'll make this up to Nishi and Hysan and the others when I uncover Aquarius's exact plans for opening the portal. It's the last thing I'll do for them before I join my brother.

"Please go, Nish," I say softly. "I woke up and left you in the Sumber when you asked me to—now I'm begging you to do this for me."

She stares deeply into my eyes, and I see something there that I haven't felt in a long time.

Trust.

"Hold on for me the way I held on for you," she says, and she squeezes my hand before turning to Blaze.

She spares him a dark glare and flashes him an obscene gesture that almost makes me smile, and then she starts walking toward the Marad soldier that just disembarked from the bullet-ship. But before she gets there, another soldier deplanes, struggling with a bound and gagged Gamba.

Nishi freezes in horror.

She turns to me with an unfamiliar expression, one completely different from the way she just looked at me moments ago. Like she's seeing me clearly for the first time.

"Rho, what did you do?"

I spin and walk away, unable to see that look on Nishi's face.

"RHO! How could you? You knew I wouldn't want this—not at this price! *How could you?*"

She keeps shouting at me, but I move onward, unwilling to hear her screams. She can hate me if she wants, but I got her out—that's all that matters. Her fate is finally in her own hands.

When I'm back indoors, I know Blaze is following me up the stairs, and after a moment I say, "I'm fine."

"Would you rather I leave you alone?" he asks.

"Can you take me to Ophiuchus?"

"Aquarius is the only one who sees him."

I figured as much. I guess that means it's time to face my other childhood monster.

"Then take me to my mother."

✦ ✦ ✦

Mom is in one of the smaller rooms belowdecks, but she has her own private lavatory and wallscreen, so it's no prison cell. Her eyes look tired and her skin is sallow, but I see no visible bruises.

I was expecting to feel sorry for her—so the anger takes me by surprise. The moment I step across the threshold, I feel like I've crossed a barrier that releases some of the darkness that's been keeping my numbness in place.

My brother died protecting a mother who stopped protecting him ages ago. A mother who lied to us every day of our lives, then abandoned us, and then replaced us with a child she chose to love honestly.

"Rho!" She springs off the bed and throws her arms around me. "Are you okay?"

It feels foreign to be hugged by her, and my arms don't know what to do, so they stay limp at my sides. After the moment we shared on Pisces, I thought the worst between us was over—only it turns out she wasn't being completely honest. I wonder if she was ever planning on telling Stanton and me about our *sister*.

"Why are you here?" she asks, pulling away, her brilliant blue eyes studying my face as she probably analyzes the possibilities.

"Gamba told me Aquarius is going to use Ophiuchus to activate the portal. Is that all you know, or do you have more information?"

She takes a step back.

The shadows under her eyes deepen and her mouth tightens, and she suddenly looks about twenty years older.

"How . . . how do you know Gamba?" Her voice fades to a whisper midsentence.

"Who is she?" I ask, and I'm fleetingly proud of how my voice stays even and my heart keeps quiet.

"*Where is she?*" demands Mom.

Her weakness for this girl makes me furious, and the anger is so near my throat that I can't keep from lashing out. "Aquarius offered me a way to save Nishi—a trade for a *less broken* Luminary. So I offered him your *daughter.*"

Pain explodes across my cheek, and I lose my balance and topple into the wall.

She slapped me. I cup the left side of my face, water welling in my eyes as I glare at her. My breaths are loud and shallow, and my vision grows red.

As Mom glowers back at me, a feral expression comes over her face that I've seen before. On the day the Maw bit Stanton. It's how she looked an instant before she destroyed it.

"I was wrong about you," I say between breaths. "You *are* capable of motherly love. I guess it was just *me* who never inspired it in you."

Her eyes grow icy, and even the temperature in the room seems to cool. We stand in silence for a moment, until she finally speaks.

"You were never mine to love." Her tone is surgical and direct, just like the militant mother I remember.

"It was always my purpose to deliver you to the stars."

✦ ✦ ✦

When I leave Mom's room, I don't know where I'm going.

My old childhood nightmare keeps replaying in my mind: The Maw that bit my brother bites me instead, and Mom never swims fast enough to save me. Every time, I'd wake up right after the monster's red eyes turned icy blue, but it's only now I understand why.

Mom rescued Stan from his fate that day, but she couldn't rescue me from mine. In fact, she built me for it. Like an animal bred for slaughter.

My whole life I assumed *she* was the problem, but what if I was wrong? What if it was me?

Mom loved Stan, she loved Dad, she even loves this Gamba girl. But my own mother couldn't love me. Even when I was just a baby, she understood that loving me could only lead to suffering.

After all, loving me got Stan killed. Loving me got Mathias captured. Loving me got Hysan jailed. Loving me got Nishi Sumbered—

"There you are!"

I turn at the sound of Blaze's voice, and I realize I've no idea where I am. "Hurry—there's a news transmission coming in that Aquarius wants you to see."

I let him pull me forward, and we cut across to the ship's west wing, where we enter some kind of briefing room where the Original Guardian is standing with a few of the Party members I met last night. At first I'm relieved Imogen isn't here, but then I see who's on the screen.

Hysan is broadcasting from Phaet with a wall of a dozen Zodai— including Eurek, Mathias, and Pandora—behind him.

"My name is Hysan Dax," he says, "and I am the true Lord of House Libra."

My mouth is arid and my knees start shaking. I feel Blaze's arm on my lower back, and I vaguely realize that he's helping me stay upright.

"Lord Neith is an android I built with my predecessor, Lord Vaz, because I became Guardian at eleven years old. I always knew there would be a day when I would share my story with you, but I hoped it would be in a time of peace, not war. I'm sorry for lying, and I will give you all the answers you deserve, but first we must *survive*."

Since I avoided looking directly at Hysan's hologram earlier, I didn't notice that a layer of stubble has crept across his face again. His golden locks look messy and unwashed, like he's been running his fingers through them often.

"None of us can escape the truth any longer," he goes on, his voice gaining volume. "The Zodiac is in danger. I understand you'd rather be living your daily lives and pretending the threat isn't real because it hasn't touched you yet, but believe me, this darkness will spread. If you choose to remain ignorant and uninvolved, you may be kissing your kids goodnight before a morning that never dawns."

He pauses, and the passion that infected him earlier flickers for a moment. But when he speaks again, he sounds as determined as before.

"Now I have a second confession to make: I broke the Taboo."

I'm definitely not holding myself up anymore, but Blaze doesn't complain as I shift all my weight to him.

"Wandering Star Rhoma Grace and I have been romantically involved since she became Holy Mother. I know her better than anyone. Which is why you have to believe me when I tell you that *she has been compromised.*"

My head is buzzing and my body grows feverish. I barely feel conscious as Hysan says his final words:

"Rho Grace is working with Ophiuchus and his master. *She is a traitor to the Zodiac.*"

26

"SHUT IT OFF," COMMANDS AQUARIUS.

I lost them all.

They hate me.

I hate me.

"Leave us."

I'm somewhat aware of everyone exiting the room and Blaze gently depositing me in a chair.

"You're not alone, Rho," says Aquarius, reading my soul as he sits beside me. "Letting go of yesterday is the most painful part of today. I don't blame your friends for wanting to hold on to what they've always known, nor should you. But you've evolved past them now."

Part of me is listening, but most of me isn't even here. It feels strangely freeing to be abandoned by everyone and everything I've ever loved, and I wonder how it will feel to die. Will Aquarius kill me himself when he learns I'm a double agent, or will he order Blaze to do it?

"Don't give up," he says softly. "You're in the embrace of a new family now. All you have to do is embrace us back. And if you'd like, your mother and the new Luminary can come with us."

I've rescued Nishi, I've cut ties with my friends, and now I have one final task. I have to uncover Aquarius's plans and feed them back to Hysan. Then he can save the Zodiac, and I can finally let go.

"Come with us *where*, exactly?" I ask, trying to pull myself together for one final push. "You keep talking about this portal through Helios, but we don't even know where it leads or that we won't get burned for flying too close to the sun. So if I'm going to go with you, I need to hear an actual *plan*."

"I understand. You proved your loyalty to me by giving up the location of the Zodai's resistance, and now it's my turn to be completely open with you." His pink eyes are glassy and clear, his voice velvety soft. "After the original earthlings settled the Aquarian constellation, I hid their spaceships and had them stored on planet XDZ5709."

"Black Moon?"

He nods. "That's why I needed the permit of exploration from the Plenum. I've been sending teams of engineers to upgrade those ships for centuries, but with all the attacks lately, my shipments from various Houses were starting to attract too much attention."

"Why not build new vessels?"

"Because I know nothing of the tunnel through Helios save for the fact that *these* ships made it through. I've outfitted them with the latest technology, and we have a full fleet ready to go. But on our way to Black Moon, you and I will make a pit stop to activate the portal."

"*Where?*"

"The Thirteenth House."

I blink. I'm certain I didn't hear him correctly.

"Opening the portal requires an enormous release of energy," he explains. "The death of a star. Ophiuchus must be killed on his own soil."

Ochus knew.

He told me on the way here that Aquarius would sacrifice him.

How much more has he been keeping from me?

"You know everything now," says Aquarius, offering me the one thing I could never get from Hysan or Ophiuchus or Kassandra: *transparency.*

Now I understand how Traxon must have felt when Blaze approached him at the royal palace and offered to tell him the truth, just moments after I refused to open up to him.

"Rho, I believe you're ready, the Tomorrow Party believes you're ready, so the last person you have to convince is yourself. You're no good to any of us if you give up or give in. I want you to want this the way you wanted to stop Ophiuchus months ago."

Aquarius's eyes glow like the holographic globes from last night's party, and I see a new universe of worlds swirling in their depths. "I want you to believe in yourself and in your species' future. I want you to care about what lies beyond that portal, to be excited to discover what kind of planets we'll find." Even his skin is blazing with light, and more than ever he looks like the fallen star he is. "Will they be ruled by scientific laws we've never heard of? Will we meet new life forms? Will there be colors and dimensions and substances we've never seen before? Will we find the answers to existence's deepest questions?

"I know you feel finished," he says, his voice becoming more Crompton-ish than godlike. "But if you're willing to depart from the mortal plane, then you've already abandoned your friends. So don't hold yourself back on their account."

Abandon. That word has always tugged at me, ever since childhood. But that's not what I'm doing. I'm helping them. I'm here gaining Aquarius's trust so I can relay his plans to them.

I've given up on myself, but not on my friends—I will always root for them.

"Death is a given, Rho," he says soothingly. "It will happen whether you race into its arms or inch toward it slowly. It's waiting for you, and it's forever. Even *I* cannot hope to grasp eternity.

"You have all of existence to spend in Empyrean—so why hasten to get there? It's coming no matter what. Life is like a candle's flame: It waxes and wanes until the wick is devoured, and then it's gone. You have so much more light to give; don't extinguish yourself."

I don't say anything, but I don't get the sense he expects me to.

"I have to take a trip to planet XDZ5709 to inspect our fleet for the final time, and then the Party will commence shuttling passengers over while I come back for you and Ophiuchus. Once the portal's been activated, we'll regroup with the others, and at the end of the seventh day we'll be on the first ship through Helios."

This is it.

He's leaving, and I know his plan. It's my chance to let Hysan and the others know what's going on.

And yet, instead of feeling energized for this last act of my life's story, I feel less sure of myself than ever. I've been pretending to be on so many sides that I'm not sure which one I'm really on anymore. Just like the artists of Artistry, I can't tell where my performance ends and the real me begins.

"Rho, this is the only chance humanity has. I know you want to believe the whole universe can be saved, but it can't, and I'd rather *some* survive than none at all."

What if he's right? asks a small voice in my head.

I may disagree with the violence of his methods, and I may regret the fact that he didn't warn us sooner so that we could have saved more people, but does that mean that everyone in the Zodiac should die just because Aquarius handled things poorly?

Even after I relay this information to the Zodai, I still don't see how they will be able to stop him—the master is too smart, and he's been planning this for too long. But maybe I can at least try to convince them to listen to Aquarius and give him a chance.

It has to be worth a shot.

"I know I'm asking more from you than anyone else," he goes on, "but I wouldn't ask if I didn't believe in you. Time is running out, and I need to know where you stand."

I feel like a once-finished puzzle that's just been disassembled into thousands of tiny pieces. I used to be so sure of what was right and what was wrong . . . and now I don't even know who I am.

"Okay," I say at last, and I know as I speak the words that I'm no longer acting. "I'll go with you."

He knows it, too, because the light in his eyes blazes back, full blast. "Then I'll see you in three days, and we'll set out for the Thirteenth House."

✦ ✦ ✦

"*Wake up.*"

I'd just fallen asleep when I'm shaken awake. The sun isn't even up yet, so my room is in complete darkness as I shove someone's fingers off my arm.

"Get off me!" I wave my hand over my head, in front of the bed's headboard, and it lights up revealing a teen girl with a mahogany face and a head full of braids.

"What did you do?" demands Ezra. "*What did you tell him?*"

"What are you talking about?"

"I haven't been able to reach Hysan since I led you to his hologram—our signal's jammed. Did you tell Aquarius anything about Gyzer and me?"

"Of course not. Hysan probably cut off communications after his broadcast as a precaution. Calm down."

She glares at me. "Gyzer was so certain you were just playing Aquarius. He insisted you'd turn around and come back to us the moment you learned his secrets. But looking at you now, you seem just as brainwashed as all the other elitists here."

"You don't know anything about me," I growl. Just like Traxon and Skarlet, Ezra is able to bring my anger out better than most people, and before I can think anything through I command, "Go commandeer us a bullet-ship."

Ezra crosses her arms defiantly. "What for?"

"What do you think for? We're getting off this planet."

✦ ✦ ✦

Just minutes later, Ezra and I meet Gyzer in the hangar deck, and we board one of the Party's black bullet-ships. They're a third the size of 'Nox and so dark that they probably blend in perfectly with Space.

"It's one of Aquarius's own designs," Gyzer says as we climb onboard. "It's the fastest interplanetary vessel in the Zodiac. We'll make it to Aries in just about fifteen galactic hours."

Hysan would probably flip for this ship, I think, and then my gut clenches at the thought of facing him.

The spacecraft's interior is as black as its exterior, and it has no cabins— just two individual sleep capsules built into the concave walls.

Even though we encountered no obstacles leaving, we're quiet until we've crossed the atmospheric barrier, which takes an alarmingly short amount of time. The three of us stay seated in the front of the ship, in a forced silence, until Gyzer finally turns from the control helm and clasps his soulful eyes on me. "Are you lost?"

"Aquarius confided his plans to me, and now I'm going to let the Guardians know . . . like I always planned to do," I say, sounding defensive even to myself.

"But you're no longer on our side." Though he phrases it like a statement, it sounds like a question.

"It's not about sides," I say, shrugging. "It's about *truth*."

"And you believe the Last Prophecy is unavoidable?"

"Can you prove that it's not?"

"I think you're brainwashed," says Ezra, doubling down on her accusation.

I wait to hear what Gyzer thinks, but he doesn't offer anything more on the subject.

"I just hope they don't shoot us down when they see we're escorting a *traitor*," Ezra goes on goadingly. "You *really* pissed Hysan off. I didn't know Librans could even get that angry—"

"That's *enough*," I say, glaring at her.

"Says the double-crosser," she snaps.

"Silence." Gyzer's mournful voice fills up the small space. He looks from Ezra to me and says, "Infighting is *not* productive."

"Gy—"

"Don't," he warns Ezra, cutting her off midwhine. "If we can't unite now, we'll fail. If you can't rise above your anger, you're choosing death for all of us."

Ezra looks genuinely shamed, and her eyes roll down to the floor as fire torches her cheeks. Gyzer turns back to the controls, and a heavy silence swaddles us until Ezra looks at me and says in a much lighter tone, "So Hysan's Guardian of Libra and Lord Neith is an android?" She shakes her braids in awe and leans in. "Show me the Ephemeris that Saw *that* twist coming."

✦ ✦ ✦

It's bright out on Phaet when we near The Bellow, the red sun barely visible at this time of day. "Something looks wrong," says Gyzer as we descend toward the landing pad—which is full of identical black bullet-ships.

"*You*," says Ezra, turning to me with fire in her eyes. "You told him the camp's location!"

Aquarius lied to me.

He brought a whole fleet of ships here, and they never left.

What if the Marad arrested everyone? What if they forced Hysan to give that broadcast? What if something's happened to him or Nishi or Mathias or Pandora or—

"You're *landing?*" asks Ezra, rounding on Gyzer in shock. "What the hell are we going to tell them?"

"That we're here on Aquarius's orders," I hear myself say. "I'll tell them he sent me here to try to recruit my friends."

Neither Ezra nor Gyzer disagrees with my plan, so we land. As soon as we disembark, half a dozen Marad soldiers approach us. When they see me, they pause.

"We're here on Aquarius's orders," I say disdainfully, and I keep walking purposefully toward the entrance into the mountain. Ezra and Gyzer keep back a respectful distance, playing the role of my Tomorrow Party guards.

Inside the mountain, there's no flurry of activity, no healers or Majors going about their work. The silence and emptiness is gloomy, and my blood chills with every step. When I eventually manage to find my way to the central area with offshoots to the hospital and The Bellow, I follow the scent of fresh air toward the smallest of the tunnels, the one that leads to Phaet's secret golden forest.

I unlock the door, and we step into a cool, sunny day. Ezra and Gyzer survey the view around us in awe—since they've been with the Party this whole time, they haven't seen this camp yet—but I hurry down the stone ramp, horrified by what I might have done.

Everything looks too still, and I scan the three fortresses ahead, wondering where my friends are.

"Which of the three holds the greatest power?" asks Gyzer, coming up beside me and staring at the same view.

"The first one has a communal reading room—"

"But barely anyone is getting visions these days," Ezra interrupts.

"The second one has our arsenal of weapons," I say nervously.

"But Aquarius already has weapons, and his are more destructive," says Gyzer.

"The third one is intelligence."

We look at each other, and immediately we head in the direction of the final Fort.

"We have no idea how many of Aquarius's people are in there," I say as we run. "We need a strategy to take back control of the camp."

"We can start a fire," suggests Ezra.

"A fire?"

"That will probably give us all the time we need," says Gyzer approvingly.

"Time for what? What are you guys talking about?"

"Just distract people," Ezra tells me. "When they're not looking, we'll do the rest."

There's no one guarding the fortress's front doors, and the planet's emptiness is becoming disturbing—but then I step into the large entrance hall full of semiprivate cubicles, and a Party member I vaguely recognize freezes.

"Oh—I didn't realize he'd sent you!" she says, seeming reassured by the sight of Ezra and Gyzer with me. "This way." She waves for us to follow.

We head down a passage that spills into a large room with a high-arched ceiling and so many windows that sunlight illuminates every corner. A dozen Marad soldiers outline the perimeter, surrounding thirteen people seated around a massive wooden table.

My heart punches my chest, and I'm as shocked to hear it as I am to see the sight before me.

Hysan, Nishi, Mathias, Pandora, Skarlet, and Eurek occupy half the seats. The other half are taken up by six Party members. The woman in the thirteenth chair has her back to me, but I recognize her sultry voice.

"We really need to get going, so for the last time: Agree to join us, or we'll lock you up along with everyone else on this planet. You have right *now* to decide."

"Captain," interrupts the Party member who escorted us. "We have a very important visitor."

Imogen turns around slowly, and when she sees me, her glossy red mouth curves into a smile. Then she spots Ezra and Gyzer behind me, and her smirk widens.

"I knew it!"

27

"KNEW *WHAT?*" I ASK AS dryly as I can, hating that my heart has chosen this moment to resurface when now, more than ever, I need to be cool and calculating. "Aquarius sent me here to try to convince them. He had a feeling you'd fail."

"Right," she says, standing on her spindly heels, her red lips still stretched in a too-confident smirk. "And you just happened to come with two of your former generals?"

"*You* were my former general," I say, softening my voice to try a gentler approach. "If your devotion to the cause is complete, why distrust ours?"

"Because Aquarius has no idea you're here," she says, resting her hands on her waist, near where she holsters her Sumber. "If he did, I would have had warning of your arrival. I have a big imagination, but even I have a hard time believing you've changed sides."

"I'm here to convince them to join us," I say, trying to keep my disdain for her out of my tone. "Whether or not you trust me makes no difference— we both still want the same thing."

Her copper-flecked eyes narrow shrewdly, and then her hands drop down at her sides. "Okay . . . go ahead."

She grips the back of her chair and pulls it out for me. "*Convince them.*"

I have no idea what Ezra's plan is or how soon from now it will take effect, so I just have to keep everyone interested. I sit down and for the first time make eye contact with my friends.

Nishi glares at me, and she looks as livid as the two Arieans beside her. Mathias is stoic and Pandora is concerned, but I only glance at them peripherally. It's Hysan my gaze locks on to.

His features are as unreadable as Mathias's, but where the latter's face is more of a familiar military mask, Hysan's is almost expressionless. His hair is scruffy, his cheeks look sunken in, and his lively eyes have dulled, like his inner sun has set for good. Yet his shoulders are squared and his jaw is hard.

I suck in a deep breath, trying to call up my words from the place behind my booming heart. All thoughts of what I would say abandoned me as soon as I saw I'd have a Tomorrow Party audience. But I also didn't realize how hard it would be to sit across from the family I deceived—and the Guardian whose secret I revealed.

Even though I'm not looking at him, I can feel Eurek's furious scowl burning into my head, like his ember eyes might have real firepower. It seems the Guardians are all in support of making sacrifices for the greater good, just as long as it's not *their* House doing the sacrificing.

"This isn't about sides," I begin, wishing I possessed some of Aquarius's or Blaze's magnetism. "*This is about our species' survival.*"

"Our ancestors came through a portal to get to the Zodiac because they, too, had a difficult decision to make, and the fact we're here at all is a testament to their strength."

Hysan looks unmoved, and I swallow and try again. "Aquarius is offering us a way out of this galaxy because Dark Matter will soon swallow our sun. I don't like the way he's gone about this any better than you—let's not forget that Pisces and Cancer sacrificed more than any other House," I add, and I venture a look at Eurek. His jaw stays clenched, but his eyes dial down their flames a little.

"Right now what matters is that we not spend this time fighting but communicating. We have to face the reality we have, not the one we want—"

"Do you really think he's working this hard to convince us to come along because we'd make a fine addition to his Zodai collection?" Hysan's voice is so soft, it's more of a murmur, and yet every word is perfectly audible.

"The six people you're closest to on this base also happen to be the Tomorrow Party's only recruitment priorities. Doesn't that strike you as strange?"

Skarlet pipes up. "I'm not close to her—"

But Hysan continues speaking in his low voice, cutting her off. "He wants *us* because he needs a way to control *you*."

Imogen cackles and perches on the table in front of me. She looks at me and says, "Now I'm not even sure *you* know what side you're on!"

"Look who's talking!" snaps Nishi, panning her scorching amber gaze to Imogen. "Aren't you the same person who came to Centaurion pledging to help defend Sagittarius from terrorists, before joining those same terrorists and shooting me into a world of my *nightmares*?"

"You broke into Blaze's files and planned to betray us," says Imogen. "But I didn't kill you, and I spared you from worse pain."

"*Worse pain?*" Nishi's face is red with outrage, and she looks at me then back at Imogen. "*Do you understand what those nightmares were like—*"

"The other pellet would have been worse," says the Geminin, and for the first time she doesn't seem to be toying with us. "To dream of everything and everyone you long for . . . only to lose it all. Again. And again. And again . . . Trust me, that takes longer to recover from."

"You're right, I really should be *thanking* you," snarls Nishi as she shoots to her feet. Only now she's directing her anger at me.

"*What's wrong with you?* Don't you realize that if Aquarius really cared about us, he would have warned the Zodiac of this danger ages ago, so we could have had time to prepare? He's only kept it to himself because *he's* the one causing the Last Prophecy—he's choosing who's worthy of survival and dooming the rest of our species!"

"He's saving us!" interjects Imogen. "He's doing what natural selection would do on its own—he's just expediting it."

"And you're fine with that justification for mass extermination?" Nishi is still looking at me.

"He doesn't have to justify himself!" shouts Imogen, at last losing her cool and leaning forward on the table toward Nishi. "We don't question the stars, *Stargazer*. We *obey* them—"

A bullet suddenly whizzes between Imogen and Nishi and hits the middle of the table, bursting into flame on contact with the wood.

Everyone dives away, and as I drop to the ground, I look up at Ezra and Gyzer. They're standing back to back with their wrists raised and Arclights aimed at the soldiers. Within seconds, they've systematically taken out every single Marad member in the room before the soldiers could even fire their Murmurs. I remember them being the best shots of anyone on Centaurion, but this is on another level—I've never seen anyone shoot like that.

Someone yells for them to stop, but I don't know who it is. Across from me, Mathias has also dropped to the floor, and he's shielding Pandora's and Nishi's bodies with his own.

When the sound of scuffling behind me cuts out, I finally sit up and look back: Eurek has single-handedly disarmed the six Tomorrow Party members, and Skarlet has Imogen in a headlock.

I hear a hissing sound and I whip around to see Hysan using a fire freezer—a small silver gun that turns the flames on the table to icy curls of smoke.

"You're going to love The Bellow," says Skarlet into Imogen's hair. "It's the perfect place to spend the Zodiac's last days."

She and Eurek tie up the Party members, including a now-speechless Imogen, but Hysan is stalking over, looking furious.

I brace myself for his words—

"You killed them!" he shouts at Ezra and Gyzer. "You shot the Marad soldiers dead!"

"Yes, and we saved your asses!" Ezra shouts back. I'm surprised she's glaring back at him just as furiously, since she usually idolizes him, but then I recognize her expression as the same one Brynda wore on Pisces. Ezra's hurt by Hysan's secrets.

After his broadcast, everyone who ever thought they were Hysan's friends realized they were wrong.

"So Party members get rounded up and arrested, but Marad soldiers get a bullet to the head? Does that sound like justice to you?" he demands. "I gave you weapons that aren't lethal, and I know you have Tasers—"

"There's no room for second-guessing in war," says Eurek, cutting off Hysan's outrage. "We need to free our camp from the Marad soldiers holding our Zodai hostage in the other fortresses. Once we've rounded up all the prisoners and locked them up in The Bellow, we'll address next steps."

His gaze stops on me and hardens. For a moment I think he's going to recommend locking me up in The Bellow, too, but suddenly Pandora comes over and links her arm with mine. "Where should we meet you?" she asks Eurek.

"My chambers. I'll arrange an urgent holo-meet with the other Guardians so we can debrief them." He looks to Skarlet, Ezra, and Gyzer. "We'll either have to take out one Fort after the other, or we can split up into two teams of two."

"I have another idea," says Hysan, and they grudgingly look to him. "You can access the central air cooling systems in the main halls of both structures, where I planted Bind bombs weeks ago, in case we ever needed them." He ignores the way the air tenses when he admits to more secrecy. "They'll disperse through the air in seconds, and everyone in both fortresses will fall asleep. Then we can arrest the Marad soldiers and explain everything to the Zodai when they wake up."

Bind is House Libra's signature weapon: a wispy white powder made from ground-up minerals found deep within Kythera's core that seeps quickly into a person's muscular system and puts the body into a deep sleep. Librans are immune to small doses of the powder from breathing in trace amounts of it every day.

Eurek finally nods. "That's a better plan," he says, biting off each word like it's bothering him. "How do we set them off?"

"I'll go with you—"

"I know how to activate them," Ezra cuts in. "You stay here and sort this shit out." She waves between Hysan and me.

"Let's go," says Eurek, marching out with his team, and then I'm left alone with Hysan, Nishi, Mathias, and Pandora.

With the others gone, Pandora lets go of my arm and returns to Mathias's side.

Only Nishi meets my gaze, and I almost wish she wouldn't. There's so much disappointment on her face that I flash back to the day at the International Village after I was stripped of my Guardianship—the day the Zodiac turned against me. Only this time, it's the people I love most looking at me like I'm worthless.

"I understand if you want to lock me up in The Bellow," I say, and at this, Mathias's indigo blue eyes shoot up to mine. He doesn't look stoic anymore . . . he looks sad.

"I came back because I don't want you guys to die," I say, realizing I'm speaking the absolute truth for the first time in a while. "If you choose death, then I'll die with you. But I'm begging you to reconsider, for your sakes."

Nishi blows out an exasperated breath and brings her hands up to her face. "You are so infuriating, Rho. You sold your soul to save my life—did you seriously think I would thank you for it? You really think I could live with that price?"

"I'm sorry, Nish—I just couldn't bear the thought of you in there another moment—"

"*You* couldn't bear it. Because it was something you had the power to fix! I was someone you could still save, unlike Stan."

The air blows out of my lungs, but new oxygen doesn't replace it. "I know I could have handled things better, but that doesn't matter now, because I brought you the information you're looking for."

Mathias and Nishi's expressions shift from upset to curious, and they edge closer. "You know how he's going to open the portal?" asks Nishi, and I nod. "*How?*"

"He's—"

"Why tell us if you think Aquarius is right?"

Hysan is still speaking in a low voice, the facial hair swallowing his usual glow.

"Because you have the right to decide your own fate."

"I don't want you to tell us," he says resolutely, crossing his arms. "Not unless you're with us again."

"*Hysan*—" starts Nishi.

But to my shock, it's Mathias who rests a hand on her shoulder and says, "Let him talk."

Hysan's green gaze locks onto mine like a lie detector. "Why did he attack your House and Virgo and Gemini?"

"To redirect the Dark Matter that was being disturbed by Guardians Origene, Moira, and Caasy's experiments."

"That's not true," says Pandora, stepping forward. "We worked it out. We believe it was to destabilize the Psy."

I turn to Hysan questioningly, and he explains. "Aquarius's plans were too close to fruition to risk the Zodai foreseeing them. So to disrupt the Psy, he had to take out its anchors—today's greatest seers. Since a Guardian's strength comes from their Psynergetic connection to their world and their people, he had to take out chunks of these worlds' populations to truly weaken the Psy's pillars."

"But the Dark Matter—"

"Is only a threat because Aquarius is a threat," says Hysan. "The signs he's been seeing started showing up the moment he set on this idea and began taking steps toward it."

I look to Mathias, who's nodding in agreement with Hysan, and I remember what he told me when he taught me about the Collective Conscious: *In the brain, everything is relative. Most of us don't intentionally try to misrepresent anything—but the lies we tell ourselves, the truths we repress, the things we conceal in the physical realm . . . they inform reality in the Psy. Even in an abstract dimension, ideas built on flawed foundations will fail.*

"Aquarius is the one bringing the Zodiac down," says Nishi. "He's a star with free will—that gives him too much power."

Everything I've learned over the past few days starts to connect in my mind, forming a new constellation of facts. Ophiuchus was meant for that role because he was Unity: It went against his very nature to think of just himself. The other Guardians weren't offered the same power because it would have had a corrosive effect—they weren't meant to hold it. By interfering, Aquarius has distorted the astral plane.

He may be all knowing, but Nishi's right: He's not just a star—he's a star with *free will*. And he keeps making the same choice as the humans he looks down on: He can't let go.

He's created his own darkness.

"Which came first: fate or free will?" I say softly, quoting Aquarius. Mallie said she joined him because she Saw herself joining the Party. But who sent her that vision?

He manipulates the Psy by creating the visions he needs, Hysan said when Crompton revealed himself as the master in the Cathedral. He's been recruiting people for his plan by altering their destinies.

"I say free will," says Nishi, and the anger in her face is gone, like a candle that's been blown out. "What do you say?"

"Aquarius is going to open the portal by sacrificing Ophiuchus on his own soil," I blurt out.

All four of them stare at me in awe.

"We have to go back for him," I say. To save the Zodiac, we have to save Ophiuchus.

28

I SPEND THE REST OF the day repeating everything I learned from both Ophiuchus and Aquarius over and over and over again.

Hysan creates a fake hologram of Imogen to field any incoming calls from Blaze or Aquarius. Funny how identity forgery used to be our greatest threat, and now it's a survival strategy. The five of us spend the rest of the day in meetings with the Zodai teams on Phaet, and the other Guardians drop in holographically at various times, until everyone has been filled in.

The plan is for a small team to fly to Artistry on 'Nox and rescue Ophiuchus and Mom and Gamba before Aquarius returns from Black Moon—which means we have to go immediately.

It turns out Ezra already sent Hysan the blueprints for the black bullet-ships, and he upgraded 'Nox's engine to equal their speed—plus, given that the Libran Talisman is built into its brain, *Equinox* has the only Psy shield that stands a chance against Aquarius. Hysan shared the master's engine designs with every House, so hopefully our whole fleet will be able to match the Marad's speed. Once we have Ophiuchus, we'll Veil from the Psy and hide him on *Equinox* until the Zodai have defeated Aquarius.

Hysan, Mathias, Nishi, Pandora, Skarlet, Ezra, Gyzer, and I board *'Nox*. Since we'll be leaving Leo with three more people onboard, we're pushing *'Nox*'s oxygen limits, but Hysan assured us that it would be okay. I go straight to my usual cabin, but I stop before turning the handle. Last time I slept in there, Stan was with me.

I look down the hall to see that Nishi is doing the same thing. Her old room is haunted by Deke's holo-ghost.

Mathias and Hysan are watching us.

"Why don't you both take my cabin?" says Hysan, and without waiting for our answer, he carries his things into the last and smallest room, the one near the storage hold, and shuts his door.

Nishi and I look at each other, and we wordlessly slip inside the main cabin. When we're alone, she just stares at me. Even though she's furious, I can't help feeling relieved that she looks so much more like herself now than she did on Leo.

"You Cancrians will be the end of me."

"I'm sorry, Nish."

She shakes her head and exhales. "The Marad soldiers let me call my parents from the ship, as long as I didn't disclose any details of what had happened. I figured they must have been going through their own night-mares over my disappearance. But when my mom answered, she and my dad were wasted at some party on Taurus. They thought I was traveling and had no idea anything was wrong."

She rests a hand on my shoulder and squeezes me hard. "I hate what you did, Rho. But I love *why* you did it."

I pull her into a hug, and as I hold her tightly to me, I'm just happy for this moment to be with her. I have no idea what will happen when we try to break out Ophiuchus. Nor do I know how we're going to keep him hidden from Aquarius now that I've given up the only secret location in the Zodiac. But I can't take another breath without her forgiveness.

"I'm so sorry, Nishi," I repeat.

"I know," she says as we pull away, and our fingers link together. "But I almost lost you."

"I almost lost me, too."

The ship begins its ascent, and we lie back on the bed, still holding hands, and stare up at the ceiling as we exit Phaet's atmosphere. From our silence and labored breathing, I know we're both thinking of the last time we did this, with Deke, right after he asked Nishi to marry him.

"I miss him, Rho."

"Me too." I squeeze her hand, and we don't say anything for a long time.

Unsurprisingly, Nishi breaks the silence with an annoying question. "So what's going on with you and Hysan?"

"Nothing."

"He seems heartbroken."

Skarlet's face flashes in my mind, and I wonder if even now, in a different cabin, she's making her move. "He'll find someone new."

"So you're over him?" She rolls onto her side to face me, and half her face is buried in the mattress. All I can see is one slanted amber eye and strands of dark hair.

"I can't think about him right now," I say, rolling to my side to face her, too. "I just want to focus on saving the universe."

Her lips curl into a smirk, and her eye grows smaller. "That should be your anthem. *Introducing the Zodiac's Wandering Star*"—her voice goes higher and becomes musical—"*She's not here to date, she's here to save the Zod-i-ac!*"

I shrug. "I kind of prefer *Trust in Guardian Rho*."

Her gaze is glassy and her smile wilts. "I wrote the new lyrics the same night you took off to Gemini to warn them about Ophiuchus, right after that meeting with your Advisors."

"What happened afterwards?" I whisper.

"A lot seemed to happen simultaneously. As soon as the song and your story got out, we received requests from schools *everywhere* asking us to come perform. We jumped on the chance to take a chartered trip to the Zodai University on Capricorn because its students have the highest test scores of any school in the Zodiac, so I figured they'd lend us the most credibility."

"I remember seeing something about it in the newsfeeds on Virgo."

Nishi smiles again, but this time the good humor doesn't reach her eyes. "Drowning Diamonds' first and last tour."

"And you went without your drummer," I say, trying to lighten the mood.

Her gaze is distant, like she's reliving the trip, and she says, "That was when Deke finally confessed his feelings."

"Tell me about it," I say softly.

"After playing the song onstage, I told the students the lyrics were real. I warned what happened to Cancer would spread unless we came together now, behind you and House Cancer, and united as one Zodiac. The school administration ushered us off the stage pretty fast after that."

Her voice is low and musical. "Kai went to bed early, but Deke and I decided to explore Tierre's terrain, and we hiked up a mountain peak where we could see the most varied tapestry of topographies we'd ever seen. The whole horizon was silver, and we took turns pointing out volcanoes and jungles and oceans. Then we lay back and stared up at the stars, and I just knew we were going to sleep out there and not go back to the room, and in that moment I decided that if he didn't finally own his feelings, I would just kiss him and see what happened. That's when he said, *I'm in love with you, Nish.*"

"What?" I ask, my eyes going wide.

"It gets better. Then, he told me that when he watched me speaking in defense of Cancer onstage, he realized how ridiculous he'd been to ever care about our Houses. He said even though we'd been born on different planets, the stars had always meant for us to find each other—that was why they'd given us each one half of the same soul."

She can't speak for a while, and neither can I. "I just remember this amazing rush of happiness," she whispers, "like every House in the Zodiac could explode, and the darkness still wouldn't be able to touch me. And the thing that scares me most now is never feeling that way again."

"You will—"

But I give up my weak reassurance when she narrows her eye. We both know the truth. Neither of us will ever be that happy again because that universe is gone.

✦ ✦ ✦

I wake up holding Nishi's hand. I only slept a little—the flight time on the wallscreen says we've been traveling for just six hours. But it's more sleep than I've gotten since the Sumber. It's the first time I've felt safe in too long.

Now that I'm up, I'm afraid to close my eyes again, so I decide to stroll through the ship. Everyone is probably still sleeping, so it's the perfect time to stretch my limbs.

As soon as I'm in the hall, I hear retching. It sounds like a girl, so it's Ezra or Pandora or Skarlet. Hoping above all that it's not the Ariean, I knock on the cabin door. "Are you okay?" I call softly.

No one answers, and I try the handle, which is unlocked, so I peek inside. There's nobody in the bed, but the lavatory door is open. On the floor is Ezra, curled around the toilet.

I shut the door behind me and come over to her. The lavatories don't fit two people, so I sit down in the doorway and ask, "What's going on?"

She groans, and an empty glass bottle rolls away from her on the floor. I pick it up and sniff the lingering licorice scent. "I didn't think Abyssthe had the same hangover symptoms as alcohol."

"I always have a . . . reaction to it," she mumbles into the cold ground.

"Can I get you anything?"

Her groan sounds a lot like the word *go*.

I keep expecting my feet to push up from the floor and carry me out of the room, but there's no pull on my muscles to move. "If you've got the hangover part covered, maybe I could help with whatever the original problem was—since Abyssthe seems to have failed you?"

"Get out," she moans, more clearly now.

"Should I call Gyzer instead?"

Her head jerks up, and she winces in pain from the movement. "*No*," she says, more pleading than threatening. "Don't tell him."

"Okay, but if you're not going to talk to him about it, then I think you should talk to me. You don't even want to be my friend anymore, so why should you care what I think? Just use me to extract whatever poison is eating at you because you're no good to this army if you fall apart."

"You really have . . . a way with words," she says, taking a breath midsentence.

"If you're too nauseous to talk, I'll wait with you."

I lean back against the doorframe and shut my eyes, nerves suddenly fluttering in my own belly. We've made the calculations, and we'll be arriving the evening of the third day. Aquarius could be back at any moment.

The plan is for me to return to the Mothership with Ezra and Gyzer by my side and tell Blaze we went to visit my friends so I could convince them, but they wouldn't budge. I'll act put out that he and Aquarius never told me Imogen would be taking over the camp, but since I also think my friends are headed to their deaths, I'm probably less angry and more sad. If Blaze wants to verify my story with Imogen, he'll have to communicate holographically since they have a Psy shield up at the camp, and our fake Imogen will confirm my report.

"I never killed anyone before."

Ezra's words hit me like a bullet, and my eyes fly open. Not just from pity, but shock that I didn't pick up on her pain earlier.

She can't be older than sixteen. Of course she's never shot a person.

I edge closer and carefully brush her braids away from her face. There are tears on her mahogany cheek, and I reach up into the wall dispenser for a fresh, warm face towel. When it comes out, I wait for it to cool a little, and then I gently mop up her skin and neck, which is drenched with sweat.

"I didn't even think of them as human," she says softly. "I just pictured monsters behind the masks." Her brown eye rolls up to meet mine. *"Risers."*

I nod without saying anything so I don't interrupt her confession.

"Hysan was right. I didn't think they were worth saving." She hinges her elbow beneath her to rise to a sitting position, and I slide back a little to give her space.

"They looked exactly like the targets in the holo-games. . . . They didn't feel real. I didn't touch them."

Tears roll down her cheeks again, and I offer her the towel. She takes it from me and blows her nose. We sit in more silence, until she says, "I thought being a double agent sounded like a dream. Hysan asked me to really think through what this would be like, but I ignored him. I thought I could pretend to be a Party member without losing myself, only . . . now that I've killed people, who am I?"

I sigh and say, "I wish I could be helpful, but as you yourself pointed out on the way to Phaet, I don't have a clue who I am anymore either. I think Eurek was right that we can't second-guess our choices in war. We have to stay present and keep moving forward. Our worlds may have raised us to think of Risers this way, but it's now up to us to change the narrative."

"But the Party members have been able to justify so much death, and I thought—it didn't seem like it could be that difficult, since they're not all bad people. A few of them I'm even friends with. How can they be okay with this?"

"I don't think anyone's okay with this," I say, suddenly feeling exhausted and ready to go back to sleep. I stand up and reach down to pull Ezra to her feet, and I help her into bed. As I'm zipping up her cocoon, I whisper, "I think win or lose, war makes victims of us all."

29

I WAKE UP STARVING.

Nishi's eyes open a moment after mine do and she says, "I'm hungry." Someone's stomach rumbles, and I can't tell if it's hers or mine.

We head to the galley to hunt for food or anything that resembles it, and we find Skarlet and Gyzer at the table. A plate stacked with what looks like sheets of brown levlan sits beside them, but they're completely engrossed in their arm wrestling match. Their faces are tight with concentration, foreheads shiny with sweat, uniform sleeves bulging with muscles.

Skarlet wins.

"Best two out of three?" he asks.

But she looks to me in the entryway and says, "Maybe later." Then she rises from her seat in one sinuous movement and knocks her rock-hard arm into mine as she edges past. I bite down on my lip to keep quiet.

Nishi approaches the levlan-like food and sniffs it. "What is it?" she asks Gyzer.

"Dried Ram meat. An ancient warrior recipe that Majors would take with them to battle. It's good," he adds, seeing Nishi's suspicious expression.

She lifts a sheet with both hands and brings a corner to her mouth and nibbles it. She chews a few times, frowns, swallows, and then her eyes grow wide. "Mmmm!"

She bites into it more eagerly now, and I reach for a square of my own. It has a hard, rubbery texture, and a smoky, spicy taste, and it's absolutely delicious.

"I'm going to check on Ezra," says Gyzer, standing up.

"Is she okay?" I ask, wiping my mouth with the back of my wrist.

"She had a headache last night, so she didn't sleep much. Going to see if she liked the Ariean food."

When he leaves, Pandora strides in. "Mathias has just taken over the controls, so Hysan returned to his cabin," she says, like it's a normal way to greet people.

"Great," I say, shrugging and ripping off another bite.

"Hysan is alone," Pandora goes on, sitting across from me and picking up a sheet for herself. "Maybe you want to talk to him and clear the air?"

Nishi frowns at her. "Hey, lavender eyes—if I thought being direct would work, don't you think I would have tried it?"

"Sorry," says Pandora, daintily covering her mouth with a hand as she chews.

"I've known her for a third of our lives, so take it from me," Nishi goes on, still talking about me like I'm not here. "She has to choose to leave her shell on her own—if you try to reach inside to pull her out, she'll only burrow deeper."

"Since you clearly don't need me here for this conversation, I'm going to wash up," I say, stuffing what's left of my meal into my mouth and heading out into the hall. But rather than tunneling to the back of the ship, where I could run into Hysan, I visit the nose.

Mathias must hear my footsteps when I cross into the front of the ship, because he looks back from the control helm and catches my eye.

"Rho." His voice is musical, and since he seems pleased to see me, my stomach relaxes. "How are you?"

"Finally slept," I say, sitting next to him at the helm and trying not to think of all the previous pilots I've sat beside in this chair.

"I'm glad," he says warmly, but his kindness only makes my guilt feel more pronounced.

"Mathias . . . aren't you mad at me? I betrayed you and everyone else who believed in me. I broke out Ochus, I didn't trust you guys with my plans, I even changed allegiances—"

"But look at where you're sitting now," he says, his baritone voice as soothing as ever. "Whatever happened, whatever you did—you never gave up on us. Even when you thought you'd changed sides, you still came back for us."

"But I—I gave up an ancient Ariean secret, I traded Gamba for Nishi, I—"

"You made sacrifices for us, ones that only you could make," he says, his tone still lacking judgment. "No one in Zodiac history has ever been put in a position remotely similar to yours, so none of us can know what it's like to be you. It wouldn't be right to judge."

Something shifts in my chest, and I have to open my mouth to pull in air. "How is it you can always forgive me?" I breathe.

For shutting the airlock door. For choosing Hysan. For keeping secrets.

"Because by now I've accepted that I'm just stuck with you in my life," he says, and when I meet his gaze again, I see that he's smiling.

"I think that's the second joke I've ever heard you make."

His brow wings up. "You're keeping count?" he teases.

I give him a small grin, and I notice the line that cuts down his neck and disappears beneath his collar is less striking. It seems to have faded a little.

The sight of his scar sends me plummeting back to the Sumber, and my grin starts to feel forced as I remember the Mathias I met in my nightmares. "So when did you and Hysan start getting along so well?"

"It was something your brother told us on the way to Pisces," he says, his expression dampening. "He told me and Hysan that if we really cared about you, we'd put the petty stuff aside and get along."

I don't tell him I overheard that conversation because the wall of ice in my chest seems to be shifting further, but I still manage to say, "I'm sorry about your sister. I didn't understand before, but I get it now."

"I'm sorry, too," he says, his voice low. He looks down, and I realize I've just made him relive those awful emotions. Sadness makes him seem younger, and I can't help but think of the Cancrian boy with turquoise eyes and sandy hair who helped me through my heartache once.

"You know . . . we could be substitute siblings," I say, channeling Deke's spirit.

Mathias's midnight eyes meet mine again. "You're already my family, Rho."

He pulls me into his chest for a hug, and even as my frozen heart welcomes his warmth, part of me wants to push him away for fear of my glacier melting. Mathias lets go suddenly, and I worry he feels the chill in my chest, but he's staring past me. I twist around and see Hysan watching us.

He turns back the way he came, and I chase after him.

"Hysan, wait," I call out, but he doesn't slow down until he gets to his cabin, and I hurry in after him before he shuts the door on me.

"I didn't mean to come between you two," he says, jaw clenched. He turns his back to me as he leans over a small desk and starts tinkering with one of his devices. There's barely enough space for one person in this tiny cabin, and my lungs feel like they're working extra hard to pull in oxygen.

"I want to apologize," I say, clearing my throat. "I know what I did on Phaet, how I betrayed you, it was—"

"The worst thing anyone's ever done to me," he finishes, twisting to meet my stare. "But at least now you can understand why I find it so hard to trust people."

His lips curve into a colder version of his centaur smile, and it seems more like the cruel smirk of the Hysan from my nightmares.

The powerlessness I felt in his presence then fuels my outrage now, and I snap, "Maybe if you'd been honest with me from the start instead of lying about the master's location, I could have trusted you with *my* plan! Did you think I wanted to do this alone? To go against my friends? If I'd thought any of you would have trusted my idea, I would have confided in you!"

"You're right, Rho." Hysan straightens and fully faces me, and I have to tilt my head up to look at him. "We've made hard choices, and maybe some of them were mistakes. But we can't judge that right now."

His leaf-green eyes pierce into mine. "Some decisions can't be evaluated on their own because they form part of a larger design. On Libra we have a saying about people who can't get past a single bad choice in their lives: *They can't see the constellation for its stars.*"

"But—aren't you mad at me?"

"Of course I'm mad!" He's so close that his breath tickles my face, and his gaze locks on to mine with an intensity that makes it impossible to pull away. "I'm mad because this isn't you. I don't think you ever woke up from that Sumber, and every day I feel you slipping further away. And the worst part is you're not even *trying* to come back to us."

With half a step, he bridges the small space between us, his voice dropping with every word. "I know this feels easier for you, but we need you here." I can almost sense the glow of his golden skin and smell the cedary scent of his hair when he says, "*I need you here.*"

His mouth moves in close enough to raise my body temperature. Only the heat doesn't warm me—it *burns*.

"I'm sorry," I whisper, stepping back lest the fissure in my glacier expand and expose me. "I just don't feel the same way anymore."

Hysan flinches, like my words have physically hurt him. "I'll leave you alone then."

And just like that, we're through.

30

WE ENTER LEO'S ATMOSPHERE VEILED from the Psy and hidden from view.

The plan is for Hysan to keep *'Nox* aloft while the rest of us pile into the two small black bullet-ships we tugged with us from Aries. There's one on either side of *Equinox*. Ezra, Gyzer, and I will take one, while Nishi, Skarlet, and Mathias take the other. Pandora will stay on the ship with Hysan. She's our *designated survivor*.

If all fails, and Hysan has to land, she'll eject in the escape capsule into the arms of the Zodai fleet that followed us from Aries and is waiting out of sight. They're our Plan B. I wanted Nishi to be the designated survivor, but the look she gave me when I suggested it made me shut up.

Thanks to Ezra's spying on Aquarius's technology, we know we can't use Veil collars on the Mothership because we'd still trigger motion sensors. So Mathias, Nishi, and Skarlet dress up in Marad uniforms we stripped off the dead soldiers. Since we still don't know how to remove the masks, even in death, the Dreamcasters on Phaet spent the day creating convincing replicas—they look just like the real thing. It's strange seeing the three all-white uniforms and knowing that behind those porcelain masks are people I love.

Well, technically two people I love and one person I tolerate.

Ezra winces when she looks at them, and Gyzer rests an understanding arm around her.

Our fake soldiers are going to rescue Mom and Gamba—since they won't look conspicuous transporting prisoners—while I get Ophiuchus. He and I, on the other hand, are bound to stick out, so if we get caught, we're counting on Ophiuchus's superstrength to help us like it did on Aries.

Hysan explained that Aquarius has been on the mortal plane for three millennia, so his body is human. But Ophiuchus has spent millennia amassing Psynergy in the astral plane, and now he's more star than man. He's become a kind of hybrid who attracts too much Psynergy—half the time it strengthens him, and the other half it leaves him drained.

We're going to be too many people to pack into the tiny bullet-ships, so Hysan will have to land 'Nox in the hangar deck to pick us up. By then, our cover will be blown, but hopefully it won't matter because we'll be back in the air.

We have exactly forty-five minutes to pull everything off. Hysan handed out yellow wristbands that will buzz once when there's fifteen minutes left, twice when there's five minutes left, and three times when he's here. Anyone who doesn't make it to the hangar deck in time will have to find another way off the planet.

Our team of Marad soldiers lands first; Ezra and Gyzer gave them directions where to go, and since Mathias is familiar with the Mothership, he shouldn't have trouble navigating it. Once Ezra, Gyzer, and I land, we dart indoors and cut across the Family Room to the south wing's spiral staircase.

"I was beginning to worry you'd changed your mind."

I turn around, and when I see Blaze I cross my arms like I'm irked. "And I was beginning to trust you—I guess we were both wrong."

He frowns as he strides over from the pale blue couch where he'd been sitting in wait. "What is it?"

"Ezra and Gyzer flew me to Aries so we could try convincing our old friends to join us. Only someone beat me to it."

Blaze exhales heavily and stuffs his hands in his white suit pockets. "Imogen is there for the same purpose as you. She's a little more forceful about it, but her goal is the same as yours or mine—we just want to save Zodai lives. Aquarius told her she couldn't force them to come."

I let sadness fall over me, willing water to fill my eyes, but it doesn't work. I've spent my whole life crying over everything, and the one time I need my tears, they won't come. Still, the expression must be convincing enough without the waterworks, because Blaze sighs. "They said no?"

I nod.

"I'm sorry, Rho."

I shrug. "It's their choice. I'm done thinking about it. I just want to sleep." Then I widen my eyes, like I've thought of something better. "Is Aquarius back? I'd put off sleep to chat with him if he's around," I lie.

"Is that why you were headed to the south wing?" he asks curiously, and I force myself to nod. "Well, he's not here, but he should be returning any moment. I'll let him know you're looking for him. But for now, sleep is a good idea—since we're leaving tonight."

"*Tonight?*" I echo in shock, and Ezra and Gyzer come closer.

"Aquarius says we're ready," says Blaze, his russet eyes bright.

I don't bother trying to return his smile because I know I would fail. So instead I frown and say, "I'll believe it when it happens. *Trust Only What You Can Touch.*"

Blaze nods approvingly. "Always."

Ezra, Gyzer, and I climb up the east staircase instead, like we're heading toward my room. Once we've put enough space between us and Blaze, we cut across to the south side of the ship, toward Ophiuchus's cell.

I try to ignore the squirming in my stomach. I know this feeling because I've already done this so many times before: thrown myself at the stars' mercy by embarking on a life-or-death adventure.

Only this time is different. My pulse isn't racing, nor am I clinging to memories of my loved ones or fantasies of my future. Instead, I'm feeling the anticipation of a spectator who's watching someone else's life unfold and wondering how it will end.

As for myself, I feel *finished*.

I want my friends to survive, and I want the Zodiac to see tomorrow— I'm just not sure I want to stick around for it.

Ezra and Gyzer wordlessly point out Ophiuchus's door, and then they speed away to help the others. Since I don't see any special technology keeping him caged in, I try twisting the handle. It's unlocked.

The Thirteenth Guardian's suite is bigger than mine. The luminous, windowed space I walk into seems to be some kind of antechamber, and there's a colorful spread of food on a glass table. I thought he'd be in a jail cell, but here he is, sitting on a cerulean throw rug, deep in meditation, his radiant snakeskin glowing with health.

His muscles bulge through the lightweight white suit he's been given to wear, and his body looks more powerful than I've seen it, like he's had plenty of time and space to recover his strength. He isn't trapped, because Aquarius knows he's not going anywhere: Ophiuchus has no intention of stopping the Last Prophecy—if anything, he's come to see it through.

"This whole time, you never really chose a side," I say, shutting the door behind me. "You've been playing us both."

He opens his starlit eyes. "I see you've chosen yours."

"You were protecting him." I lean against the wall and cross my arms, squinting into the reddening light of the sunset streaming through the windows. "Even after all he did to you and your people."

"I was protecting you, too." His voice is so deep that it rumbles through me like thunder.

"You lied to me," I say, glaring at him. "You knew exactly how he'd activate the portal. You knew he needed to bring your House back to do it. Then you willingly traveled here to be sacrificed. And in all the conversations we've had in the Psy the past few months, you never said a word about any of this."

"Stars exist to illuminate your path. Not to tell you why you're on it." His inky-black hair is like an oppressive cloud of Dark Matter pressing down on his youthful face.

"Or maybe you just couldn't See which side would win."

Ophiuchus plants a clawed foot on the ground and rises to his full height, towering a few heads over me. "Is that what you think I was doing?" he asks, his voice booming through the room.

I straighten and drop my arms to my sides. "Just tell me the truth for once. *What is it you want?*"

"Same thing I've always wanted."

"*Unity?*" I ask, scoffing. "Your beloved Aquarius destroyed any semblance of unity we ever had—"

"And you humans are so much better?" he growls, and the glass windows tremble. "I've watched you from the beginning. Why is your species so deserving of a tomorrow? What have you learned? How have you grown? You're still the same petty, greedy creatures you've always been."

"Maybe we could have aspired to more if our stars hadn't failed us!"

His murderous eyes flash to mine, and I hear my heart starting up. "You let Aquarius get the best of you, and you were too weak to even accuse him." My pulse pounds harder with every word, so I throw everything I have at him. "You're pathetic! What kind of *god* lets his power get taken from him and dooms his people to suffer a maniac's twisted rule just because he's too scared to get his heart broken—"

My lungs run out of air as Ophiuchus lifts me off my feet and shoves me into the wall, pinning my shoulders there with his fists. His mouth is inches from mine as he says in a low voice, "I know what you want from me. I know who you need me to be. But have you even considered what it's doing to me to treat you this way?"

"You've done far worse," I say, my breathing choppy. "And why should you care? You only needed me around to end your despair, and now you have Aquarius for that."

"You've made bad choices," he whispers, his cold breath blowing on my face. "You are not the first. But you can still make new ones."

"And what—what if I just wanted it to end?"

My mouth is dry and I can barely believe I'm saying the words out loud. "Would you offer me the same courtesy I once offered you?"

Even though I'm literally in his hands, he looks at me helplessly, like I'm beyond his reach. His voice dips, and he speaks in the same intimate tone I heard him use with Aquarius—like we're equals. "I need to know you can come back from this."

Before I can stop it, I feel the revulsion showing on my face, and I spit, *"You want me to forgive myself because you want to be forgiven, too."*

I sound aghast. "You really think you can come back from all you've done? Because you can't." His eyes widen slightly, like some part of him actually thought he stood a chance of being forgiven. "You've murdered whole worlds—don't you get that? You're a *monster!*"

His knuckles press into my shoulders with such force that I'm certain bruises are blossoming beneath my tunic. His starry eyes go supernova and his snakeskin darkens until even the room seems to dim, and he looks like the monster every child in the Zodiac was raised to fear. *The darkness we created.*

Terror makes my heart beat faster until it's all I hear, and I feel Death's presence like a shadow that's just entered the room.

"*Tempting*," he growls, "but I would hate to end your torment prematurely. Not when you have so much more suffering to endure."

The pressure in his grip eases a little, and at last I see his threats for what they've always been—*empty*. He's not going to end me. I'm still too powerful a game piece to trade amongst him and Aquarius and the Zodai.

I sigh in resignation and ask, "What was it about Aquarius you loved?"

"His light." Ophiuchus's answer is so quick that it's more reflex than reflection. "I fed his fire because I longed to see how brilliant he could burn. I tried to check his flames to keep them from consuming him, but I didn't condemn his thirst for power. . . . I was too in love with his blaze."

Ophiuchus lets go of me, and my feet slide back down to the ground.

"I can't force you to leave this place with me," I say, glancing at the yellow wristband which hasn't buzzed yet. "But if you stay, the whole Zodiac dies. Are you really going to let your world disappear a second time?"

"Aquarius promised to return my descendants to my House. My people may be gone, but he's Seen that my planet has been protected by the Dark Matter, and it will continue to endure after Helios goes dark. *The Thirteenth House is the only world that will survive the Zodiac's apocalypse.*"

That's why Ophiuchus came so willingly.

His House was never in any danger. Which means I have zero leverage to convince him to betray Aquarius.

"So you're going to let him annihilate the Zodiac?"

A shadow crosses his snakeskin face. "I didn't see any of the other Houses rushing to help *my* people when we were destroyed."

"And your solution is to let the star you claim to love become the universe's ultimate monster?" I ask, grasping for anything that might make him reconsider. "Is that what you want for him?"

It's obvious from his hesitation that this isn't what he wants.

And as I study Ophiuchus's expression closely, I recognize a feeling that's completely out of place in our current predicament. It's *hope*.

"*Holy Helios*," I breathe, my eyes widening as I finally understand his behavior. "You still believe he can change," I say incredulously. "You think you can actually save him. *You're insane!*"

Ophiuchus drops his gaze, and after a moment he says, "I'll go with you."

I can hardly believe it, and every cell in my body exhales with relief. I have no idea why he's helping me, but I just want to get going before he changes his mind again. "Great! Let's—"

"But not without my Star Stone."

I stare at him in utter bewilderment. "*You're joking*. Aquarius probably took it with him—"

"I can feel its presence. I was never meant to meet a true death, so to die properly I must destroy it."

My wristband buzzes—we have fifteen minutes left before Hysan lands. "Okay, fine, but we have to hurry."

Ophiuchus leads us out of the room, and I keep close to him as we meander through the Mothership. I hear Party members talking and dragging luggage as they outfit ships for tonight's takeoff, yet somehow we manage to avoid running into any of them. I wonder if the reason we're taking such a roundabout path is that Ophiuchus can sense their Psynergy signatures.

We end up on the ship's top level in the Holy Mother's reading room, the round hall with crystal windows where we met Aquarius when we first arrived. "It's in here?" I ask, staring skeptically at the open space. I don't see anywhere to store anything like a Talisman.

Ophiuchus closes his eyes and concentrates, like he's trying to pick up his Stone's scent. Outside, the smaller Leonine sun is already out of sight, and Helios has mostly set, so the skyline is tinged with pinks and purples. The blue sea beneath us is dark and still, and the horizon is flat on every side.

Aquarius could return at any moment. The Mothership is already crawling with Party members making preparations. And Hysan is going to land in the hangar in under fifteen minutes.

Success is sounding less and less probable by the second.

"Where is it?" I demand impatiently, glancing at my wristband in anticipation of the five-minute warning. "We have to get going!"

Ophiuchus's eyes open, and he looks deliberately behind me like he's spotted the Talisman. I turn to follow his gaze, and I see it, too.

Nestled in Aquarius's hand.

31

"RHO, PLEASE GO TO THE hangar deck and board our ship with Blaze," says the master in a parental tone. "Ophiuchus and I will join you soon."

How will Hysan land if the Tomorrow Party ships are already here?

A pair of Marad soldiers marches into the hall to escort me, but Ophiuchus says, "She's part of this now."

He stares down the masked Risers—*his people*—and they stop moving. They look from one Original Guardian to the other, and then they leave the room without me, apparently obeying their true master.

Aquarius looks impressed, and I'm reminded of the way he and Ophiuchus used to take pride in each other's victories. "It appears you are ready to return to your world."

Now Ophiuchus directs his stony stare at him. "I have been waiting in the room where you left me for a week, and you have yet to come see me."

"I've been busy."

"Will you speak to me now, or did you only bring me back to life to murder me again?"

Aquarius's expression is pleasant, but a muscle quivers in his cheek. "We have a long trip to your House—why don't we speak on the way?"

But Ophiuchus moves toward him, and as I watch his powerful strides I wonder how Aquarius intends to see his plans through since the Thirteenth Guardian physically outmatches any mortal I've ever met.

"After you and the other Guardians assassinated me, my Talisman alone wasn't enough to retain my essence. Especially not when most of my people were gone and the whole Zodiac had forgotten me. I knew someone powerful had to be anchoring my soul."

He stops when he's face-to-face with Aquarius. "The only reason I didn't completely lose myself was the hope that you couldn't let me go. But it was your pragmatism, not your heart, that held on to me."

"All this time and you still try to attach sentimentality to my motives," says Aquarius in a pitying tone. "I may have lived among humans for millennia, but I am not one of them. If I were, I would be unable to push forward with the plan you thwarted three millennia ago."

"That's because you have never given people a chance. You never let anyone in. It's why you have followers but no friends: You can't trust anyone who isn't you. Not even your *soul mate*."

The term seems to anger Aquarius because his velvety voice unsheathes a sharp edge. "I know you want to think you operate from a place of moral supremacy, but let's not forget that you were always guaranteed immortality. You knew the rest of us would perish and you alone would live on, and you were fine with that. It's easy to be grandiose when you have nothing to risk."

My wristband buzzes with Hysan's five-minute warning, but before I can tell Ophiuchus, his booming voice cuts through the air.

"It took me just as long as the rest of you to uncover the secrets of my Talisman!" His words make the crystal walls around us quiver. "When I learned of this power and my ultimate purpose, I immediately set to work trying to harness it to share with others. Had you ever known me to think only of myself?"

Aquarius shakes his head resignedly, like he doesn't want to argue. "Why do you insist on the past so much when it's just dead time? Even *we* do not possess the power to change it."

"If the past poses no threat, why do you refuse to look back?" asks the Thirteenth Guardian, still staring at him intensely.

"Because the present is all that matters. I don't concern myself with anything beyond my control—it's just a distraction."

"If that were true, moments wouldn't leave imprints. Our minds wouldn't make memories."

"Careful, you're starting to sound like an old man," Aquarius cautions him. "Memories are all mortals have left in the end, so they *have* to assign them importance. Otherwise, they'd have to face the futility of their lives and how truly meaningless they are."

"Yet memories were all I had for millennia," says Ophiuchus softly. "And I found them to be loopholes in the construct of time. We can't change the past, but we can relive it. Memories store the answers to the riddles of the present. It's just as the wisest of us, Capricorn, always said."

"House Capricorn's obsession with the past will cost them the future," says Aquarius disdainfully. "It's how I've kept Sage Ferez distracted for months—I made him think I stole a Snow Globe from one of his precious Membrexes so he'd be so focused on uncovering what it was that he'd disregard the present."

I gasp.

He tricked Ferez.

"Would the mere memory of me have sufficed for you?" Aquarius asks Ophiuchus, and for the first time the master sounds as breakable as the rest of us. "When we passed on and you remained with the humans, would remembering me have been enough?"

Ophiuchus moves closer, leaving too little space between them, and though he's physically superior, I'm scared for him. No one in the Zodiac has managed to outwit Aquarius in the history of humanity; I wouldn't get that close to him if I were the Thirteenth Guardian.

Yet the latter seems willing to accept any destiny Aquarius wants to deal him. The original Ophiuchus would probably be appalled by the new him. How far I—

How far *he's* fallen.

"I would never have abandoned you," the Thirteenth Guardian murmurs.

Aquarius raises his hand, and I'm certain he's about to strike—but then the room blackens, and I realize what's happening. He's cueing a memory.

When the darkness lifts, we're in a hall with sandstone walls that seems familiar . . . the Aquarian royal palace. A holographic solar system orbits us, and it's so detailed that it must be projected by a Talisman.

I stare at the brightest blue light that was the crown jewel of the Zodiac, and when I pull my gaze away from home, I notice there's something different about the constellations. There's a large gap between Houses Scorpio and Sagittarius . . . and as I look closer, I see the Dark Matter. It's not near Pisces the way it is now.

Does that mean the Thirteenth House wasn't really number *thirteen*? Was it actually located between the Eighth and Ninth Houses, like this Ephemeris shows?

Beneath the star map is a round table, where fourteen people are gathered. Two of them are identical, so they must be the Geminin Twins. Everyone here looks human, which means this is after the Original Guardians died out.

I scan the faces until I spot an Aquarian with long platinum hair and pink eyes.

"Wandering Star," says the Guardian dressed in red, "we must have your tie-breaking vote. Prophet Draema has foreseen a threat to our galactic sun, and she believes we must create a commission of Zodai from across our worlds to investigate the Dead Zone between Scorpio and Sagittarius and see what we can learn. She thinks they might be connected."

"What's the argument against?" asks Aquarius—and with a jolt, I realize he's this era's Wandering Star.

"The Stridents who've studied that area have discovered a destructive substance they've been calling Dark Matter, and it seems to have latched on to a planet and consumed it," says the Ariean General. "Supreme Guardian Forsythe has foreseen that our team of Zodai will accidentally trigger the Dark Matter's spread and cause the sun's darkening that we're trying to avoid. So, the question is—would investigating it save us or damn us?"

Aquarius nods, his eyebrows pulling together like he's deep in thought. There's no doubt in my mind that he sent his House's Guardian that vision of doom. After a long moment of consideration he says, "I have always believed free will sets fate in motion, so I must vote against."

"Then the matter is settled."

We fast-forward in time, and now the same group is meeting in a different location, and once more the spectral star map hangs over them. I gasp as I take in the deep blue lapis lazuli walls around me—they look like water that's fossilized into stone—and I know where we are.

Cancer.

There's no roof over our heads, just the infinite blue sky I grew up staring at, and I could cry from happiness to be seeing it again.

"This is the first year that the Helios's Halo effect has stopped happening," says a gray-clad woman with delicate features. "It's a sign of the prophecy I've Seen. We *must* investigate," insists Prophet Draema.

A small voice a couple seats over says, "I've Seen something, too."

Everyone looks at the Guardian in olive green—the youngest of them by far—and I get the impression she doesn't speak often. Her brown skin pales as all eyes focus on her. "I think the Dark Matter is connected to a vision I had—"

"Speak up, honey, we're not all twenty," says an old man in black. Nice to know Scorps have always been charmers.

The Taurian looks like she's not going to finish her sentence, but then the Cancrian Guardian—a stunningly beautiful woman who looks familiar—leans into the table and says to the Scorp Chieftain, "If you're going deaf, maybe you should build yourself a better hearing aid."

Then she looks down the table to the Taurian and says, "Take your time, and speak at any volume you'd like, Vecily."

Vecily Matador.

I ogle at the short-haired, almond-eyed Taurian, and then I swing my gaze to the Cancrian beauty I should have instantly recognized. *Brianella Amarise*—the Guardian who led our House into the Trinary Axis.

She's just as breathtaking as history says—her long blue-black curls cascade down to her waist, and her dark skin holds hints of light, making me think of the black opal Talisman. But most striking of all are her crystal blue eyes, which are spiderwebbed with faint lines, like fractured crystals.

I look one seat over to the Leonine man beside Brianella—*Blazon Logax.* He has a square jaw and facial hair, and his arms are covered in tattoos. He looks more like a musician than a politician.

"I've Seen that a Guardian from the past has betrayed us all, and we won't escape darkness until their treachery is brought to light." Vecily says it all in one long whoosh, and from her insecure delivery it's clear that no one at the table takes her vision seriously.

Except Aquarius. He's staring at her through murderous pink eyes.

"Is there anything else before we close this session?" asks the Ariean General, dismissing Vecily completely.

I look to see if Brianella will defend her again, but she's gazing adoringly at Blazon, who's edged his chair closer to hers.

"I'd like to introduce a motion," says Aquarius, and I notice he's watching the Cancrian and Leonine Guardians, too.

Everyone looks to the Ariean General questioningly, and I realize it's probably taboo for the Wandering Star to propose something. When he nods, Aquarius says, "I've come across texts saying the first Aquarian Guardian believed we should each live on our own House, among our own people, so we could focus our efforts on designing our worlds and evolving to suit our environments. But it's now been two millennia and our worlds are developed, each House with its own sense of identity—so isn't it time we came together and lifted the ban on inter-House marriage?"

And there it is.

The seed for the Trinary Axis.

Fire ignites in Blazon and Brianella's eyes, and the flames look like they come from the Everblaze—the kind of blaze that can't be stomped out. With a few words Aquarius got the entire universe to look down instead of up.

Arguing breaks out immediately.

It's obvious he's not the first to consider this measure, but he is the first to say it out loud in this official forum. Everyone is shouting over each other, and there's no hope of shutting this down. And as the whole meeting devolves into chaos, Aquarius quietly slips out the diamond-bright Talisman under the table and closes his eyes.

Suddenly, every Guardian keels forward, squeezing their heads like they're hearing the screeching noise of Psynergy. A vein is popping in Aquarius's forehead, and it looks like whatever he's doing is costing him every ounce of life force, and as I look around I notice a shifting in the stars.

The holographic map is shaking, like the very galaxy is becoming unstable, and it seems like what happened at the Piscene Cathedral is about to take place, as lighting streaks across the galaxy. Only instead of uncovering the Ophiuchan constellation, the Dark Matter begins to drift away until it's at the edge of our solar system, just beyond Pisces.

When it's over, everyone slumps forward, unconscious. But Aquarius rises. He eagerly looks around the room, like he's expecting to see someone, and then he stares up at the stars—and cries out in horror.

He rushes to the place where the Dark Matter has strayed, at the very edge of our universe. "I'm so sorry," he whispers to the stars, tears rolling down his cheeks. "I thought I could bring you back to have a life together . . . but I have to wait for the portal. There's no other way."

I watch Aquarius's grieving face until the emotion recedes from his eyes, and I realize he probably designed this particular body for this life cycle because he thought he'd be reunited with Ophiuchus.

He wanted to wear his original eyes.

Watching him I understand what's happening: His window for love has just passed. The next time he sees Ophiuchus will be to kill him so he can open the portal. I see the emotions sliding down until they're so deep within him that he can only access his mind, not his heart.

I know the look.

It's the face of letting go.

32

WHEN THE MEMORY IS OVER, it takes me a moment to readjust to the Mothership's crystal-walled reading room.

By now the sky has cooled to a dusky violet, and silver stars are starting to peek out overhead. Panic snakes through my insides as I realize too much time has passed. Hysan must have taken off by now.

I turn to Ophiuchus in alarm—and I gasp.

The Thirteenth Guardian is curled into himself on the floor, looking ancient and near death, like his lifeforce was just sucked out of him.

No, not sucked.

Psyphoned.

Aquarius didn't pull on the Unity Talisman's Psynergy, or even his own, to play us these memories. He distracted us with the past so he could steal Ophiuchus's power in the present.

Life is a dance of illusions, he said to me at the Cathedral. *With the right distraction, you can make a person believe anything.* It's always the same trick, and we're always falling for it.

I glower at Aquarius, only he's also looking down at Ophiuchus, and something in his face has shifted. Seeing the Thirteenth Guardian reduced to this half-dead state, and knowing he's the one who's caused his condition . . . He's not as indifferent as he'd like to think.

I decide to drop all the acts I've been balancing and just go back to what I know best—*honesty*.

"Please don't do this to him," I say softly. "Hasn't he been through enough?"

"I told myself I wouldn't go through with this plan if humanity proved itself worthy," says Aquarius, still staring at Ophiuchus while speaking to me. "If you evolved, if you were a species worth saving . . . But I've watched you since the beginning, and you're *not*.

"Just like your predecessors, you can't come together for the greater good. Even in your ancestors' world, humans have always needed tragedy and violence to learn their lessons. Your species doesn't do subtle."

"Please," I beg, moving closer to him. "I know you want to see what's beyond that portal, but how much more do you need? You've been a *star* in the *sky*. You've been immortal for millennia. Please don't take more from us. We can be better, I know we can."

He finally looks at me, and I notice the star-kissed glow of his skin has dampened. He looks less like Aquarius and more like Crompton. "You still don't understand," he says sadly. "I'm not doing this for myself anymore. . . . I'm doing it for *you*."

His eyes beam at me, cutting a pink path through the darkening air. "This whole time you've managed to see how special everyone around you is, but the only person you've never seen is yourself. Do you know how many events had to play out just so for you to be here, before me, burning brightly despite everything?"

"You're right," I say, once I manage to find my voice again. "I don't understand."

He walks up to the crystal wall and stares out at the purpling horizon. "I found you the first time you Saw Dark Matter. I *felt* it. At the time you didn't know you were Seeing it, but I've been using much of my Psynergy to veil the Thirteenth House from the Psy, so when you Saw through it . . . I couldn't believe a human was capable of that."

He turns to me with a warm smile, and he seems like a proud parent. "When I looked into you, I learned that you were different. You didn't show your work at the Academy when you made your predictions. Your mediocre instructors faulted you for this, but they were the ones in the wrong."

I can't help flashing to one of Mom's favorite phrases from my childhood—*Your teachers are wrong.*

"In fact," he goes on, "you've always been the perfect student: You learn from everyone and every situation. You *remember* things because you're *paying attention.* You strive to be better because you respect the people and the world around you."

He starts striding toward me, his eyes bright and his voice gentle. "In a school that was almost entirely Cancrian, you chose a Sagittarian for your best friend. Of all the potential love interests available, you chose the top-ranked university student to admire and live up to." His voice dips with heaviness as he says, "I felt you through the Psy when you fought with your friends on Elara and nearly suffocated on the moon's surface minutes before curfew. I was moved by your resourcefulness and heart and drive to survive."

Once he's standing right in front of me he says, "I protected the crystal dome from the power outage when your House fell so that your story wouldn't end on Elara. I have always been with you, Rho."

I can't even blink. Or breathe. Or think.

"I now see that your Cancrian and Ophiuchan heritage—Unity through Nurture—made you uniquely qualified to bind us together," he goes on, not realizing that I'm barely digesting any of this. "But ultimately, it was your choices that cemented your worthiness. You're not the first person to have a militant mom—but rather than rebel, you opted to excel at her teachings, and later you continued your own training. When you faced Ophiuchus and he threatened to kill you if you spoke of him, you chose to warn the other Houses anyway. When the Plenum laughed in your face, you chose to go before them again. And again. And again. And now, when the Zodiac has shunned you, when you've lost everything that matters to you and I offer to take you to a new universe and give you a supreme amount of power no man has ever had—you choose to save everyone else rather than seize it."

"I . . . I can't," I sputter, only now fully appreciating how insane Aquarius is.

"When you're as large as I am, Rho, you realize attaching too much meaning to individual members of a species is a downfall. It's tragic to send so many people to Empyrean so soon, I know, but they're sacrifices for the evolution of your race. They will all die anyway—we're just moving up their time lines. The earthlings who settled the Zodiac also left most of their people behind on a dying Earth, and aren't you better off for it?"

He cups my cheek in his palm for an instant, and I feel the same buzz I've felt every time I've touched him and Morscerta. It's not the Barer's electricity—it's his Psynergy I've always been able to sense.

"The irony is," he says, his pink eyes bright with warmth, "now at the end of the worlds, I finally love a human. I haven't felt this way since . . ." He clears his throat but doesn't look at Ophiuchus. "You are the child I always hoped to lead, but this galaxy can't appreciate your light. I want to gift you a universe that's worthy of you."

My brain is completely blank. Aquarius is out of his mind, and Ophiuchus is dying at my feet. No one is coming to rescue me.

It's up to me now to save them.

I can't stop Aquarius with violence, which means meeting him on his own playing field. I have to use my *words*.

"You say it's weak of me to attach so much meaning to individual members of my species, but do you know what I find most amazing about humans?"

He quirks his head curiously at my question, and I answer, "How at times a single person, or small group of people, can lift our entire species onto a new rung of evolution. How a single achievement can thrust us all forward in time, and all of a sudden what was unknown is known, and we're ready for what's next.

"Like Galileo Sprock's creation of the first holographic communication, or Tinga Baron's invention of Abyssthe. Or think of the first Wave, the first Zodai Ring, the first Ephemeris. The social impact of visionaries like Empress Wen, who came up with the axiom *Trust Only What You Can Touch*; or Sage Huxler, who was the first to coax the other Houses into sharing their secrets with the Zodiax. Sometimes something as seemingly small as a single individual can change the entire course of a species' future. And that means within each of us lies the potential to be infinite."

Aquarius is nodding vigorously. "That's beautiful, Rho. It's exactly how a leader ought to feel about her people. And that's why you deserve this."

"You're not hearing me," I say, my tone growing exasperated. "At the Tomorrow Party's ball, you said change is the universe's only currency and that it's human hubris holding us back—Plenum politicians who won't let go of their power. But the flaw you're most passionately set against in *us* is the one you're blind to in yourself. *You* aren't growing or evolving because you won't give up your immortality. You won't follow your own advice and *let go.*

"You think you're the exception to the rule because humanity needs you, and your mission matters so much that you have to stick around to lead us. I bet you even think you're coming from an altruistic place. But your naked need to survive and see more is as human as it gets. It's *greed.* Or do you honestly believe in your heart that you've been a better Guardian for us than Ophiuchus might have been?"

In my peripheral vision, I notice the Thirteenth Guardian twisting around to look at us. He seems so pathetically weak that I don't return his stare. I've failed us. I've failed the Zodiac.

I drop my gaze to the floor. "You said once that I was only good to you if I wanted this," I say softly, "and I don't. So if you're going to force me like you did Ophiuchus, just know you've killed us both. I won't be that leader you admire anymore, and my light will go out."

Aquarius is silent for so long that I make myself meet his eyes, and I'm startled by the change that's come over him.

He looks as defeated as Ophiuchus, his hair less silver than gray, his features sunken in. "Of course," he says to himself, and his mouth curves into a sad smile. "The right person would refuse, wouldn't she?"

His gaze pans from me to the Thirteenth Guardian, and he seems to be seeing his legacy in one shining moment of lucidity. "Your parents couldn't appreciate you or raise you right," he says to me suddenly, "because you're a child of the stars. But I'm going to love you the way you deserve."

He kneels down beside Ophiuchus. "You were right, my love. I couldn't kill you then. And I can't kill you now."

All the air rushes out of me in relief.

I can hardly believe it.

I stopped Aquarius with my *words*.

He leans over and presses a kiss on Ophiuchus's forehead, and he stays there a moment, like he's giving him a blessing. "I'm sorry I was blind," he says gently. "You were always the star for this job. Unite this species. Take them to new worlds. Give them the hope I couldn't bring."

He stands up and faces me. "Killing Ophiuchus on his planet was only the plan because you're right—I am greedy. I believed humanity would need me forever, so I planned on taking his Star Stone with me through the portal. Only you've given me a greater purpose to serve."

He bends down and presses a kiss on my forehead, and I feel tingly Psynergy come over me, like the stars of the Zodiac have just blessed me.

"I'm doing this for you, Rho. I'm so proud of you, and based on everything I just heard I know more than ever that you will be a great leader who will heal humanity's wounds. Remember me, and I will always be with you."

He takes out the Unity Talisman and wraps his hands around it.

His forehead suddenly begins to bulge, and his glow grows so bright that I have to fall back a few paces and shield my eyes.

Then Aquarius falls, his body limp and lifeless, and the Stone explodes into a massive cloud of Psynergy.

The molecules of air around me start jittering, and the whole world seems to be undergoing a metaphysical earthquake. I can hardly catch my breath. The sky outside lights up with small flashes, like a whole galaxy of shooting stars, and some part of me feels Aquarius's soul returning to its rightful place among the stars.

It's over.

Ophiuchus gasps, and I kneel down beside him. "He's gone," I say, my eyes shiny and wide. "We're okay."

"No," he manages to get out. "He just activated the portal."

33

WHITE MIST FROM THE TALISMAN'S explosion hangs in the air, turning the room into an Aquarian thought tunnel, and I watch someone's silhouette charge inside.

A Marad soldier armed with a Murmur.

I don't shield myself or bother fighting now that I know I've failed us. In seven days the portal will be fully open, and as soon as the first ship goes through, the Zodiac will be undone.

The soldier rips off their mask.

"Nishi!" I run over and crush her to me in an embrace. "What are you still doing here?"

"I'm not leaving without you," she says when we pull apart.

"It's too late!" I say, shaking my head. "He's done it—Aquarius killed himself with Ophiuchus's Talisman and activated the portal." Her face pales, and her eyes grow glassy. *"It's over—"*

"No, it isn't," she says, hope coursing through her voice. "We'll find a way to close it. We *always* find a way. But we have to get out of here now, before Blaze—"

"What about me?" asks the white-haired Leonine, cutting through the rapidly dissipating mist. "Nice outfit," he tells Nishi, a sardonic smile on his face. "I didn't think you wore anything that wasn't couture—"

He notices Aquarius's body lying beside Ophiuchus.

"What—"

He runs over to Aquarius's side, shaking him. "No, no, no," he moans, and soon sobs choke his words. "How—why—*what happened?*"

He whirls on me, and Nishi instinctively raises her Murmur and points it at his chest.

"He killed himself," I say, "and he activated the portal. Blaze, if you know how to undo it, you have to tell us."

But he doesn't seem to be listening. "He . . . he killed himself?"

The Leonine's explosive russet eyes are far from the conversation, far from logical thought. "Then it was a *sacrifice*. . . . He did it for a reason."

He focuses on me again, and a new emotion begins to line his face. It looks a lot like hate.

"*You.* This is *your* fault. I did everything he wanted, I'm a better speaker than you, I'm much more like him—and yet he chose *you*."

"Blaze, whatever he made you think or feel, it wasn't real," I say, too ashamed to admit that I'll miss the way he made me feel sometimes, too.

"Let's go, Rho," says Nishi, but I'm looking at the Thirteenth Guardian, who is too weak to move on his own. Do I abandon him here?

Blaze turns his back to us, and he drops down beside Aquarius again. Since he doesn't seem intent on stopping us, I say, "Let's grab Ophiuchus. We can carry him out together."

"You can leave alone, right now, with your lives," warns Blaze, twisting his neck to look up at us, "but if you try to take Ophiuchus, this place will be surrounded by Marad in seconds, and you'll never make it out."

"Fine," I say, eager to get Nishi out of here. My only priority is that she survives. "We're going." I grab her arm and pull, but she doesn't budge.

"*No.*"

ROMINA RUSSELL

I turn to her in alarm. "Nish, come on!"

But she's watching Blaze with a calculating look. "The portal's already open. Why do you need Ophiuchus?"

"I'm going to count to ten," says Blaze steadily, taking a step closer to us even though Nishi's still pointing her Murmur at him. "If you're not gone, I will sound the alarm through the Psy, and you'll never get out again."

My heart catapults into my throat. "Nish, please, let's go, we'll worry about him later—"

"*He's* how we close the portal, isn't he?" she asks Blaze, her reasoning outspeeding mine as usual. "If it takes a star to open it, then logically it must take a star to close it."

I look at Blaze's hands—he's not wearing his Ring. Aquarius was careful about limiting access to the Psy from his stronghold. "I think you're bluffing," I say, now taking Nishi's side. "I don't think you have a way of calling out to everyone. And since the plan was for you guys to take off now to Black Moon, I'm fairly certain most people are already on their way—"

Blaze lunges at Nishi, knocking the Murmur from her grip. They both fall to the ground, and the cylindrical weapon clatters away from them. His hands wrap around Nishi's neck, and I grab his shoulder and try pulling him off my best friend, but he's too strong.

I run for the weapon instead, and then I swing it across his head. There's a loud *thwack* as it cracks against his skull, and he instantly crumbles into a heap on the floor.

I help Nishi to her feet. "*Stellar*," she says, breathless but smiling.

I return the grin, and we run to Ophiuchus, who seems to be regaining some of his energy. We each lift one of his arms and manage to pull him to his feet.

"Where do we go?" I ask.

Just then, an engine's deafening roar rumbles through the crystal room, and Nishi and I duck to the ground, dropping Ophiuchus with us, and we

250

cover our faces as the wall farthest from us shatters. When we look up again, the nose of a familiar bullet-ship has blasted through it.

Equinox can't fit inside the hall, but a round escape capsule disengages from its side and shoots inside, hovering beside Nishi and me. Hysan must be controlling its flight.

Gusts of wind blow more shards of crystal into the air, and I shout at Nishi, "Get in!"

"Ophiuchus first!" she shouts back, and we each pull one of his arms around our shoulders and drag him into the capsule. It looks like it'll barely fit the three of us, but we'll make it work. He seems to be growing heavier as I shove him through the opening, but I push harder, using all my strength, until he's in. Then I wheel around to tell Nishi she's next.

But Blaze has her in a one-armed headlock, one side of his head bleeding. His other hand is holding the Murmur.

"Step inside that pod, and she dies."

"Okay," I say, walking away from the capsule. "I'll go with you anywhere you want. Just let her go."

"I don't want *you*," he spits out. "Or *her*. I want *him*. Bring him out of there, and you two can go."

"Rho, *DON'T DO IT!*" cries Nishi. "Remember, this isn't about *us*, it's about the *Zodiac*—"

Blaze's hand muffles Nishi's mouth, cutting off the rest of her words. "What's it going to be, Rho?"

"I'll do it!" I say, my heart going too fast to give me any space to think or breathe. "I'll get him out! Just, please—don't hurt her. You can have Ophiuchus, okay?" I look into Nishi's sparkling amber eyes. "Nish, it's going to be fine. We'll find another way. I promise."

I poke my head inside the capsule. "Get out here," I command Ophiuchus, but he doesn't move. I can't even tell if he's conscious anymore. So I step into the pod and go around him to shove him out—but the moment I cross the threshold, a glass door comes crashing down, sealing me inside and muffling every sound.

"NO!" I shout, pounding on the glass, my voice too loud in this small chamber. "Let me out! *HYSAN, LET ME OUT!*"

Blaze throws Nishi away from him, and she stumbles to the floor. Then he raises the Murmur at me and shoots blue light at the ship, but it does nothing.

The pod begins to rise into the air, and I'm pounding desperately against the glass, my throat raw, my fingers clawing at every button to try to open the door again. But the capsule just keeps going higher, and I look down in despair as my best friend watches me go.

Maybe Blaze won't hurt her. After all, she's his only leverage. Maybe he'll reach out and offer a trade.

I'm still hitting every button in sight, and suddenly, the glass door slides down.

I shout in triumph. "Blaze, it worked! Don't hurt her!"

"Push him out!" he demands.

The pod is hovering in midair, but Ophiuchus is tall enough that it's just a small jump for him. I turn and tug on his arm. "Please, you have to go," I beg him.

"Rho."

I look down to see Nishi staring up at me, with Blaze behind her, his weapon aimed at her head, executioner-style.

"This is my choice," she says, tears streaming down her cheeks. "You risked the Zodiac's fate for me once already. Don't put that on me again."

"Nishi, *please*—I can't live without you," I say, yanking again on Ophiuchus's arm. But he's as immovable as stone.

"You're better than this," she says strongly, fighting against her tears. "I told the Zodiac to *Trust in Guardian Rho*. Don't make me a liar."

For a second that feels timeless, we watch each other, and deep down I know it's the last time I'm seeing my sister. And I hate them all for making me choose a murderer over an angel. None of their souls are worth this price. She's too good for us.

Though my throat's shrinking, I get out my last words to her. "You're my everything, Nish."

And despite the terror in her amber eyes, she manages a small smile. "I'll save you a seat in Empyrean."

Then she spins around to face Blaze, who's just realized what's happening. He swings the Murmur from her to me, but before he can shoot, she tackles him.

"NISHI!" I scream, but the glass door is closing again on its own, and the capsule is rising once more.

I watch them struggle, but Blaze easily overpowers her, pinning her beneath him. Nishi knees him between the legs, and he cries out in pain and falls off her as she stumbles to her feet and starts racing out the hall.

But Blaze springs up too fast and aims the Murmur.

He fires.

She falls.

34

IT'S BEEN FIVE GALACTIC HOURS and three galactic minutes since we left House Leo. Since Aquarius activated the portal. *Since Nishi—*

I'm still in the escape pod, even though it's docked on 'Nox. When the metal door to the ship slid open, I let the others remove Ophiuchus, and I told them the portal was triggered and will be active in seven days unless we can shut it down—and that the Thirteenth Guardian is the only one who can tell us how. "Hysan can figure out a plan," was the last thing I said.

Then I shut the pod's glass door and stayed inside.

Hysan deactivated all the controls so I can't shoot myself away—not that I have anywhere to go. I've been watching the holographic numbers of the flight time ever since we left. My leg has a cramp, and I've had to pee for two hours and eighteen minutes, but I'm dreading going inside that ship.

I don't want to lead anyone.

I don't want to do anything.

At five hours and thirty-three minutes, the pain in my bladder becomes unbearable, and I finally follow the instructions Hysan gave me to open the door. I slip into the nearest lavatory, and when I'm back in the hallway, I hear Ophiuchus's deep voice coming from the front of the ship.

"Without my Talisman, it will take more time to locate where I first crashed as a star, and Aquarius's army will be waiting to stop you. They know they just have to hold us off until the seventh day." I walk into the nose and find Ophiuchus sitting on the floor, facing an audience made up of Hysan, Mathias, Pandora, Skarlet, Gamba, and my mother.

Everyone turns to me at once, but I survey the Thirteenth Guardian. There's something different about him. He's still the same stature, but he seems diminished somehow.

"What's happened to Ezra and Gyzer?" I ask, anticipating the worst.

"They took one of the Tomorrow Party's ships and regrouped with the rest of our fleet," says Hysan, rising from his pilot's chair and offering it to me.

I don't take it. "What's the plan?"

"We're meeting all the Guardians and our full Zodai army on Libra, where we'll refuel before flying to the Thirteenth House," he reports. "With all the travel time taken into account, we'll have exactly two galactic days to close the portal once we land. Ophiuchus knows what to do, but first we need to find the place where he first landed as a star. Without his House's Talisman, we'll need to track the trail of Psynergy."

I study Ophiuchus again, trying to pinpoint what's different.

"The division of Psynergy between my Talisman and my soul is what made me unstable, giving me superstrength and superspeed part of the time, and weakening me the rest of the time," he says, answering my unasked question. "Now I am . . . normal."

It sounds like a joke, since there's nothing normal about him, but I nod. "Sounds like you have everything covered. I'm going to sleep."

No one objects as I turn and tunnel deeper into the ship, but after a few steps I realize I don't know where to go. I can't bear to return to the main cabin where Nishi and I spent her last night alive.

"You're in the room to your right."

I don't turn around at the sound of my mother's voice. I just open the door she referenced, and the first thing I see is my traveling bag on the floor. When I go to shut the door, she sticks her boot in the threshold and forces it open.

Reacting would be giving her what she wants, so I just cocoon myself inside the bed and stare up at the ceiling. In my periphery I see her pull down on the seat that hinges from the wall.

"I'm sorry, Rho," she says, not sounding sorry at all.

I'm not sure I'm going to answer, but then I hear myself ask, "For abandoning me? Replacing me? Slapping me? You'll have to be more specific."

In a voice almost too low to hear, she says, "For everything."

I roll my head to the side to see if the emotion in her words is real or fabricated, but her bottomless blue eyes look like they've hit bottom at last. She seems to have shed all her layers, and I'm staring at what's left of her.

"I'm sorry about your friend."

My insides harden, and I face the ceiling again.

My *friend*. She can't even bring herself to use Nishi's name. She never even met my best friend, I realize. My *sister*. She has no idea who I am. She may be my biological parent, but Aquarius knew me better and had more compassion toward me than she's ever been able to show.

"I know you're hurting, but you can't fall apart." Her voice grows familiarly businesslike. "You need to pull yourself together, because now is when the Zodiac needs you most—"

"Screw the Zodiac," I say tonelessly, turning to look at her again. "And *screw you*."

Her face becomes a military mask, only I realize now it's not a mask—this is her real face. It takes more effort for her to show emotion than to conceal it. She really isn't Cancrian at all. She never belonged on our House, just like she never belonged in our home. Our family was just one of her masks.

"Rho, this person you're becoming," she says, attempting a softer tone that doesn't suit her, "she isn't you."

"How the hell would you know?"

"I know I've failed as your mother, but blaming me isn't going to do anything for you." An old darkness infects her words, the same iciness she would use to frighten me into cooperating when I was just a small child.

I unzip the cocoon because my body feels too hot, and I sit up and finally say the words I've always dreamt of saying to her.

"You're a *bitch*."

Without missing a beat, she retorts, "I guess that's where you get it from."

I'm relieved she's fighting back. Because now I can tell her *everything* I think.

"You ruin everyone you touch," I say, the blackness within me rising to my surface, like it's eager to come up and breathe fresh air. "You think *I* had the worst of it? I *lived*—I moved to the moon, I made best friends, I became Holy Mother of a House I've always loved and belonged to. But what about Dad and Stan?"

Her face looks like it did the first time I brought up Gamba. Like I've found another of her weaknesses.

"*You ruined their lives.* Neither one of them ever got over your abandonment. You forced Stan to grow up too soon by making *him* head of the house, and you left Dad in a stunted state he never shook off. And now they're both dead, and they never even got to live for themselves, and that's on *you*."

I missed this anger. It swirls in my chest like a tonic to numb my pain, and it hardens every part of me until I don't have to feel anything else. I'll do whatever I have to do to keep it in place. I'll stay angry forever if that's what it takes.

"You're right," she says, her face pale and blue eyes overly bright. "I have a lot to answer for, but those are *my* sins to carry—not yours."

She reminds me of Hysan. No one can ever get to know either of them because they're ensconced in secrets, and they refuse to see how the things they keep hidden affect those around them.

"I know our relationship is beyond repair," she says, standing up. "Even if you forgive me—and whatever your feelings on the matter at this moment, I know your heart, and I know you won't hold on to this anger forever—I still doubt you would *like* me. We're very different people, you and I. That indestructible heart of yours will beat again, and it will lead you to true happiness, something I myself will probably never experience."

If this were a holo-show, she and I would probably be crying and forgiving each other by now, like we started to do on Pisces. But real life isn't scripted by writers—it's written by *us*. And our own conclusions are far less satisfying.

Stan died before he got to live for himself.

Deke and Nishi died before they got to live for each other.

And in seven days, when the first ship goes through the portal, the whole Zodiac is going to die—unless we can find the exact spot where Ophiuchus crashed to mortality more than three millennia ago, on a planet no one has ever seen and that might be completely uninhabitable.

"I'm so grateful you're nothing like me," she says, coming closer, "because even if you don't believe me, I will always care for you and want what's best for you."

She stops when she's standing over me. "This blessing is overdue, as you outgrew your childhood long ago. But despite all my failings, I am still your mother, and you are still Cancrian, so I owe you at least this much."

She closes her eyes and touches my forehead, just as Agatha did the day of my swearing-in ceremony as Holy Mother.

"May you remember the worlds of yesterday, may you transform the worlds of tomorrow, and may you unite our worlds today."

✦ ✦ ✦

When we enter the atmosphere of Libra's lemon-yellow planet, Kythera, we land on the smallest of the floating silver bubbles, the one that houses the International Village.

We dock on the rooftop landing pad of the Libran embassy. I don't see Hysan again until we disembark, and then I do a double take.

He's shaved his face and brushed his hair back, and there's a bitter determination on his face that reminds me of when he stood up to Aquarius in the Cathedral.

We follow him down an elevator to the hotel's black-and-white lobby. The place is startlingly empty, and the few Librans who are here all glare at Hysan, their expressions ranging from distrusting to disdainful. Yet Hysan holds his head high and meets their eyes. I wonder how soon before they strip him of his Guardianship.

The next person the Librans' eyes jump to is Ophiuchus, whose height eclipses every human in sight. He might be less powerful now, but he'll always be undoubtedly supernatural.

Hysan guides us to the exit, and as soon as we step outside, I stop moving.

There must be at least ten thousand Zodai gathered here, donning their House uniforms. There's no weather inside Libra's flying cities, so the Plenum meets outside, on an elevated stage, in the center of the round village—and atop the elevated platform are all the House Guardians and Plenum Ambassadors.

I finally force myself forward on the cushiony, plexifoam ground, and this time Hysan falls back, along with the rest of my friends, leaving me in the lead.

The clouds above look woolly green through the city's transparent skin. A path parts for us in the crowd, and hands reach out to touch me as I go; I think we could all use the tactile reassurance that this moment is really happening.

The scene around me isn't color coded: Zodai aren't standing in front of their own embassies, among their own people—they're intermixed, like a tapestry woven with rainbow threads.

Once we're closer to the stage, I spot Ezra and Gyzer standing by the steps, awaiting us. I'm relieved to see they look unharmed and resolute. Gyzer steadies me as I climb up the stairs, and it's only when I feel his firm grip on my elbow that I realize I'm trembling.

He lets go when I get to the stage because Brynda and Rubi engulf me in their arms, and I'm grateful for their armor. When they pull back to look at me, Brynda's amber eyes and cinnamon skin remind me so much of Nishi that I can't catch my breath.

"I'm sorry," she says, and tears skate down her face. "I'm so sorry."

"Me, too," says Rubi, and when I turn to look at her, I'm stunned to see how much more she's aged since I last saw her. She still has a prepubescent figure, but her features have grown lined and heavy, reflecting the truth: She's an elderly woman in a child's body.

Time seems to be speeding up for her, probably because she's no longer undergoing the cell regeneration procedures. And I recognize the look in her deep, tunnel-like eyes: After over three centuries here, she's ready to join her brother in Empyrean.

"I know it feels like you've lost him," she says, squeezing my hand, "but he's part of you. And when it gets so loud here that you can't hear his voice, just do what I do . . . visit the stars. He's up there, you know."

Even her voice and demeanor seem to have matured, and I nod in acknowledgment because it's the most I'm capable of doing right now.

Next to greet me is Sage Ferez. His hundred years of life make him look as frail as he is wise, and I can't help hoping that he isn't planning on coming with us.

"Some fights are worth fighting at any age," he says to me, his inky-black eyes bright as we trade the hand touch.

Hysan is behind me, and the three Guardians I just greeted greet him just as warmly as they did me. Yet as we continue down the line, the rest of our worlds' leaders don't seem as ready to acknowledge his place in their ranks. Chieftain Skiff won't even look at him; but as he bumps fists with me, the red-eyed Guardian dips his head a fraction and says, "If we're still here tomorrow, you're welcome on Scorpio any time."

From Ferez's awed expression, I think it must be the highest compliment the Scorp has ever given.

The Guardian of Taurus shakes my hand next, and she flashes me a rare smile. "I see I'm not alone with my Riser parentage," says Fernanda in a conspiratorial tone. "I knew there was something I liked about you."

Agatha is beside her, and she eagerly wraps me in a warm embrace that's more motherly than any hug I've had in my seventeen years.

"I've never been prouder of anyone in my life," she says in my ear, and when we pull away, her misty gray-green eyes have filled with water. Sirna stands at her side, and when I look into her sea-blue gaze, there's so much I want to say. But we trade the hand touch silently because I can't speak.

House Aquarius has named a new Supreme Advisor, and when I turn to greet him, I recognize his face.

"*Revelough.*" It's the first word I've spoken since setting foot on Libra.

His eyebrows rise to his hairline. "You do me the greatest honor by remembering my name, Wandering Star," he says, bowing. He was the only Elder who stood up to Pollus when the latter gave permission for me to speak to Crompton as they were escorting him to the dungeons. *Your lack of subtlety, Revelough, is what keeps you from moving up the ranks,* Pollus said to him then.

House Aquarius is changing. *Politics* are changing. If those who didn't want to play the game, people who spoke up and spoke out—like Revelough and me—are becoming the new leaders, maybe Aquarius was wrong. Maybe we *can* do better. Maybe there is hope for the Zodiac.

. . . If we survive.

After I've greeted the remaining Guardians, General Eurek steps forward and addresses the crowd, a black volumizer floating around his head.

"The end of the Zodiac is upon us."

The whole village goes deathly silent.

"You are here today because you have chosen to fight for our very existence. You are also here because after we defeat our enemies once and for all, you are not ready to go back to the way things were before. But above all, you are here today because many months ago a girl raised her voice to call for unity, and you listened."

Clapping breaks out, and someone squeezes my arm, but I don't even turn to see who. My gaze is unfocused, and all I can concentrate on are Eurek's words.

"Prophet Marinda is too ill to make this journey, but she is watching us from Pisces. There were very few Piscenes off-world when the plague hit their constellation, and we've been protecting them on our various Houses, as they are the last of their people. But I want the whole solar system to know that every last one of those Piscenes chose to come here today. Even though their House rarely takes sides in times of war, they are here to make their final stand alongside us, for they know that sometimes neutrality *is* a side and cannot be endured."

The whole village breaks into applause again, and as my vision begins to focus on the crowd, I spy a small group of Piscenes in the front. Hexel and Jox from Centaurion are here, and I'm relieved to know they're okay. My gaze drifts past them, and I see Mathias's parents, and Strident Engle from Scorpio, and Arcadia from Taurus who took me to see Vecily's house, and the Cancrian Candela who on Centaurion reminded me what we're fighting for, and Qima of Virgo, and Numen of Libra, and others. I almost gasp when I notice the red-haired sisters, Lola and Leyla, sitting at the end of the row.

All the faces from my travels have come. Every person I'm still fighting for is gathered here.

"You'll notice an unfamiliar presence on this stage," Eurek goes on, once the clapping ends. "A Thirteenth Guardian."

I turn to see Ophiuchus, who stands at the far end of the platform like he's just as uncomfortable as I am with the attention.

"*Ophiuchus is real,*" Eurek says loudly, his voice echoing through the silence. "Tonight, we set off for that world. That House our ancestors betrayed and abandoned is where the Zodiac will make its final stand. And now I will turn things over to the commander of our army, the leader whose voice has brought us all together, whose courage is unmatched and whose spirit is unbreakable—our one and only Wandering Star Rhoma Grace."

The crowd breaks into rousing roars of applause, but it's Agatha who steps forward instead of me, leaning heavily on her cane. They quiet down again.

"I would like to add one more title to Eurek's beautiful words." She turns and bestows on me a loving smile as she pulls out the black opal Talisman and offers it to me. "Welcome home, *Holy Mother.*"

All at once, every Guardian and Ambassador onstage bows—including Brynda, whose people bow to no one. My gaze pans over the crowd, and everyone else is bowing, too, even the Sagittarians.

The volumizer zips over to me, like even the device knows it's my turn to speak. As heads pop back up, everyone is watching me with hope shining in their eyes, and the dignitaries beside me all step back, leaving me alone as they await my speech.

I clear my throat, but I can only think of one thing to say.

"I'm sorry. I can't lead you."

And I turn and leave the stage.

35

I FLEE TO THE CANCRIAN embassy, and duty bound to me once more, Sirna follows.

I cross the plank and enter the second bungalow, and then I climb up the stairs until I'm on the rooftop with the aquarium beneath me. I try not to think of how much Stan would have loved to see it.

"Rho."

"Don't lecture me," I snap, whirling on Sirna. "You know I'm doing the right thing. You saw through me from the start. You always knew I didn't have what it takes to be Holy Mother, but I was too naïve to listen. You were right: I was unprepared, I was selfish, and I took everything personally. I was wrong for this role since the first day, and deep down, I knew it."

"You're right," she says, and I savor her honesty the way a parched person savors water. "I thought you were a fame-seeking child who would only manage to alienate our House from the rest of the Zodiac at a time when we needed the others' help more than ever."

She gestures to the people in the center of the village. "But one look at what's happening down there is all it takes to prove how wrong I was."

"They're not here for me. They're here because they don't want to die—"

"They're here to *fight*. And you're the one they're asking to lead them."

"Well it's just as crazy as when they asked me to lead the armada. They should be looking to Eurek or Ferez or Hysan—"

"Who told us about the Dark Matter?" she demands. "Who told us about Ophiuchus? Who told us about the master?"

"If not me, someone else would have uncovered this stuff—"

"But it *was* you, Rho." Sirna's ebony face fills with light, and I've never seen her look so hopeful.

"And to be clear, I saw how wrong I was about you two minutes into our first conversation."

I frown. "That's not true—"

"It is. We were in my office, and I'd just told you that your dad and brother were lost again. Then I cruelly pressed on with the political agenda, and I waited for you to fall apart so I could be proven right in time to spare Cancer the humiliation of you standing on that podium and name-dropping Ochus. I remember you shut your eyes, and I was sure you would break down. But when you opened them again, I didn't see a girl in pain. I saw a Guardian."

Her eyes are still bright as she rests a hand on my shoulder and brings her face so close that I feel her warm breath on my skin. "You plowed forward with our agenda, and in your voice I heard Holy Mother Origene's resolve. And I knew then that you would always protect us, even when you had nothing left for yourself.

"I may not have agreed with all your choices, and I will probably continue to disagree with you from time to time. But I had the same relationship with Mother Origene—as you've seen, I'm not one to keep my doubts to myself." She allows herself a small smile, and it makes her look so much younger. "But I have no doubts you're our true Holy Mother, Rho. And neither should you."

As if to prove it, she takes something out of her pocket.

It's the Cancrian Star Stone.

"This belongs to you now."

I don't want to accept it, and yet just like the first time I laid eyes on it, I can't help myself from wanting to touch it. She sets the smooth black opal in my hand, and goose bumps race across my arm.

It feels fated to be standing here, having my Guardianship restored in the same spot where it was once stripped from me. After all, every Holy Mother's ceremony must be blessed by the Cancer Sea.

"We leave for planet Ophiuchus tonight, and we're counting on the Thirteenth Guardian to close the portal," she says, reverting to her all-business demeanor. "We anticipate the enemy knows our plan and will do whatever they can to stop us. Ophiuchus has the strength of a mortal now, so if they kill him, it's over. We need you in this fight."

"I'm not a fighter, Sirna."

"No, but you're our best *seer*. And when we get to that world, we're going to need our Guardians to work together to pick up the Psynergy trail to Ophiuchus's crash site."

"I haven't accessed the Psy in a long while," I admit.

"Then I suggest you use this time wisely and go square things up with the stars."

✦ ✦ ✦

Black opal in hand, I visit the reading room on the top floor of the third bungalow, where I helped Mathias find his Center again after his capture.

I feel along the Talisman's ridges to unscramble the constellation puzzle and unlock it.

The Archer. *Sagittarius*.

Nishi drowns my thoughts, and I immediately descend to my Center. I didn't think it'd be this easy, but at the mere thought of my best friend, it's practically unavoidable. She *is* my soul.

Now that Aquarius is gone, I'm not afraid to enter the astral plane—but the Psynergy is still erratic. I have a feeling the only way to heal the Psy is to heal ourselves.

I stare at the stars and try pushing down my pain so I can See something. Only instead of my eyes registering movement, it's my ears that hear a sound. It's indistinct muttering . . . and it's coming from Helios.

As I approach the holographic sun, I flash back to when I met Ophiuchus in the slipstream and I hesitate. But curiosity gets the best of me, and I reach out to touch it.

The reading room disappears, and I'm transported to a vast, grassy field that extends endlessly in every direction. I take a few befuddled steps forward and gaze in awe at the greenery around me.

No time to dawdle, we don't have long.

I spin around to see a familiar wizened face.

Moira!

You sure took your time finding me. I don't know how much longer I could have held on.

But you're—

In a coma, yes, but my spirit is free in the astral plane. It's strange seeing her without her Perfectionary in hand. *Before I move on to Empyrean, I have a message for you from the Luminaries, and I don't have long.*

There are Luminaries with me, I cut in, frowning. *Why couldn't they tell me?*

Because they don't know this information, and if you continue interrupting me, you won't either. She knits her eyebrows, adding more wrinkles to her olive face, and I determine the best course of action is to stay quiet.

The Luminaries were formed by Empress Virgo, my House's Original Guardian. She Saw the Last Prophecy, and she suspected one of her brethren to be behind the vision, so she couldn't confide in any of them. Instead, she broke off a piece of her Talisman and gave it to her most trusted Advisor and instructed her to form the Luminaries.

The Virgo Star Stone contains a true Psy Veil, so the person using it can enter the Psy invisibly, without being seen by anyone—including Aquarius. That's how the Luminaries have kept their location secret this whole time.

Moira's mossy eyes fix on mine with deadly focus, and since she's usually a multitasker, it feels like a lot of pressure to hold her full attention.

We are the last outpost of the astral plane, she says heavily. *We're why the Last Prophecy vision has never gone away. As long as we've been here to anchor the Psy, he couldn't twist it too far. That's why it's imperative no one ever know where we are—we are the only safety net the astral plane has. Of course, it's all moot if the Zodiac dies.*

Remembering what Aquarius wanted from them, I ask, *Where does the portal lead?*

Moira dismisses my question with a curt wave of her hand. *The stars of the Zodiac cannot See beyond their own existence.*

But Aquarius said the Luminaries were hiding a prophecy from him—

That's because we wanted him to think that, she says with a note of pride.

You were baiting him? I ask, staring at her in shock.

The Luminaries have always hoped to prevent the Last Prophecy by uncovering the Guardian's identity before he could set it in motion, so we tried luring him out. But when he realized we were searching for him as hard as he was searching for us, he stopped chasing our fake vision, and—

She seems to sense something in the air because she starts speaking faster than usual. *You need to know that it will take the same amount of energy to close the portal as to open it. So without the Unity Talisman, you must find the spot where Ophiuchus crashed onto his planet, as the soil there will still retain remnants of his Star Stone—*

We already know all this, I say, and then I inhale sharply as the greenery around us flickers. *What was that?*

The portal's activation is accelerating the Psy's instability. Moira is still speaking too quickly. *The Psynergy being Psyphoned from Pisces has opened a* doorway through the Dark Matter. *If you can release that energy back to Pisces, it will restore that House, and that act will balance out Aquarius's death.*

Can Ophiuchus do that?

The ground beneath our feet starts quaking violently, and Moira has to raise her voice over the noise. *He has a role to play, but yours is more important.*

Mine? I shout back as the shaking grows deafening.

Ophiuchus will serve as a conduit for absorbing the excess Psynergy—but as there is no Talisman to destroy, you'll need to do the Psyphoning.

I feel my presence in this dimension fading, like the Psynergy is trying to buck me off, and I struggle to cling to my Center. *But I've never—*

Psyphoned? Why do you think I've been waiting around all this time? The ritual requires someone strong enough in the Psy who can pull on Psynergy from the whole Zodiac, she explains. *But if the process kills you, all will be lost. You must survive it.*

And how exactly do I do that? I call back over the noise.

You'll need an anchor. Something in this world with a strong enough pull on your soul to ground you here. Someone worth coming back for.

The one thing I don't have.

She seems to know that already because she comes closer and says, *If you want to save the Zodiac, you have to jumpstart that oversized Cancrian heart.*

36

WHEN I LEAVE THE ASTRAL plane, I set out for the Libran embassy. There's no judge or jury in the courtroom, so I go straight through to the hotel, which is equally void of people. The emptiness is becoming disturbing, and as I cut across the dichromatic lobby with white marble walls and black floors, a wallscreen catches my eye.

Hysan is addressing a crowd of Librans somewhere in this hotel, and from the ticker text scrolling beneath the footage, it seems like his message is being broadcast through his whole House. I move closer, and once I step within the radius of light on the floor, the audio pops on.

"My story begins with two Knights in the service of Lord Vaz's Royal Guard. Their names were Helen and Horace Dax."

Hysan is standing in front of a golden wall designed to look like the Libran flag, his voice as somber as his expression. "My parents died before my first birthday, and they left me in the care of an android into whom they'd programmed all their teachings. I followed in my inventor father's footsteps, and it was one of my designs that caught Lord Vaz's eye at the

Pursuit of Justice Symposium when I was nine. I received private tutoring from him until the day he confided in me that he had Seen his death and planned to name me his successor. Only he didn't believe anyone would willingly follow an eleven-year-old boy, and he needed his jury to approve of his selection. So we created Lord Neith."

Hysan pauses and his chin tilts down a fraction, his gaze dropping to the floor for a few breaths. It's the first time he doesn't seem cool and in control in front of a crowd, and I realize this is probably the hardest thing he's ever done. By exposing all the secrets that have defined him, his old way of life is lost to him forever.

His nest is gone.

"We each view the universe through our own telescope, so I don't expect any of you to see this from my perspective," he says, lifting his eyes to the crowd again. "I only hope you will try to understand it.

"Until recently, I didn't think there was anything wrong with my keeping this secret from you. I thought that as long as I protected my House and my people, as long as you were well taken care of, it didn't matter who the man was behind the android. I guess you can say that mindset is a product of how I was raised. But over the past few months, my eyes have been opened to how wrong that was, and how unjust I have been to you. *I should have trusted you.*"

Even though he's addressing his House, I can't help feeling like he's speaking directly to me. Then again, probably every friend of his watching this feels that way. It's part of Hysan's charm.

"In a few hours, we will embark on a journey that could either be the end of the Zodiac or a new beginning for all of us. There isn't time to go through a proper trial or cross-examination now, but if we survive, I vow to submit to any fate I am sentenced to. I am profoundly sorry for deceiving you. It has been an honor to serve you these past seven years, and whatever happens next, I will always be proud to be a Libran Knight."

As I watch him up there in his golden suit, his gaze focused and his jaw set, I no longer see the cocky teen Guardian with mysterious eyes and a mischievous smile.

I see a man.

✦ ✦ ✦

I take the elevator up to the penthouse suite even though I know he's not there yet, and I prepare myself to wait. But as soon as I lean against the wall, the door swings open.

"Lord Neith!" Without thinking I wrap my arms around the android, and I'm surprised when I feel him hugging me back.

"Lady Rho, what an honor it is to see you again."

We pull away, and I see actual tear tracks on his Kartex cheeks. I'd always wondered if he could cry.

"You were watching Hysan's speech?" I ask as I follow him into the workspace.

"Every word."

"I'm so relieved you're okay," I say as I walk through the holographic facts and figures floating in the air. "You had us worried back on Pisces."

"Hysan could not risk reactivating me while Aquarius was alive. Lady Rho, I must apologize to you for how I behaved the last time you saw me—"

"You weren't yourself," I say quickly. "It's not your fault."

The door opens, and I spin to see Hysan entering the penthouse. His head hangs down and his hair falls over his face, and he looks despondent—then he glances up and sees me.

His shoulders roll back, and light flashes in his eyes. "My lady."

"I must recharge," says Lord Neith, and he goes up to Hysan and lays a hand on his shoulder. "I've never been prouder of you," he says in an undertone. "I know Lord Vaz feels the same way, for much of my personality was molded after his. Right now he would be saying: *You are a true Lord and Knight.*"

Hysan's ears go pink, and I look down so I won't intrude. Then he and I wind around the worktables and enter the main suite. "May I offer you anything?" he asks once we're in the living room.

I shake my head and say, "I just spoke with Empress Moira."

His brow wedges with concern. "In the astral plane?"

"Yes." We're standing behind a levlan couch that looks a lot like the one from the suite on Aries where I first kissed him. I angle myself away from it.

"She told me how to close the portal. It's a ritual that takes place in the Psy, so Ophiuchus and I will need to be protected while we perform it."

He nods, and the green of his gaze fades like he's multitasking. He's probably inwardly accessing his Scan. "Would you like to select the members of your regiment, or would you rather General Eurek assign his best Majors?"

"I . . . there's something else," I say, steeling myself for what I came here to tell him. "I think you should lead us."

"And why is that?" he asks, his tone tensing.

"You're smarter than me," I say, not meeting his eyes, "and you're better at telling people what they need to hear." Since he doesn't disagree, I go on. "You know every world almost as well as your own. You had the best strategy for taking back our camp on Aries. You figured out Aquarius's plan before anyone else—"

"So use me."

In my shock I look up. His green gaze is electric.

"If I'm such a good strategist, use my mind to strategize," he clarifies, but I can't escape the feeling that there was an accusation in his words. *Use me.*

Have I used Hysan?

"But I still haven't heard a single good reason why I should lead over you," he finishes, crossing his arms and leaning on the couch's backrest.

"Then tell Eurek to lead," I say, suddenly wishing I hadn't come here. "I'll play my part with Ophiuchus and do what Moira asked of me, but I won't be placed in charge of an army against my will again."

The last part comes off sharp and accusatory, and I bite my lip to shut myself up and keep from wreaking more damage.

"My turn to make my case for your leadership?" he asks, and I shrug to avoid arguing. "You inspired me to trust others and let go of my secrets. You inspired Mathias to be more open-minded and let go of what's past. You inspired Pandora to speak up and let go of her fear. You inspired Nishi to fight the system and let go of her personal pain—"

"Stop!" The anger comes with such force that I feel something in my chest fracturing. "It's *you* all who inspired *me*—Nishi gave me confidence, Mathias gave me strength, you gave me hope—"

"*Exactly.*" Hysan moves closer so I'll look at him, but when I don't lift my gaze, he lowers his voice and murmurs, "You inspired us all, and we inspired you back. Each of us let you in, but you let *all* of us in. That's why it has to be you, Rho—because inside that beautiful Cancrian heart, you carry a piece of all of us."

My *heart*.

Everything keeps coming back to that: A dead organ that can't find its beat.

The anger rushes to my chest again, like it's determined to punch through my glacier. "How can my heart stand up against their hate?" I ask, my voice rising until I'm shouting. "Pretty words are nothing next to the Marad's weapons! A Murmur murdered Deke. A Murmur murdered Stan. A Murmur murdered Nishi. I loved them more than the Zodiac, and my *heart* failed to protect them." I'm yelling at the wall, the floor, the couch, at anything but him.

"How the hell can you still believe in me?" I demand, sucking in a raking breath. "How have you always been so sure my light can stop any of this darkness?"

He's quiet as he bridges the small space between us and gently cups my cheek with his hand. "Violence isn't an ending—it's a cycle. Someone will always build a bigger weapon. I can design a device more powerful than a Murmur, but tomorrow our enemies will design something even deadlier, and on and on we'll go until we end up here, on the brink of our mutual destruction. You don't fight fire with fire, Rho," he says, his voice husky. "You quell it with water."

His mouth is close enough to kiss, and I finally look into his vibrant eyes. The golden star of his right iris sparkles, and I try calling up some of the magic I once felt when I looked at him. But the ice in my chest is too cold for love's warmth.

"I'm sorry, Hysan," I say, falling back a step. "You mean a lot to me, and I wouldn't have made it this far without you, but I'm not the same person you knew. And the truth is"—I suck in a quick breath because the fissure in my chest is widening again—"I'm not in love with you anymore."

I'm too much of a coward to look into his eyes when I say it, so my gaze finds the marble floor. My gut churns from how much I hate hurting him, but I don't have the energy to keep playing games. I just want to do my part to close the portal and then disappear.

"I had amazing parents who raised me," he says unexpectedly.

I wrinkle my brow and look up.

"Only problem is they weren't real. They were androids." He sounds less sad and more somber, the way he did when he addressed his House. "My family was a lie, and I couldn't escape the knowledge of that because I was the forger. For most of my life, everything has been under my control: My House, my home, my heart. Until I fell for you."

"Hysan, stop," I say, drawing back, away from him. "You can't charm me into feeling something that I don't." I stand against the far wall and cross my arms over my chest. "I just need you to be my *friend*—"

"I can't," he says, and his voice breaks on the word. "I can't give up on you."

There's a shine in his eyes that robs me of speech.

"When everything in your life is fake, you know something real when you find it." His green gaze smolders as he strides over, and I try to move but my legs won't work. "So if you think I'm just letting you go, then as you Cancrians would say, *you're dreaming.*"

My pulse leaps to action, and I say, "Hysan, *don't—*"

But his fingers dig into my curls and he pulls my face into his, and before I can push him off, his lips part mine.

The Abyssthe-like rush of his kiss fills my mind with buzzing, and his hand cradles my head protectively as he pushes me into the wall, the warmth of his touch igniting my skin too fast, like a fire that's been fed an accelerant—

And I gasp as the glacier in my chest bursts.

37

MY GUARD COMES CRASHING DOWN, and flames engulf my insides until I can't breathe through the flood of feelings surging through me.

Hysan's kiss lifts my curse, and all the pain I'd been stockpiling rushes to the surface, and for the first time since the Sumber, I break down in horrible, soul-scratching sobs.

Stan and Nishi are gone.

Hysan scoops me up in his arms and carries me into a bedroom, depositing me on the bed. Then he presses me into his chest and kisses my hair as I cry hysterically, his hand caressing my back gently as he whispers, "You're not alone, Rho. I'm here. You're loved, and I'm not going anywhere."

I can't breathe. I lost Stan. My brother isn't here because Aryll killed him—the traitor Hysan warned us about but we refused to see. "*Stan,*" I groan between sobs, and Hysan tightens his hold, his heart racing faster in my ear.

He kisses my head again and whispers, "I'm so sorry, Rho."

"I abandoned Nishi," I choke out. I lost my brother and my sister, the only family I had left, my best friends and the best people I've ever known.

Everything in me has shattered, and just gasping for breath scrapes my throat.

I can barely see through my puffy eyes, and the knot in my chest won't loosen, until my heart feels like it will give out and my limbs start shivering uncontrollably. "I c—can't stop shaking," I stammer, and Hysan rubs my back and arms to generate heat.

"It's okay, Rho," he says soothingly. "You've never abandoned anyone."

"I—I became a monster," I say, fighting down more sobs. "I'm no better than Aquarius. When I had to, I betrayed Risers. I turned over Gamba, I *tortured* Corinthe—"

"Shhh," says Hysan, and he takes my chin in his hands to look at me. My eyes are so weighed down with tears that his face looks like a low-resolution hologram. "You're not perfect. None of us are. But you have to forgive yourself right now because you're our leader, and we'll follow your example. If you hold back, so will we."

"Hysan—I've just lost my family," I say, scowling at him. *"I can't lead this army."*

He wipes the wetness off my face with his fingers. "You're this army's leader whether you acknowledge it or not. Even if you stand in the background, every Zodai here will still look to you for their cues. You've been a leader from the moment you left the Crab constellation against your Advisors' wishes, so forget the titles you've worn; they're just words. Whatever you call yourself, it will never change what you are."

I shake my head in defeat. "And what am I?"

He plants a soft kiss on my cheek, near my ear. "You're the brightest star in the Zodiac. *Hope.*"

✦ ✦ ✦

My eyes are still red and puffy when we board *Equinox* just a couple of hours later, and then our army of over twelve thousand Zodai takes off for House Ophiuchus.

'Nox is in the lead, and behind us flies the rest of our fleet. Most of the Tomorrow Party members aren't fighters, so we're counting on them being busy boarding the ships on Black Moon in anticipation of going through the portal. But the Marad was promised their planet back, and they're not going to want us anywhere near it.

After everything the Zodai have put Risers through, this is their chance to make us feel as homeless and desperate and unwanted as they've felt for three millennia. And from the intelligence the Zodai gathered on Phaet, there are at least a hundred thousand soldiers.

Our only advantage is that imbalanced Risers can't Center themselves. They won't be able to sense the Psynergy, so they won't know what part of the planet to protect. Whereas we have Ophiuchus, and his close connection to his home should enable him to pick up on that Psynergy so we can land in the general vicinity of what's left of his Star Stone.

Our army will have to fend off the Marad while Ophiuchus and I go seal the portal.

I spend my first day on 'Nox training with Mathias in the storage hold, the largest private space on the ship, so that I can learn to shield myself from the Murmur with my Barer. The Zodai believe these shields are our best chance against the Marad since they render the Murmurs useless.

"The trick is coating the blue energy with Psynergy and bonding both elements," he says in a deep, meditative voice, our eyes closed as we slowly cycle through Yarrot. "Let the electric tingling in your skin match the buzzing of your blood, until there's a balance between your inner and outer selves, your physical and metaphysical states. . . ."

By our second day of training, I can shield myself at a moment's notice, and we turn the room over to Ezra and Gyzer, who have also been using it to train, while Mathias goes to take his turn at the helm.

I dart to the main cabin, which I'm sharing with Hysan, to avoid running into anyone; Ophiuchus, Gamba, Pandora, and my mother have taken over the front of the ship, where they're meditating and trying to locate the Talisman.

"Why am I here?"

Skarlet's statuesque figure steps into my path right before I reach my room, her arms crossed and brow puckered.

"You'll have to ask your parents—"

"*Answer me, crab,*" she demands, blocking my body with hers as I try to go around.

"Don't you want to be here?" I snap, frowning up at her. "*You're* the one who's always going on about how you're a leader and deserve to be treated as one."

"I could be on General Eurek's ship."

"Then why aren't you?"

Her shoulders pull back with a pride she can't repress. "Hysan said you invited me to be in your party."

"And you accepted. So what's the problem, *ram?*"

She swallows down her attitude and says in a slightly less entitled tone, "I just want to know why."

Since she's trying to be sincere, I decide to answer with the truth. "Because you're one of the most physically powerful warriors in our army, yet your weapon of choice is your voice." My face heating up a little, I add, "And for the record, if I were Hysan, I would have picked you."

I leave her standing dumbstruck in the hallway and slip inside the cabin. But as soon as I do, I see Nishi again. She's all I ever see in here.

I approach the bed slowly, looking at the space where her body lay beside mine as we slept, hands clasped together. For all my pain, I know her death hasn't fully hit me yet. Nor has Stan's. I haven't had the luxury to grieve them right.

And I'm not sure if I'm more afraid of feeling those feelings or dying.

I get the sense the experiences won't be very different.

I switch on the black opal and try to push those emotions back so I can See. The room is drowned in stars, and I orbit the lights, searching for a sign of what's coming. Since I let the Zodai down on Libra, I want to at least be useful in some way. And contributing from in here, alone, is far preferable to doing so out there, with the others.

Though I know I should be focusing on the Dark Matter by the Thirteenth House, I suddenly feel a pull toward Cancer that I can't ignore. The beautiful blue of our world is barely visible through the belt of broken moons that engulfs it, and I long to see it again the way it looked in Aquarius's memories.

A bright light abruptly blazes above the Crab constellation, and I feel a familiar presence in the Psy.

I know it's crazy and it can't be real, but I think my brother is trying to talk to me.

I close my eyes to tunnel deeper into my Center—and as soon as the holographic stars disappear, there he is.

Stanton stands before me in a Cancrian blue uniform, like a vision that's been waiting just behind my eyelids.

His pale green eyes are luminous, his curls are bouncy, and his aura is glowing. *Stan?*

Hey, sis.

At the sound of his comforting voice, every other concern in the Zodiac melts away. *But—how? Is this real?*

I leap up to hug him, but my hands go right through his body, like he's a hologram.

You'll have to redefine real, he says with his goofy grin. *But I think so.*

Are you in Empyrean?

His radiant eyes dim a little. *Not yet. Not until I know you're okay.*

I can hardly breathe. Cancrians believe those who pass on with unsettled souls become constellations in the sky and eventually return to life to complete their unfinished business. Could it be that Stan might come back?

I don't think so, he says sadly. *And yes, I can read your thoughts in here.*

I shake my head in utter bewilderment. *But then why haven't you moved on yet?*

I think because I can't let go. Not until I know you've got this.

Well I don't want you to go, so I'll be a perpetual wreck if that's what it takes—

Rho. His voice grows parental, and I miss it so much that I'm torn between smiling and crying. *Do you remember the story I told you about the girl who was swept away from her planet and landed on a feathery world with a talking bird?*

I nod and it doesn't surprise me he's brought it up, as I've been thinking a lot about that tale.

In the story, little Rho had a choice to be sad about the past or to exist in the present—to smile or frown. It's the lesson of your favorite Stantonism: Don't fear what you can't touch.

It was a naïve lesson, I can't help saying.

Then you misunderstood it, he says, and his face is so close that it's like some new form of torture to be unable to feel him. *What little Rho can touch is the grass beneath her feet. What she can't touch is her home. She's creating a fear that doesn't exist—her home is fine without her—and what's worse is that fear isn't doing her any good.*

He looks so young and healthy, and he sounds so sure of himself that it seems impossible he's really gone.

When you awoke from the Sumber, he says gently, *you couldn't get past every second of Nishi's suffering enough to focus on the present. And now, you can't get over Nishi's and my passing—but I'm not gone yet, Rho. I continue to exist, but only if you do.*

He reaches out with his hand, and I can almost feel his skin stroking my cheek. *If you fade, you erase me, too. And Nishi. And Deke. And Dad. But if you let us in and let us become part of your light—if our memory shines through your words and your actions—then you honor us, and we're not gone. Don't doom us to the darkness. Bring us into the light with you.*

Tears streak down my face, and I'm not sure how much more crying my eyes can take. *But what if this conversation is only happening in my head?*

It is, and you're doing it again: You're looking for reasons to frown instead of smile.

But what if I'm scripting your words even now?

So typical of you to take credit for my brilliance. You can't let me have anything, can you? Not even this last moment to shine.

I laugh for the first time in months, and the change is startling. The reaction loosens my chest, and it's only through this flicker of levity that I register the weight of everything I've been carrying.

But my relief doesn't last long because just like when I spoke with Moira, my session in the Psy is cut short as the ground starts shaking.

Stan raises his voice over all the noise. *Rho, forget the past for now, and don't fret about the future! Remember that every second is a choice you make.*

I love you so much, Stan! I cry out as his image starts flickering, and somewhere in the back of my mind, I'm certain I heard him say *I love you, too.*

✦ ✦ ✦

I race to the control helm, where Hysan and Mathias are laughing about something. They both grow alert the moment they see me. "What is it?" asks Hysan.

I look from one to the other.

"I'm ready."

38

I STAND IN THE NOSE, nerves buzzing in my stomach, as Hysan cues up the transmission. He contacted every ship in our fleet so they'll broadcast my message.

Everyone on 'Nox has gathered around to watch, and even Ophiuchus leaves his Center to be present. I close my eyes and take a deep breath, hoping I'll see Stan behind my eyelids again. But even though he's not there, I still feel his presence.

Rubi was right. Our brothers never leave us.

I take another moment for myself, and then I open my eyes and nod at Hysan to begin the broadcast.

"I stand before you," I start, "not as some shining beacon of perfection, but as the most flawed among you."

I look away from the recording device and let my gaze trail across my friends. "I've hurt the people I love most," I say, gazing from Hysan to Mathias. "I've led an armada of Zodai right into the enemy's hands," I say, looking into Pandora's amethyst eyes. "I've betrayed my family"—I stare at Mom and Gamba, then Gyzer and Ezra—"and my friends. I fell so far that I even became the monsters I was trying to defeat," I say, thinking of Corinthe.

"And I broke the Taboo." My gaze returns to Hysan's, and he's watching me with such fierce love in his eyes that I feel my inner flame growing to new heights.

"Yet, whether or not I deserve it, you have all found enough love in your hearts to forgive me, and I'm so grateful. But now I want you to do something infinitely harder—I want you to forgive yourselves."

I stare into Ophiuchus's starlit eyes.

"The past is important only insofar as it informs the present—but when memories grow so powerful that they drag us back rather than propel us forward, they're not worth lugging with us anymore." Looking into the device again, I speak to the whole fleet. "If you can absolve someone who's sinned as much as I have, you can absolve yourselves."

I can't help pausing and looking at Mom. I think she was right: We'll never have the mother-daughter relationship I longed for as a child. . . . But I'm no longer that child.

My nest is gone because I don't need it anymore.

Thanks to Stan, I can fly.

"Leave your guilt and your self-doubt and your fears on these ships," I say, my voice gathering strength, "because when we land on the Thirteenth House, we can't carry them with us. For too long we have been leading with our fear and not our faith, because no matter how unfulfilled we feel today, we worry tomorrow could be worse. We are an army of seers, yet we've become so blind that none of us knows what tomorrow will bring, or if it will even dawn at all.

"This whole time it's not the stars who have been our enemies—not even Aquarius or Ophiuchus. It's been *us*. The master's plans only worked because we let them. Our distrust broke our Unity, and then he slipped in through the cracks. And just like in the Libran alphabet story, we were too busy pointing fingers at each other—our fellow letters—to look up and notice the eraser.

"We've defeated ourselves by forgetting the lessons of our past. Our choices have led us to this fate, not the stars—but that means our choices can also bring us to a new fate. Only our *true* survival depends on whether we learn anything from what we've survived.

"Will we continue to define ourselves by where we're born? Will we continue to distrust those who look or act differently from us? Will we continue to be a tribal species that's only comfortable living among others who are genetically like us? Or will we finally be ready to admit that there aren't twelve or even thirteen types of humans in the Zodiac?"

I cast a glance at Mathias, who looks just as proud as Hysan, and as I'm watching, he takes Pandora's hand and her face lights up like a sun.

"We are one people." I look at Mom and Gamba, Risers and yet also my family. "Risers are not abominations—they are descendants of House Ophiuchus. They are members of a repressed race, and our ignorance has created their condition. We are doing this to them by putting so much value on fate and not enough on free will—but Risers are the future," I say, thinking of the prophesy Ferez once shared with me and understanding at last what it means.

"None of us can truly be defined as *one* thing. We are all born as curious creatures with boundless imaginations. We are all seekers of justice and wisdom. We are all at times passionate and philosophical and nurturing and industrious and innovative. We all have a spiritual side that connects us to the stars, and we are all charged with the stewardship and protection of our land and environment. We are all warriors, especially today. And that means *we are all Risers.*

"What we're missing is the glue that gels together all these pieces of us: *Unity.* The only way we will save the Zodiac is together. So don't spend the rest of the flight reviewing strategy or anticipating our fate. Spend it getting to know the Zodai next to you. Forget whom we're fighting against and instead focus on whom we're fighting for—because the most important weapon we can bring to the field of battle isn't the one we can touch. *It's hope.*"

Hysan shuts off the broadcast and pulls me into his arms, lifting me off my feet with his kiss. Mathias hugs me next, and then Pandora, Ezra, and Gyzer come over to congratulate me. Even Skarlet bumps fists with me.

Ophiuchus goes back to meditating, but I didn't really expect him to do anything else.

Mom and Gamba approach me last, and the others busy themselves with other things to give us some semblance of privacy.

"Did you really mean what you said about forgiveness?" asks Mom.

"Yes," I say softly, thinking of Stan and what he would want for us. "I forgive you, and I also release you. You don't owe me anything. Just *be happy.*"

She stays silent, and I read it as just part of her stoicism, but then Gamba rests a hand on her lower back, and I realize Mom's moved. I guess it'll take some time to get to know the real Kassandra.

But at least I'll have that chance.

I look into Gamba's tourmaline eyes next, knowing now it's my turn to ask for forgiveness. "Gamba, I'm—"

"Forgiven," she says simply, and there's no rancor in her voice. "I know I'm a stranger to you, and we look nothing alike, but I would really like to be your sister, if you'll let me."

I consider the three of us—a Cancrian, an Aquarian, and a Capricorn—and my lips stretch into a smile: We're the family of the future. "I'd love that."

Gamba grins, her white teeth bright against her dark skin, and even Mom's mouth curves into a small smile. The first real smile I ever remember seeing on her face.

And I wonder if she might be feeling her first flicker of happiness.

"Rho, I think you have some admirers to greet," says Mathias, and I turn to see Pandora smiling beside him. "There's a cue of calls coming in from every ship—should I patch the first one through?"

"Sure."

After fielding congratulatory calls from every Guardian, I cast my gaze around for Hysan and realize he's not in the nose anymore. Mathias is in the pilot's chair, and Pandora sits beside him. I go check out the galley, but I only see Skarlet, Ezra, and Gyzer. The Ariean is arm wrestling Gyzer again, and Ezra is refereeing.

I crack open the door to the largest cabin, and I find Hysan sitting cross-legged on the bed, beaming out a series of screens from his Scan. His hair is as long as when we first met, but he seems larger now, like he takes up more space than I remember. Or maybe the room has just grown smaller.

I slip inside and lock the door behind me.

"Just checked on Neith, and he's almost at full charge," he says without looking away from the holograms he's scanning. Neith is plugged into the ship, since Hysan thinks he can be a useful warrior with his super strength and speed. "I just had this idea for upgrading the—"

I place my hand under his chin and tip his face up. "You're defying my orders, Lord Hysan. I said no more strategizing."

If I'm going to follow Moira's instructions, I need to ground myself in the present. I need to remember how good love can feel. I need Hysan's sunlight to take on so much darkness.

He blinks, and all the screens vanish at once. "Apologies, my Zodiac Queen."

I smirk and swing a leg around him, pulling myself onto the bed by straddling him. He hooks his hands on my hips and slowly slides them up to my waist.

"When I spoke to Moira," I whisper, his touch making my breaths shallow, "she said that to tether myself strongly to this plane, I'll need an anchor."

His hands stop at the small of my back, and he frowns a little. "Rho, you still haven't given me any details about that ritual."

"You don't have to worry. I know what to do." I cross my legs behind him and pull myself all the way forward, until my chest is pressed against his and our faces are touching. I feel his body harden beneath me as I whisper, "You just have to give me a reason to return."

His lips lock with mine, and we rest there. Then his hand hugs my head, and his mouth trails down my chin and neck, his touch igniting my skin. I moan softly, and his mouth meets mine again. He kisses me gently, like he's savoring my taste, the way he did the night I lost my virginity to him.

His tenderness only makes me want him more, and I slam both hands onto his chest and push him down on the bed. I lean over and kiss him savagely, and his hands reach up to pull off my blue tunic as my fingers work to free him of his golden suit. We're down to our underwear in seconds.

Hysan wraps a hand around my lower back and tries to flip me over so he's on top, but I pin his biceps to the bed. "It's *my* turn at the helm."

Dimples dig into his cheeks. "You sure you can handle this engine?"

We both burst into laughter, and when I see his ears are pink with embarrassment, I lean down and kiss him. "Hmmm . . . maybe just a test ride then," I whisper in his ear in a seductive voice, and then my mouth travels slowly down his jawline and neck.

His body tenses at my touch, his breathing growing labored. I spy his fingers twitching with the itch to take over, but I trust him not to touch me until I've given my consent. And now I'd like for him to trust me back just as completely.

"You're cruel," he groans as I inch my way even more leisurely down the smooth skin of his chest, and the ripples of his abs, and the lower I go, the more I feel his muscles submitting to me, until—

Someone pounds loudly on the cabin door.

I fall off Hysan and burrow beneath the sheets, my heart racing, and Mathias shouts, "Hysan! Why is your door locked? We need you up front *now!*"

Hysan curses under his breath.

"*Are you listening?*" demands Mathias, who's still hammering on the door. "Why aren't you answering on your Ring?"

"He'll be there!" I call out.

Hysan suddenly rolls on top of me, his body stiff against mine, his green eyes ravenous as they gaze into me. He kisses me with such force that my mouth opens fully for him, and every clenched muscle loosens until I feel like I've dissolved to a puddle of seawater.

As he pulls away, he says huskily, "You better come back from all this and finish what you started."

39

"WHAT IS THAT?" I ASK as soon as Hysan and I enter the nose, short of breath and with our suits disheveled. Everyone else is already gathered, and they're staring wide-eyed at the streaks of lightning flashing through the glass—except for Mathias, who's looking back at me.

His midnight eyes are soft, and his face is paler than usual, and I understand what he's feeling because watching the early stages of his romance with Pandora has hurt me, too. Even if I don't want to admit it.

We may not be able to affect the past, but the past can still affect us. Mathias and I may have made our choices weeks ago, but our hearts haven't finished paying the price.

"It's Dark Matter," says Hysan, taking over the control screens from him. "We can't see it, but according to our coordinates, we've just entered the Thirteenth constellation."

"I will guide us," says Ophiuchus, leaning forward from his spot on the floor, and I hear a new energy in his deep voice.

"Mathias, send a message to the other ships to form a line behind us," instructs Hysan. "Tell them they'll need to stick to our exact flight path so we don't risk hitting anything our sensors can't pick up."

Hysan buries his face in the controls as Ophiuchus provides directions, and Mathias leaves to pass on Hysan's message to the fleet. Pandora is glued to the window, same as Gyzer, Ezra, Skarlet, Gamba, and Mom, so I slip away and follow Mathias out.

He opens his Wave and transmits the data to all our ships at once, and when he turns to return to the nose, he sees me.

Neither of us says anything, but before it's too late, I break our silence.

"What do you imagine would have happened if we'd spoken that last morning in the solarium?" I ask, repeating the question he once asked me.

His indigo blue irises swirl like whirlpools of the Cancer Sea, and he murmurs, "Maybe I would have asked you for your name."

"And I would have said, *I'm Rho*." I hold out my hand for the Cancrian greeting.

"Nice to meet you, Rho," he says musically as we bump fists. "I'm Mathias."

His fingers wrap around my hand, and he holds on to it. "This might sound strange," he says, his baritone voice deepening, "but I've really enjoyed sharing these mornings with you. More than I ever realized."

Warmth tickles my face as I channel the girl I was then, and it feels good to finally give her what she most wanted. "Being around you," I whisper, "makes me feel safe. Your dedication to your routine, the peaceful aura around you, the way you're so comfortable with silence . . . you remind me of home."

His face softens, and he interlocks his fingers with mine. "Today is my last day of university," he says, "but would it be too forward to ask for your information so we can keep in touch?"

"I'd love that," I say, and though my face is still warm from the interaction, I feel tears forming in the corners of my eyes.

"I would have Waved you every day," he breathes, his thumb drawing small circles on my hand. "And as soon as I got to know you, I would have fallen irreversibly in love, and I would have never let you go." His midnight eyes are glassy and bright. "Hysan wouldn't have stood a chance. By the time you met him, our bond would have been unbreakable."

And neither of us would have fallen in love with someone from another House, I realize. We would have clung closer to Cancer, and we wouldn't have opened our minds to the change we needed. Our hearts would have stayed strictly Cancrian, rather than expanding to encompass the whole Zodiac.

Mathias and I had to fall in love with people different from us to understand that, deep down, we're all the same.

My eyes fill with so much water that his face blurs. "You still would have doubted Ophiuchus's existence, while Hysan would have supported me," I say with a small laugh, blinking to clear my view. Tears streak down my cheeks. "And I still would have shut the airlock door to try to protect you," I say more seriously. "Pandora still would have saved you."

His gaze grows distant, and I see the events playing out in his eyes; when he focuses on me again, I know from his defeated expression that my math was right. Whatever we do, we always end up back here.

It's just our nature.

He drops my hand, and the warmth in my skin recedes, like the sea's tide pulling away from the shore.

And now that it's gone, I identify the feeling.

It's closure.

✦ ✦ ✦

The Thirteenth House is completely covered in Dark Matter, but Ophiuchus guides us through the pathway created by the Piscenes' Psynergy. He seems to be the only one who can See through the darkness, though I'm willing to wager Aquarius's technology can navigate it.

Our whole fleet lands in the same area because it's where the Thirteenth Guardian directs us to go.

"The Marad may already have us in its sights," says Hysan before we disembark. "Everyone has to be armed and ready."

Every ship brought stores of Barers and pistols with them, in addition to their House's signature weapon. I stick with just my Barer, and Ophiuchus is the only one who doesn't take any weapon at all.

When I step off 'Nox, I join thousands of other Zodai who are looking up in bewilderment. The Dark Matter in the atmosphere completely blocks out the sun's rays, so the planet is shrouded in eternal night. The small hole in the atmosphere through which we flew in is the only place where silver starlight is visible, and every now and then it sends tendrils of lightning streaking through the sky.

Scientifically, life shouldn't even be possible here—yet the temperature is balmy, and we're breathing fresh air. Only the oxygen tastes slightly different . . . almost like Abyssthe.

Licorice-flavored air.

Since there's barely any light coming through the blanket of blackness above, this world's illumination comes from the plant life.

We're surrounded by a massive and seemingly impassable swamp. The wild and overgrown trees are tall and spindly, their limbs crisscrossing with each other, and their leaves glow with silver light, like Ophiuchus's eyes.

They look like stars hanging from tree trunks.

Just like its Guardian, this planet never died. It got caught between states—not quite part of this world, and not quite part of the next.

While the other ships find places to land and more Zodai disembark, I glance at Hysan, who's ogling at everything and for once looking just as mesmerized as the rest of us. "Guess I finally brought you somewhere you've never been before," I say.

His lips hitch into his centaur smile, and it's like a small sunrise in the midst of an everlasting night.

Then I notice Ophiuchus.

His wide eyes are taking up his whole face, and he looks smaller somehow. He drops to the earth and touches the loamy soil with his bare hands, the way one would caress a long-lost lover. I feel like I'm intruding, so I turn away to let him have his moment.

If I had the chance to return to Cancer, I would be on my knees, too.

As the rest of the army joins us, I notice most people are in their Zodai suits, but some are donning their House's actual warrior uniforms, like the ones worn during the Trinary Axis.

The Arieans' armor is a bloodred fireproof fabric made from the wool of their House's Rams. It's woven so tightly as to be as impenetrable as the toughest of metals. But the most striking part of their getup are their metal helmets, which have Ram horns sticking out from either side—when coupled with their huge bodies, they look terrifying.

The helmet is Aries's signature weapon. It's called the Helm, and it provides a polarized, panoramic view of the battlefield and alerts them of incoming attacks or problematic vitals.

A different herd of horned beasts emerges from the swamp, and after a moment I realize it's the Taurians, who are dressed in their own fear-some battlefield regalia. The House's Promisaries wear formfitting olive green uniforms adorned with shoulder epaulets that resemble the horns of a Bull.

I quit scoping out the Houses' getups when General Eurek says, "We should assemble the Guardians quickly, before the Marad catches up with us."

I search for Ophiuchus, and when I spot him tenderly touching a silver leaf, I call out, "Can you feel the presence of your original crash site?"

He turns and strides over to us. "The whole place is buzzing with Psynergy. It's too busy to locate a particular place."

Hysan comes closer, frowning, and before he says anything, I say, "We need to find Sage Ferez. I think I have an idea."

Eurek dispatches a Major to fetch Ferez from his ship, and when the Capricorn Guardian joins us, I don't waste any time. "You once told us that uniting the four Cardinal Stones might lead us to the Unity Talisman—but do you think it could also lead us to the Talisman's original landing place?"

"A wise theory," says the Sage, nodding.

"My Talisman is built into my ship, so we'll need to do this from 'Nox."

We follow Hysan inside, and he activates his Stone's Ephemeris in the ship's nose. I switch on the black opal next, and then Eurek and Ferez do the same with theirs. Four star maps overlap with each other, and the four of us close our eyes to Center ourselves, creating a Quorum. Ophiuchus stands in the middle of our group, and we channel his Psynergy to help reconnect him with his birthplace.

At first I don't sense anything, but then a light begins to glow inside me, like I'm carrying new life in my womb. I feel overwhelmed with compassion and care and concern, like a new mother, and as my body swells, so does my heart, and I realize I'm embodying *Nurture*.

I can sense the presence of Wisdom and Justice and Military might nearby, and as our energies combine, our individual essences are united into a single purpose.

"I know," says Ophiuchus, and I open my eyes. He's staring directly at me. "I know where we have to go."

We regroup with all the Guardians while the commanders of every troop gather their Zodai. "Ophiuchus has located his crash site," announces Eurek once the Guardians are assembled. "Report your findings."

Neith joins our group and stands by Hysan's side, and the other leaders stare at him.

"Most weapons won't function here due to this world's different scientific and metaphysical laws," says Ferez, breaking the uncomfortable silence. "We've tested the Shrill, and it won't sound in this air."

"Bind won't disburse properly in this atmosphere," says Hysan, and he directs himself to the Leonine and Scorp Guardians, who are scowling at him.

"Our Veils aren't camouflaging us here," says the interim Virgo Guardian. "This air won't accommodate invisibility collars."

Virgos fight with the Veil and Thorn: They vanish and sneak up on their targets with an elegant and small-but-deadly dagger called a Thorn. It's often dipped in poison, sometimes meant to paralyze and sometimes to kill.

"The Scarabs work just fine," says Skiff proudly.

"Our Swaths won't function without solar energy," adds the Guardian of Leo, Holy Leader Aurelius. Their weapon is a sword with a handle covered in microscopic mirrors that traps rays from the sun and produces a focused beam of solar energy that consumes whatever it passes through.

"The Tremble can't produce earthquakes in this soil," reports Fernanda. "So what does that leave us with for protection?"

"Everyone has been trained using a Barer." I turn to look at Rubi and Brynda, who are standing beside me. "Gemini and Sagittarius's weapons will also be fine. We'll have to defend ourselves with what we can."

"Remember that if we're encountering technology constraints, odds are so are they," Hysan points out. "Aquarius's technique was sophisticated, but this place is primal and untamed, down to the very particles of air. Their Veils likely won't work here either, and the Marad will be limited to their Murmurs, which we can fend off with the shield produced by our Barers."

Brynda faces me. "Rho, do you know where you're going and what you have to do when you get there?"

I nod and look to Eurek. "Should the whole army march there as one?"

"We'd be leading the Marad right to you," he counters. "The best strategy is to split up into factions so they don't know where you are. Remember they're only here to get Ophiuchus—and they win by either taking him away from us or waiting out two more days until the portal fully opens. The more confusion we create, the better."

"Then we'll divide into teams," I say, "and we'll stay in contact through our Rings. If anyone needs reinforcements, just call out to the Collective Conscious. And if we close the portal, we'll send the alert to the rest of you so we can regroup and get out of here."

"I'm on Rho's team," says Rubi, but Eurek shakes his head.

"Guardians are all targets. We should split up."

Hysan takes my hand, and I know he's coming with me no matter what the Ariean General has to say about it.

We disband to regroup with our teams, but before we can do anything, an army ten times larger than ours creeps out from the swamp's trees, like they've been waiting for us to corral ourselves.

They're all in white with porcelain masks, and they move with a confidence that feels like they're already native to this land. Their Murmurs are trained on us, and even though our Zodai shout and lift their weapons, nobody shoots. The standoff seems to be because the Marad is expecting something. Or someone.

And then a figure in all white steps forward through their ranks, the only one not wearing a mask.

It's *Blaze*.

40

HIS FACE IS A KNIFE blade to my gut.

Hysan's hand squeezes mine, but I can't focus on anything but Nishi's killer.

"My name is Blaze Jansun, and I am the leader of the Tomorrow Party," he says, his voice amplified. "I've come to bring you *hope*. If you let down your weapons and join us, we will not harm you, and you may come with us through the portal to discover a new universe."

Silence meets his words, and a few more people in white, also without masks, come up beside him, and I see Traxon and Mallie and Barg and Geneva and June in her hover-chair—all the people I met and liked from his Party. Blaze learned well from Aquarius: He's baiting me with empathy.

"All we ask is that you hand Ophiuchus over to us," he goes on, "and you will be saved."

The Thirteenth Guardian is surrounded by a platoon of Arieans, but I can see his face through their ranks, and he looks like he's resigned to any fate. Just as he struggled between his conscience and his love for Aquarius,

I wonder if now his loyalty to his people will keep him from saving the Zodiac.

It seems impossible to ever know what side he's on.

As I pan across the familiar faces next to Blaze's, I know that just like all the Zodai here, these teens don't deserve to die. They've been manipulated—we all have. But there's a better weapon than violence for undercutting lies.

Traxon was right.

It's time we told the truth.

I let go of Hysan's hand and step forward into the empty space between our army and Blaze's. "The sun going dark isn't inevitable!" I shout to them.

My voice isn't amplified but it's still strong, and the Party members look to me. "Trax, Mallie, Barg, Geneva, June—you guys aren't fighting for our universe's survival but its destruction. I know you're afraid to trust that because Aquarius was so convincing and you're afraid of staying and dying, but if you don't believe me, you'll be wiping out our entire solar system!"

Hysan is already next to me again, a pistol in his hand, and Mathias and Pandora come up on my other side with their blue-bladed Barer swords out. The three of them scan everyone around us like they're ready to defend my life with their own.

"You have a choice," I go on, avoiding Blaze and addressing the Marad soldiers and Party members. "You can trust your fear, or you can have some faith. As someone who's trusted her fears her whole life, I can tell you it doesn't lead anywhere good. To the Marad soldiers, I myself hail from your lineage. My mother is a Riser. My mother's mother was an imbalanced Riser. Ophiuchus, your own Guardian, stands with us. I know you've been wronged, but you don't have to do this—we can choose to be better than the generations that came before us."

The same silence that met Blaze's words meets mine, and my shoulders slump in defeat. But then the guy next to Blaze begins to move forward.

Trax, with his shaggy mane of hair and pierced eyebrows, steps across the divide. When he's in front of me, he says, "I'm sorry. I was just tired of the lies . . . and I thought I was finally hearing some truth."

"I understand," I say, and he hands me something small and shaped like a scorpion. The Echo Stan stole from Link on Scorpio.

I take the device in my hand, and it reminds me of my brother's pluck and protection and sacrifice. And touching this piece of proof that he lived and fought once makes me feel stronger. "Thank you," I whisper.

He nods and stands beside Hysan, who rests a comforting hand on the Leonine's shoulder. Traxon's face immediately burns bright red.

I look over to the other Party members beside Blaze, hoping they'll follow Trax's lead. But no one else comes over.

On our side, people from every House have now stepped up beside me. Brynda, Rubi, Eurek, Fernanda, Ezra, Gyzer, Mom, Gamba, Skarlet, Engle, Numen, Qima, Hexel, Jox, and more, until we're one indivisible, colorful mass of Zodai from across the universe. And from this gesture, it's clear that everyone in our army is willing to give their life for the Zodiac.

Just as Nishi did.

This isn't hate: We're fighting with *love*.

"Rho, this is silly," says Blaze, like we're old friends having a private conversation and not enemy generals meeting on the battlefield. "You're going to get everyone here killed. We outnumber you ten to one. You can at least save these people—it'd be such a waste to let these Zodai die just because you can't let go of the past."

One of the Marad soldiers steps up and rips off his mask, revealing yellow eyes I'll never forget.

My brother's murderer.

"You're testing our patience," he says, only he's talking to Blaze. "This is our home now. That was the deal we struck with Aquarius. Whether you people make it through your portal isn't our concern—this planet will survive, and so will we. We want you *all* off our land, same way you wanted Risers off yours. So get your guy and screw off."

Aryll doesn't even care enough for his own Guardian to use his name. Then he turns to me, but he doesn't raise his Murmur yet. He doesn't have to—not when his brethren are already pointing theirs.

"But Rho is mine."

Hysan and Mathias block me from view with their bodies, and it looks like things are about to get violent—when suddenly, there's a shuffling noise on both sides of our armies, and we all turn to look.

A collection of strange creatures slithers out from the swamp. They walk on four legs and make raspy sounds that almost seem like part of a language, except it's unintelligible. There are enough of them that they surround both our armies, and the Marad doesn't seem quite as sure what to do—some aim their Murmurs at them and some keep them pointed at us.

"What are those?" I hear Brynda ask.

A few of the creatures start rising up on their hind legs, revealing humanlike bodies, and they lift their faces to stare at us. They have skin just like Ophiuchus.

Holy Helios.

This world's population didn't die out—it mutated over the millennia. *These are the last Ophiuchans.*

At the sight of his people, Ophiuchus springs out from his hiding place amid the Ariean Majors and moves desperately toward the creatures.

"KILL HIM!" Blaze shouts, and every Murmur suddenly points to him. Then everything descends into chaos.

I'm jostled among the Zodai as both armies start shooting at each other, and the Ophiuchan creatures jump into the fray, attacking with their sharp jaws and claws. Zodai or Marad, we all look like threats to them, and they don't differentiate.

I feel Hysan pulling me with him, and I realize Eurek, Neith, Mathias, Skarlet, and Gyzer are ahead of us, and they're pushing a heavy weight in front of them. It's Ophiuchus—they need their combined strength to force him away from the creatures he's so desperate to touch.

Pandora appears on my other side, and she's already glowing with the blue shield from her Barer. I don't see many others shielding themselves—most of our Zodai probably don't have enough focus to pull it on while they fight.

"Rho, raise your shield," Hysan instructs me, and I reach down for the electricity in my hand and the Psynergy in the air, and I breathe in deeply as I bind them together in my mind. Then I pull the energy across my body. I'm sure I'm leaving some holes, but it's the best I can do.

Brynda suddenly joins us, her wrist raised as she walks backwards, shooting at the soldiers coming after our group. Bodies are dropping so quickly that I sway, dizzy amid so much death, and Hysan holds me tighter.

Rubi and Ezra and Engle and other Zodai join Brynda, until there's a wall of people protecting Ophiuchus and me from the Marad as we run to put an end to this.

A loud explosion distracts everyone as an Ariean ship is blown up. "Duck!" shouts Brynda, and we all hit the ground as flaming pieces of metal fly everywhere—but the flames die quickly; whatever brand of oxygen this is can't sustain fire for long.

Hysan pulls me to my feet right as a maskless Marad soldier breaks through the mob, gunning for us at top speed.

Aryll goes straight for Brynda, who's causing the most damage to his ranks. She raises her Arclight, but she's out of bullets, and without giving her time to reload, he tackles her.

He loses his Murmur as they roll on the ground, and Hysan and I tear through the throng of fighters to reach her. Hysan shouts at the top of his lungs to all the Zodai nearby: "Help Brynda NOW!"

But even as we sprint, I know we're not going to make it. Brynda looks like she's been dazed by the fall, because when Aryll lifts his head, she doesn't get up. Rubi is closest to them, and she's running with her Barer's shield on.

The Geminin Guardian is still a few feet away when she raises her gun to shoot Aryll, but he yanks down on a masked soldier's sleeve, using him as a human shield, and the bullet lodges in the soldier's chest.

Aryll tosses the dead Marad soldier at Rubi, and then he draws a dagger from his waistband and turns to stab Brynda.

But Rubi easily dodges the body, and she uses her suit's levitation boots to launch herself at Aryll's head. She yanks on his hair, and he shrieks and raises his blade to stab her, but she flies off him too quickly.

While the diminutive Guardian buzzes around Aryll and distracts him, Hysan, Pandora, and I drag Brynda away from the chaos. I've no idea where Mathias and the others have taken Ophiuchus, but I hope they're safe. Once we get away from Aryll, we'll locate them.

Ezra charges toward her Guardian, leading a platoon of Sagittarians, and she shouts to us, "Go! We've got her!"

Relieved, I turn around to help Rubi, who's half running, half flying toward us, her copper curls bouncing wildly. I don't see Aryll, but there's no time to stick around and search for him.

"Rubi!" I call when she's within shouting distance. "The Sagittarians will protect Brynda, but we have to go—"

Her eyes grow wide, like she's seeing a threat behind us, and I wheel around in fear of what I'll find. But when I hear Hysan shouting "NO!" I realize what's happening.

I turn back just as Rubi falls, the dagger's black handle sticking out from her back.

41

"RUBI, *NO!*" I CRY OUT, my voice breaking as blood spreads through her orange fabric like spilled paint.

Aryll stands too far away, and through the smoke and bodies and flashes of blue light, I see he's smiling. Then he melts into the mob behind him, growing more dangerous by his disappearance.

A swarm of Dreamcasters descends on their fallen Guardian, and I take one last longing look at Rubi—who gave her life to spare Brynda's—and as tears spill from my eyes, Hysan and Pandora take my arms and pull me away.

The three of us are shielded as we dodge the chaos of fighters, and I'm startled by the viciousness of the Ophiuchan creatures, who are taking down people in packs and eviscerating them with their ferocious jaws. The corpses of Zodai and Marad Risers lie side by side on the battlefield.

Fear must be the most destructive power in the universe.

It births monsters.

Hysan uses his Scan to illuminate a pathway through the tangled trees, and their branches scratch at our uniforms as we burrow as deep as we can into the silvery swamp. When the noise of the violence fades, new sounds take over.

The high-pitched buzzing and chirping of unknown insects is underscored by the drone of deep and unfamiliar animal calls, all of it muffled and echoing, like we're underwater. I touch one of the large silver tree leaves, and it's the strangest texture I've ever felt: It feels like water, but it's a solid, and when I dip my finger in it, my Ring buzzes. This whole planet is living, breathing Psynergy.

Rho? Are you safe?

I touch my Ring at the sound of Mathias's voice.

We're in the swamp, and we're fine. Pandora is with me, I add quickly, to ease his mind. *So is Hysan. How are you?*

We're safe, too. We have Ophiuchus, but it's proving difficult to get him to stay with us—he's desperate to reconnect with his people, and I'm worried they'll kill him if he gets too close.

How will we find each other? I ask.

Meet me in the Collective Conscious, and I'll guide you to us, the way I came to you in the Aquarian palace.

I turn to Hysan to let him know the plan. His brow is furrowed, and I realize he's also in conversation with someone. When his gaze refocuses, his eyes look pitifully sad. "We've lost two thousand already."

Pandora and I hang our heads for a moment in respect of the fallen. Hysan had the idea to create necklaces with trackers, like the one Sirna gave me, to keep track of our soldiers. Only in place of a pink nar-clam pearl, Hysan's version holds a pulse reader that transmits Zodai's vitals to the people we left behind at the International Village.

"Mathias and the others are safe," I say, breaking the silence, and I see Pandora exhale. "We need to get to Ophiuchus so we can end this. Mathias is going to guide me to his location through the Psy, so follow me."

I shut my eyes and twist my Ring, and I enter the solar system of souls. I see a light a great distance away, and instead of moving toward it, I feel like the world is moving around me.

When the light jolts into me, I open my eyes with a gasp—and I see Mathias's face in front of me, his blue eyes like twin midnight skies.

I reach out and touch his cheek, which has a bloody scratch on it. "Is this real?" I whisper breathlessly.

"I'm here," he whispers back, resting his hand over mine.

I hear movement behind me, and I turn to see a panting Hysan and Pandora surfacing from the swamp, and I realize we're standing in some kind of crater that looks like it was once a body of water.

Mathias dashes over to Pandora and wraps her in his arms, while Hysan comes up to me. "I've never seen anyone but Neith run that fast," he says, his voice choppy.

"I was running?" I ask in awe. "I didn't feel anything!"

"Your connection to the stars is so strong that when you gave yourself over to Mathias's Psynergy, it pulled you forward at such a brisk pace that Pandora and I could barely keep up."

"Where is the location where you first fell?" I hear Eurek shouting.

Hysan and I run over to where the Ariean Guardian and Ophiuchus are facing off. Gathered in a protective circle around them are Neith, Gyzer, Gamba, Mom, Skarlet, Traxon, Engle, Numen, Qima, and half a dozen other Zodai I don't know.

"Ezra isn't answering me!" says Gyzer the instant he sees me.

"She's fine, she's with Brynda," I say quickly, and his whole face slackens with relief. "What's happening here?" I demand, looking from Ophiuchus to Eurek.

"He won't tell us where to go," says Eurek angrily. "We're running out of time and Zodai, and he still hasn't made up his damn mind what side he's on!"

Ophiuchus glares defiantly at me, like he's bracing himself for my outburst. But I don't say anything. I just approach him slowly, the way one would a wild animal, and I lay a gentle hand on his arm. Then I close my eyes, and I channel the Psynergy surrounding us until I've penetrated his consciousness.

You may be a star, I whisper into his mind, *but like Aquarius, you've been given the power of choice: You can be our light or our darkness. You can save the Zodiac or doom it. You can be the monster the Original Guardians invented . . . or you can reclaim your place as the Guardian of Unity and teach us what it means to stand together.*

When I pull away from him, he opens his eyes, and his starlight bathes my face as he whispers, "This is the place."

So he did bring us to the right location.

He rests a hand on my arm now, and my heart is suddenly infused with emotions that aren't my own. My eyes shut, and I see how ever since the armada he's been helping us, even though his heart has questioned his actions. He's acted on his faith in Unity, though his fear has made him doubt his path. His fear of us and how hateful we can be as a species.

But for the first time, seeing new generations of Zodai from across the Houses come together like this, he has hope.

"Spread out," commands Eurek to the others. "Rho and Ophiuchus are going to enter the astral plane and close the portal. We need to buy them all the time necessary."

Hysan turns to me, and he cups my face in his hands. "You're my hero," he says, and he kisses me gently—like it's only a short goodbye and I'll be right back.

But when it's over, his lips linger on mine for a moment, and he breathes, "I'm so proud of you, Rho. Come back to me, please."

I circle my arms around his neck and hug him, holding him close to me, and I whisper, "Meeting you is the best thing that's ever happened to me. And I'm not saying that because I'm not coming back—I'm saying it because I am. We have too much unfinished business."

When we let go, I turn to face Ophiuchus. I don't say bye to Mom or Mathias because I intend to come back. I refuse to let this be the end of the Zodiac.

Ophiuchus walks away to the center of the crater, and I understand this wasn't a body of water—this is where he crashed as a star when he landed on this planet. When he gets to what could be the midpoint, he digs into the moist soil with his bare hands, until I hear his nails scrape against something solid.

Then he closes his eyes to Center himself, and standing across from him I do the same. Within seconds, I feel my soul completely leaving my body and accessing the astral plane. Only when I open my eyes, I'm still standing in the same place.

I watch Ophiuchus step out of his skin, like a hologram, and I leave my physical shell, too. I turn around and scan everyone around us—they don't seem to see our ghosts. They're still staring between our frozen bodies and our surroundings, making sure no one finds us.

The Thirteenth Guardian's skin alternates from dark to light as he comes closer, his Dark Matter hair falling into his panoramic eyes, the silver irises bright and alive. *Are you ready?*

I nod.

He closes his eyes in concentration, and he begins to tug on the Psynergy from his land. I feel the pull immediately, and I see that Hysan and Eurek do, too, because they clutch their chests. After a while, Mom and Gamba do the same, until all the Zodai around us can feel the yank on the Psynergy they're breathing.

The air molecules start shaking around us, like an earthquake in the sky, and I hold tightly to my own Psynergy so I don't lose my Center.

Suddenly I hear scratching noises, and I look around to see the Ophiuchans crawling out from the swamp and approaching us slowly. My friends all gather closer to our bodies, facing the creatures with their Barers out, their bodies curved inward from the pain in their chests.

But the Ophiuchans keep slithering forward until they're standing next to the Zodai, watching us. And all at once, they close their eyes.

Suddenly I feel an influx of Psynergy in the astral plane that blows me back a few steps. Ophiuchus opens his eyes and sees his people, who've come to donate their Psynergy to him.

I'm shocked to see tears streaming down Ophiuchus's snakeskin cheeks, and I feel him growing stronger in the Psy, until the Psynergy swirls around us like a hurricane, and at last he begins to glow like a true star.

This is where my part comes in.

I take a deep breath and step forward. Then I take his hand, and I begin to pull in his Psynergy. Once it filters through me, the Psynergy is no longer trapped on Ophiuchus, and it's free to return to Pisces.

It feels like I'm overdosing on Abyssthe.

Feelings and sensations that have nothing to do with the present begin to pass through me, and my mind is hit again and again and again with pieces of people's lives, like I've inhaled the stardust that makes up existence, and now the whole universe is being processed through my brain. If not for Hysan anchoring me—if not for my longing for a life with him and my hope to see him again—I don't know that I could hang on.

I think only of his golden face as I'm racked with phantom pains and emotions, and I try to hang on to who I am while the energy of others stampedes through me.

The transferring process seems to be speeding up, and the whirring of Psynergy grows too intense until I can't catch my breath, and my heart is beating too fast, and I fall forward to my knees.

Ophiuchus draws his hand away from mine, and as the dizziness ends, I open my eyes.

Did . . . did we finish? I ask, breathless.

Almost, he says, his eyes shining brighter than I've ever seen them, like pure starlight.

I look up, but the Dark Matter is still in the sky, and the Psynergy is swirling around us. *It's not working.*

Because there's one step left, he says, and then he falls to his knees, too, and looks at me, his whole being glowing with beautiful silver light.

Dread fills me so that I can't even speak. I've suspected this, but Moira didn't say, and I was hoping it wouldn't come to it.

Rho, you must kill me.

No, I say, and I get up and take a step back.

It's the only way. The death of a star opens the portal, and the death of a star closes it. The same release of energy. You must do it now—it must be timed with the release of Psynergy.

I—I can't. I've never killed anyone—

Please. You promised me.

But when I promised, I hated you. I blamed you for the deaths of my dad and Mathias, and now I know the truth.

It's more than that, though. Ophiuchus is the only person who truly knows me. He's seen all of me, my soul and my darkness. He understands both because he's made of light and shadow. And he started out just like me—hopeful and warm, a champion of Unity among the earthlings. He deserves a chance to live among his people. A chance to tell his tale to the worlds. A chance to redeem himself.

Don't you care what this will do to me? I ask, echoing his old question.

It will keep you honest, he says gently. *I'm helping you keep your word to the stars. There's no other way, and we're out of time.*

I close my eyes and fall out of my Center.

When I open them again, I'm standing in front of Ophiuchus, and he's on his knees before me, just as he was in the astral plane. Only now we're back on reality.

With everyone watching us, I make a fist and activate my Barer. An aqua blade shoots out from the handle, and I choke as I whisper, "I promise the Zodiac will know your story . . . and your people will never be abandoned again."

"Thank you," he says softly, and then I steel my muscles, fighting against the nausea and clamminess trying to take me over.

And I plunge the sword into his heart.

42

THE ZODAI AROUND US GASP as Ophiuchus falls forward, and Traxon cries out in horror to see his beloved Thirteenth Guardian vanquished once and for all. I drop to my knees, sobs erupting from deep within me, because something inside me just died, too.

Hysan's arms are the only thing tethering me to life. He kisses my hair, my forehead, my wet cheeks, but I can't stop crying. "I'm so sorry," he whispers, understanding better than probably any other Zodai here how much this act of violence just shredded my soul.

The Dark Matter begins to grow less opaque, like a day that's dawning in extreme slow motion, and we know it worked.

The portal's window has closed, and the darkness that stained the Zodiac millennia ago, with Ophiuchus's betrayal, is receding. The Thirteenth House is back—and that means the Psynergy is being returned to Pisces, renewing that world, as well.

The Zodiac lives to see another day.

Suddenly everyone starts cheering, the delayed reaction unanimous, and Hysan and I stand up. I watch as Mathias hugs Pandora, and Skarlet hugs

Eurek, and Quima hugs Numen, and Mom hugs Gamba. The Ophiuchans are watching the lightening sky overhead like they've never seen anything like it; then, without warning, they scatter back to the swamp's darkness, like the light is a threat to them.

"This change will affect this species and this world's topography," I say, sniffling. "They'll need our help."

"And they'll get it," says Hysan, wiping my tears with his thumbs.

"It's over," says Eurek, his white smile bright against the dark air. "Wandering Star, it was an honor—"

"Are we celebrating something?"

I spin to see Aryll strutting over from the swamp. "Why wasn't I invited?"

Before his question is even out, a swarm of Marad soldiers charge at my friends, and Eurek shouts, "Activate your shields!" right as the Murmurs begin shooting blue light. He, Mathias, Skarlet, and Gyzer rush forward to meet the soldiers, and soon almost everyone is battling someone—but not Hysan and me.

Nobody interferes with us as Aryll casually saunters over, and Hysan grips my hand in anticipation.

Then Blaze comes roaring into the clearing, his eyes rimmed red and his face set in a scowl. "WHAT DID YOU DO?" he booms at me. "YOU'VE RUINED OUR ONLY CHANCE!"

"It's over," says Hysan as his former friend joins Aryll.

"It's not over until that bitch is dead," says Blaze, glaring at me.

"You're not touching her." Hysan's voice is low and deadly, a darkness rising in him that I've only glimpsed a few times before.

"He doesn't have to," says Aryll merrily. "That's what this is for."

He raises his wrist, and I recognize the black band—it's a Scarab. "I got this especially for Rho, so she can experience the pain she put me through."

Hysan tugs on my arm, and we start running. I try to concentrate on keeping my shield up, even though it won't protect me against the Scarab's poison—the Barer can only deflect technological attacks.

Something white suddenly collides with Hysan, and we drop each other's hands as we fall to the ground. I look up to see a Marad soldier wrestling with him, and as they struggle, Blaze rushes over, lacking his usual swagger.

I have no time to defend myself as his hand closes around my neck, and he lifts me off the dirt. But before he can shatter my throat, a fist blows into the side of his head.

Blaze is blasted back ten feet, and I drop to the ground.

"Are you okay, Rho?" asks Neith, offering me a hand and pulling me up.

"Now I am," I say, my throat sore. I search for Hysan. He's fighting off two Marad soldiers at once, and I start to run to him, but Neith won't let go of my arm.

"I'm sorry, Rho, but I've been programmed to protect you and Ophiuchus at all costs. Even if the price is Hysan's life."

"*What?*" I whirl around to look at him, and I see tears in his eyes. He's struggling against the directive, but he can't defy it. He's a machine.

Pandora runs over to me, still shielded by her Barer. "Mathias is helping," she assures me, and sure enough I look over to see that Mathias has materialized at Hysan's side, and when they've fought off the soldiers, they run over to us.

"Hysan, order Neith to stop protecting me!" I demand.

"Rho, I can't—"

"Hysan, *please*! We're all putting our lives on the line here. He deserves to make his own choices. You can't control all our destinies."

He sighs and looks into Neith's eyes, beaming something out from his Scan. After a moment, the android's shoulders sag with relief. "Thank you," he says to me.

"We have to help," I say, seeing some of my friends battling up to three Marad soldiers at a time. Mom, Gyzer, Skarlet, and Eurek can hold their own, but Engle, Gamba, Qima, and Numen are struggling.

I run into the fray, and the others follow. The Marad are no longer fighting with their Murmurs because the Zodai are all shielded, so most have resorted to hand-to-hand combat, though some carry daggers or pistols.

I force a shield around me, and I make a fist until I've grown a set of electric brass knuckles, and then I come up behind one of the soldiers fighting with Gamba and land an electric blow into his unprotected neck. He falls immediately.

I run and do the same with one of the three soldiers Engle is fending off, and when I turn, I'm face-to-face with Mallie of Aquarius.

She raises a pistol.

"Mallie, do you even know what you're fighting for?" I ask as she cocks the gun.

Her eyes look glassy and lost, and her suit is covered in dirt and blood. She has no idea what she's doing, but she's given up so much of her soul to this cause that she can't stop now.

"Sorry," she says, a tear falling from her eye, and she fires.

My whole body hits the ground, and it takes me a moment to realize I wasn't shot—I was shoved. I look up to see a dark-skinned woman wearing Cancrian blue disarming Mallie and knocking her out with the butt of her own gun. Then Sirna turns and offers me a hand.

"You sure took your time getting here," I say, grinning as she pulls me up.

"Mind if I apologize later, Holy Mother?" she asks as bullets sail over our heads.

"Sounds good!"

We race through the chaos, and I'm relieved to see only a few Marad soldiers are still fighting—we've beaten most of them back . . . or worse. Then I see the fallen Zodai on the ground. Numen. Qima. *Traxon*.

Before I can mourn their deaths, I notice that Mom and Gamba are outnumbered, and I point them out to Sirna. "Can you help my family?"

She nods and immediately goes, while I look around to see who else needs help, and I spy Hysan's golden figure racing over. "Are you okay?" he asks, and I nod, pulling him into a tight hug.

"We need to get back to the ships," I say.

"Let's get—"

"Now where were we before that rude interruption?"

Aryll appears behind us, the Scarab on his wrist aimed at me. "I believe I was going to share some empathy with Rho. But I had a better thought."

Hysan shields my body with his, and Aryll laughs. "You really are a mind reader! That's exactly what I was thinking. To kill a Cancrian properly, first you must take out her heart."

He's going to shoot Hysan.

I wrap my arms around him and try to push him out of the way, but Hysan is too strong, and he won't let me. "I'm sorry, Rho," he says, blocking me from Aryll's view.

Then he turns his head slightly in my direction and shouts one final word at me: *"RUN!"*

"NO!" I hug him tightly as Aryll presses down to shoot—but something huge soars in front of Hysan right as the poisonous dart flies out.

"NEITH!" shouts Hysan as the android falls before us.

"He's okay—" I start to say, then I remember Scarab poison renders technology useless. Neith's mouth is open, his eye twitches, and smoke comes off his Kartex skin.

I fix my eyes on Aryll and start walking toward him. "You're dead," I growl, but he doesn't bother to raise his Scarab. He doesn't look scared at all. He looks amused.

"Oh, Rho," he says when I'm just a few feet away. "You're just so . . . adorable."

I raise my Barer in the shape of a sword.

Hysan springs over, and even though his expression is broken, I can see that he won't let Aryll hurt me.

"Mathias!"

At the sound of Pandora's piercing scream, Hysan and I look away. A Marad soldier has injured Mathias's right arm, and he can't raise his

Barer. Pandora leaps in front of him, and I turn to Hysan desperately. "GO!"

He looks from me to Aryll like he's going to disagree, and I say, "Hysan, *trust me!*"

And he does.

When he runs to help Mathias, I face Aryll again.

"That is some impressive pet training," he says, his yellow eyes dancing. "You'll have to show me that trick sometime."

I raise my electric sword. "Let's do this."

"You think you're so dark!" Aryll laughs at me as I approach. "All because you lost some people and had a few nightmares?"

He pulls out a dagger that looks like the one he used to kill Rubi. "You're not dark, Rho. You only dream of darkness." His voice drops to a whisper, like he's sharing a secret. "True dark dwellers dream of *light*."

He raises his dagger to stab me, but I dodge him. Then I shove my sword forward, but he dodges it, too.

"Your real name is Grey Gowan," I say as we circle each other. "You were born on Capricorn. You had pale skin and black eyes and you were thirteen when you started shifting for the first time."

"That's a pretty story," he says, flashing his sharp teeth in a cruel smirk. "But do you really think you can play on emotions that aren't there?"

"You left behind a Snow Globe for your family, and Ferez found it. That's why you didn't like being on Capricorn when we were there. Some part of you realized you were home."

"I'm home *now*," he says, and there's an edge in his voice that proves he's not as indifferent as he claims. "And I'd say it's time you went home, too—and reunited with your brother."

He raises the dagger just as a flash of blond hair comes up behind him, and Aryll freezes as Mom presses a pistol to his temple.

"A family reunion!" he says gleefully. "Too bad there are no Grace men left to rescue you—"

Mom fires.

Blood gushes everywhere as Aryll's head explodes. I recoil in shock as blood sprays my face and uniform, and I stare at Mom aghast.

There's no emotion or hesitation on her face. There's only the feral look she wore when she killed the Maw that attacked Stanton. And now she's taken out the beast that murdered him.

"*Mom*," I gasp, my hand clutching my chest. "Thank you."

Her face softens. "Rho—"

A blade suddenly bursts through her chest.

"MOM!" I shout as her eyes fly open in horror. The metal withdraws, and she falls into my arms, blood spurting out of her wound.

We drop to the ground, and I stare into her pallid face, her bottomless blue eyes fading fast. "No, please, hang on," I say, my tears dropping onto her. "Please don't go, *please*. . . ."

But her death is instantaneous—the blade went right through her heart—and I look up to see Blaze holding the bloody sword that killed her.

"Oh, Rho," he says, his face pinched in faux pain. "My *deepest* condolences about your mom."

43

THE BLOODY POINT OF BLAZE'S sword slides under my chin and tips my face up. "On your feet," he commands, and I rest Mom on the ground and rise.

I can barely see Blaze through the field of red that fills my vision. He's murdered my mother and Nishi. I don't care what Hysan would say—Blaze doesn't deserve my mercy.

He deserves death.

"I'm not sure what I want to do with you," he says, tilting his head, the cold metal still touching my chin. "You monopolized Aquarius's attention. You impeded my plans to leave this universe. And now you've stolen my power."

"Sounds to me like you're a sore loser."

"Well I'm still standing, so it sounds to me like the game isn't over."

"Put down your sword, Blaze."

Hysan's voice is void of light. He strides over to us and stands beside me, equally covered in blood and dirt and gashes. "It's over."

Mathias comes, too, Pandora propping him up since he's injured. Sirna also approaches, and then Eurek and Gyzer and Skarlet and Engle, and other Zodai I don't know. They all form a circle around Blaze, whose sword is still touching my chin.

In the distance, I hear a girl's voice calling out for her mother, but I ignore it.

"Put down your sword," commands Eurek.

Blaze looks desperate but unwilling to submit.

"You're all fools! You know the Zodiac won't change. It'll be just like after the Trinary Axis—this will be another war for the history texts that will start out as a cautionary tale until someone gets the itch for some excitement and starts riling people up again. Aquarius was a visionary—he understood that we need to start anew! You're just recycling the same bad foundation—"

"Drop your weapon," Hysan repeats, and there's so much strength and power in his voice that Blaze stops speaking.

His head hinges down, and to my surprise he drops the sword tip to the ground. And I hear the girl again, calling my mom's name.

I start to turn to go to her, right as Blaze raises the sword again and moves in to drive it into my heart. I have no time to run or defend myself as the blade flies toward me—

A metal dart shoots into Blaze's throat.

Beside me, Hysan is holding the small golden gun he used to stop Neith on Pisces. Blood fountains from the Leonine's neck as he falls facedown on the ground, the sword still in his hand.

It's finished.

"MOM!" calls Gamba for the third time, and I turn to see her flipping over bodies, searching for our mother's face. She's probably already glanced this way and seen that Mom isn't one of the people standing here—what she can't see is her body because it's lying on the floor beside Blaze, inside the circle.

I move toward her, and when Gamba sees me, she freezes.

"No," she says, stepping back from the truth she reads on my face. "No, she can't—she's not—"

She tries fighting me off, but I pull her to my chest and hold her there as she breaks down into sobs. We cry together, both of us sisters, both of us orphans, and we don't stop until hands pull us apart. Hysan helps me to my feet, and I see that the Zodai have started gathering all those who have fallen on both sides.

The Dark Matter has thinned even more, and the sky looks like a gray dusk. More silver stars are visible as the hole in the blanket of blackness expands. We carry as many corpses between us as we can to the ships, where we find the rest of the Zodai survivors.

"Gy!"

Ezra comes running, and Gyzer drops the body he's carrying to catch her as she leaps into his arms. When he sets her down, she turns to all of us, and without anyone having to ask she says, "Once the portal closed, those Ophiuchan creatures slipped away, and most of the Marad went with them. They just . . . stopped fighting us."

We regroup with the rest of our fleet—which has been cut in half—and we begin to sort through the fallen bodies as every House claims their dead to send to Empyrean through their own customs. We position the fallen Marad soldiers against the tree line so their brethren can decide how to lay them to rest.

Every Tomorrow Party member Blaze brought with him died in battle. My gaze lingers on Mallie, and for some reason I think of the young girl in the pink spacesuit who froze to death on Elara. Both senseless deaths, yet the Cancrian has been cast as a victim and Mallie a villain. But Mallie was a victim, too.

Suddenly the whole camp falls silent, and I look up from Mallie's pallid face to a solitary Marad soldier who's just stepped out of the swamp.

The Zodai point their weapons, but since she's not holding a Murmur, nobody shoots. Then she rips off her mask, revealing a snakeskin face and lime-green eyes that are looking right at me.

"We outnumber you," she says in a raspy voice. "You either agree to leave this planet and never return, or we'll finish off what's left of you."

I step forward. "We're sorry for the way Risers have been treated, and we want to offer you a place in the Zodiac."

"You may feel that way, but the rest of the universe doesn't. We don't want your help. And we never want you coming back."

"You have the technology to reach us if you ever need anything," I say. "We *will* come if you call."

She nods and retreats into the swamp. After a moment's delay, activity resumes, and I hear a familiar voice that makes me ache with relief.

"You're not touching me with that needle!"

I jog over to the makeshift medical area, where Brynda is sitting on a fallen tree trunk and being treated by an Ariean healer. "Don't be a baby," says the fiery-haired woman.

"You have a great bedside manner," snarls Brynda. "I bet everyone raves about it."

"No one's complained about my manners in bed before," says Kenza, shrugging. I recognize her from when I awoke from the Sumber.

"That's not what I said, *Red*."

Since Brynda's expression is looking lethal, I jump in and say, "Hey, Brynda! You okay?"

"Rho!" she immediately turns away from Kenza and surveys me with her amber eyes, and once she's sure I'm unharmed, she smiles. "I'm glad you're okay. I'd be much better off if I had a proper healer—OW!"

Kenza used my distraction to stab Brynda's arm with a needle, and as the Sagittarian Guardian raises her wrist like she's going to fire a bullet from her Arclight, the Ariean flashes her an annoyingly antagonizing smile and darts off.

"You're totally marrying her," I say, and Brynda shoots me a glacial glare that has me walking my words back. "Sorry," I say quickly, and I sit down beside her on the log.

"Hysan told me about your mom," she says, her face and voice softening. "I'm sorry, Rho."

"We've all lost people," I murmur. I'm not ready to process it yet.

"I know . . . but sometimes it feels like the stars are picking on you the most. You've given up so much more than the rest of us."

Home. Dad. Deke. Stan. Nishi. Mom. It's hard to argue with her, so I don't. "I'm sorry about Rubi. I know you two were close."

She looks down at the marshy ground. "She was always doing something stupid—like dying to save my life. I wish I could yell at her for it." When she lifts her gaze again, there are tears in her eyes.

"I know how you feel," I say, thinking of Nishi. "We were lucky . . . to have friends like them."

✦ ✦ ✦

Most ships have already taken off to their home worlds, but the Arieans, Scorps, and Librans remain, overseeing the last of the cleanup.

"Wandering Star," says General Eurek. "We've just heard from Prophet Marinda, whose health is improving by the minute. She reports that most Piscenes are coming out of their comas."

I feel my face glowing with delight. "Thank you so much for telling me."

"Thank *you*," he says, and he offers his hand for the greeting. I reach out to bump fists with him, but he takes my fingers in his, and he plants a kiss on my skin.

Now my face begins to burn, but he spares me the struggle of speaking by saying, "It has been an honor to serve with you." His orange-red eyes simmer with emotion as he adds, "You will always be welcome on House Aries."

When he turns to go, I see Skarlet behind him, hidden by his burl and bulk. Even the cuts on her forehead and cheeks do nothing to mar her beauty or dampen the shimmer of her bronze brown skin.

"I'm going to hitch a ride back on an Ariean ship," she says. "I just wanted to say I'm sorry for being a bitch."

"Not your fault," I say with a sly smile. "You can't fight what you are."

Her cat-eyes widen in shock—and then we both burst into sudden laughter, and when we try to stop, our gazes cross and we start up again, until we're both clutching our stomachs and gasping for air.

Once I've calmed down enough to speak, I say, "I'm sorry, too."

"I was thinking we could combine forces to see what we can do for Risers," she says tentatively, "and try to make some changes in the Zodiac."

"I'd like that."

She nods, and we bump fists before she turns to go. But she's only taken a step when she spins around and says, "For the record, I think Hysan made the perfect choice."

✦ ✦ ✦

When most of the Zodai have cleared out, I spy a glimmer of gold, and I see Hysan on the ground, tending to someone. As I move closer, I recognize Lord Neith.

The android's nose is tipped open, and Hysan is uselessly trying to spark the Guardian back to life, but nothing is happening. Before I can say anything, Strident Engle comes over and rests a hand on Hysan's shoulder.

"The Scarab's poison can't be extracted from a machine," he says softly. "I'm sorry."

Hysan doesn't answer him, and he keeps trying to revive Neith, like a healer who won't give up on his patient.

Engle spots me and he comes over, his red eyes mournful. The sky is dark enough on this planet that he doesn't need to wear sunglasses. "I'm sorry about Skiff," I say.

I saw Sage Ferez earlier, and he told me the Scorp Guardian went down fighting. The only reason the Capricorn centenarian survived is because Skiff had him locked up on one of his House's ships to keep him safe. He was a loyal friend to the end.

"So am I," says Engle sadly.

I look at Hysan again, who's now reviewing information from his Scan and still refusing to resign. "I don't understand," I say, speaking softly and hanging far enough back that Hysan can't hear me. "He synced Neith with his ship on our way here—can't he just download the data into a new body?"

Engle shakes his head. "That's not how his artificial intelligence works. He could create a new Neith that has the same knowledge as this one—but it would never possess the same subtleties or . . . for lack of a better word, *emotions*."

"So he's . . . *gone?*" I ask incredulously, my heart plummeting for Hysan.

Engle frowns and nods. "I'm sorry, Rho."

"I need to go to him, but I'll be in touch soon," I say, thinking of what Skarlet said about getting organized. Engle would make a good addition to our team—as would a lot of the Zodai here.

Kneeling next to Hysan I say, "I'm so sorry." When he turns to me, there are tears in his eyes.

I'm so startled that I reach out and envelop him in a hug, the way he'd do for me.

"You were right," he says when he pulls away, his green eyes so bright they glow. "What you said to me on Aries—I've never lost anyone before. I've never felt . . . *this*."

He suddenly sits up, like he's remembering something, and his eyes widen. "I should be comforting you, Rho. You lost your *mom*—"

I rest a hand on his cheek. "Don't worry about me. Take care of yourself," I whisper, and I hear Nishi speaking through me as I repeat what she once said to me. "*It's okay to feel your pain before walling it off.*"

He kisses the inside of my palm, and I lean into his chest and keep him company as we stare down at Neith in silence. In the distance, I spot Gamba digging a shallow hole in the ground that's the length of . . . Mom.

"Go to her," says Hysan, who's following my gaze. "She needs you."

I press a kiss on his lips, and they taste salty. "I'll be quick."

Gamba must have seen me coming, because when I'm just a few feet away she says, "I told Mom once how on Virgo they don't launch their dead to Space—they bury them in the ground to become part of the soil." She doesn't look up from her work while she talks. "She told me that's what she wanted when she went."

"Can I help?"

"I'm done," she says, standing up and wiping her hands on her pants. "Pretty sure it's not deep enough, but she'll decompose anyway."

She kneels and lifts Mom's corpse by the shoulders, and I pick up her feet to help her. We gently deposit her body in the hole, and then we look at her for a long moment. "I didn't mean to take her from you," says Gamba, her voice tight.

"You didn't," I say, fighting back my own tears. "I think you saved her."

Gamba turns and starts shoving the soil over Mom, and I help her until her whole body is covered. Wiping my hands on my suit I ask, "Ready to get going?"

She finally meets my gaze. "I'm staying."

"*What?*"

She sighs. "I may not be imbalanced like the Marad members, but I am a Riser, which means I hail from this world, and I clearly had a strong enough pull to it to change Houses. I've left the Luminaries, which means I can't go back . . . I don't belong anywhere else."

"You belong with *me*," I say, and the words come out almost angry. "We're sisters."

She looks at me and smiles, and a tear spills over her eye. "I guess that means I'll have a place to crash when I'm ready to leave this world."

✦ ✦ ✦

Since Ezra and Gyzer left with the Sagittarians, it's just Hysan, Mathias, Pandora, and me on *Equinox*.

We're going back to Libra, and I'm excited at the thought of seeing Hysan's home for the first time. None of us are sure what we'll do tomorrow, but I'm not thinking about that. I'm still too caught up in yesterday.

Hysan is manning the helm, and Mathias and Pandora are in a cabin as I roam the ship, missing Nishi and Stan and Deke, who by all rights should be here with us.

And yet I know they are. Because I can feel them. It's like Stan said—they're in my heart, feeding my light, making me who I am.

I watch the mythical House Ophiuchus recede through the glass, and so much of the Dark Matter is gone by now that it must be visible to astronomers and seers alike. There won't be any denying its existence anymore—but we'll have to make sure no one disturbs the Ophiuchans as they rebuild their home.

The greatest danger now is forgetting.

I slip into the seat beside Hysan, whose furrowed brow tells me he's still thinking of Neith, the only true friend he had his whole life. I plant a kiss on his cheek, and he turns to me, and his mouth curves into that irresistible centaur smile.

"I love you," I say.

"I love you more than everything, Rho."

As we soar through Space, I think about Ophiuchus and Aquarius, and I wonder if they're watching us now and guiding our destinies. And even though I've always loved reading the stars, I no longer think their visions are all that important.

Prophecies are helpful, but they're not real. What's real are the people we surround ourselves with, the ones we love and admire and rely on. The stars do what they can, but ultimately, we have to trust only what we can touch.

An Ephemeris can show us a million different futures, but the only one that counts is the one we make for ourselves.

✦ ✦ ✦

THE END

✦ ✦ ✦

ACKNOWLEDGMENTS

THANK YOU, THANK YOU, THANK YOU, THANK YOU, THANK YOU.

Writing this series has been *the most rewarding experience of my life, and I will be forever grateful to everyone who's been a part of it.*

To every single reader who's stuck by Rho through all four books—*in any language*—I am beyond mind-blown that you've taken this trip to the Zodiac with me. Hearing from you guys has brought me so much joy and love and laughter, and I am so grateful for your support. I'm always happy to answer your questions about the series, just find me on social media.

Marissa Grossman, thank you for guiding me through this darkest part of Rho's journey and for shining your brilliant light whenever I couldn't find my way.

Ben Schrank and Casey McIntyre, thank you for taking this chance on me and making my dreams come true.

Vanessa Han, thank you for a fourth fabulous cover and for designing the best-looking series I've ever seen!

Laura Rennert, thank you for fighting for me and for believing in me and for *always* being there.

Morgan Rhodes, thank you for your beautiful blurb—I've loved seeing it on every Z cover!

Thank you to the stellar teams at Penguin Random House, Del Nuevo Extremo, Oceano México, Ediciones Urano Colombia, Michel Lafon, Piper Verlag, Pegasus, AST Mainstream, Karakter, Grupa Wydawnicza Foksal, and Alpha Books Company.

Thank you to the booksellers and librarians and educators and bloggers and reviewers and everyone else who spends any part of their day promoting reading to teens. You are my heroes.

Thank you to all the local LA authors and aspiring authors I've met along the way—I've learned so much from you, and I love being part of such an active and caring community.

Thank you to all my friends and family who have been so supportive of me the past few years. Now that I'm back from the Zodiac, I hope to see more of you!

In particular, I need to name-drop a few friends who got me through the end of this series (in alphabetical order because I'm a Virgo): Tomi Adeyemi, Lizzie Andrews, Caden Armstrong, Jay Asher, Russell Chadwick, Aurora Lydia Dominguez, Corinne Farkash, Vane Florio, Will Frank, Aditi Khorana, Tomás Lambré, Nicole Maggi, Ashley Moore, Robin Potts, Robin Reul, Luli Sulichin, and of course, Liz Tingue, whose faith changed my stars.

Fanny, te adoro. Brillas más que Helios. Gracias por compartir tu luz tan especial con todos los que te rodeamos.

Baba y Bebo, los mejores abuelos del mundo, los extraño todos los días.

Pa, Ma, Meli, y Andy—Los adoro. Me pone tan feliz poder compartir esta aventura con ustedes. Son lo que más quiero en el universo y son mi inspiración en todo lo que hago. Gracias por ser mis mejores amigos.